LORENZO'S ASSASSIN

by John Van Roekel

2016
Triptych Press

This is a work of historical fiction. Apart from well-known actual people, events and locales that figure in the narrative, all other names, characters, places, and incidents are the products of the author's imagination or are used fictitiously.

Published in the United States by Triptych Press

lorenzosassassin.com
johnvanroekel.com
facebook.com/johnvanroekel
john@johnvanroekel.com

Cover design by Lori Mitchell and John Van Roekel

The cover art is from the original painting *Florence, 1478* by Lori Mitchell and commissioned by the author. The maps were drawn by Chris Erichsen.

Lorenzo's Assassin is based the historical events now known as the Pazzi Conspiracy. It contains minor deviations from historical accounts, while remaining true to the overall story. See the Appendices for more information about historical accuracy.

The author commissioned a new translation of Giovan Battista da Montesecco's confession from the original Italian by Jenny Gherpelli. This version is used as a basis for the confession quotes in the text and is included in the Appendices.

First Edition, June, 2016
8/2/16

Triptych

A picture on three panels. Each panel tells its own story and contributes to the picture as a whole.

Each of John Van Roekel's novels tells a story from three intertwined points of view.

A portion of the reverse side of the Stefaneschi Triptych by the Italian painter Giotto. Pinacoteca Vaticana, Rome.

The *camiciaia* worked for individual clients from her own home or convent.

Carole Collier Frick
Dressing Renaissance Florence:
Families, Fortunes, and Fine Clothing

For it is ill living in Florence for the rich, unless they rule.

Lorenzo de Medici

For Pam

Table of Contents

Characters

Rome

Giovan Battista da Montesecco
Captain of the Apostolic Palace Guard and Commandant of Castel Sant'Angelo. Loyal to Count Riario and Pope Sixtus IV.

Archbishop Francesco Salviati Riario
Archbishop of Pisa and a nephew of Pope Sixtus IV.

Francesco de' Pazzi
A banker in Rome from the powerful Pazzi family of Florence.

Count Girolamo Riario
Count of Imola and Forlì and a nephew of Pope Sixtus IV.

Francesco della Rovere, Pope Sixtus IV
The current Pope.

Filiberto
A soldier under Giovan's command.

Father Nicolo
Giovan's friend and confessor.

Paulo
An altar boy serving as an aide to Giovan.

Florence

Alfeo
Giovan's guard in the Palazzo della Signoria tower cell.

Fioretta Gorini
Mistress of Giuliano.

Lucia
Servant and friend of Fioretta.

Antonio Gorini
Fioretta's father.

Lorenzo de' Medici
Also known as Lorenzo the Magnificent. The powerful political leader and art patron of Florence.

Giuliano de' Medici
Handsome and popular younger brother of Lorenzo.

Stefano
Servant of Giuliano.

Bruna
Stefano's mother, also a servant in the Medici household.

Sandro Botticelli
Painter and friend to Fioretta and Giuliano, as well as Lorenzo.

Jacopo de' Pazzi
Former Gonfaloniere of Justice and leader of the Pazzi family.

Antonio Maffei
A clerk in the Inquisitor's Court of Florence, originally from Volterra.

Cesare Petrucci
Current Gonfaloniere of Justice.

Lucrezia Tornabuoni Medici
Mother of Lorenzo and Giuliano.

Simonetta Vespucci
La bella Simonetta, a great beauty and Giuliano's first love, died 1476.

Nóna
A woman in Lucia's village.

Pisa

Thadeous Phylacus
Greek tutor of Raffaele Riario.

Raffaele Sansoni Riario
A nephew of Pope Sixtus IV, studying at the University of

Pisa.

Dante Carpani
Librarian and friend of Thadeous.

Tessa Carpani
The wife of Dante Carpani

Father Bernardo
Raffaele's religious tutor and confessor.

Constantinople - 1453

Young Thadeous Phylacus
Protégé of Pletho.

George Gemistus (Pletho)
Greek philosopher, scholar and writer.

Lauro
Mercenary soldier from Genoa, serving under Giovan.

Young Giovan Battista
Mercenary hired by the Byzantine Emperor.

Constantine XI Dragases Palaiologos
Emperor of Byzantium.

Giovanni Giustiniani
Leader of all foreign troops in Constantinople.

Mehmed II
The Ottoman sultan attacking Constantinople.

Rome - 1523

Giulio di Giuliano de' Medici
Son of Giuliano.

Stefano
Servant of Giulio.

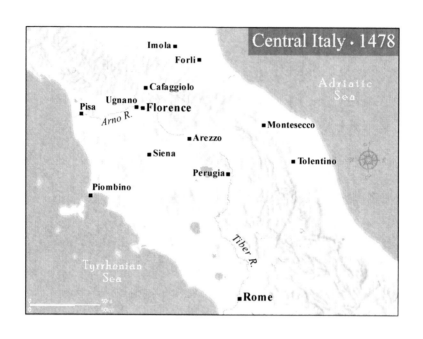

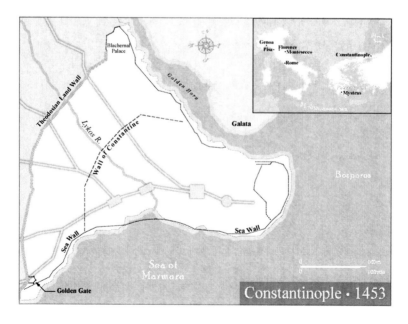

Chapter One

May 3, 1478

Eight Hours Until Dawn

The Arno was turbid with spring rains and invisible in darkness below, as were the sixty thousand Florentine citizens in their houses, all of whom wanted Giovan to die. He gazed out the cell's window into the moonless night, noting a lonely campfire flickering in the hills beyond the city walls. Perhaps it belonged to some poor goatherd who knew nothing of the turmoil that plagued this city and was ignorant of Giovan's great crime.

Giovan felt a vibration rumbling up through the stone floor as the mechanism of the massive clock turned below. A lever dropped into a slot on its count-wheel, and the clock bell struck three times, marking the hours since the sun had fallen behind the Tuscan hills.

It was an odd place for a prison cell, high in the clock tower. With barely room for a bed and a little table holding paper, a quill pen and an inkpot, the cell stank of burning olive oil from its single lamp. The guard—his name was Alfeo—sat on a stool in front of the ironclad door, and more guards stood watch outside in the stairwell.

Giovan turned away from the window, and the wool of his winter camicia rubbed against the open wounds on his back. Despite the chill in the cell, beads of sweat appeared on his forehead.

"I told them…"

Alfeo stirred. "What?"

"Nothing, you brute. Go back to sleep."

Alfeo grunted and fell silent.

Giovan had told them from the beginning that he would

write the truth, but still they used the scoriada, and only when he'd been beaten into unconsciousness did they stop, afraid he would be unable to complete his final task.

He returned to the bed, sat behind the table and picked up the pen. He wrote.

> *In this confession I will make known how His Holiness the Pope commanded the murder of Lorenzo de' Medici and his brother Giuliano.*

Three bell strikes—three hours since sunset. As it was early May, he had another eight hours or so before dawn spread out across Florence. He was to finish his confession by then. After that, they would take him to the Podestà. He wrote.

> *Firstly, I spoke about this in Rome with Archbishop Salviati and Francesco de Pazzi.*

He let the feather touch his lip for a moment, remembering.

One Year Earlier

Giovan hated the burners of marble.

Standing atop the Bastion of Saint John, Giovan scowled as white plumes, like the smoke of funeral pyres after a battle, rose above the city across the Tiber. Once, he had led some of his soldiers over the Sant'Angelo Bridge and confronted a man at the ruins of Caesar Augustus's mausoleum. A Hungarian ex-slave, he was chipping away marble blocks each day and burning them on his charcoal fire for lime, which he sold for fertilizer and whitewash. He pleaded that he had no other way to feed his family, so Giovan gave him some coins. Then Giovan had drawn his longsword and chased the marble burner away.

It had done no good, of course. Today, a smoke column again rose from poor Augustus's grave, as well as half a dozen others places across the city. Giovan shook his head and sighed. The ancient Rome of the emperors was disappearing before his eyes. The wind blew from the south, and the smells of the new Rome assailed his nose: dead mules and dogs, garbage and sewage in the streets. In the Forum Magnum, cows grazed among the broken columns.

Bang!

Giovan started and then grinned. "Filiberto, you waste too much powder," he shouted down at the leader of the gun crew below him. The sweet scent of gunpowder wafted up to him.

Filiberto, a portly soldier standing with his men beside a bronze cannon, grinned up at Giovan and gave a careless salute. After a lazy hour of mock firing, Giovan had allowed them to discharge a single shot with no ball and only half a powder charge.

"That was hardly enough for a good fart," Filiberto shouted, and Giovan laughed.

The Bastion of Saint John stood in the southeast corner of the massive fortress, Castel Sant'Angelo. As captain of the Apostolic Palace Guard, Giovan also commanded Sant'Angelo and had walked its ramparts for eight years, inspecting its walls and the soldiers who manned them.

Giovan had been a soldier for forty years, first as a mercenary and then in service to three popes. Years of riding had left him bowlegged, which he knew exaggerated his short stature, and these last years of garrison duty had added a paunch that made his sword belt uncomfortably tight. That morning his servant had offered to poke a new belt hole, but Giovan had boxed his ears in reply. Unlike the nobles and clerics he dealt with daily who wore their hair fashionably long and were clean-shaven, Giovan's wispy blond fringe gave the appearance of baldness, and he took pride in his neat goatee.

Giovan pulled himself up ramrod straight, his hands clasped behind his back, and slowly turned, surveying Sant'Angelo. Deep inside was the tomb of another Roman emperor, Hadrian. Giovan had been in charge of the castle's renovation since His Holiness's election, and he had tried to protect the vestiges of this once magnificent mausoleum. Sadly, from where he stood, it was completely obscured by the brickwork of the fortress's ramparts and bastions.

"Captain Giovan Battista da Montesecco?"

Giovan turned and saw an unfamiliar servant, his elaborate uniform edged in red piping indicating he was from a bishop's household. Giovan nodded.

"My master, The Most Reverend Francesco Salviati Riario, Archbishop of Pisa, commands you to attend him in his Vatican apartment."

Salviati? Giovan hadn't heard that the Archbishop had come to Rome. His Holiness, Pope Sixtus IV, had numerous nephews, and Salviati was reputed to be a favorite. Two years earlier Sixtus had appointed him to the bishopric of Pisa, but there had been some sort of trouble about it, something about Lorenzo de' Medici.

Giovan arched an eyebrow. "Your master commands me?"

The messenger swallowed, but stood his ground. "Yes, Captain. He wishes me to remind you that he is cousin to His Excellency, Count Girolamo Riario."

"Ah."

That made a difference. Another favorite papal nephew, Count Riario was rumored to be the Pope's illegitimate son. So while Giovan's official loyalty lay chiefly with His Holiness, he had gladly provided many services to Count Riario over the years, such as chasing off a gang of bandits that had been plaguing his small principality.

"When does the Archbishop wish me to attend him?" Giovan asked.

"Now, if it is convenient."

Giovan glanced down at his uniform: leather breaches, linen shirt and a doublet, its red color indicating fealty to His Holiness. His pointed shoes were scuffed and his hose drooped a bit below the knees. He could change, but he decided his appearance was adequate for a mere archbishop.

"Fortunately, I am available to His Eminence now," he said.

A parapet walk ran atop the outer rampart, and they followed it around to the Bastion of Saint Mark on the opposite side of the fortress. As they entered the tower, Filiberto and the men from his gun crew emerged from a passageway and watched.

"Filiberto, come with me," Giovan said as he strode by.

"But, Captain, it's almost time for our noon meal."

"Missing a meal will do you no harm," Giovan called out over his shoulder. Filiberto's men laughed.

Filiberto grumbled and hurried to catch up, falling into step beside Giovan and puffing a little.

"What's this about?" he asked.

Giovan ignored him.

Before them, the ancient Totila Wall stretched out straight as a bowstring toward the Vatican, a half-mile away. Years before, Giovan had supervised the rebuilding of this old wall and added a parapet walk on top which provided easy communication between Sant'Angelo and the Apostolic Palace.

As they followed the messenger, Giovan glanced back. High above the great hulking fortress, the plumes of the marble burners were still visible, climbing into the Roman sky. Yes, they were like the pyres after the Battle of Rimini— where Matthias had died.

A few minutes later, they descended a stone staircase and entered the papal palace. Giovan knew that besides the Pope's chambers, the palace contained a number of residences, apparently including one for Archbishop Salviati. The corridor had no carpets, and several of the colorful floor tiles were cracked or broken. Faded tapestries lined the walls between a half-dozen nondescript oak doors. The palace had fallen into disrepair during the Avignon papacy, and His Holiness had not yet acquired sufficient funds to rebuild it.

The messenger stopped in front of an unmarked door. "I will announce you." He slipped inside.

Filiberto gazed at the decayed splendor around him, and Giovan guessed he'd never been inside the Vatican proper.

"I'm to meet with Archbishop Salviati," Giovan said. "You stay here and rescue me when the noon bell rings."

Filiberto nodded, his insolence forgotten in the face of papal elegance, faded though it was.

The door opened, and Giovan stepped through into a windowless room where a man in a fine red cassock sat writing at a polished walnut table. A carved and painted coat-of-arms with a distinctive stair-step pattern on its shield hung on the wall behind him. Giovan assumed it belonged to the Salviati family.

Glancing up, Archbishop Salviati lay down his quill pen and stood to greet Giovan. He held out his hand.

"Your Eminence." Giovan bowed and kissed the episcopal ring.

"Captain," Salviati said with a slight tilt of his head.

Giovan noticed a man sitting in one of two carved chairs in front of the table. This man now stood. He was short, plump and dressed in a bright green tunic, its hood carefully folded across his shoulders in the style currently fashionable in Rome for powerful, worldly men. In contrast, Salviati's unadorned cassock, while clearly of fine wool, seemed modest.

"I have the pleasure of introducing my dear friend, Signore Francesco de' Pazzi," Salviati said, "the director of the renowned Pazzi Bank here in Rome."

Francesco blushed with pleasure at this compliment. He had straight blond hair falling in bangs over his forehead. Even longer on the sides, he tucked it back behind his ears as he stepped forward and bowed slightly.

Giovan hesitated, unsure about the proper response. He knew Francesco was a member of a powerful banking family based in Florence, but he was not of noble birth. He returned Francesco's bow with the same limited degree of respect.

Francesco recoiled at this and glared at Giovan, who returned the gaze, guessing that he had made a miscalculation.

Salviati stepped around the table and stood between them. "Gentlemen, please." He touched Francesco's elbow and did the same with Giovan. "We meet today for the glory of God and in service to His Holiness. I pray we will all become great friends."

Both Giovan and Francesco crossed themselves. Then Giovan bowed with exaggerated formality to Francesco, and the man responded with a satisfied smile.

"Please." Salviati gestured that they should sit, and as he returned to the other side of the table, Giovan and Francesco stood eyeing each other. They sat in unison as the archbishop settled into place and gazed at them.

"His Holiness has asked me to perform a service," Salviati said. "He is vexed by the situation in Florence." He paused. "As am I." He glanced at Francesco.

"I also," Francesco said.

"The Medici forget themselves, Lorenzo in particular," Salviati said.

"They call him *Magnifico,*" Francesco said. "At twenty-eight years old. And his brother, the handsome one, is even younger."

Salviati looked at Francesco with a hint of impatience. "This is true. But, more bothersome to His Holiness is that Lorenzo reaches beyond Florence."

"Pisa," Giovan said.

Salviati's cordial countenance gave way to a flash of anger, and Giovan wondered if he'd made another mistake. He remembered that Lorenzo had opposed Salviati's appointment as Archbishop of Pisa and had even prevented him from taking up residency for a year.

Salviati's fists clenched on the table surface before him. "Yes." he said, his voice barely controlled. "Pisa is, of course, a source of annoyance to His Holiness. And to me. Lorenzo has no right to interfere with the papal prerogative to appoint archbishops." As he said Lorenzo's name, he banged the table top with his fists.

"Of course," Giovan said.

Salviati gazed at him as though he was trying gauge Giovan's true sympathy.

Giovan wasn't sure what he thought yet. "How can I be of service?" he asked.

"The important thing," Francesco said, interrupting, "is you must understand that this is a secret. You must not speak of what we discuss today."

Giovan kept his expression neutral. To Salviati, he said, "I hope Your Eminence knows of the many services I have performed for His Holiness and Count Riario. Do you doubt me?"

"No, no. Of course not." Salviati glared at Francesco and added, "Among Captain Battista's many virtues is confidentiality."

"Of course," Francesco said.

Another pause. Giovan waited.

Salviati shifted in his chair. He picked up his quill pen and then set it back down. "Captain," he said. He cleared his throat. "We propose to change the state of Florence. Do you take my meaning?"

Giovan blinked. Change the state of Florence? An odd phrase. "I'm sorry, Your Eminence," he said. "I am a soldier and don't understand politics."

Salviati's eyes bored into Giovan's. "You're too modest. We are determined to do this. We think your talents will be helpful."

Giovan dropped his gaze, thinking. Change the state of Florence. By force. "You propose a military solution," he said, looking at Salviati.

Both Salviati and Francesco smiled.

"Yes, a military solution," Francesco said.

"What do you want to do, specifically?" Giovan asked.

"We're not experts in this." Salviati spread his hands in front of him. "What do you suggest?"

"Me? Why, I have no idea." Giovan thought for a moment. "I could lead an attack on Florence."

"No," Francesco said. "I am a Florentine first. I won't allow my city to be attacked and to become a vassal of Rome."

"Yes," Salviati said. "We prefer something a bit more subtle."

So they meant assassination. They had no idea how to do this and wanted him to propose some kind of plan. "I am the servant of His Holiness and of Count Riario."

"We understand," Salviati said. "I assure you that our ideas meet with their approval."

Giovan wasn't sure he believed this. It was difficult to imagine the Pope, the successor of Saint Peter, countenancing political assassination. He glanced back and forth between the shifty-eyed Francesco and the stone-faced Archbishop Salviati.

"Tell me more about why this is necessary," he said.

"My family is the oldest and most esteemed in Florence," Francesco said as he leaned forward in his chair. "The Medici are upstarts. Yet they control everything in the city."

"Forgive me, sir," Giovan said. "I thought Florence was a republic. You select your leaders by drawing names from some kind of bag."

"Yes, the *borse*," Francesco said. "But who controls the names going into it? Lorenzo and his cronies. He pulls the strings and only his marionette friends benefit."

"Ah, I see," Giovan said. "Very unfair."

"There is a commercial aspect," Salviati said. "Come, Francesco. Now is the time to be frank."

"Yes, well, that's true. The Medici Bank has branches in many foreign cities. When a member of our Weaver's Guild wishes to buy wool in England, he need not carry the gold florins with him. The roads and seas are too dangerous. Instead, he takes a paper from the Medici Bank in Florence, and the London branch gives him the money to make the purchase, minus a large commission, of course. Lorenzo's grandfather, Cosimo, perfected this system, and it has made the Medici family the wealthiest in Florence, perhaps all of Italy."

"Doesn't your bank do the same?" Giovan asked.

"We do," Francesco replied. "But it will be more convenient without the Medici family."

Giovan knew he meant more profitable. He turned back to Salviati. "I understand your anger at Lorenzo because of Pisa," he said with care. "But why would His Holiness desire such a drastic action? And why would Count Riario agree?"

"I assure you, they have their reasons," Salviati replied. "Of course, we cannot speak for them."

"I see." Giovan thought for a moment. "You said the Medici *family*."

"The brother, Giuliano," Salviati said, "is also popular—"

Someone knocked on the door and, as they all turned toward it, Filiberto stuck his head in. "Noon bell, sir."

Giovan stood. "As I said, I am the servant of His Holiness and the Count. Now, if you will excuse me, I must go to prayer." Giovan bowed, and as he followed Filiberto out of the room, he glanced back and saw that the faces of the archbishop and the banker bore astonished expressions, as if Giovan had just burst into ribald song or pissed in the corner.

In the hallway, Filiberto gave him an appraising look. "They're powerful men," he said.

Giovan touched a tapestry hanging by the doorway. The wool felt damp and moldy beneath his fingertips. "True. But now they know I owe them no fealty." He shrugged.

A moment later, they climbed the stairway to the top of the Totila Wall, and Giovan saw Sant'Angelo in the distance. Most likely this will come to nothing. Francesco was a silly fop. But Salviati… That man wanted revenge. And he had the ear of the Pope.

Fioretta Gorini eyed the men around her, wondering about their *camicia*, their underwear. She ignored the weavers, shoemakers, dyers and the other workmen because they had no money, and money had been on her mind lately. She was only interested in well-dressed gentlemen who could afford to pay for new camicia.

"Some of them must be unmarried and have no mother," she said to Lucia, who walked at her side on the Via dei Benci.

The narrow cobblestone street was thronged with Florentines who had come to watch the jousting.

"Or sisters," Lucia replied. "Perhaps, one in a hundred will have no women to sew for him."

That didn't sound hopeful. She had asked Giuliano about camicia, but with a mother and two sisters, he gave no thought whatever to his underwear, and certainly not to the underwear of other men.

Giuliano! Her heart gave a little jump in her chest. Giuliano de' Medici, the second most powerful man in Florence, and the most beloved by the people—Giuliano, twenty-five years old, and so handsome and brave and athletic. Her Giuliano, her lover. Thoughts of money and camicia flew from her head like pigeons on a piazza scattered by a running child. She skipped ahead and then walked backward through the thickening crowd, facing Lucia.

"Have you ever seen Giuliano joust?" Fioretta asked, her voice lilting with excitement.

"I've never seen *any* jousting," Lucia replied. Two years older than Fioretta, short and buxom, Lucia's skin was darkened by years of work in the vineyards near her home village outside Florence. Lucia was the only servant Fioretta's father could afford, but Fioretta often confided in her, especially when they were away from the house together.

Fioretta knew they made an odd couple, as she herself was tall, slim and fashionably pale—Giuliano said he loved her ivory complexion. She sometimes played a game when she and Lucia walked together on the street, and she observed the eyes of men as they approached. Their gaze would flit back and forth between her and Lucia and then settle on one of them, and most often it was Fioretta. She'd been a plain and gawky young girl, but adolescence had brought a beauty that surprised her still as she approached her eighteenth birthday. Her auburn hair with its gentle curls contrasted with her green eyes and light complexion, giving her an appearance that Giuliano had described in a love poem as a marriage of the setting sun and the rising full moon.

"Ouch, you pig," Lucia cried out. She turned and punched the shoulder of a boy walking next to her, striking him hard enough to knock him back into the arms of his laughing friends. "He pinched me."

Fioretta smiled in sympathy. In Fioretta's game, sometimes the eyes of the men, especially the young ones, came to rest on Lucia. Fioretta guessed they valued a big bosom over pale white skin.

Clang, clang, clang.

Over the chatter of the crowd and the shuffling of feet, the bells of Santa Croce rang nearby, signaling that the parade would soon begin. They were getting close to the piazza. As Fioretta returned to Lucia's side, she heard the staccato beat of the tabors and the taratantara call of trumpets. The crowd surged ahead.

Something else happened when Fioretta and Lucia walked together. Lucia complained that her short legs made it difficult to keep up. But Fioretta had noticed that when Lucia was excited, the reverse was true. Today, Lucia grabbed Fioretta's hand and pulled her along.

"Did you see the last joust?" Lucia asked, looking back over her shoulder.

"Oh yes, two years ago. It was so exciting. Although it's not like the knights of old that you hear about where they charge at each other. Now they just charge at the *Saracen*."

"What's that?"

"It's this straw dummy with a shield for a target," Fioretta said. "That day was the first time I ever saw Giuliano. He rode Samuele, of course, and he never missed the target." Samuele was Giuliano's black stallion, a gift from the Duke of Urbino. "Of course, he paid no attention to me. I was just one of a hundred young girls calling out his name as he rode past during the parade. Out in front of him, Stefano carried a banner painted by Sandro Botticelli."

"Stefano?" Lucia slowed to walk beside Fioretta. Stefano

was Giuliano's favorite servant, and Fioretta had seen him and Lucia exchange glances.

"Yes, Stefano. Why, do you ask?"

Lucia blushed and shook her head. "So, Sandro Botticelli painted the banner," she said. "He's the one who painted that portrait of you."

"Yes." Giuliano had hired Sandro six months before, soon after she had begun to share Giuliano's bed. She had sat, quiet and still, for days, but Sandro was entertaining and by the time the portrait was finished, he'd become her friend. The painting hung in Giuliano's bedroom.

"What was the banner like?" Lucia asked.

"A pale shade of pink with gold letters saying *La Sans Pareille*—that's French for *The Unparalleled One*—and a beautiful portrait of Athena."

"And you were the model?"

"I *told* you, we hadn't even met." Fioretta said. "So how could I be the model?"

"Oh, sorry." Lucia looked surprised. "Do you know who was…" She trailed off as she saw Fioretta's scowling at her.

Fioretta was too embarrassed to tell her that the model had been Simonetta Vespucci. All Florence had adored her, the most beautiful woman in Italy, and they called her *La Bella Simonetta*. It was the custom for a competitor to dedicate his joust to an older, married woman, and while Simonetta was married, it had been a little scandalous that she was young. Darker rumors claimed that she and Giuliano were lovers.

How I had envied her. Despised her. But no longer. La Bella Simonetta is dead, died of consumption last year. Now Giuliano belongs to me alone.

"Perhaps he'll have a banner with your portrait this time," Lucia said, eyes dancing with excitement. "He should."

Fioretta shook her head. "Not today."

"Oh, phah. So what if your father finds out about Giuliano? It won't kill him."

"It might."

"Still, if ever he was to announce his love for you," Lucia said, "wouldn't a banner today be just the best way to do it?"

Fioretta shook her head again. Giuliano would follow the custom. But what if Lucia was right? Imagine it—her likeness on his banner. Sandro had painted her portrait once before after all, so it *was* possible. Such a romantic, chivalrous gesture would be so typical of Giuliano.

Fioretta and Lucia emerged onto the Piazza Santa Croce, the largest public square in Florence. The immense Basilica di Santa Croce loomed over the piazza, and thousands of people, citizens of Florence and many from the neighboring towns and farms, filled it from one end to the other. The drums beat out a continuous thunder that echoed from the buildings around them.

Lucia pulled Fioretta forward, pushing people aside, shouting, "Make way, make way for a lady." Fioretta blushed at this. She wore the lovely red cloak that Giuliano had given her, but beneath it she wore a plain cotton dress, not very different from that worn by Lucia and many of the common women around them. Even so, she must look like a lady as the people cleared a space in front.

The drums stopped, and the square still seemed to reverberate with their beating. Shop girls and wealthy wool merchants alike cried out in excitement as the trumpets announced the parade. Marshals struggled to clear a way through the crowd, which surged forward and back as everyone pushed to see.

First came the procession of the religious orders: the Dominicans first, of course, followed by the Franciscans, the Servites, the Carmelites and the Cistercians. As the priests and monks shuffled past in their robes, cassocks and vestments, Fioretta crossed herself, as did the people around her. Knowing something of Lucia's experience with priests, Fioretta was not surprised when Lucia glared at these men of God and kept her hands at her sides.

Next the *batteristi* marched past pounding the tabors,

followed by the *sbandieratori* swinging and tossing their colorful silk flags high into the air. Again everyone raised their collective voice in continuous cheers.

At last, the jousters paraded before them on their powerful, nervous steeds, each with a banner carried in front by an equerry. From the four districts of the city, each team wore colored surcoats over their armor: the Blues from Santa Croce, the Whites from Santo Spirito, the Greens from San Giovanni and last, Giuliano's team, the Reds from Santa Maria Novella.

Fioretta's cloak was of fine English wool, dyed deep crimson to match Giuliano's team color.

Fioretta and Lucia stood on their tiptoes, peering down the line of marching men and horses. There — a bright red banner.

"I see them," Fioretta cried, one hand grasping Lucia's shoulder, the other waving a red handkerchief above her head. They bounced up and down in excitement.

The red banner must belong to one of Giuliano's teammates, as Giuliano, on the best horse with the most beautiful livery and regalia, would come last. As the parade passed by, the Reds came closer. Fioretta leaned forward, trying to catch sight of Giuliano, wondering about his banner and what Lucia had said. Would her picture be on Giuliano's banner? No, it was impossible.

The cheering dropped to an excited murmur as Fioretta caught a glimpse of a pink banner. Standing in front of her, Lucia turned and gazed up at Fioretta. "Is that…"

It couldn't be. Fioretta saw the banner in full. Tears welled up in her eyes as she recognized the French words and the portrait of that woman. The dead Simonetta.

The tabors and trumpets were silent now, the sbandieratori stood motionless, their flags furled at their sides, and whispers rustled through the crowd like a breeze through dried oak leaves.

All Florentines knew Giuliano's history, of course. Many of them must recognize the banner, must think that Giuliano still loved La Bella Simonetta. What were the people around her whispering? Where they casting furtive glances at her? Did they know about her? Did they pity her?

Sobbing, Fioretta covered her face in shame, turned and tried to force her way back through the throng. The people were packed so tight that she could couldn't move. Lucia pushed from behind and shouted, "Make way. This lady is sick."

They escaped the crowd. The sun had crept behind the buildings facing the Via dei Benci, leaving it shrouded in shadow. Fioretta Gorini, stumbling over the cobblestones, ran down the street with Lucia trailing behind.

The front door was stuck again. Fioretta wiped the tears from her cheeks and pushed. Her father's ramshackle single-story house sat just inside the town wall and had been in his family for generations. While she and Lucia worked hard to keep it clean and neat, the house itself had fallen into disrepair since Fioretta's mother had died seven years before. The red tile roof leaked in the frequent Tuscan rain storms. Lucia joined her at the door and together, they forced it open and went inside.

Antonio Gorini rose from his chair by the fireplace and came out into the hallway. He stared at Fioretta's red cloak.

"Papa, I thought you were visiting..." Fioretta stopped as she noticed her father's friend, the odious Father Maffei, sitting by the fire. "Oh. Hello, Father," she said, with a cursory nod. Even though Maffei was not a priest, just a clerk in the Inquisitors Court, he still demanded that she and Lucia call him *Father*. He wore a priest's ankle-length cassock and, as always, it was soiled and stained.

"Fioretta. And the delightful Lucia." Maffei's voice was unctuous. As he stood, his eyes flitted between Fioretta and Lucia, and then focused on Lucia's chest. "How good to see you both."

Lucia gave the briefest possible curtsy.

"Where did you get that cloak?" Gorini said. "Tell me."

"We made it, Papa, Lucia and I." The lies came easily now. She took off the cloak and folded it over her arm.

Her father stepped closer, seized the cloak's hem, and rubbed the fabric between his fingers. He'd once been a successful wool broker. "And the cloth? This is good quality. What did it cost? Where did you get the money?"

"Uh... Uh..." Fioretta stammered, trying to think.

"It was a gift." Lucia said. "The cloth is from her Aunt Maria."

Fioretta thought it was a good lie. Maria was the sister of Fioretta's dead mother, and she lived in Siena, two days distance by horseback. Her father wouldn't trouble himself to write to her and if he did, she most likely wouldn't reply.

Gorini turned on Lucia, his face twitching. "You kept this secret from me. You sleep in my house, you eat my food, and you keep secrets from me?" He grabbed her shoulders and shook her so hard that her head jerked back and forth.

"Papa." Fioretta grabbed his arm.

Gorini wrenched his arm free and raised it to strike Lucia.

"Stop, Papa, please," Fioretta said. "I told her not to tell you. It's my fault."

Gorini lowered his arm and gave Lucia a final, violent shake. "Your loyalty is to me, not her. Understand?"

"Yes, sir." Tears ran down Lucia's plump cheeks.

Father Maffei, who had been watching, stepped close to Lucia. "Saint Peter tells us, 'Servants, be in subjection to your masters with all fear.' Be a good girl, Lucia, and do as Our Lord commands."

Lucia said nothing and turned away. With her back to Gorini and Maffei so only Fioretta could see, she made the obscene sign of the fig, clenching her fist with the thumb thrust between the first two fingers. She retreated into the kitchen, and Fioretta heard the rear door slam as Lucia went out into the alleyway behind the house.

"You went to watch the jousting," Gorini said. "An idiotic waste. The looms are idle. The market is closed. Phaah. Lorenzo and his cronies—"

"Would you like something to eat?" Fioretta asked. "Father Maffei, we've some fresh plums. Or today's bread?"

"Perhaps a cup of wine?" Maffei said.

"Yes," Gorini said. "Fioretta, tell that girl to bring us wine."

"Yes, Papa."

They returned to their seats by the hearth, and Fioretta knew they'd resume their political talk. Her father would rant about Lorenzo and the men who ruled the city with him. Maffei would recount how years before the young Lorenzo had ordered his hired troops to sack Volterra, Maffei's home town. She'd heard their complaints a hundred times.

Fioretta went into the kitchen and closed the door, leaning against it.

Some mornings, after creeping home from a night with Giuliano, she lay in her bed shaking in fear that father would somehow find out she was the mistress of Lorenzo's brother. At such times she hated her father. He was a fool who had bungled the investment for her dowry, which left her with no possibility of a proper marriage.

She needed to move out of this house. And for that, she needed a way to make money. Giuliano had offered to help, of course. But the events of the day had convinced her that she needed to be independent of her father, of Giuliano, of all men. Both she and Lucia were excellent seamstresses. Fioretta was certain they could support themselves making camicia—if only she could convince Lucia.

Fioretta went through the back door to the alleyway. Lucia stood leaning against the wall, a half-eaten plum in one hand, more cradled in her arm, and a small pile of pits at her feet. She looked at Fioretta with defiance, plum juice on her lips and chin.

"Give me those." Fioretta pointed at the uneaten plums.

"Yes, madam."

"Oh, stop." Fioretta rolled her eyes as she took the plums,

sticky with juice. "Still enough for Papa tonight. Wipe your face."

Lucia ran her sleeve across her mouth.

"I'm sorry," Fioretta said. "Papa used to be different, before you came to us, before my mother died…"

"I know. You've told me."

Fioretta leaned back against the wall next to Lucia. She closed her eyes and sighed. "I thought today was going to be wonderful."

She had pushed the memory of Giuliano's banner from her mind, but now it roiled up in her consciousness like a black thunderhead presaging a spring storm. Tears filled her eyes, and a band of iron seemed to tighten around her chest. Oh, Giuliano…

"I hate men," Lucia said.

"What? *You* hate men? Hah." Fioretta pulled out her kerchief. "Priests are the only men you hate." She dabbed her eyes. "Maybe you're right, though. Me, too. Today, we hate men together."

Lucia grinned at her. "And tomorrow?"

"Tomorrow, we think about money. And camicia. Right?"

Lucia shrugged, and Fioretta put her arm across her shoulder. Together, they walked back into the kitchen. "They want wine," Fioretta said.

Lucia nodded and took out two cups. "This is for Father Maffei." She spat into it.

Fioretta put her hand to her mouth in horror. Then she laughed.

Flames fill the tunnel, searing his bare legs and arms. A thousand tons of stone press down from above, and the shouts of the Turkish miners fill his ears. He must escape, run back to the entrance twenty yards behind him, but he can't move his feet. Fire fills his lungs. He falls to his knees, gasping.

Thadeous sat up in his cot, shaking and sweating, twisted in his blanket. Relief flooded through him as he looked around his tiny room, up under the palazzo's eaves, his books and writing materials scattered on the table and floor. It had been a quarter-century, but still these nightmares plagued him. With a trembling hand, he grabbed the water cup he kept on the little table and gulped down what remained.

A beam of morning sun shone through the single window, promising a new spring day. Below him, he heard the sounds of the household, though it was less busy lately because the Archbishop was in Rome. In the courtyard, the old cook sang without a care as she removed the morning bread from the oven, and he smelled its comforting aroma.

Was Raffaele up? The boy had a lecture this morning, and he had gone out the night before with his friends to celebrate his sixteenth birthday. Thadeous used the chamber pot, pulled a shawl around his shoulders and hobbled down the stairs to Raffaele's room.

Raffaele Sansoni Galeoti Riario, his student and nephew of both the Pope and Archbishop Salviati, lay sprawled across his bed, fully clothed and snoring.

Shaking his head, Thadeous struggled back up the stairs, pausing when he reached his room to catch his breath. He'd give Raffaele a little more time, and then he'd push the boy out the door with no breakfast. It would be a good lesson. Still wheezing, Thadeous dropped back onto his cot and glanced at the book of Greek history he'd been reading. Eventually, the rasp of air through his damaged lungs quieted.

On the table next to his empty water cup lay a stack of blank paper sheets, a bundle of goose-wing quill pens and an inkpot. He had used Archbishop Salviati's money to purchase a new inkpot for Raffaele and had kept this old one, which was still one-quarter full. Thadeous stared at the blank pages. He knew he should start. Instead, he shifted around on the bed so they were out of his sight.

Thadeous picked up the book of Greek history. There were advantages to being the tutor of a wealthy young man studying at the University of Pisa. The library was excellent, and

Thadeous often borrowed books using his young master's name. After a few minutes of flipping through the pages, he tossed down the book. It contained only the briefest description of the Byzantine Empire that had lasted a millennium, and mentioned the fall of Constantinople in a single paragraph.

Thadeous of Constantinople, as some knew him, had been in Italy since that catastrophe, but when he closed his eyes at night, he still heard the crash of the stone cannonballs against the great Theodosian Land Wall. When his hand cramped from too much writing, he remembered his mentor Pletho standing over him, urging him to work faster even as the savage cries of the Ottoman Janissaries came closer. And when he was at the library and opened an old parchment sealed with camphor, the smell took him back to the fire tunnel deep beneath the wall.

For twenty-five years, he'd wanted to tell this story, and yesterday he purchased the paper and quill pens with his own money. His master was often occupied—sometimes with his studies—and this left Thadeous time to do as he pleased. At fifty-three years old, lame, hunched over and his lungs scarred by fire, he knew he had few remaining years. As a scholar, he was determined make a contribution to history.

"I don't feel good," Raffaele croaked, leaning against the doorjamb.

Startled, Thadeous looked up at his pupil. Even in his disheveled state, Raffaele was a handsome boy, a little chubby, but with straight black hair that fell over his eyes.

"You should hurry, otherwise you'll be late for your lecture."

"Ecclesiastical law. Memorization." Raffaele sighed and recited, "Canon 12, 'Universal laws bind everywhere all those for whom they were issued.'" He rolled his eyes.

"*Repetitio est mater studiorum.*"

"Oh Thadeous, it's too early."

"Translate," Thadeous said.

Raffaele furrowed his brow. "Repetition is the mother of studies."

"Good. If you join the Church one day, knowledge of these laws will be useful."

"I pray every night to God that He will not call me to his Church. Is that sacrilege?"

Thadeous laughed carefully, not wanting to trigger a bout of coughing. "You'll have to ask Father Bernardo."

Raffaele glanced at the writing materials on the table, noticing his old inkpot. "Are you working on something?"

"*Procrastinatio odiosa est*," Thadeous said. "You should leave now." He knew his position as the boy's tutor was dependent on Raffaele being successful in his studies; Archbishop Salviati had made that clear. "There are some apples in the kitchen. Take one to eat on the way." Raffaele liked apples. "There's a lecture on Greek architecture this afternoon."

Raffaele perked up, ran his fingers through his hair, and straightened his wrinkled tunic. "Do you want to come to the architecture lecture?"

Thadeous shook his head.

"You could teach it," Raffaele said over his shoulder as he started down the stairs.

As Thadeous shook his head at his young charge, he felt a scrabbling in his chest. He focused on it, slowing his breathing. In his mind, he saw a rat gnawing at his lungs, but by force of will, he drove the rat into a wooden box and latched the lid. The urge to cough abated. He inhaled and felt relieved—it didn't always work.

The empty pages beckoned. He had at least two hours before his master returned.

For years, he'd planned out the story, revising the opening sentence a thousand times. He just needed to write it down, to make a start. With a trembling hand, he selected a quill pen and sharpened it with the little knife he kept for that purpose. He opened the inkwell and dipped the pen. He wrote.

> *I am now called Thadeous of Constantinople because in the year 1453, I was present when the great city of that name fell to the evil and barbarous Ot-*

toman Turks, led by the wicked Sultan Mehmed II.

He worked for an hour, filling the sheet. He described his childhood on Cyprus, where as a young man he'd worked for a time with his father in the vast and ancient copper mines. The work didn't suit him, and his father managed to send him to a school in the Greek Peloponnese. He had done well and eventually became a student of the famous theologian George Gemistus, often called Pletho, and moved with him to the mountain village of Mystras. There they studied old manuscripts, especially those of Plato and Ptolemy, talking and writing about Greece, its history and its problems.

Thadeous wrote another paragraph, describing the event that had changed their lives forever. Emperor Constantine, the eleventh Byzantine emperor to hold that name, had sent a secret summons requiring Pletho to come to Constantinople. With foreboding, they arrived just before Easter in 1453.

All of this was easy to write—like the opening sentence, he'd planned it out for years. Now he finally had to decide whether to tell the full story or not. In the clash of two empires, one ancient and faltering, the other boisterous and savage, in the last great city of Greece, at this momentous event of history, he'd found Lauro, the great and only love of his life.

Twenty-Five Years Earlier

Young Thadeous hunched over a battered table, writing on a parchment sheet.

"How many pages today?" Pletho asked, standing at his shoulder.

"Three."

Pletho leaned down so his nose was close to the half-filled sheet, his weak eyes scanning back and fourth as he struggled to make out the Greek text. Keeping his place by touching a word with his finger, he moved over to the page containing the original, muttering beneath his breath.

Thadeous slid off the bench he'd occupied for hours, standing and stretching and then hurried over to the chamber pot in the corner of the room. When the Emperor had summoned Pletho, Thadeous had assumed their accommodations would be sumptuous and clean, but this room with its tiny windows, cracked walls and dirt floor was the opposite. The sour stench from the pot filled the air.

As he buttoned his trousers, a thunderous crash shook the room, and particles of dust fell from the ceiling. Thadeous hurried back to his master at the table. "That one was close."

The house stood near the immense Theodosian Land Wall, three Roman miles in length. The thirty thousand residents of Constantinople hoped it would protect them from the Turks attacking from the west, the land side. Several times a day, a stone ball from the largest cannon ever forged smashed into the wall, and every time it seemed that it would bring down the crumbling ceiling on top of Thadeous's head.

"Here, the word is θεός, not θέμα." Pletho swept dust from the page Thadeous had copied. "Any half-educated schoolboy would know the difference."

"Sorry, master." Thadeous took the offending sheet, sat down and started to make the correction. "You want me to work quickly—"

"That's no excuse for sloppiness. Do this page again."

This copy was for the Emperor, so it must be perfect. Stifling a sigh, Thadeous grabbed a fresh sheet and resumed his endless task. He averaged five or so pages each day, and there were hundreds of pages that had not yet been copied. When he had a chance, he'd count them, trying to get an idea of how long this work would take—and how long before they could return to Mystras.

Thump, thump, thump. Someone hammered at the door.

Pletho stood. "Keep working."

Thadeous kept his eyes down but listened.

"What do you want?" Pletho asked, opening the door.

"How many men are in this house?" a voice asked. His

Greek was awkward, halting, but still commanding.

"Phah. I've no time for this," Pletho said. The hinges of the door squeaked as he tried to force it shut.

"Stand aside. I come at the command of the Emperor."

Thadeous looked up. A soldier, wearing armor under a dirty white surcoat emblazoned with a red Greek cross, longsword at his side and his helmet under one arm, pushed his way in. His face was framed by dark curly hair so long it swung out from his head when he turned. Beneath coal-black eyebrows, intelligent blue eyes swept around the room, taking in their mean pallets, table and little else beside the chamber pot. Thadeous swallowed when they fixed on him.

"Just the two of you?"

Pletho said nothing, so Thadeous nodded, unsure what else he could do.

"You." The soldier pointed at Thadeous. "Come with me."

Thadeous stood.

"Stop. The Emperor commands us, too. Look." Pletho pointed at the table and the stacks of parchment. "This is for him."

The soldier walked over to the table and picked up the sheet on which Thadeous had been writing. He seemed to be able to read it. He surveyed the stacks—empty pages, originals, copies—and turned to Thadeous. "You've been busy." His voice was softer. "But you still have much to do."

"Yes. And it's important," Thadeous said. He wished he had emptied the chamber pot.

"No doubt." The soldier dropped the page. "But if the land wall falls to the enemy's cannon, then none of this will matter. We need men to rebuild the damage at night." He turned to Pletho. "You're too old, but I'm taking your young friend."

"I'll speak to the Emperor about this outrage."

"Go ahead. He's busy trying to save his empire." The soldier motioned to one of his men standing outside, pointing at Thadeous. "Take him."

"I'll come," Thadeous said lifting his hands in surrender.

He'd known about the danger to the city, of course. How could he not, with cannonballs crashing nearby? But for the first time, he envisioned thousands of Turkish Janissaries swarming over the broken wall, ransacking the city, sweeping into this very room and killing both him and the illustrious Pletho. This handsome young soldier was part of a colossal effort to stop that from happening.

"When will he come back?" Pletho asked.

"Every morning. To sleep."

"I'm sorry, master," Thadeous said.

"Just go."

Thadeous stepped out onto the street where he found a dozen more unarmed and disheartened men. They marched west, toward the wall.

The blue-eyed soldier walked beside Thadeous, pulling his helmet on over his curls, tying the strap beneath his chin. His arms were tan, and muscles bulged beneath his armor.

"Your Greek is good," Thadeous said.

"You mean for a foreigner." He stared ahead at the great wall rising before them at the end of the street. "I'm from Genoa, in the north of Italy. The Emperor hired three hundred of us to defend the city."

"A mercenary."

The solder turned to look at Thadeous, his cerulean blue eyes bright with enthusiasm. "There's the wall. Come on! Maybe we'll kill some Turks today." He punched Thadeous in the shoulder and added, "My name is Lauro."

Chapter Two

Seven Hours Until Dawn

Again the clock bell struck, four slow clangs echoing through the tower. As Giovan laid down his pen, he heard regular soft wheezes that told him Alfeo was asleep on his stool. Another hour gone, and he had so much more to write. Picking up the pen and dipping it into the inkpot, he continued.

> *One day, the Count asked me to join the Archbishop and himself in his room, where he started to talk again about this thing.*

Eleven Months Earlier

Giovan swayed as he stood, his mind empty except for the sound of the choir as it finished the Sanctus.

> *Benedictus qui venit in nomine Domini.*
> *Hosanna in excelsis.*

Three weeks after his meeting with Archbishop Salviati and Francesco de' Pazzi, Giovan now clasped his hands tight against his chest as the chapel returned to an echoing silence. The smell of incense hung in the air.

When he opened his eyes, Giovan saw his friend, Father Nicolo standing before the congregation. Nicolo turned to face the altar for the long Eucharistic Prayer, ignoring the missal held for him by the altar boy.

Giovan knelt, his joints crying out to him, telling him that he was getting old.

Nicolo prayed.

> *Te igitur, clementissime Pater…*

Giovan repeated the words. Then he departed from the

canonical text and continued in Italian beneath his breath, "…
to pray for my son, Matthias, who was lost to me nine years
ago." His throat tightened as he remembered his only child,
just sixteen when an enemy arrow had struck him down. "If, in
your wisdom, you have placed him in Purgatory," Giovan
continued, "please give him the strength to complete his task
so he may join you in heaven and spend eternity with your
Son, Jesus Christ. Amen."

Brushing aside a tear, Giovan returned his attention to
Father Nicolo's prayer.

The Church of San Pellegrino stood inside the Vatican
walls, and it took only a few minutes for Giovan to walk from
Sant'Angelo, something he tried to do every day. In the vaulted apse above Father Nicolo and the altar boy, a medieval
fresco of Christ standing before a golden sky gazed down on
Giovan. Like much of Rome, the fresco was in disrepair,
cracked and smudged by centuries of candle smoke, but Giovan still found comfort in the sad eyes of Jesus, his left hand
holding the Gospel, his right hand lifted in blessing.

The prayer ended, and the altar boy rang the Sanctus Bell.
Giovan made the sign of the cross and climbed to his feet with
the other worshipers. The bell signaled that Communion was
to begin and, as he'd positioned himself at the rear of the nave,
Giovan slipped out the door. He hadn't taken Communion in
nine years. He had accomplished his main purpose in attending today—praying for poor dead Matthias.

Emerging onto the street, he bought an orange from a
vendor. He peeled it as he walked down Via del Pellegrino,
went around the corner and came to the church's back
entrance, where he stepped inside.

The sacristy was cluttered and dusty, reflecting Father
Nicolo's casual approach to the material aspects of his calling.
As he'd done many times before, Giovan sat in the single chair
and waited, eating his orange and licking the sweet juice from
his fingers.

The sound of *Benedicamus Domino* came through the door

leading to the sanctuary, and a moment later Nicolo came into the room, followed by his altar boy.

"Giovan," he said. "I hoped you'd come by for a chat."

Giovan stood and embraced his friend. He stepped back so the boy could remove Nicolo's plain blue stole and hang it on its hook. Unlike many priests, especially in Rome, Nicolo eschewed rich vestments.

"So, Paulo," Giovan said to the boy. "How do you hold up that heavy prayer book for so long? You must be getting very strong."

The boy blushed and said nothing as he took off his own cassock and surplice.

"I don't know why you do it," Giovan continued, "since Father Nicolo doesn't need it."

Paulo glanced over at Nicolo and then whispered, "Sometimes he peeks."

Giovan laughed and tussled the boy's hair. "Remember, Paulo, when you're sixteen, come and see me at the castle. I'll make a place for you as a guardsman."

"If Father Nicolo allows it," Paulo said.

"If your *mother* allows it," Nicolo said. "You'll have more trouble with her than with me, I think. Now thank the good Captain for his offer and then go. I'll see you at Vespers."

Paulo bowed to Giovan and then dashed outside, the door slamming behind him.

"I fear his sixteenth birthday," Nicolo said. He pulled a wide-brimmed felt hat from a peg beside the door and together, he and Giovan stepped outside. "Watch over him, Giovan."

"Oh, he'll be safe enough with me in Sant'Angelo. Italy is at peace and will probably stay that way."

"You sound wistful for more combative times."

"I am a soldier for His Holiness and for our God," Giovan said. "But I am still a soldier."

They walked in silence for a while along the dirty street.

"I have been thinking about Matthias today," Giovan said.

"Ah, yes. Today is his name day. May 14th, good Saint Matthias."

"Sadly, my Matthias was no saint. And so he in Purgatory."

"Yes," Nicolo said.

"Nine years. I pray every day for his soul."

"As do I. Every day. And as does Rachele, I'm sure."

Rachele was Giovan's wife of twenty-six years. She lived in his home town of Montesecco, far to the north, and he had not spoken to her since just after the death of Matthias.

Giovan stopped walking and turned to Nicolo. "I have a theological question for you, Father."

Nicolo's eyebrows rose.

"How will I know when he has gone to heaven?" Giovan continued. "When will I know that I can stop praying for him?"

"Is praying for the soul of your only child such a burden to you, Giovan?"

"No, no. Of course not."

"Then perhaps it is God's will that through our prayers for departed ones, we are brought closer to Him."

Giovan thought about this. It seemed to him now that his question had showed terrible selfishness. Nicolo must be correct. "Yes," he said. "Thank you, my friend."

"Captain!"

Giovan turned and saw a familiar servant running down the street toward them.

"This can only be trouble," he muttered to Nicolo.

"Captain," the servant said, out of breath. "My master, The Most Reverend—"

"Yes, yes, I know. Archbishop Salviati. What does he want now?" Giovan put his hands on his hips and glared at the unfortunate messenger.

"My master is with Count Riario in the palace and requests your presence."

"The Count," Giovan said. "Lead the way." Looking back over his shoulder, he called out, "I must go, Nicolo. Many thanks."

"Go with God, Giovan."

Giovan knew Count Riario owned a palazzo on the east side of the Tiber, but His Holiness had also given him the use of some rooms in the Vatican Palace. As Giovan visited Riario there often and knew the way, he followed the messenger with impatience through the narrow Vatican streets.

In the section of the palace where the Count lived, the servants swept the corridors and the tapestries lining the walls were rich with color. The messenger slipped inside to announce him and then beckoned him to enter the familiar room.

Count Girolamo Riario, Lord of Forlì and Imola, stood to greet Giovan. A rotund man in a bright green tunic edged with gold cord, Riario had the appearance of powerful man. Having worked with him for many years, Giovan knew him to be a man of only modest intellect. Archbishop Salviati stood next him.

A pair of papal nephews, Giovan thought. "Your Excellency," he said, bowing to Riario. "Your Eminence," he added, turning to Salviati, who made a little gesture that indicated that kissing his episcopal ring was not necessary. Was the Archbishop being magnanimous because he wanted something?

"Captain," Riario replied, also bowing, but to a calculated lesser degree. "Please sit," he said. "Bring us wine," he shouted, and a moment later a servant appeared with three silver goblets on a silver tray. Giovan noticed that the Archbishop took only a small, polite sip, and so Giovan did the same.

"Ah, that's good." Riario smacked his lips. He looked from Salviati to Giovan. "The Archbishop tells me you've already discussed a certain matter that His Holiness has put into our hands. What do you think?"

"I don't know what to think, Your Excellency," Giovan replied. "I don't understand what you want. Once that is clear to me, I'll be happy to say."

Salviati scowled. "When we met before, didn't I explain to

you how we want to change the state of Florence?"

"Yes, Your Eminence. You told me Lorenzo and his brother must be removed from power, but you did not tell me *how* you want to do it."

"And I explained that this is why we need you, a military man."

Giovan said nothing, waiting.

Salviati stared at him for a moment. Riario took another deep drink.

Finally, Salviati said, "Of course. You expressed concern as to whether His Excellency the Count is supportive of this plan."

Giovan nodded and turned to Count Riario. "And do you support it, Excellency?"

Riario's face was flushed as he nodded and said, "Yes." It appeared that he didn't want to explain further.

This puzzled Giovan. Why was Riario so reticent to express his opinion? Giovan was anxious to be of service to him, as he often had in the past. In return, Count Riario used his influence with his uncle, the Pope, to advance Giovan's career and provide funds for improvements to Sant'Angelo.

Giovan did know that some years ago, His Holiness had tried to buy the principality of Imola for Riario so he'd have more lands to rule over and could claim the title of Count. But Lorenzo refused to let the Medici bank finance the purchase because he had his own designs on Imola. Sixtus was forced to go to Lorenzo's rival, the Pazzi bank.

Giovan had a thought. "When we last met," he said to Salviati, "Francesco de' Pazzi was with us."

"Francesco has his uses," Salviati said, rolling his eyes ever so slightly. "But it wasn't necessary that he join us today."

Pieces of the puzzle were dropping into place. Francesco was a buffoon. Salviati was the force behind this plan, and Count Riario was content to let him take the risk.

"And His Holiness?" Giovan asked.

Riario stood. "Enough. Come with me," he said over his shoulder as he bustled from the room. Salviati shrugged and gave Giovan a tight smile. Together, they followed Riario.

Outside, the new chapel being built for His Holiness rose before them. Construction had started four years before and the outer walls, with their massive plain buttresses, were complete. The sounds of hammering, sawing and workmen's shouts came from high over Giovan's head, where work on the roof was progressing.

Count Riario led them through piles of lumber, red roof tiles and trash to a small doorway in the chapel's near wall and then up a steep, winding staircase. Giovan hadn't seen the interior of the new chapel and he was curious. He smiled as he heard the Count puffing from the exertion.

They emerged into the largest room that Giovan had ever been in and he gaped in wonder. Next to him, a wooden scaffold stretched all the way to the vaulted ceiling, which must have been at least five stories above them. Giovan moved to the center of the room, gazing up. The earthy scent of fresh cut oak surrounded him. At the top of the scaffold, workmen were fitting an immense wooden beam into place.

"When it's completed, this will be the finest chapel in all the world," Salviati said, turning around and gesturing at the walls. "Pilgrims will come from all over Europe to see it."

"Bringing their money," Riario added.

"Yes. Alms for the Church, and business for the merchants. All of this is the good work of His Holiness. He has magnificent plans for our Church." He turned to Giovan. "How much Latin do you know?"

"Some, Your Eminence."

"In Latin, the possessive form for *Sixtus* is *Sistina*, did you know that? Already people are calling it the *Cappella Sistina*."

Riario ushered them toward the far end of the sanctuary. A group of men stood before the unfinished altar platform, and they parted to reveal an old man sitting in a gilded chair, wearing a white cassock and short, red cape. He had watery eyes, and his was face fleshy but smooth with a long, hooked nose. Giovan had met His Holiness, Sixtus IV, only a few times over the years because when his services were required, he usually dealt with papal officials.

Sixtus was listening to a well-dressed man that Giovan didn't know, but he turned as the three men approached. The stranger continued to talk, but Salviati hushed him. Sixtus twitched the fingers of his right hand, and Giovan dropped to his knee and kissed the papal ring.

"Ah, Captain," Sixtus said as Giovan returned to his feet. "We are pleased to see you again." He spoke to the men around him. "We have entrusted this able man with the command of our Apostolic Palace Guard and Castel Sant'Angelo."

"Your Holiness is too kind," Giovan said. "It is my life to serve you."

Sixtus nodded. "Have you met Maestro Sandro Botticelli of Florence?" he asked, gesturing at the stranger, who stood between two large sheets of paper unrolled on the floor. On each was a drawing in charcoal.

Botticelli ignored Giovan. "You see, Your Holiness," he said, resuming his earlier speech, "how in this *cartone* we see the trials of Moses. It will go there." He gestured at a section of nearby wall. "And this," he added, pointing at the second drawing, "shows the temptations of Christ. It will go there," indicating the section of wall opposite the first. "I will tell two parallel stories, that of Moses and Our Savior."

Giovan edged closer and peered down at the drawings, focusing on the face of Christ in the second. It was roughly done, smudged, and bore no resemblance to the serene image he'd seen in the apse of San Pellegrino.

Sixtus gazed at the drawings and then glanced up at the wall sections where Botticelli had pointed. "So, what do we think?" he asked his retinue. There were low murmurs of tentative approval. Both the Count and the Archbishop said nothing and kept their eyes on Sixtus.

"We are surrounded by weak old women," Sixtus

muttered. Then, with a mischievous smile, he said, "Captain, perhaps you have an opinion."

Botticelli's jaw dropped in surprise at this.

Giovan tried to think what he should say. He leaned forward, studying the sketches. Again, his eyes went to the face of Christ. "I'm a mere soldier, Your Holiness," he said.

"Do not try our patience, Captain," Sixtus said.

Giovan swallowed. "I think the face of Our Savior does not inspire me."

Sixtus had bushy eyebrows, and they arched up in surprise. He peered at Christ's face, and then began to nod.

"But Your Holiness," Botticelli protested. "These are mere sketches. And this man is, as he admits, just a soldier."

Sixtus seemed amused. "Yes, yes. We understand. But still, Our Savior's face must be perfection, and alas, here it is not." He paused and thought for a moment. "We have been informed it will be a year yet before the chapel is ready for decoration. Maestro, thank you for this presentation. We will summon you when we are prepared to continue."

Botticelli stared at the Sixtus. Giovan guessed he'd come to Rome hoping to receive a papal commission now. Turning to Giovan, Botticelli put his hand on his sword hilt and leaned forward, whispering, "Don't ever come to Florence, *soldier*," his lips curling on the last word.

Giovan gripped the hilt of his own sword, and the men around him stepped back. Sixtus said nothing, but as he watched, his eyes crinkled.

Giovan said, "I travel wherever His Holiness sends me. I've killed a hundred men, some of them surely Florentines. One more, an unknown *artist*, will hardly matter to me." The old familiar rage of battle began to grow in Giovan's gut, his breath quickening, his muscles tensed. He'd slice this fop from his weak chin to his shriveled little cock. Giovan started to draw his sword, but then he stopped. While the chapel was not yet consecrated, God would surely see his actions here. And, of course, His Holiness and Count Riario were watching.

"Enough," Archbishop Salviati shouted, as he stepped between them. "His Holiness commands you to cease this foolishness at once."

Giovan blinked and forced himself to relax. His Holiness commands. Giovan took a breath and told himself that he wouldn't fight today after all. He watched Botticelli, who appeared to be relieved, and when he lifted his hand off his sword hilt, Giovan did the same.

Without a word, Botticelli bowed to the Pope, backed away and retreated into the gloom.

Chuckling, Sixtus pulled a lace handkerchief from his sleeve and dabbed at the corners of his eyes. "My dear Captain, we hope you let that young man live. He does have talent."

"I am your servant, Your Holiness."

Count Riario stepped forward with the archbishop at his side. "If I may change the subject, Holiness. We've spoken to Captain Battista about the matter of Florence," he said.

"Ah, yes. Lorenzo," Sixtus replied, his voice hissing with contempt. "The man is a trial to us. Imola. Pisa. He thwarts our every project. We feel like Moses attacked by the Egyptian." He gestured at the first drawing.

"Tell me how I can serve you, Your Holiness," Giovan said.

"The rest of you, leave us," Sixtus said, his voice loud. The others in the retinue retreated to the far end of the nave, leaving only Riario, Salviati and Giovan standing in front of him.

"We wish to change the state of Florence," Sixtus said.

Giovan, the warm blood of possible combat still running through his veins, felt impatient. They all used this phrase, *change the state of Florence*. It was to time be sure what this meant.

"These gentlemen," Giovan gestured at Count Riario and Archbishop Salviati, "think this change cannot be accomplished without the death of Lorenzo and his brother Giuliano.

Is this what you want?"

"No, we do not wish anyone to die," Sixtus replied.

"Then I think this is not a military problem, Your Holiness," Giovan said, feeling both relieved and disappointed. He bowed, and began to edge away.

"Wait, Captain," Salviati said. He turned to Sixtus. "Your Holiness, if we accomplish what you want, and do everything we can to avoid unnecessary deaths, then will you absolve everyone who is involved?"

"We are telling you that we wish no one to die."

"Yes, Holiness. But will you grant us absolution if we accomplish all you want?"

Sixtus sat for a moment, his watery eyes glistening as he thought. Finally, he sighed and said, "You are a beast, Archbishop."

They waited.

"But yes, we will absolve you for everything if you rid us of Lorenzo and his brother."

They took their leave of Sixtus and retraced their steps back out into the midst of the construction debris outside the chapel. They stopped next to a pile of bricks.

"You are clear as to what His Holiness just said?" Salviati asked.

"Yes," Giovan said. "He cannot bring himself to say it, but if we must kill Lorenzo and his brother, then he will accept it. And we are all agreed that their deaths are necessary." He looked back and forth between Count Riario and Salviati. They nodded. "Good," he said. "It's settled."

They resumed walking back toward the papal palace.

"It's not enough to kill them," Giovan said, pondering what should be done. "We'll need troops to control of the city."

Count Riario grinned and said to Archbishop Salviati, "You see? Captain Batista is just the right man for this work. Now that his duty is clear, he will be like a terrier dog, refusing to let go of the hare."

"Please forgive me for any past doubts, Captain," Salviati said, his voice soothing. "I understand now that your initial reluctance, before hearing His Holiness's wishes, does you honor." He bowed.

Giovan returned the bow. "Thank you, Your Eminence," he said. Then he added, "I must tell you, it will be good to start a new campaign, to have something new to do."

"Didn't I tell you?" Count Riario cried. "When we are finished, His Holiness will rule half of Italy."

Salviati shrugged and nodded. "It will be a great accomplishment for Mother Church and for the glory of God."

"So what do we do next?" Riario asked.

"We'll need more troops—more than I have," Giovan said.

"Would it be possible to use only foreign soldiers?" Salviati asked. "If you take the Apostolic Guard to Florence, that will surely create suspicion. And the Pazzis won't like it."

"I can provide twenty men," Riario said. "There are many other lords who consider Florence to be a threat. I'm sure we can convince them to support us."

"Can you give me a list, Excellency?" Giovan asked.

Riario nodded.

"Good. I will go and meet with these lords," Giovan said. "I'll need money for the travel and for bribes."

"Money won't be a problem," Salviati said. "That's why we have Francesco."

They reached the entrance to the palace and stopped. Salviati cleared his throat and glanced around. He said, his voice low, "There is another thing. We are agreed Lorenzo must die."

"And his brother, Giuliano," Count Riario added.

"Yes, but Lorenzo is the most important," Salviati continued. "My question is: Who will do it? Who will assassinate this man they call Lorenzo the Magnificent?"

"Oh. I thought that was obvious." Giovan put his hand on the hilt of his sword. "When the time comes, I will be Lorenzo's assassin."

Fioretta awoke with a start and sat up. Pearl gray light seeped into Giuliano's bedroom from the window facing the central courtyard, and Fioretta lay back, relieved. She had a little time before she needed to go home. The evening before Papa had been drinking again with the priest Maffei, so he would sleep late this morning.

Beside her, Giuliano slept on, his handsome face untroubled. Careful not to wake him, Fioretta snuggled deeper into the big bed, luxuriating in the softness of its down stuffing and the Flemish linen sheets, so much nicer than her mean little cot at home. Last night Lucia, with the help of Giuliano's servant Stefano, had again sneaked her into the huge Medici palazzo.

It had been three weeks since the affair of the banner. The next day, Stefano had appeared at Fioretta's door with a letter. Fortunately her father was not home. Lucia told her to refuse the letter, to make Giuliano suffer for a while, but Fioretta couldn't do this. She tore open the letter and wept as she read. Giuliano pleaded for her forgiveness. He included a poem he had written, and having learned it by heart, she now recited the last lines to herself.

I earn her fame, and every thought of mine,
only of her, and shared with no one else.

In the letter, he had begged her to meet him that afternoon at a local goldsmith shop, and when she arrived the proprietor ushered her into the back room where Giuliano waited. On seeing her, he dropped to his knees, pleading that she try to understand. He said that on the morning of the joust, a wave of sadness for an earlier time in his life had struck him. He didn't say Simonetta's name. He had made an ill-considered decision to use the old banner, despite Stefano's reservations, and standing behind his master, tall and solemn, Stefano nodded in confirmation. But, Giuliano continued, he understood that his past was his past, and the present, the beautiful Fioretta, stood before him.

She had wanted to ask about the future, but before she could summon the courage, Giuliano gestured to the goldsmith who stepped forward carrying a pink velvet-covered box. Inside lay a gold pendant with a large emerald, surround by four enormous pearls.

So she had come back to his bed—happy, she thought now, fingering the necklace. She always wore it when she was with him, and never at any other time.

"The emerald brings out the green in your eyes," Giuliano said, awake beside her.

"So you've told me a hundred times." Smiling, Fioretta rolled into his arms. "I think you really are a banker at heart, wanting to get the maximum value for your investment."

Giuliano laughed. "Oh, the horror of that idea. My grandfather, Cosimo, was the banker. I'm just the profligate grandson." He kissed her.

Tisp-tisp-tisp. The call of a song thrush drifted up from the open courtyard below.

Together, they lay back on the pillows and listened. Fioretta thought Giuliano might slip again into sleep, but instead, he laid his cheek on her bare shoulder, and a day's growth of beard rubbed against her skin. She reached out and traced each of his eyebrows with her fingertips. He tilted his head so her fingers passed over his closed eyes, brushing against his long lashes, past the patrician nose to his full lips. He kissed her fingers. He sucked them into his mouth, his tongue stroking the tips. With her other hand, Fioretta pressed his head lower, down to her breast, and she felt his tongue along side her own fingertips inside his mouth, caressing her tingling nipple. She trembled in pleasure. She withdrew her wet fingers and traced a path down his chest, lingering at each taut muscle and rib, until she reached his flat stomach. He caught his breath as she lowered her hand still farther and gently stroked him. Her own breathing quickened.

He rolled onto his back. She threw her leg across his body and lifted herself so she was astride him, guiding him into place, his hands grasping her hips. Giuliano gazed up at her, his face still relaxed with a little smile curving the corners of his mouth. He began to thrust, without hurry, and warmth radiated up her body, across her skin. Her thighs, her breasts and her lips burned. As the first wave of pleasure crashed over her, he kept his eyes on hers. She gasped for air. The song of the thrush, the soft sheets, the morning light, even Giuliano's face, they all faded into nothingness. There was only the waves, in rhythm with his steady strokes, sweeping through her body.

His hand touched her face. Her eyes fluttered open and she saw him, his gaze still locked on hers, but his jaw clenched, his lips pressed tight as though he were suppressing a shout. His body arched up, and her eyes closed again as the waves came faster and harder. It seemed to go on forever and this is what she craved, but finally she felt his release and a last shuddering thrust. She collapsed onto his chest, both of them panting, her body swathed in cozy, tingling warmth.

Oh, Giuliano, my love. My life.

They lay for only a moment, then the door opened and Lucia stepped inside, followed by Stefano.

"Oh." Fioretta rolled over to lie next to Giuliano and pulled the bedcovers up over her breasts. She knew that in the Medici household servants entered rooms without knocking, but it disconcerted her when she was in bed with Giuliano.

"Lady, it's getting late." Lucia used the word *lady* in front of Giuliano and Stefano.

Stefano carried a pitcher and a cup, which he set next to the washing basin by the window. He drew back the window's curtain; morning sun flooded in, and Fioretta again heard the tisp-tisp-tisp of the song thrush. Larger than all the rooms of her father's house put together, with a high ceiling and walls of pale yellow and contrasting rich red draperies, Giuliano's bedroom reflected his famous refined taste. On the wall opposite the bed hung the portrait of Fioretta painted by Giuliano's friend, Sandro Botticelli.

"Don't go," Giuliano said.

"I need to get home before Papa wakes," she replied. "You know that."

"But why?" He sat up, and ignoring the two servants, took her hand in his. "Fioretta, my love, let me help you. Thanks to my beloved grandfather, I can afford a hundred houses in Florence. Let me buy one for you."

Lucia stared at Fioretta from the foot of the bed. Her face showed both her desire for a change to her own life and also her resignation, knowing Fioretta's likely answer.

"We can't talk of this in front of them," Fioretta whispered.

"Oh?" Giuliano's eyes danced with merriment. Louder, he said, "Stefano, tell me, how did you know to come in just now?"

Stefano came and stood next to Lucia. They glanced at each other, and then Stefano answered, "We listened for you to finish. It's what good servants do."

"You see," Giuliano said. "We have no secrets."

Fioretta's mouth fell open as she blushed.

Giuliano grinned at her. He said to Stefano, "You may leave us for now."

Lucia and Stefano slipped from the room.

"You live with your spiteful father because you think you have no choice," Giuliano said, laying back on the pillow. "But you do."

They had talked of this before. He wanted her as his true mistress, not someone who sneaked into his bed whenever they could arrange it. He had offered to provide a house, money, servants and food from the Medici estates.

"My darling, please listen," Fioretta said. "I remember when Papa was a good man. He took me picnicking in the country. He and I lay on our backs in the grass, with me tucked up under his arm, and we watched the swallows flying over-head. He told me stories of wood elves and unicorns, of King Arthur and his knights."

Giuliano gazed into her eyes and waited.

"Then my mother died."

"So let me help you."

Fioretta shook her head. "I cannot bear the thought that he might know about us, that he would think of me as a kept woman. If I move out of his house into one you provide, surely he will find out."

There was more to it, of course. Papa's wool business had fallen apart soon after her mother's death, which was also about the time Lorenzo came to power. Caught up in his grief, it had been easy for Papa to blame his failure on Lorenzo's policies rather than his own neglect of the business. Now, with hatred of Lorenzo consuming Papa's days and nights, how could Fioretta ever admit to him that she loved Lorenzo's brother?

"I suppose it's God's will that even as adults," Giuliano said, "we still worry about what our parents think of us. My own father has been gone these eight years now, but my blessed mother still tries to control my life, and every day I try to make her happy."

"She wants you to marry." Fioretta watched him.

"Of course. As does Lorenzo. I'm a valuable family asset to be used to the best advantage possible." He smiled. "An asset. Maybe he and I are bankers after all."

Fioretta knew Giuliano must marry someday. It might be soon, and due to her own low social position, it wouldn't be to her. Lorenzo would find the daughter of a powerful family, probably outside Florence, and so cement another political alliance.

But Giuliano had assured her it would be a marriage of convenience, and Fioretta would still be the only woman he loved.

"I think there is another way," she said. "Lucia!"

Stefano and Lucia hurried back into the bedroom.

Fioretta continued. "I have a plan to let me be independent of Papa without breaking his heart. If it works, then we can be together whenever we want. Isn't that right, Lucia."

"Yes, lady." Lucia shrugged.

Ignoring her, Giuliano said, "Tell me more."

Fioretta put a finger on his lips. "Not now, my love. We have no time." She glanced at the sunlight streaming through the window and then at Lucia.

"All men out, please." Lucia clapped her hands. "Lady needs to dress."

Giuliano obediently swung his legs out of the bed and climbed to his feet, completely naked. His lack of modesty always surprised Fioretta. He stood before them all, proud of his muscled, athletic physique, like the bronze David by Donatello in the courtyard below. As Stefano stepped forward with a robe, Lucia stared without embarrassment at Giuliano's now indolent penis.

"I'll have a bath." Giuliano bent down and kissed Fioretta's cheek. "Farewell, my love." He strode from the room with Stefano following.

After the door closed, Fioretta stood, also naked, crossed to the basin and began to wash herself with warm water from the pitcher and some lemon-scented soap. Lucia unpacked the clean clothes they'd brought with them. Next to the cup, Stefano had left a small pile of carrot seeds.

"He's your first, isn't he?" Lucia asked. "In bed, I mean."

"My first and only."

"I know something about cocks. Dear lady, I think this man has spoiled you for life."

She meant it as a joke, of course. Fioretta started to laugh, but it caught in her throat. She grasped the basin with both hands and leaned over it, her tears dropping into the soapy water. Had Giuliano spoiled her for life? Could she ever have a real husband, children? Did she really want them?

Lucia rushed to her side. "I'm sorry."

"If I ever lose him…"

"I know." Lucia glanced down at the carrot seeds and filled the cup with water.

Fioretta wiped her eyes. She swept the carrot seeds into her palm, tossed them into her mouth and washed them down.

Lucia starred at her with a questioning look. "Did you chew them?" she asked.

Ignoring her, Fioretta returned to the bed and put on her camicia. "I trust you made it home last night without trouble," she said.

"I stayed here." Lucia helped Fioretta pull on her clean dress.

"What? Where did you sleep?" Fioretta asked as her head emerged.

Lucia grinned.

"Oh, of course. Stefano," Fioretta said.

"His bed is much better than mine at home."

"And Stefano? How was he?"

Lucia shrugged.

Smiling now, Fioretta sat on the bed, pulling on her stockings and shoes. "So there's no the possibility of love with the stern-faced Stefano?"

"I love his bed."

They both giggled. The door opened, and Stefano came in. "My master wonders if you need any assistance." He walked to window and glanced down at the spot where the carrot seeds had been.

"I'm ready," Fioretta said, standing and pulling a shawl around her shoulders.

Giuliano's bedroom occupied one corner of the Palazzo Medici, away from the rooms of Lorenzo's family and his mother. After Stefano scouted ahead, they hurried through the corridor, down one of the back stairways to a servants' entrance, and then out onto the already busy Via de' Ginori.

In the doorway, Fioretta thanked Stefano, and he bowed. Then he gazed at Lucia, and his stern facade softened. "Goodbye, Lucia," he said. He reached out to touch her arm.

"Bye," Lucia replied as she turned away and started down the street.

As Fioretta followed, she glanced back and saw a look of sad desperation on Stefano's face as he slipped inside and closed the door. "He's in love with you," she said.

"They always are."

They giggled as they dodged people on the narrow street—wool carders, laborers, candle makers and others—each scurrying to their place of work. The sun hadn't risen high enough to reach the street, so Fioretta shivered and pulled her shawl tight as they hurried to get to the house, still ten minutes away.

"I told Stefano about your idea, about a camicia shop," Lucia said as she struggled to keep pace.

"Oh. What did he think?"

"Sandro Botticelli stayed with Giuliano after he came back from Rome. Stefano told me his camicia is terrible. Almost rags."

"A customer."

Lucia shook her head. "It's not enough. How much would he pay? How many other customers could we find? How much would the rent be?" She pulled Fioretta out of the crowd into a dark doorway. "We both want to leave your father's house. But if we cannot make enough money—if we fail—then what do we do? He'll take you back, but not me."

"You could find another house to serve."

"I can't take that chance," Lucia said. "And I can't go home. There are too many mouths to feed in my family as it is."

"So what are you saying?"

"I'm sorry, Fioretta. I cannot join you in your camicia business."

Thadeous struggled up the stairway leading from the piazza to the library entrance. A few more steps, and he would be amongst hundred of books where he would surely find answers to his questions about Sultan Mehmed II. Raffaele held his arm, steadying him as they climbed.

His lungs were burning, so Thadeous was forced to pause.

He focused on his breathing, oblivious to the young students running up and down the stairs around them. After glancing over at Raffaele with appreciation for helping him today, he took another shallow breath and they continued.

"Well, look at this," a voice shouted from above. "It's a couple of Roman *froci*."

Thadeous and Raffaele looked up and saw a sandy-haired young man standing at the top of the narrow stairs with two other boys, and while they stood with deliberate casualness, they had their hands on the hilts of their daggers.

"That's Benedetto," Raffaele whispered. "He's a Medici."

Thadeous understood. Four years before, a generous gift from Lorenzo de' Medici had resurrected the ancient University of Pisa from decay, and the long-standing animosity between Pisa and its neighbor Florence had subsided. But this meant that the Medici clan considered the university to be their own private school.

"Ignore them," Thadeous whispered.

They climbed another step.

"You're not wanted here." Benedetto's lips curled with disdain. "Pisa belongs to Florence." He looked around as though he was challenging anyone to object. Other than his friends, no one seemed to be paying attention. "Just ask your uncle Salviati. He thinks he's our archbishop, but where is he?" Benedetto gestured, his arms sweeping around him. "Why does he spend all his time in Rome?" His hand gripped and ungripped his dagger's pommel.

Thadeous glanced over at Raffaele. The boy's eyes were big, and they twitched back and forth between Benedetto and Thadeous.

"Raffaele, did you know," Thadeous said, his voice loud, "that I once tutored Lorenzo and Giuliano de' Medici?"

Raffaele stared at Thadeous for a moment, and then he too raised his voice and replied, "No, Thadeous. I did not know that. Did you live in the Medici household?"

They climbed another step and were now level with

Benedetto. He edged back.

"Why yes, I lived there for three years, as I remember. Lorenzo and Giuliano were just boys, of course." Thadeous kept his eyes on Raffaele. "But I think they were very fond of me." Together they put their heads down and pushed past Benedetto and his friends and into the building.

"A fine pair of *froci*," Benedetto called. He didn't follow them inside.

They stood in the hallway of the main university building. Thadeous put his hand on the wall as he struggled to get his breath.

"They were ready to draw their daggers," Raffaele said. "That was a good story."

"But I did teach the Medici boys. Didn't I tell you?" Thadeous said. "Look, Benedetto and his friends are cowards at heart. I don't think they would have caused any trouble with so many people around."

More students swarmed past them, heading for the stairway leading to the lecture hall on the second floor.

"Go on, get a good seat," Thadeous continued, glancing at the door leading to the library. He needed to get to work, but then he put his hand on Raffaele's shoulder to stop him. "Wait a moment. They called us *froci*. What does that mean to you?"

Raffaele shrugged. "Nothing. It's just an insult." He started toward the stairway, but then turned, adding over his shoulder, "I'll come down to the library after the lecture. We can walk back together if you're finished."

Thadeous watched him run up the stairs, disappearing into the crowd. *It means nothing*, Raffaele had said. At least he had no suspicion of Thadeous's secret. He took another breath and then stepped through the door to the library.

Lorenzo had a famous love of books and old manuscripts, and he had made this obvious with the library of the University of Pisa. Polished oak shelves lined both walls of the long, high-ceilinged room, and a stained glass window looked out onto the piazza at the far end. In contrast, the air was heavy with mold and damp.

A few students sat at the single long table running down the center of the room. They glanced up at Thadeous and then returned to their whispered conversation.

Beneath the window, Dante Carpani, the *bibliotecario*, sat at his little desk with a book open in front of him. In his late forties, he was almost as old as Thadeous, but he was a bull of a man, his ruddy face radiating good health that belied the long days he spent buried amongst his books. Dante saw Thadeous and leaped to his feet. "Professore Thadeous, it's so good to see you." He rushed forward and ushered Thadeous to a chair next to his desk.

"Many thanks, Dante." Thadeous took a careful breath as he sat. "Do you know a boy named Benedetto, a Medici?"

"Yes. He and his gang are a bad lot. Why?"

"They gave Raffaele and me some trouble just now. This enmity between the Pope and Lorenzo can have no good outcome, I'm afraid. But no harm today. So, how are you, Dante?"

They chatted for a few minutes, with Dante doing most of the talking as Thadeous continued to get his breath back.

"I was speaking to my wife about you last night," Dante said. "I'm instructed to ask you to come to dinner this Sunday. You can meet her and the children. She makes a wonderful *ribollita* with cannellini beans, carrots, silverbeets and onions." He kissed the tips of his fingers. "I'll come with our neighbor's donkey cart to carry you. We can talk about books."

Ribollita. With the Archbishop away, the cook at Palazzo Salviati had been providing very plain meals lately, often just cheese and bread. Thadeous felt his mouth watering. "Let me think about it. My health troubles me."

"Of course." Dante's kind eyes showed concern. "Your breathing is worse?"

Thadeous shrugged. "Some days worse, some days better. But today we walked here with no coughing. A good day."

"Excellent. How's the boy?"

"Like my health, Raffaele is good some days, but some days not. But he was brave just now."

Dante nodded with understanding and then pointed at the book in front of him. "Perhaps this would interest him. *Decameron*. I just obtained this copy."

"Ah, Boccaccio. I'm familiar with it, of course." Thadeous glanced around at the books lining the walls. The Sultan Mehmed. He needed to get to work.

"Yes, but have you read the Tenth Tale of Day Three?" Dante asked. "The unexpurgated version?"

Thadeous thought for a moment. Decameron was divided into ten days, with ten individual tales on each day. One hundred tales, and he didn't remember them all. "Unexpurgated, you say?"

Chuckling, Dante leaned over, his nose close to the book, and read.

> *Then, having divested himself of his scanty clothing, he threw himself stark naked on his knees, as if he would pray; whereby he caused the girl, who followed his example, to confront him in the same posture. Whereupon seeing her so fair, he felt an accession of desire, and therewith came an insurgence of the flesh, which she marking with surprise, said, "What is this, which I see thee have, that so protrudes, and which I have not?"*

"Ahem." Thadeous wasn't sure what else to say.

Dante waggled his eyebrows at him. "There's more. I'm sure Raffaele would appreciate it."

"No doubt. However, I can't risk word getting back to his uncle, my patron."

"I understand. Well, perhaps you'd like to take it home, eh? For your own enlightenment."

Thadeous glanced at Dante, relieved. He thinks I lust after women, as he does. Like Raffaele, he does not suspect. "Alas," he said. "I'm old and infirm. Thank you for your offer."

"Just as well," Dante replied. "I should like to keep it awhile longer for myself."

"Yes, well. Dante, while I enjoy your company, I must get to work. I have limited time."

"Of course, of course. How goes the writing?"

Thadeous stifled his irritation, knowing Dante meant well. He also needed Dante's help. "I'm making some progress. It's been three weeks now, and I've written a good introduction, I think. There's some background about Emperor Constantine and the terrible state of the Byzantine Empire. It had degenerated into little more than the city of Constantinople, a few islands, and the Peloponnese."

"Where you lived, in Mystras?"

"Yes, Mystras. It's a fortress town. Did you know that? It held out for six years after Constantinople fell. But alas, I never made it home."

Thadeous sat silent for a moment, thinking of Mystras and his happy years there studying with George Gemistus Pletho. That was before they were summoned by the Emperor.

"But life goes on," Thadeous said. "Today, I'm thinking I need to know more about the Ottoman sultans, and Mehmed II in particular. What have you got for me here, Dante?"

Dante leaned back in his chair and thought.

Another boy entered the library and approached them, but seeing the two older men conferring together, he sat at the big table and waited.

Dante stood and crossed to one of the bookshelves. He wore a fine cotton apron, no doubt sewn for him by his wife. Dante tapped his chin with a finger while the other hand ran down the line of books, caressing them. Many had plain spines, and Thadeous guessed that Dante intimately knew every book in the room by its cover's color, thickness and texture.

"Here it is," Dante cried out. He pulled out a volume and wiped it on his apron. "You read Arabic, do you not?"

"Yes. In Mystras, half the books we studied were in

Arabic."

"Well, this should suit you." He handed the book to Thadeous, proud of his bibliographic skills.

The book was almost new. It would need to be if it told the story of Mehmed II, who, as far as Thadeous knew, still lived. Thadeous pulled his chair around so he could sit at the table and examined the book. Its fine kidskin cover was dyed deep green with no printing or decoration of any kind. Using his fingertips, Thadeous opened it to the first page, hearing the lovely sound of its spine creaking and admired the fine cursive Arabic calligraphy. He read for several minutes, flipping back and forth through the pages. It was a history of Ottoman empire, and the last few pages were about Sultan Mehmed II, conqueror of Constantinople. He grinned.

"It will suit?" Dante asked.

"Oh, yes." Thadeous looked at Dante, thinking he was as close to being a friend as anyone Thadeous knew. Dante liked Thadeous, and they shared an interest in books and history. "Dante Carpani," he said. "You're a true friend. I accept your generous invitation to dinner."

Dante clapped his hands together in delight. "I'm relieved," he said. He lowered his voice. "I was a little afraid to go home tonight as my wife can be, well, formidable when she doesn't get what she wants. She'd blame me, of course."

"Well, we can't have that." Thadeous gave Dante directions to Salviati's palazzo, and they set the time for noon on Sunday.

Thadeous turned back to the kidskin-bound volume, settling into place to read. After a while he stopped and stared at the page without seeing it, remembering the day twenty-five years before, remembering when he saw Sultan Mehmed II—and remembering what followed.

Twenty-Five Years Earlier

"There's the Sultan's tent," Lauro said, standing atop the great land wall and pointing. Below them, tens of thousands of

Turkish soldiers filled the plain to the horizon.

Peering in the direction Lauro pointed, Thadeous spotted the enormous red and gold tent near the River Lykos. Every day the Turkish cannon, visible not far from the Sultan's tent, pounded at the wall. For the last three nights, Thadeous, Lauro and a multitude of soldiers and citizen workers had piled up stones and broken masonry, and had built temporary wooden palisades to protect Constantinople.

As the sun rose higher above the city behind them, stone cannonballs would again crash down, making it impossible to continue their desperate repairs. Workers were creeping away to find safety and to sleep for a few hours, leaving Thadeous and Lauro standing alone.

"I see horsemen by the tent," Thadeous said. "And camels."

They watched as scores of mounted men rode toward them led by a dozen camels with barrel-sized *kös* drums slung on either side, their thunder rolling across the plain, along with the clang of cymbals and the screech of *kurrenay* horns. On either side of the entourage, thousands of soldiers dressed in bright green, red and purple uniforms lined the route, shouting *Rahim Allah! Kerim Allah!*

The party came closer, and one rider in the center stood out, his large white turban distinctive even in the distance.

"That's Mehmed." Lauro said, pointing. "The Sultan."

They stopped a hundred yards away, and Thadeous was barely able to make out Mehmed's face. He seemed to be laughing as he surveyed the previous night's repairs. Even at that distance, Thadeous thought it was a cruel face.

"He's only twenty-one years old," Lauro added.

Thadeous had heard this. Again, he gazed at the tens of thousands of soldiers spread out before him, arrayed in disciplined camps and fortifications. He knew that behind him, on the other side of the city, beyond the eastern sea wall, Mehmed's vast fleet filled the Sea of Marmara and the Bosporus Straights. Thadeous found this overwhelming, and it was all the result of a twenty-one-year-old's desire to expand his realm. By doing so, he would extinguish the last light of the thousand-year-old Byzantine Empire.

An arrow thudded into a waist-high woven basket filled with earth that stood next to them. Workers had hauled dozens of these baskets to the top of the repaired wall, forming merlons behind which defenders crouched.

"Perhaps we should move." Thadeous stepped behind the basket.

"There won't be a general attack today." Lauro continued to study the trenches and assembled troops. "So far, we are keeping ahead of them."

"So far?"

"We only have to hold out until the Venetian ships arrive."

While the schism between Roman Catholicism and Easter Orthodoxy had lasted four hundred years, the Emperor had still pleaded for help from his fellow Christians in the West. Genoa and Venice responded with mercenaries like Lauro. The Roman Pope, Nicholas V, had supposedly paid the Venetians for a fleet of ships to bring more soldiers and much needed supplies to Constantinople. Rumors constantly swept through the embattled city: someone had sighted the ships, or they would arrive soon, or the Pope had lied and there were no ships at all.

A puff of white smoke blossomed at the mouth of the largest Turkish cannon, and both Lauro and Thadeous ducked behind the basket merlon as a stone cannonball crashed into the wall just above where the river flowed through an immense iron grate.

"It takes them an hour to reload." Lauro stood to observe the new damage.

Thadeous, worrying about arrows, stayed crouched behind the basket, gazing up at Lauro. They were both filthy as a result of their toils, but Lauro still cut a striking figure. When he took off his helmet, dark curls framed his face. There was a softness around his mouth that struck Thadeous as a sign of sensitivity in contrast to his tough soldier's bearing. Thadeous ran his fingers through his own long hair, guessing he must look dreadful, as bad as when he had spent a long day in the copper mine with his father.

"I'm tired," Lauro said, turning. "I—" He stopped as he saw Thadeous's face. "I—" He closed his mouth, gazing into Thadeous's eyes for a second, and then looking away.

"Where will you sleep?" Thadeous asked.

"I have blanket in a nearby church."

"Come with me. You can use my master's bed." Thadeous wanted to reach out his hand to Lauro, but resisted, afraid that he might be rebuffed, that he had misunderstood.

Minutes later, they entered the tiny house where Thadeous had started his copying labor with Pletho and where he still slept during the day. The main room was empty. Thadeous crossed to the worktable and saw a scrap of paper tucked under the inkpot.

With the Emperor

Familiar with the bureaucracy and formalities of the Byzantine court even with the city under siege, Thadeous knew Pletho might be gone all day, certainly all morning. They'd have the house to themselves.

"So what is this work?" Lauro said, standing beside him and picking up a copied manuscript page.

"The Emperor has commanded us to make a copy of my master's—"

"A copy? Ah." Lauro grinned at him. "I remember you were writing when I first came here." He sat down and glanced around the table. He found the original page, set it out in front of him, and pulled a blank page from its stack. Using Thadeous's quill pen, he wrote with confidence while Thadeous leaned over his back and watched, amazed. Thadeous knew that Lauro was more than an ignorant soldier —this had become clear to him during the past few days—but it appeared that he was also a skilled scribe. In less than half the time it had taken Thadeous, Lauro completed the page and leaned back, pleased with his work.

"What do you think?" he said, spreading out the three pages: the one he'd done, the one that Thadeous had copied, and the original written in Pletho's hand.

Thadeous lifted Lauro's page and examined it closely. "It's the best of the three."

"I studied back home with a Greek teacher," Lauro said. "What's the subject? It's hard to tell from this one page."

"It's new. My master, George Gemistus—"

"Pletho? So that old man I saw here was the famous Pletho? I've read his *De Differentii*s. I thought his support of the Platonic conception of God was a little strange." Lauro glanced at Thadeous, smiling. "He's really something of a pagan, isn't he?"

"He calls it a book of laws, the *Nómoi*," Thadeous continued. "It brings together all the ideas of his life. And he's so old that I fear it's his last work."

"And this is the only complete copy?"

Thadeous nodded.

"And if Constantinople falls and the barbarians overrun the city," Lauro continued, "it could all be lost."

"Yes. Almost surely."

"You and I must complete the copy." Lauro glanced up at Thadeous. "The day we met, you said this was important. Now I understand. The siege may go on for weeks, maybe months. We'll work on the wall at night and copy during the day." He glanced over at the two pallets in the corner. "We'll need some sleep, of course."

Thadeous tried to understand what was happening. A few hours before, he had been hauling stones to rebuild a wall while thousands of Turks waited for an opportunity to kill him. His hands were rough and blistered, as were Lauro's. Now, he was about to return to the world of scholarship, trying to save the masterwork of his famous mentor. And this soldier who sat before him, so unlike the academics he'd known, would be the answer.

"We need to rest," Thadeous said. "Then we can work."

He found the water bucket and was grateful that Pletho had left it half full. Turning his back to Lauro, he stripped off his clothes, crouched in front of the bucket and washed as well as he could. He dried himself with the rag towel they used and then stood, trembling, holding the towel in front of him.

Lauro watched, his mouth slightly open, his eyes traveling up and down Thadeous's slim young body. Lauro stood, took off his uniform and moved to the bucket while Thadeous stumbled to his bed. Thadeous could hardly breathe as Lauro splashed water over his muscular body and dried himself. He stood, dropped the towel to the floor and walked to the bed, naked and aroused.

Chapter Three

Six Hours Until Dawn

Giovan sighed and squinted at his quill pen. Its tip was worn to a nub, but it was the only one they had given him, and they had taken away even his penknife. "Wake up, you oaf," he shouted to Alfeo, who was asleep on his stool by the door.

"What?" Alfeo said, shaking his head and standing.

"Sharpen this."

Suspicious, Alfeo took the pen and examined it. It occurred to Giovan that the man had never used a quill pen in his life, that he was illiterate.

"You have a knife, don't you?" Giovan glared at him. "If I don't finish this, they are going to blame you."

Alfeo stared back at him for a moment and then pulled a knife from his boot. He held the pen in one hand and the knife in the other, unsure of what to do. With a shrug, he handed both to Giovan. "I'm watching," he said as he returned to his stool.

Giovan glanced down at the knife. It seemed familiar. He turned it over his hands and saw the word *Sicarius* carved into its handle. It was Paulo's dagger! How was that possible? He glanced at Alfeo, about to ask him, but the guard sat with his eyes glazed over, almost dozing. Let the fool go to sleep. With a sleeping guard and a weapon something might be accomplished.

But not now. Giovan sharpened the pen and set the dagger on the table in front of him. He thought for a moment and then bent back to his task.

...we concluded that the task His Holiness had set for us required the death of Lorenzo The Magnificent and of his brother.

* * *

Five Months Earlier

"Thank the heavens," Filiberto said as he climbed off his mule in front of the inn.

Giovan silently agreed as he swung his leg over the back of his own mule and dropped to the frozen ground. He had chosen mules for this trip instead of horses because they were better on the icy mountain roads they had just left behind. Still mounted, Paulo took the reins of the other mules and led them around to the stable in the back.

Seven months had passed since His Holiness had blessed this endeavor, and the days were getting shorter in the early Italian winter. Giovan stomped his feet, trying to warm them, and then led Filiberto through the inn's door into the gloomy common room, which smelled of sweat and garlic. A smoky fire burned in the big hearth, bathing the room with its welcoming warmth, and before it stood some rough tables, chairs and benches. Two men, sitting at the fire, turned to look, grasping wine cups in their hands.

"Innkeeper," Filiberto shouted. "This is a pigsty," he said to Giovan, his voice only slightly quieter.

"It's the only inn for miles," Giovan replied. "Would you prefer to tempt bandits on the road?"

"Hah. We are a match for any bandits."

"Perhaps. So you prefer to keep riding and sleep out on the ground again?"

Filiberto gave an exaggerated shudder and again shouted for the innkeeper.

Giovan stepped up to the fire, unbuttoning his overcoat to let in some of the heat. "Good evening," he said to the two men who were inspecting him with obvious curiosity. Giovan pulled back his coat, revealing the hilt of his longsword, and when Filiberto joined him, his sword was also visible. Neither of them wore their papal uniforms, as their mission required discretion, but Giovan knew that they were intimidating none the less.

The men seemed unperturbed and didn't appear to be armed. They wore simple peasant dress, and Giovan guessed they were locals who had come to spend the evening drinking wine.

"Good evening to you, stranger," said the older of the two. "What news have you?"

Letting Filiberto take care of the obligatory conversation, Giovan pulled up a chair and sank into it. He thought about pulling off his boots, but decided to wait until Paulo could help him after bedding down the mules. Paulo had been a blessing on this trip, and Giovan was glad he had convinced the boy's family to allow him to come. Giovan's friend, Father Nicolo, had resisted because Paulo was one of his altar boys, but had relented when Giovan had promised that the boy would merely work as servant, not a soldier.

"My apologies, good sirs," an rotund man cried coming into the room. "I was helping in the stable. We have nice rooms for you with soft beds. My daughter is preparing a meal."

Filiberto's head jerked around. Giovan guessed that the words *daughter* and *meal* had both captured his interest.

"Some wine for us," Filiberto said.

"And another cup for our new friends," Giovan added, indicating the two locals.

The men lifted their cups in thanks as the innkeeper shuffled from the room, returning a moment later with three pewter cups and a bottle. Paulo followed, carrying their saddlebags. Giovan reached around and pulled another chair up to the fire for him, and the boy sat down without a word.

When the innkeeper left the room again, Filiberto leaned toward Paulo and said, "The daughter, did you see her?"

Paulo glanced at Giovan, who said nothing. Paulo nodded.

"Is she a beauty?" Filiberto asked.

Paulo grinned.

"That may be promising," Filiberto said.

Giovan leaned back, not listening as Filiberto and the two locals discussed the innkeeper's daughter. Paulo followed the conversation silently but with keen interest.

With this trip, finally there was progress. The summer and fall had been endlessly frustrating for Giovan as Count Riario, Cardinal Salviati and that fop Francesco de' Pazzi argued and dithered back in Rome. Francesco, or *Franceschino* as they called him when he was not present, contributed nothing to the planning, and was parsimonious when it came to actually disbursing the necessary funds.

At least now, away from Rome and working independently, Giovan had accomplished something. During the past three weeks they had visited Tolentino, Imola and Perugia, and had just left Ravenna the day before. In each city, Giovan had discreetly consulted with the local lord and military leaders about the plan to overthrow the Medici in Florence. He needed soldiers because following the dual assassinations, it was inevitable that there would be turmoil in the streets.

The discussions had been tricky. After Lorenzo and Giuliano were dead, everyone would rush to support His Holiness and Count Riario. But Giovan's plan required troops waiting outside the city walls, ready to rush in when the cry went up that the evil Medici were overthrown. There was hesitation, of course, but in the end, they all pledged their support and claimed they would supply troops when the time came.

When the time came. That was the problem. So far, it had not been possible to plan the details of the actual assassinations because Giovan knew hardly anything about Lorenzo, Giuliano or Florence. Then, while they had been in Ravenna, a message had come from Count Riario: Giovan was to go to Florence to meet a man named Jacopo de' Pazzi who could help them.

"I have dinner for you," the innkeeper said, reentering the room with a tray holding three bowls and a loaf of bread. As the door to the kitchen closed behind him, Giovan caught a glimpse of a dark-haired girl wearing an apron—the daughter. He noticed Filiberto and Paulo both staring at the now-closed door. He smiled, remembering what it had once meant to be young. There was a time when he too would have stared, as he had once gawked at Rachele.

"I'll wash first," he said to the innkeeper. "You, too," he added to Paulo, who gazed at his steaming bowl with longing. Filiberto had started eating, and Giovan knew it was pointless to get him to wash.

The landlord led them to nearby washstand with a basin and brought lukewarm water from the kitchen. Paulo waited as Giovan scrubbed the road grime from his face and hands and then hurriedly did the same. They shared a stained towel and returned to the table.

Paulo stopped, frozen, staring down at his bowl. He pointed.

Filiberto looked up, his face blank. "What?" he asked, his voice sweet and innocent.

Paulo was breathing hard. He glanced at Giovan, pleading in his eyes. The boy's bowl clearly contained less stew than Giovan's full one. And the bread was half gone.

"There's plenty more. Right innkeeper?" Filiberto said.

The men at the fire turned to watch.

"That's not the point," Giovan replied. "You broke the seventh commandment, 'Thou shalt not steal.'" There was still some stew in Filiberto's bowl, and Giovan picked it up and dumped it into Paulo's. "Two more bowls, full ones, and another loaf," he said to the innkeeper. "But no more for him," he added, nodding at Filiberto.

Filiberto snatched up his bowl and noisily licked at what was left. Then he slammed it down on the table.

"And no more wine, either," Giovan said.

"I have my own money," Filiberto said, snatching his cup. He shoved back his chair and joined the men at the fire.

Paulo glanced back and forth between Filiberto and Giovan for a moment, and then he grabbed his spoon. Giovan put out his hand and stopped him. The boy looked up, momentarily surprised, then with resignation clasped his hands together on the edge of the table.

"Dear Saint Christopher, protect us in all our travels..." Giovan started, his own hands folded in front of him. After droning on for a while, he said "Amen" and crossed himself, with Paulo doing the same.

Paulo grabbed for his spoon and began shoveling stew into is mouth.

"Humph," Filiberto spat into the fire.

Giovan ignored him, picking up his own spoon. He ate quietly. The stew contained lamb, carrots, big chunks of soft onions and was, as expected, heavily seasoned with garlic. When the innkeeper appeared with more stew and bread, the boy finished his second bowl quickly and wolfed down half of the bread. Giovan pushed the remainder across, and Paulo grabbed it. After a lifetime with young soldiers, Giovan knew how teenage boys ate.

"Help me with these boots," Giovan said when Paulo had finished, stretching one leg out toward the fire. Paulo leaped to obey and, after some tugging, managed to pull off both battered traveling boots. He set them before the fire to dry.

"That's better." Giovan stood, unbuckled his sword belt and laid the longsword in its scabbard on the table while Paulo watched.

Giovan dropped back into his chair and took another deep gulp from his wine cup. The warmth of the fire was starting to seep through his clothes and into his old bones. Thoughts of intrigue, mules and murder slipped away as his eyelids became heavy. Paulo was a good boy...

"He's only sixteen," Rachele had shrieked as Matthias cowered behind her, staring at Giovan.

"Old enough," Giovan had replied. "Older than many of my troops."

"But he knows nothing of soldiering."

"I agree. That's why he needs to go with me. He needs

toughening, some time in the open air, among men."

Matthias had a sallow complexion and his blubbery lips quivered as he stared at the father he hardly knew. His finely embroidered tunic and cape, as well as his perfect hosiery, failed to hide a plump frame.

"And what right have you to decide this now? You, who have not been home one day in ten."

"I've been making mercenary wages so you and he could live your comfortable, protected lives."

"Comfortable? When he was born, I lived in a tiny room in my parents' house while my husband was a thousand leagues away in Constantinople."

"Constantinople is not a thousand…but no matter. I was fighting for Christianity against the infidel Turks."

"And were you paid? Did you bring home riches for us?"

Giovan had sighed. It was an old argument. "He is my son. I have decided. He goes with me."

And a month later, fighting in service of the old pope, Matthias had stood trembling at his side.

"I want a sword," Paulo whispered.

Giovan roused himself. Across from him, the boy sat with Giovan's unsheathed longsword in his hands, his eyes downcast, the German steel flickering in the firelight. Paulo was nothing like Matthias, except possibly when it came to eating.

"Let me see your dagger," Giovan said.

Paulo set down the sword and pulled his dagger from its sheath, handing it to Giovan.

The blade was clean, the edge sharp. Giovan nodded in approval. Then he noticed some letters had been carved into the chestnut handle. "Sicarius?" Giovan asked.

Paulo looked at him sheepishly and replied, "Assassin."

"You know Latin?"

Paulo nodded. "Some. Father Nicolo has been teaching me."

Giovan looked into his wine cup and was pleased so see it wasn't empty. He drank what remained and smacked his lips.

"So then, Paulo. Have you heard the story of the Roman frog who learned how to write?"

"No, sir." Paulo stared at Giovan in astonishment.

"What did this literate frog say?"

Paulo shrugged.

"Scribit. Scribit."

Paulo's eyes got big, and his mouth dropped open. He burst out laughing and slapped his thigh. "Scribit," he repeated. He faced the men at the hearth. "Hey, Filiberto, the Captain told a joke."

Filiberto turned to look at him. Paulo repeated the story, but when he finished, Filiberto just stared at him.

"It's Latin. *He writes. He writes.*" Paulo explained. "Filiberto, it's funny."

Filiberto's eyes narrowed, then he shook his head and turned back to the fire and his new companions.

Paulo looked crestfallen.

Giovan patted the boy's arm. "Don't worry about him. He's just angry because he wants to go back to Rome. Like we all do."

Paulo nodded. "If you would just tell us why we are—"

"So, this is a fine dagger," Giovan said, interrupting. He hefted it, liking its balance and weight. Neither Filiberto nor Paulo knew anything about their purpose.

"Does your sword have a name?" Paulo asked.

"I don't name my weapons," Giovan replied. "Before we left Rome, I went to the Sant'Anglo armory and picked the best German longsword I could find. And this excellent dagger for you," he added, handing it back to Paulo. "For me, a weapon is a tool, like a hammer for a carpenter."

"I'll shave off the name," Paulo said.

"No, no. It's fine. Sicarius is a good name. Your dagger is enough for now," Giovan said. "It's the right weapon for a boy."

He had given Matthias a longsword.

* * *

"How many fingers are you using for the waistband?" Lucia asked. She picked up the stretched-out, ragged under-breeches from the bed next to Fioretta. "One, two, three…" she counted, using the width of her forefinger to measure while Fioretta waited. "…sixty, sixty-one, sixty-two. Well, he's a big man, isn't he, so we'll need lots of the material. I wonder if he's big here." She pushed her finger into the pouch-shaped crotch and stuck it out toward Fioretta, wagging it back and forth.

Fioretta forced a laugh, knowing Lucia was trying to cheer them both, trying to jest like she used to. Lucia had so much strength. Fioretta snatched away the under-breeches and put her hand over Lucia's, folding the trembling finger back into her palm. As Lucia started to turn away, Fioretta saw a gleam of tears in her eyes.

"But, the cotton has been stretched," Fioretta said, and Lucia turned back to her.

Fioretta held out the camicia, trying to guess the size when it had originally been sewn, knowing they must get this right. She hadn't been able to measure their client. That morning, one of his servants had brought his old camicia and a bolt of cotton cloth to her shop with instructions that his master required a dozen sets of undershirts and breeches before he left for Milan in three days. The fee was huge, eighteen silver soldi, almost a gold florin. They could survive on eighteen soldi for another month.

"Fifty-four?" Fioretta asked. "What do you think?"

Lucia shrugged.

"Yes, let's use fifty-four for the waistband." Fioretta tried to sound confident.

Lucia went to the door and the stairs leading down to the first floor where she worked—worked that is, when they had a customer. She slept in the tiny back room, which also served as a kitchen, while Fioretta sewed and slept on the second floor. This house was much smaller than her father's and shabbier.

So far, as well as Fioretta knew, her father and Maffei did not know where she and Lucia lived.

Lucia stopped in the doorway and glanced back over her shoulder.

"Go on," Fioretta said. "I'm fine."

Lucia disappeared and soon a sad song drifted up the steps.

Fioretta blew into her cupped hands to warm them. They had no money for firewood. The early winter cold seeped through the room's single window. Its wooden frame was rotten and some of the panes were cracked, but it was unusually large for such a modest shop. It provided good light for sewing, and she could see the tower of the Palazzo della Signoria peeking above the low buildings on the other side of the street. It's clock showed twenty hours since the last sunset— only four more hours of daylight. Fioretta picked up her needle and pressed her mother's pewter thimble onto her forefinger.

An hour later, Fioretta put down the half-completed undershirt and stretched out her tired, cold fingers. Needing to cut a piece of fabric and realizing her scissors were getting dull, she stepped over to the one good piece of furniture in the room, her mother's marriage chest, sitting next to the window with its lid open. At one time painted panels had adorned its front and sides, but years before her father had pried them off and sold them. Now, as Fioretta rummaged in the old chest, inhaling the familiar cedar aroma while searching for her whetstone, she saw the single remaining painting on the inside of the lid.

Saint Anne held her adult daughter Mary on her lap, gazing down at her with adoration. Mary, her face also radiating love, leaned over, reaching for the baby Jesus who played with a lamb. It was the story of two mothers and of motherhood. Unable to find the stone, Fioretta collapsed back onto the bed, sobbing.

In six months, *she* would be a mother, or so the midwife said. Fioretta laid her hands across her stomach, sure she felt a bulge. Her breasts were already larger and more tender. She had no husband, nor any prospect of one. Ever. Giuliano shared her little bed, said he loved her, still wanted to give her money. And there had been no further occurrence of melancholy over his former love, the dead Simonetta. But, Lorenzo was rumored to be negotiating Giuliano's marriage with a family in Piombino. Giuliano continued to profess that such a marriage would make no difference to them.

But how could he know? What if the proposed wife was beautiful? What if he fell in love with her? Would he really still have time for Fioretta? Would he still love her? Did he truly love her now?

She must do everything she could to hold on to Giuliano. It was the only path before her. He loved her. He said so often, and he was so sincere. She had to believe him, have faith.

But she hadn't seen Giuliano for a week.

And he didn't know about the baby.

"I have some watered wine," Lucia said, standing at the door. "Like the midwife said." She came and sat on the bed, handing the cup to Fioretta, who sipped at it. "Drink it all," Lucia said, and Fioretta forced herself to gulp down the remainder.

"How goes the work?" Fioretta asked.

"I finished two breeches." Lucia picked up the partially completed undershirt. "Is this all you've done?"

"We've still got a few hours of daylight. I can finish this one and start another. Tomorrow, we'll work from sunrise to sunset."

Lucia said nothing.

"I'm working as fast as I can," Fioretta said.

"Perhaps I should work on the shirts—"

There was a noise in the street, the sound of horses' hooves on the cobblestones and men's laughter. *Giuliano!* Fioretta hurried to the window and there he was, swinging off his favorite horse, Samuele, along with Stefano. A third man that Fioretta didn't recognize stayed mounted and took the reins of the other two horses.

"Quick, my mirror," Fioretta said.

Lucia grabbed Fioretta's hand mirror from the chest and held it up.

Fioretta wiped the remains of her tears from her cheeks with the back of her hand and stared at herself in the mirror. She was so pale.

Bang, bang, bang. Giuliano's knocks sounded impatient.

Fioretta pinched her cheeks. She shook loose her hair, which had been tied back so she could work, and used the brush Lucia offered. It would have to do. She strolled to the door and stood at the top of the steps, gazing down to the main room below as Lucia rushed down to open the front door.

"Fioretta, my love," Giuliano called out as he burst through the door and bounded up the stairs, leaving Stefano with Lucia. He grabbed Fioretta's waist and twirled her around. "I have missed you so much," he cried. "And I've written a new *sonetto* for you."

He stepped into her room, tugging at her to follow.

As Fioretta closed the door, she caught sight of Lucia putting her hand on Stefano's chest, pushing him away and shaking her head.

Giuliano enveloped her in his powerful arms, smothering her with kisses, his lips still cold from the ride.

"Where have you been?" She pulled back a bit. "It's been a week."

"Surely I told you Lorenzo and I were hunting at Cafaggiolo." He gazed at her with concern. "Didn't I?"

Fioretta said nothing. She waited.

"My darling," he continued. "I'm so sorry. I'm such a fool. Did you worry? Did I tell you I wrote you a new sonetto?"

In some ways, this was a game they played. He was inconsiderate in a small way, she pouted, he dissolved into abject apology, and she forgave him.

"You're here now," she said, smiling. "That's all that matters."

He crushed her to him, covering her mouth with his, his

tongue touching hers. She gasped, feeling her nipples tingle as she slipped her hand inside his tunic, searching for bare skin while he reached for her breast.

A thought forced its way into her consciousness. "Stop," she said, gasping and trying to push him away. "Giuliano, please stop." She realized that if they made love, he'd surely notice her growing breasts and belly, might somehow feel the baby. And that wasn't how she wanted him to find out.

He stared at her, confused.

"I want to, my love," she said. "Soon, I promise. But first we must talk. Please." Despite herself, tears began to roll down her cheeks.

Giuliano saw the tears, let her go and drew back. She saw him take a deep breath, and then he gave her a wan smile. "It's difficult, you know." he said, "for a man to stop like this." He sighed.

She took his hand, and they sat beside each other on the bed. He handed her a handkerchief, and Fioretta dabbed at her tears. His eyes wandered around the room, and settled on the marriage chest. "I've not seen your chest open before. That's a lovely painting. Sienese, I think."

"The chest was my mother's."

"A marriage chest—ah." He turned to her. "We've discussed this before. When I marry, it must be for the good of the family. You have always known this." He shrugged. "I don't know what else to say."

"I know."

"But still, it makes you sad. I'm sorry. Is this what you want to talk about? Again?"

Fioretta shook her head. She started to put her hands on her stomach but snatched them back, afraid he would guess the meaning of this gesture. But she wanted to tell him about the baby. Didn't she?

"When did you get back?" she asked.

"Just this morning. I rushed here as soon as I could." He grinned at her. "Stefano wanted to see Lucia."

"Oh, so that's why," she replied, forcing a smile. Then, remembering, she added, "I fear she is not so happy to see him."

"And what's this?" he said, seeing the uncompleted undershirt and her sewing things on the bed. "You have a customer? Is it a big commission?"

"Enough money to last us for a while. But there is so little time, and we are not sure about the measurements. And the work is going so slowly—"

"Stop, my love. We'll come back tonight, when it's too dark to work. And I'll stay the night, if that suits you."

"Oh, thank you. But stay just a bit longer now. It's so good to see you."

In the distance, the sound of the hour bell rang out across Florence. Giuliano stood, stepped over to the window and peered out.

"Fioretta, I know you won't let me support you," he said, "But please consider again my offer to invest in your enterprise."

Fioretta pressed her finger against his lips. "No money from any man," she said. "Unless I've earned it. I can never take money from you. If I did, I'd be nothing more than a—"

"Stop. Don't say that. Have you heard from your father?"

"Not since Lucia and I left."

It had happened four months before, on the Nativity of Mary feast day. Fioretta and her father had been walking home from Saint Joseph's, their neighborhood church, avoiding puddles from the afternoon rain.

"She lives under my roof," Antonio Gorini had said.

"Yes, Papa. You're right, of course," Fioretta replied. "She should have come with us."

"Next time, I'll use my belt. She'll do as she's told."

"But, Papa, you know that only makes things worse."

Gorini grunted and said nothing.

As they approached their house, a scream stabbed through the night air.

The door refused to open, swollen by the rain. Gorini threw his weight against it, but her father was not a large man and it did no good. Fioretta gathered herself and threw her body alongside him, and finally the door burst open into the hallway. They rushed inside. The fire burned low in the hearth, and by it's light she saw the main room was empty. Fioretta opened the door to the kitchen.

They found Father Maffei standing in front of the cupboard, fumbling with the buttons on the front of his cassock. He looked up, his face pale, contorted.

"She seduced me," he said.

Lucia sat on the floor, leaning against the back wall, her shift pulled up to her thighs. Glassy-eyed, she stared down at her bare legs, stretched out in front of her. Fioretta leaned down beside her. "What happened?" she asked, already knowing the answer in her heart.

Lucia said nothing. She continued to stare at her legs.

"It's not my fault," Maffei said. "We all know what kind of woman she is."

Fioretta tugged Lucia's dress down as far as she could manage. She put her hand on Lucia's shoulder, but Lucia shrank away. Fioretta leaped up and charged into Maffei, her fists beating against his chest. "Bastard!" she shrieked as he fell back onto the cupboard, and the crockery rattled inside. The sickly sweet smell of wine was strong on his breath.

"Stop," her father shouted, and Fioretta felt him grab her arms, dragging her away. "Father Maffei, what happened here?" he asked.

"I came to see you, and she let me in." His speech was slurred. "She smiled, showed me her bosom. I am a man of God, but I am also a man. She has the fault."

They turned to Lucia on the floor, who said nothing.

"She'd never do that." Fioretta struggled against her father's grip. "She hates you."

"Daughter," Gorini shouted. "Be silent. This man is a priest. He says she's at fault."

"What? You believe him? You know Lucia would never —"

"Be silent," Gorini said. "Everyone knows she's a whore."

Fioretta stared at him. Her father was taking the side of his friend, ignoring what was obviously a great sin. She pulled Lucia to her feet and left the kitchen.

During the next hour, while her father assisted Maffei back to his abbey, Fioretta stuffed as much as she could of her and Lucia's belongings into her mother's marriage chest. Once Lucia understood they were moving out of that house, she rallied and helped. Fioretta went next door and returned with the two brothers that Fioretta knew Lucia was friendly with, and they hauled the chest to Saint Joseph's. The priest there, like so many people around them, disliked her father and was happy to provide sanctuary for a time. Within a few days, they'd moved into this shabby little house, where Giuliano now stood beside her at the window, four months later.

She hadn't told Giuliano the whole story, of course, because Lucia was insistent that Stefano must never know. All Giuliano knew was that there had been a falling out, and he was happy she'd finally left her father's house.

"You know," he said, "being a father must be difficult, especially trying to raise a daughter without her mother. Perhaps you should let him know you are safe. Have Lucia take a note."

"No!"

Giuliano looked at her, surprised.

She turned away and gazed out the window, speaking softly, "So have *you* thought about being a father?"

"Maybe I already am," he cried. "So many happy women."

Fioretta spun around and hit his shoulder as hard as she could. "How can you say that to me?"

"My dear," Giuliano replied, surprised and rubbing his shoulder. "You know I've been with other women. We've joked about it before."

"So fatherhood means so little to you?"

"Why? What has brought this on?" His eyes traveled down her body, stopping at her breasts, her belly. His mouth opened a little, his eyes widened.

"Yes," she said. "In six months, I think."

This was the moment. The rest of her life depended on how he reacted now.

Giuliano stared at her belly. When he reached out to touch it, she felt a flash of hope. Then his face contorted in disgust. He withdrew his hand and walked to the door, where he stopped, turned and said, "You told me the carrot seeds would prevent it. You deceived me." He pulled a slip of paper from his pocket and dropped it on the bed. "The sonetto." Then he shouted, "Stefano. We're leaving," and she heard the clomp of his boots on the stairs.

Stunned, Fioretta stayed at the window, and seconds later she saw Giuliano leap onto Samuele and gallop up the street, his guard and Stefano racing to catch him. What had just happened? She felt Lucia come up behind her and slide her arm around Fioretta's waist.

"These stupid, stupid, highborn men," Lucia said. "And their stupid fear of being with a pregnant woman."

She handed Fioretta the slip of paper, and Fioretta read the first two lines.

> *To savor the sweet roses I was fain,*
> *But to describe their loveliness was in vain;*

Sweet words. But he'd written them before he knew about the baby.

"Hello, Tessa," Thadeous said, bowing as deeply as he could manage. "Thank you for letting me visit you again."

Tessa Carpani stood in the doorway of the small, sturdy cottage and gave him a quick curtsy. "You're my husband's friend, so of course you are welcome, Professore Thadeous."

It had been six months since Dante had first invited Thadeous to come to his house and meet his family, and since then he had visited many times on Sunday afternoons, with

Dante and his oldest son driving a donkey cart to fetch him at the Cardinal's palazzo after Mass. The cart was necessary as it was almost a mile to the outskirts of Pisa where they lived.

"Come sit by the fire and talk," Tessa added. "We'll have supper soon." Her words had a forced, formal quality, and she exchanged a look with Dante that always made Thadeous wonder how welcome he actually was.

It rarely snowed during the Pisan winter, but it was cold today, and Thadeous, Dante and the boy were wrapped in blankets from the ride. Thadeous kept his as he entered the house's main room and crossed to the big chair by the fire reserved for him. He suspected it was normally Dante's chair, but he sank into it gratefully. He said hello to the second oldest boy who brought him a cup of warm wine.

During the next hour, Thadeous and Dante discussed local politics, Dante's interest in the underrated *Paradiso* by his namesake, and Thadeous's progress on his book about the fall of Constantinople. The two girls came in from the kitchen to join their brothers while Thadeous told a story about Galahad rescuing Sir Percival from twenty knights and saving a maiden in distress.

The youngest child, a boy of about five years, stayed back in a corner, as he usually did. After Thadeous's first visit, as Dante drove him home in the donkey cart, he had explained that the boy was completely deaf and had never spoken a word.

After the story, Dante suggested that they let Thadeous rest for a while until supper was ready. He refilled Thadeous's cup. The girls returned to the kitchen, and the two older boys worked with their father at carving a toy boat.

Thadeous had been reluctant to talk about the Constantinople book. He was making less progress than he had hoped because whenever he sat down to work on it, the memories flooded back. He gazed down into his wine cup, tapping the side with his finger and watching the ripples expand and collapse on the wine's surface.

Thadeous drank down the remains of the wine, set the cup on the floor, and stared into the fire, remembering the night with the ripples in the water bucket, the same night when Lauro had introduced his fellow mercenary, Giovan Battista from Montesecco.

His reverie was interrupted as he realized that a small body was climbing onto his lap. He glanced down in surprise to see Dante's youngest boy staring up at him, his eyes big and fixed on Thadeous's face. Wrapping his arm around and under the slight body, Thadeous wondered if, with four older siblings, the boy got enough to eat.

"Hello," Thadeous said.

The boy didn't react.

Thadeous moved his free hand next to the boy's ear and snapped his fingers. No response whatever.

"I'm sorry," Thadeous said. "I'm afraid I don't remember your name."

The boy turned away.

"He's called Luca," Dante said, continuing to carve at the toy boat's mast.

Thadeous touched Luca's chin and gently pulled his head around so they faced each other. "Are you a good boy, Luca?" he asked.

He wasn't sure, but Thadeous thought he saw the pupils in Luca's eyes expand slightly as he said *Luca*. After a moment, they shrank back.

"Is your name Luca?" Thadeous studied boy's face.

Again, the pupils widened and contracted.

"Is your name Thadeous?"

The boy looked away.

"Dante," Thadeous said. "I think he recognizes his name."

Dante stood up, skepticism on his face, and came over, followed by the other boys.

"Watch his eyes," Thadeous said, tugging Luca's chin around. "Is your name Thadeous?"

No response.

"Is your name Luca?"

The boy's mouth twitched slightly and then something happened that Thadeous hadn't seen before. Luca smiled.

"But how?" Dante asked.

"He watches my mouth," Thadeous replied. "I think he recognizes the movement of my lips."

Dante looked thoughtful. "He does smile, but we always thought it was for no particular reason." He turned and shouted, "Tessa, come here."

Tessa Carpani came into the room, wiping her hands on a rag. "We're almost ready, so why do you—" She stared at Thadeous and Luca. "What's he doing there?" she cried out. "Get him away from that man."

"What?" Dante said.

Tessa strode across the room, grabbed Luca's arm and yanked him away from Thadeous. She shoved the boy into his corner and spun around to face to Thadeous. "Get out of my house. You filthy *frocio.*"

Usually, when Dante drove Thadeous home through the streets of Pisa, his oldest son accompanied them. But not this night. Dante said nothing as he sat next to Thadeous, seemingly focused on directing the donkey. Wrapped again in blankets against the winter chill, they rumbled over the rough dirt street in silence.

"My friend," Thadeous said finally. "What happened?"

It was hard to see Dante's face in the gathering darkness. "Tessa wants to protect her youngest child, her baby."

"From me? Why?"

"You've never married."

There it was. "Yes. And how does that make me a threat to Luca?"

"Men who do not love women, well…"

"You think I prefer men," Thadeous said.

Beneath his blanket, Dante shrugged. " Do you deny it?"

"If that were true," Thadeous replied, carefully choosing

his words, "how does it make me a threat to your son?"

"It happens."

"Yes. But look at it this way. You prefer women, right?"

"Of course."

"Does that mean you're a threat to five-year-old girls?"

"No. The idea is offensive." Dante tugged at the reins, and the cart came to a halt. "It's not the same. God condemns men being together."

"We've had many discussions as friends. At the library, in your home. This is the first time you've resorted to God to make a point."

"Get out." Dante gestured at the street. "We're close enough."

Stunned, Thadeous glanced around and realized they had come only half way. He wanted to remind Dante of his difficulty walking, even breathing, but surmised that it was futile. He climbed down from the cart, landing in a puddle of icy water. He saw ripples spread out across it's surface as he stepped out and began trudging toward Salviati's house.

"He's my son," Dante called out behind him.

Thadeous didn't look back. Instead he stumbled ahead into the winter darkness, his mind working. If he had lost Dante's friendship, what would happen to his life? He had come to cherish these visits, and now they were surely finished. And what about the library? Would he be welcome there now? He need access to books so he could finish his own.

The edge of the scarf covering his mouth slipped, and a blast of cold air blew down into his damaged lungs. His chest seemed to explode with the cough, and he stopped, doubled over and spat blood onto the street. He still had a long way to go. Covering his mouth again, he took a slow breath and started walking, shivering.

It had been warm in Constantinople. And Lauro was there. Lauro, who had never lost faith in him.

Twenty-Five Years Earlier

A ripple appeared on the water's surface, spreading out and colliding with the sides of the bucket, and then reflecting back to the center where it disappeared. A moment later, it happened again.

Thadeous stared down at the half-full water bucket, not understanding. He sat on a stone block at the base of the great land wall, waiting for the signal that he and Lauro and a hundred other workers would once again swarm up the rubble from the day's cannonade. Like Sisyphus, each night they hauled the broken stones back to the top, all the while wondering if their labors would be enough to keep out the Turkish hordes for yet another day.

He and Lauro had slept for only a few hours at Pletho's house after slaving at a different labor, both of them copying the manuscript with Pletho hanging over them, cajoling and correcting. Exhausted, and with Pletho always nearby, they had not made love since that first night.

Another ripple appeared and disappeared.

Thadeous looked up, wondering if somehow raindrops were falling from the darkening but clear sky. He put out his hand and felt nothing. He listened, but heard only Lauro's regular breathing as he dozed on the ground next to him. The other workers around them were silent, resting, dreading the backbreaking night that once again lay before them.

Pletho had told Thadeous about this great land wall, the Theodosian Wall, built a century after the Emperor Constantine had moved the failing Roman Empire to Byzantium and renamed the city for himself. It had protected the city for a thousand years, and now they repaired it every night, hoping that they could hold out for a few more days, when the relief ships sent by the Pope would surely reach them. And in a few more days, Lauro and Thadeous would finish copying Pletho's manuscript.

The sound of shuffling feet roused Thadeous, and when he looked up he saw a ragged line of dirty men trudging past. Thadeous recognized the pickaxes, shovels and pikes they carried, all tools used by his father and himself back in the Cyprian copper mine.

Puzzled, he turned to Lauro. "Are those men copper miners?"

"What?" Lauro replied, his voice hoarse as he climbed his feet, shaking his head to clear it. "Oh, them. They dig for Turks, not copper," Lauro said. "The enemy has their own miners tunneling under the wall. They want to dig out a large area called a gallery, prop it up with timbers, and when all is ready, they will set the timbers on fire. The tunnel collapses into the gallery, and the wall comes down."

"And those men are digging to find the Turkish tunnels?"

"Yes. Can you imagine the fighting when they find one?" Lauro grinned at him. "You're underground with the largest, heaviest wall of the world over your head. You fight in narrow, dark, muddy passages with barely room to swing your sword." He took out his short sword and swung it back and forth.

"You've never been in a mine, have you?" Thadeous said. "My father was a copper miner. I worked with him for a year before he sent me off to school."

Lauro returned his sword the its scabbard and put his hand on Thadeous's shoulder. "We know so little about each other."

Thadeous stood, gazed into Lauro's eyes and shrugged. "Yes. Because of all this." He gestured at the men who were beginning to stand, at the wall before them, and at the Turks he knew were just hundreds of yards beyond.

Lauro pulled him close, pressing his lips into Thadeous's neck. Thadeous returned the embrace for a moment and then turned his mouth to Lauro's, luxuriating in his soft lips, wanting more.

They each stepped back, and Thadeous was relieved that nobody seemed to have noticed them or seemed to care.

"Of course," Lauro said, his voice businesslike now, "the problem is that this great wall of ours is over three miles in length. Where do our miners dig?"

Thadeous, still savoring the memory of Lauro's touch,

hardly listened. Then, he remembered the ripples. He looked down at the water bucket. It happened again.

"Lauro," he shouted, pointing at the surface of the water. "Watch."

Puzzled, Lauro leaned over and joined Thadeous in peering into the bucket.

Nothing happened.

A horn sounded nearby, and it was repeated up and down the wall.

"It's time," Lauro said, turning to join the workers who had started to scramble up the rubble.

"Wait. Please. This can help us."

Lauro stopped, even as the other workers swarmed past him. Sighing, he came back to where Thadeous stood next to the bucket. "What?" he asked.

Thadeous pointed. A ripple appeared and disappeared.

Lauro glanced at Thadeous, his brow wrinkled as he struggled to understand. "You've seen this happen before?"

"Several times since we got here. When everything was quiet. There's no rain, nothing else to cause it."

Another ripple.

"It's from digging in a Turkish tunnel," Lauro said. "There must be one near here."

Nodding, Thadeous glanced around, wondering how close the tunnel might be. He had taken some comfort in knowing that the masses of Turkish soldiers were on the other side of the wall. But perhaps the Turks were much closer, maybe just a few yards below where he and Lauro now stood.

"Do you understand what this means?" Lauro voice rose in excitement. "This gives us a way to detect the tunnels. We can post men with water buckets up and down the length of the wall. We'll know where to dig. Come, we need to see Captain Giovan."

Chapter Four

Six Hours Until Dawn

The fresh scoriada wounds on Giovan's back rubbed against his camicia, so he paused and shifted his body, trying to find a position that eased the pain. As he did so, he eyed Paulo's dagger still on the table next to the inkwell. Giovan glanced over at his guard, who was again asleep on his stool. It would be an easy thing to do; he had killed men in their sleep before. But then what? This cell was in a tower, high above the street, and there were more guards in the stairwell. And the door was bolted on the outside.

No, it was hopeless.

Giovan clasped his hands together on the edge of the table, squeezing his eyes shut. As so often happened when he prayed and was troubled, the sound of the glorious Sanctus, sung by the small choir in Father Nicolo's church, crept into his consciousness. A vision of Jesus Christ against the golden sky floated before him, the sad eyes of Jesus gazing into Giovan's soul, his hand raised in blessing. Silently, with his lips barely moving, Giovan repeated the *Padre Nostro*, Our Father, three times.

His hands relaxed. I've taken on the task of writing my confession, he said to himself, and I'll finish it. He picked up the quill pen and resumed where he left off.

> *The Archbishop and the Count sent me here to Florence, so that I could have a chance to see the city and meet Lorenzo the Magnificent.*

Five Months Earlier

Giovan sat on a marble bench in the Palazzo Medici's

central courtyard, trying not to look at the bronze statue in front of him. He had been waiting for over an hour. He understood that Lorenzo de' Medici was undoubtedly a busy man, but waiting had never been easy for Giovan. Soldiers should have patience—they must wait for orders. In Rome, the city of popes, archbishops and cardinals, Giovan often had to wait, and he considered it the bane of his career.

"Captain Giovan, welcome to my home." Lorenzo emerged into the courtyard spreading his arms wide in a gesture of greeting and beamed as he joined Giovan who leaped to his feet. With a wave of his hand, Lorenzo dismissed the attendants who were following him.

"Thank you, Magnifico." Giovan bowed.

He had been wary of finally meeting Lorenzo de' Medici, the man everyone called *il Magnifico*. All of Europe knew of Lorenzo. He had come to power in Florence at age twenty after his father's death and after serving for many years as a young diplomat. During Lorenzo's eight-year reign, the economy of Florence had flourished. Archbishop Salviati and Francesco de' Pazzi claimed that the people of Florence hated him, but so far Giovan had seen no evidence of this.

"How was your journey?" Lorenzo asked, taking Giovan's elbow. "Have you come from Rome? Please, sit. You must tell me everything." His lack of formality was disconcerting.

They sat on the bench facing the bronze statue, a nude boy with an oversized sword in his hand, his foot resting on a severed head. Giovan stared at the boy's sensuously curved body with its prominent, if dainty, penis, and then turned away, embarrassed. He glanced over at Lorenzo who was gazing at the statue.

"It's David and the head of Goliath," Lorenzo said. "Isn't it splendid? My grandfather commissioned it from Donatello di Niccolò."

Lorenzo was not a handsome man, with a squashed nose dominating his flat, swarthy face. He wore a simple woolen tunic. Giovan was surprised at this because the men with wealth and power that he knew wore silk. However, it was easy to see that the wool was of the best quality, tightly woven, and dyed a deep luxurious crimson. His hose matched the tunic. Giovan could not help but notice his ornately tooled green leather shoes with pointed toes. This was the fashion.

Paulo had thoroughly brushed Giovan's battered traveling boots that morning, but still Giovan pushed his feet out of sight beneath the bench.

"I know little of art, Magnifico," he said. "I am merely an ignorant soldier."

Lorenzo continued to smile, but his eyes narrowed as he said, "I doubt that very much, Captain."

Startled, Giovan kept his expression calm. What did Lorenzo know? He was reputed to have spies in every major town, and especially in Rome. Lorenzo knew of Giovan's high military rank, of course, and of his loyalty to the His Holiness and the Count. But did he know of Giovan's travels around northern Italy? Was it possible that Lorenzo suspected that Giovan, the man he had so warmly welcomed, would return one day soon to kill him? Giovan glanced around the courtyard, looking for armed guards. He saw none.

Lorenzo had turned back to the statue. He said, "My mother thinks it's scandalous."

"I think I agree with her, Magnifico."

Lorenzo laughed. "You are a wise man, Captain. I've learned that agreeing with my mother is always a good idea. But turning to business, your note said that you had a letter from my great friend, the estimable Count Riario."

That morning, Giovan, Filiberto and Paulo had arrived in Florence and had taken a room at the comfortable Inn of the Bell. Giovan had sent word to Lorenzo that he carried a letter from Count Riario, and the messenger returned with an invitation to dinner. Back in Imola, the Count had shown the letter to Giovan before it was sealed. It was a mere pretext that would allow Giovan to meet Lorenzo.

Giovan pulled the letter from the pocket inside his doublet

and handed it to Lorenzo, who broke the seal and read it.

"The Count expresses his sadness for the death of a mutual friend," Lorenzo said, shrugging. Then his demeanor brightened, and he added, "Come. Now that we're done with that, let me show you more of my treasures."

They wandered through the rooms adjoining the courtyard with Lorenzo showing off his collections of ancient manuscripts, precious stones, carved gems and his Marango glass figures, as well as a number of oil paintings and more statuary. They stopped in front of a large canvas depicting the Nativity, with Mary, the baby Jesus, the three Magi and a crowd of onlookers.

"May I ask a question about his picture, Magnifico?"

"Of course. If I can enlighten you, it will give me great pleasure."

"The sky…"

"Yes?"

"It's blue." Giovan pointed at the top corners of the painting were the pale blue sky peeked through the ruined wall that provided the backdrop for the scene.

"Of course."

"But isn't it traditional to paint the sky gold?"

"But our sky is not gold, is it? This is in the new style, where we value realism."

Giovan said nothing for a moment, remembering the fresco over the altar at the Church of San Pellegrino, back in Rome. It's background was gold, of course, just like every other fresco or painting he had ever seen.

"You don't approve, Captain?"

"I think there is a reason why sky is painted as gold. It shows a better place than our ugly world."

"A better place." Lorenzo took a step back and peered at the sky in the painting. "Perhaps you have a point."

Giovan's eyes were drawn to the right side of the painting, to a haughty young man staring directly out of the canvas, his lips full and curling with contempt. Giovan knew this man.

"That's Sandro Botticelli," Lorenzo said, noticing Giovan's interest. "The artist. It's just like him to paint himself as the largest figure in this holy scene."

"We've met," Giovan replied, keeping his voice flat. "In Rome." He remembered the confrontation in His Holiness's new chapel, and Botticelli saying, "Don't ever come to Florence, *soldier*."

Lorenzo laughed suddenly. "You're the one. Sandro told me about you. He was still angry when he got home, even after riding for three days."

Giovan stood silent, unsure what to say.

Lorenzo touched his arm. "Sandro is a hothead, of course. But he's a good friend to my brother and me."

Giovan nodded, understanding. As it was best that he remain in Lorenzo's good graces, he would avoid Sandro Botticelli while he was in Florence. "I've been admiring your city," he said.

Lorenzo smiled at him. "The most beautiful in Italy. You must visit the Palazzo della Signoria, the seat of our republican municipal government. It's easy to find. You can see the tower from anywhere within the walls." He paused for a moment and then went on. "Did you know that a century ago there were twenty great towers in Florence, each built by a powerful family. When fighting broke out, as it often did, a tower provided a safe haven and a military base."

"I've seen such towers in other cities."

"Yes. But Florence isn't like other cities. Years ago we tore them all down, and we're now a peaceful republic. We have only the one great tower at the Signoria. It represents our unity."

Giovan realized that Lorenzo, no longer smiling, was making a political point, wanting Giovan to know that Florence was unified against any external threat. "I'll tell that story to the Count and His Holiness," he said.

"Do that."

Giovan followed him back out into the chilly but bright

courtyard.

"We've had our squabbles here, of course," Lorenzo continued. "My grandfather, Cosimo, was imprisoned in that same tower, forty-five years ago, in a little cell above the clock. But soon the people of Florence saw the error of their ways, and he returned to power."

"You said Florence was a republic."

"And so it is. My grandfather, my father, and for the last eight years, myself, have only provided guidance. Did you know that Cosimo was so well loved that he was known as *Pater Patriae*, the Father of his Country."

"And you are known as *il Magnifico*," Giovan said.

"A source of embarrassment, I assure you." Lorenzo bowed slightly and made a deprecating gesture with his hands. The man was charming.

"And you were so young, just twenty years I believe," Giovan said.

"I've done the best I can for my people," Lorenzo replied.

It was clear to Giovan that the man was enjoying these complements. "And you have military experience, too," Giovan added. "When Volterra revolted—"

Lorenzo swung around and glared at Giovan with such intensity that Giovan took a step back.

"Please, your pardon, Magnifico." Giovan bowed deeply. Clearly he had gone too far.

"Lorenzo," a voice shouted.

They turned and saw two men entering the courtyard. The taller was perhaps the most handsome man Giovan had ever seen, his features similar to Lorenzo's but with an aquiline nose and a ruddy complexion. His cape and coat were the same deep crimson as Lorenzo's, but they had the sheen of silk and had flamboyant embroidery. He moved with the easy grace of an athlete, and Giovan guessed that this must be the younger brother, Giuliano.

"A message from the London branch, I'm afraid." Giuliano indicated the man in traveling clothes next to him.

"Can't you deal with it?" Lorenzo replied, clearly irritated.

"I'm so sorry, Magnifico," the messenger said. "The report is to be delivered to you personally."

Lorenzo's shoulders sagged. Then he turned back to Giovan and, once again the gracious host, he said with a slight bow, "I'm sorry, but I must take my leave." He put his hand on Giovan's shoulder. "Please do me a great kindness. When next you see Count Riario, tell him of my good wishes. And when you return to Rome, tell His Holiness that I love and revere him. It serves no one if there is tension between us."

"Of course, Magnifico." As Giovan returned the bow, he wondered if this man was sincere or merely the skilled politician that he was reputed to be.

Lorenzo introduced him to Giuliano, and then he strode away with the messenger trailing behind him.

"Did I hear you say something about Volterra?" Giuliano asked.

"A mistake, I'm afraid."

Giuliano nodded. "It haunts him."

"What happened?"

"It's not for me to say. We don't talk about it within these walls."

"I'll take my leave then," Giovan said, starting to bow.

"No, no. You're from Rome." Giuliano took Giovan's arm. "What news have you? But wait—how about some wine? Come up to my rooms, and we'll have a cup or two. I insist."

Despite Giovan's reluctance, moments later they were sprawled on a comfortable divan in Giuliano's sumptuous, if untidy bedroom, looking out over the courtyard, each with a full cup of excellent red wine. Giuliano took a deep drink, smacked his lips, and Giovan sipped at his appreciatively. Giuliano talked about his visits to Rome, his hunting, the jousting tournament he'd won that summer while Giovan carefully spoke of nonpolitical topics, which seemed just fine with Giuliano. These two Medici brothers were so different.

Giovan noticed a painting of a young girl hanging on the

wall nearby. He got up and stood before it. Blue sky shown through the window behind her. Another modern painting. "She's lovely," he said.

Staying in his chair, Giuliano sighed. "Yes, she is. Alas."

A servant entered the room. "Dinner will be served soon," he said. "Perhaps your guest would like to wash?"

Giovan again became aware of his bedraggled appearance. "Please," he said.

"Show him the way, Stefano." Giuliano was now lost in thought, staring into his cup.

"If I could ask a favor," Giovan said. "I've been traveling for almost four weeks now. Can you recommend a tailor?"

"Yes, of course," Giuliano replied, distracted.

"And, this is a little embarrassing, my camicia is, well…"

Giuliano's head jerked up. He and the servant exchanged a look, and then he said, "As a matter of fact, I think we can help you with that."

Three hours later, Giovan took his leave and Filiberto joined him, having spent this time in the servant's quarters. The Via de' Martelli was bustling with activity as Giovan and Filiberto left the Palazzo Medici, starting the short walk back to the inn where they had left Paulo.

"Thank you for coming with me," Giovan said. "I know you have no love for the Medici."

"Captain, I follow your orders, even when they are unpleasant." He was a little drunk. Apparently, the Medici servants had treated him well.

Smiling at this, Giovan said, "You've never told me of your grievance against the Medici."

"We're returning to Rome soon, right?" Filiberto asked, stopping and turning to Giovan.

"First I need to meet with another man. Then yes. You'll be in bed with your young wife in five days time."

"Thank the heavens." Filiberto raised his eyes skyward and then his expression became serious. He glanced back over his shoulder in the direction of the Palazzo Medici. "Why do I despise the Medici? Because Marta is from Volterra."

Volterra again. Giovan only knew that some years before, during the early years of his reign, Lorenzo had put down a revolt by the town of Volterra. This seemed to be something any powerful ruler might need to do.

"What did Marta tell you?" Giovan asked.

"She says Lorenzo hired five thousand mercenaries from Urbino. The siege lasted a month, but in the end the town surrendered. They *surrendered*. And yet, Lorenzo ordered his mercenaries to sack the town. For two days, those Urbinese beasts raped and pillaged."

This was neither shocking nor surprising to Giovan. Terrible things happen in war. "Your wife's family? Marta?" he asked.

Filiberto shook his head and said nothing.

Giovan remembered how both Medici brothers had reacted to the mention of Volterra. This seemed to be a source of embarrassment or shame for the Medici family, and he wondered if there was some way to use this against them. There must others in Florence who hated the Medici.

"What was it like with the servants?" Giovan asked. They resumed walking toward the inn.

Filiberto shrugged and said, "They eat and drink well in that house."

"Did you hear any complaints?"

"The usual, I suppose. I've heard worse at Count Riario's house."

"In Rome," Giovan said, "they say the Medici are not popular here."

He studied the people around them, and they seemed much like the citizens of any northern Italian city. Perhaps they were a little better dressed. Certainly Giovan had seen no obvious dissatisfaction.

Were his fellow conspirators—Count Riario, Archbishop Salviati and Francesco de' Pazzi—all wrong about the popularity of the Medici brothers? Were they good men and not knaves as the others claimed?

Giovan had promised Count Riario he personally would assassinate Lorenzo, and he would. As a soldier, he wasn't troubled by the possibility that Lorenzo might be a good man. It had been necessary for Giovan to kill many men on the battlefield and elsewhere, and some of them must have been good men. All that mattered was Giovan's loyalty, and in that he would not fail.

That still left the troubling question: If the Medici brothers were not despised in Florence, why did the others in Rome make the claim that they were? Did they have bad information? Were they fooling themselves? Or were they lying to him?

No matter what the reason, this did not bode well for Giovan. He needed to better understand this confusing state of affairs. He glanced at Filiberto.

Giovan liked to think he was good at knowing whom to trust; he could not have survived and risen to his position otherwise. He put his hand on Filiberto's shoulder and said, "I've decided to tell you the purpose of our journey. You are not to speak of it to anyone, including Paulo. And not to Marta when we return to Rome. Understand?"

Filiberto's heavy eyebrows shot up in surprise. "I swear to God to keep this secret," he said, his voice solemn as he crossed himself.

Giovan drew Filiberto into a dark doorway and looked around, not wanting anyone to overhear. He explained that His Holiness had given him the task of overthrowing the Medici rule in Florence, and described what had been decided in Rome. Filiberto's jaw sagged open as Giovan spoke. When Giovan finished by saying that this would include the killing of Lorenzo and Giuliano, Filiberto grinned broadly. He grasped his sword hilt and looked around, apparently expecting the Medici brothers to appear at any moment.

"You can tell Marta when the deed is done," Giovan said.

Filiberto nodded, his eyes gleaming. Again he swore to keep silent and crossed himself again. They stepped out of the doorway and resumed their way south.

The narrow street widened into a broad piazza with the immense but plain-faced Cathedral of Saint Mary of the Flowers, usually called the Duomo by the Florentines, looming over them on the left. An oddly shaped smaller building, the Baptistry of Saint John, stood before it. Giovan and Filiberto turned to gaze up at the cathedral and at Filippo Brunelleschi's towering dome, completed sixteen years earlier.

"Before we leave Florence," Giovan said, "I'll attend Mass here."

Filiberto shrugged.

In the distance, farther down the street, Giovan spotted the tower of the Palazzo della Signoria, the one Lorenzo had mentioned. The hand on its clock face pointed to *XX*, twenty hours since the last sunset, so four more hours of sunlight remained—plenty of time to arrange the meeting with Jacopo de' Pazzi. Lorenzo had said there was a prison cell high in the tower, above the clock. It was an odd location, but it had the obvious advantage that escape would be difficult, if not impossible.

A few minutes later they arrived at the inn and Paulo was waiting inside.

Giovan sat down at a table and asked the innkeeper for pen, paper and wax. He wrote a brief note, folded and sealed it. "Paulo," he said. "Find out where Jacopo de' Pazzi lives and take this to him."

"Yes, sir."

"Who is this Jacopo?" Filiberto asked after Paulo had left.

"He's Francesco de' Pazzi's uncle. According to Archbishop Salviati, he's the second most powerful man in Florence."

The nearby Signoria clock struck twice—two hours after sunset—and Giovan wanted to go to bed. Gone were the days when he would drink and gamble all night. He squirmed in an uncomfortable chair, watching Filiberto teach Paulo to play the dice game known as *Marlota*. If Paulo pulled out his purse with the few coins Giovan had given him, then Giovan might intervene. But perhaps not. It might good for the boy to learn a lesson…

The inn's front door slammed open and a tall man stood in the doorway, surveying the room. Jacopo de' Pazzi, no doubt. He had no resemblance to Francesco, being thin, gaunt even, and more conservatively dressed.

Giovan stood and approached him.

"Are you Giovan Battista?" the man demanded.

"I am." Giovan bowed. "I assume you are the esteemed Jacopo de' Pazzi."

"What do you want? And what's this about my nephew Francesco? I'm a busy man, a past Gonfaloniere of Justice, for Mary's sake."

"My dear friend Francesco sends his greetings from Rome," Giovan said. "Come, let's talk privately. I have wine in my room."

Jacopo hesitated for a moment and then followed Giovan upstairs. On the floor above, Giovan ushered him into his room, the best in the inn, with the remains of a fire still smoldering in its small fireplace. Giovan gestured for Jacopo to sit in one of the two chairs placed in front of the fire while he stirred up the coals and added some wood from the cast iron rack. As Giovan had arranged, a bottle and two pewter cups sat on the mantle. He filled both cups and handed one to Jacopo.

Sitting in the other chair, Giovan raised his own cup and said, "To Francesco."

Jacopo eyed him with suspicion, then raised his own and took a sip. Two fingers from his left hand were missing. "Well?" he said.

Giovan took two sealed letters from his tunic pocket and handed them to Jacopo, who turned in his chair so he could read them by the firelight. The first was from Count Riario, and Jacopo's face grew less annoyed as he read it. He said nothing when he finished. Looking at the second letter, Jacopo started when he saw the papal seal, and his eyes widened as he read. When he finished, he sat staring into the fire for a moment. Then he took a deep swig from his wine cup and looked over at Giovan, waiting.

"His Holiness commands me," Giovan said, "to come to Florence and ask for your help." This was a small lie as it was Count Riario who had instructed him to come.

Jacopo's eyes shifted, glancing around the room before settling back on Giovan. "Of course, Captain," he said, "I will do whatever His Holiness asks of me. What is this request?"

"His Holiness said to me, 'We wish to change the state of Florence.'"

"So? What does that mean?"

"We wish to end the control of the Medici faction."

"I see." Jacopo's eyes narrowed. "That means Lorenzo must die. His brother, too."

"His Holiness says he wishes this to be done without anyone dying."

"Impossible."

"I agree. Fortunately, His Holiness is a practical man. He also told us, if deaths are necessary he will absolve those involved."

Jacopo nodded. "And who else *is* involved?"

"Besides Count Riario of Imola and your nephew, there is Archbishop Salviati."

"Yes, that makes sense. Because of Pisa." Jacopo leaned back in his chair, thinking.

Giovan took a sip of his wine and waited.

"What do you want of me?" Jacopo asked.

"We need a strong leader to take control, someone who can govern. I've arranged for foreign troops to help, but you must gain the support of the people."

"Yes, I can do that," Jacopo said, nodding. "The people love me. And hate the Medici. They'll follow me, I'm certain." There was a gleam of firelight in his eyes. "But…"

"Yes?"

"After the deed, after the turmoil, His Holiness must name me Duke of Florence."

Giovan was stunned. Florence had been a republic for hundreds of years. "Surely the people would rebel," he said.

"Let me worry about that."

"I have no authority to make such a guarantee."

"Then we have nothing more to discuss."

Giovan stared, astonished. How could he accomplish his task without the help of this man? "You refuse His Holiness?"

"With regret, Captain." Jacopo gulped down the last of his wine and stood. "As anyone in Florence will tell you, I am a gambler. His Holiness wishes me to put my fortune and my life on the gaming table. A good gambler measures the risk against the potential gain, and if the risk is to be great, then so must the gain."

Fioretta pulled the red cloak tight around herself, grateful for its warmth.

"How much is left?" Lucia asked, shivering.

They stood outside the front door of the shop, trying to absorb a little heat from the weak winter sun. As frugal as they were with firewood, they had burned their last sticks the day before. Even in this cold weather, the sewer running down the center of the narrow street stank, and Fioretta knew it would be unbearable come summer.

"Only a few denari," Fioretta replied, her trembling finger pushing around the copper coins in her palm. "What food have we?"

"Just some flour and some beets. I can try to make some sort of pie."

"So tomorrow we go hungry."

"I'm hungry *now*," Lucia said. "What are we going to do? The landlord comes next week, and we didn't pay him last time."

"I know."

"We could sell something. The chest. It must be worth a few soldi."

"That chest belonged to my mother."

"But we need money," Lucia said. "If only you..."

"So it's all my fault," Fioretta cried out. "That's what you want to hear, right?"

Lucia stumbled back, her lips trembling.

Fioretta slumped against the doorframe. "After Giuliano left, I couldn't work. You should understand." They had failed to complete even half of the camicia for the gentleman traveling to Milan, and so he had refused to pay them anything.

And she hadn't seen Giuliano since he found out about the baby.

"So what am I to do? Starve?" Lucia glared at her. "Go back to your father's house? I'd rather die."

"I don't..."

Lucia stepped close, grabbed Fioretta's shoulders and shook her. "Enough," she shouted. "You need to eat. You need food for the baby."

An old woman passing by stared at them, turned away and hurried on.

Fioretta placed her hand on her swelling belly and sobbed. "I know. But I don't..."

Lucia shook her again.

"Stop, please," Fioretta said. "He was everything to me."

Lucia lowered her arms. "You're right," she said. "*He's* the problem." A look of cunning appeared on her face. "In my village, there's a woman who can help."

"What do you mean?" Fioretta stared at her, confused. What was she talking about?

"She knows about these things. She has ways, magic ways, to help. Let me see the money."

Fioretta held out her hand.

"I don't think it's enough," Lucia said, taking the coins.

"But I don't understand—"

"Fioretta! Lucia! My lovelies."

They turned and saw Sandro Botticelli striding down the street toward them, a broad smile on his face that disappeared as he got closer.

Lucia slipped into the shop.

"What's wrong?" Sandro asked, his face showing concern. He opened his arms to Fioretta.

Trying to wipe her face with a corner of her sleeve, Fioretta accepted his embrace. "Oh, Sandro, it's so good to see you."

"You are sad. Oh, of course. Giuliano." Sandro touched her chin. "He told me."

"Did he? What did he say?"

"I think Giuliano misses you very much."

"Then why haven't I seen him? Is it because..." She stopped herself. Did Sandro know about the baby?

"Like all men, Giuliano is a fool." Sandro said, stepping back. "He doesn't understand women, so he's confused." Putting his hand on the hilt of his sword, he cried, "Do you want me to kill him for you? I'll run him through." He pulled the sword part way out of its scabbard, and then slammed it back with a clang. "I'll skewer him like a roast boar. Anything for you, my love."

In spite of herself, Fioretta found herself laughing, and she put her hand over her mouth. "Oh, Sandro," she said. "I'm so glad you are here."

She had met Sandro Botticelli when Giuliano had commissioned Sandro to paint her portrait, and the days she spent in his studio had been among the most enjoyable of her life. Sandro talked while he worked, and had kept her entertained with funny—and sometimes crude—stories of the powerful citizens of Florence, including even Lorenzo and Giuliano. And, despite Fioretta's modest background compared to most of his clients, Sandro had treated her with unceasing respect.

"Come, let's go in," Sandro said. "You can give me some wine."

"Yes, but..."

Fioretta led Sandro into their tiny first floor room. He

glanced around, and Fioretta winced as he noticed the empty fireplace. She gestured towards the single rickety stool that Lucia used when she sewed, but Sandro shook his head. Lucia was not in the room.

"We have no wine," Fioretta said.

"And no firewood. So the business—it does not go well?" Fioretta nodded.

Sandro pulled a velvet purse from his waistband and opened it. "Let me help you. Here, take a florin."

A gold florin—more than they would have made on the lost job. It would buy food, firewood and pay the landlord. And perhaps Lucia would stop being angry with her.

"No, Sandro. Thank you."

"But I have plenty." He jingled the purse. "What's a man to do with his money if he can't help his friends?" Sandro looked thoughtful and then raised his hands in triumph. "But, I forget. That's why I came to see you. I am working on a wonderful new painting about spring. When I lay in my bed at night, I envision Venus standing in a lush and beautiful woods. And, she has *your* lovely face. You can model for me. I'll pay you for your labor. You see?" He handed the coin to her and stunned, she accepted it.

Lucia came down the stairway from Fioretta's room carrying a bag.

"Lucia," Sandro cried, "You can be the cherub."

Lucia ignored him. "I packed some things," she said. "We need to leave now."

"You're leaving?" Sandro asked, looking back and forth between Lucia and Fioretta.

"No," Fioretta said.

"Yes," Lucia said.

"But Sandro will pay me," Fioretta added. "To model for a painting. Oh, wait." She paused. "My dear friend Sandro," she continued, blushing. "I'm afraid I've changed since last you saw me. I'm fatter here." She pointed at her protruding abdomen and at her breasts. Would he guess? Did he already know?

Sandro dismissed this with a wave of his hand. "That's of no concern. I am a great painter. I only need your face, and I must tell you, it's lovelier than ever."

Excited and pleased, Fioretta turned to Lucia, saying, "You see. He'll pay me. It solves the problem. Look at this." She held out the gold coin.

Lucia snatched the florin from her, shouting, "Money is not the problem, Giuliano is. We need to leave." She threw the coin at Sandro who caught it.

There was a knock at the door. "Hello," a man called from outside. "Fioretta Gorini?"

Startled, Fioretta went to the door, pulled it open, and saw a bowlegged man with a neat goatee.

"I'm Fioretta Gorini, sir," she said.

"Good day, my lady. I'm Giovan de Montesecco, Captain of His Holiness's Apostolic Palace Guard." The man bowed. Seeing Fioretta's confusion, he added, "Giuliano de' Medici sent me. I understand you make camicia."

Now even more confused and not knowing what else to do, Fioretta curtsied and said, "Come in, Captain."

The man, this Giovan, followed her inside.

Sandro turned to them. "You!" he said, his face dark. He placed his hand on his sword hilt, this time clearly with menace. "I warned you not to come to Florence, *soldier.*"

Giovan froze where he stood and reached for his own sword. "Yes, I *am* a soldier—in the service of His Holiness, your Pope."

"Phah. We have no fear of your pope here."

Lucia stood beside Fioretta and whispered, "What is this? Some kind of feud?"

Fioretta shrugged. It made no sense to her.

"I want no trouble from you, *artist*," Giovan said, his voice even. "I have papal business here in Florence, and killing you will not serve my master."

"You think you can kill me? You're an old man."

"True. I've been a soldier for forty years. I've killed scores, hundreds. But never an artist, I think. Perhaps that changes today."

Fioretta felt Lucia tugging at her arm. "Let's go," Lucia said. She still held the bag she had packed.

Fioretta ignored her. Sandro was hotheaded, but Giuliano had told her that he was not a skilled swordsman. "Sandro, please," she pleaded, grasping his sword arm. "He'll kill you."

"Listen to the woman," Giovan said.

"Keep out of this," Sandro said, shaking Fioretta loose and pulling out his sword. He wheeled on Giovan and stepped forward. "In Rome, I gave you fair warning, *soldier*."

With a look of tired resignation, Giovan drew his own weapon. They each took a step back, attempting to find space to maneuver, but the room was so small that Sandro bumped into the wall behind him. Giovan kicked Lucia's stool out of the way.

The tip of Giovan's sword traced slow, tiny circles, and Sandro's eyes followed it. Giovan kept own his eyes on Sandro's, waiting.

Fioretta gasped as Sandro leaped forward and stabbed at Giovan, who deftly turned the blade aside. Giovan lifted his sword's hilt and clipped Sandro on the jaw with the pommel as he stumbled past.

Sandro wheeled around and faced Giovan. He shook his head to clear it, moving his jaw back and forth. Fioretta heard the short, rapid bursts of his breathing.

"Stop," Lucia shouted. Dropping the bag, she stepped into the tiny space between the two men and held out her arms, the palms of her hands facing them. "This is our shop. Respect that."

Both men ignored her, moving sideways, trying to get a clear path to the other.

Fioretta watched, uncertain. What was going to happen? Glancing at Sandro's face, she saw that his eyes were big. There was a spot of blood on the corner of his mouth.

"Yes, stop," Fioretta cried, joining Lucia. "I won't have one of you killed here."

Sandro and Giovan continued to stare at each other for a moment, and then Giovan lowered his sword. "I respect your wishes, Signorina Gorini."

Sandro did not move, his body tense and ready.

"Please Sandro. I thought you were my friend," Fioretta said.

"This is not a suitable place," Sandro replied. He pointed his sword tip at Giovan. "Tonight. On the Ponte Vecchio. One hour before sunset."

Giovan sheathed his sword and bowed. "Agreed." He gave a brief bow to Fioretta, saying, "My apologies. Please take this for the trouble I may have caused you." He took a silver coin from his purse and tried to give it to her. When Fioretta refused it, he offered the coin to Lucia, who snatched it. He left.

Fioretta turned to Sandro. "You fool," she said. "He'll kill you."

"That old man?" Sandro replied, still breathing heavily. He glared at her as he returned his sword to its scabbard. "You bring me dishonor, Fioretta."

"How?"

"He thinks I am protected by a woman."

Fioretta threw her hands into the air. "You men and your honor," she said. "I'm sick of the lot of you."

Sandro glared at her for a moment and then turned and stalked out the door.

Picking up the bag, Lucia stood in front of Fioretta.

"Oh, God," Fioretta said. "The job as a model. The money he promised."

Lucia opened her hand to show the silver coin Giovan had given her. "We have enough. If we leave now, we can be there before dark. My family will feed us."

Fioretta stared at her. What was she talking about? Why would they go to Lucia's family?

Lucia grabbed Fioretta's elbow and pulled her toward the

door. "Then we visit Nóna," she said.

Thadeous glanced at Raffaele, worried. Yesterday Father Bernardo, the boy's confessor and theological mentor, had complained that Raffaele would surely fail his examination in Canon Law. He had also made it clear that he blamed Thadeous and so would Archbishop Salviati.

They were seated at the table in Raffaele's cluttered room, with books, pens, an inkpot and loose sheets of paper spread out around them. The boy sat across from Thadeous, his fingers smudged with ink, a page covered with his scrawled handwriting front of him and an ecclesiastical volume beside it. He stared at the wall behind Thadeous, his face blank.

Thadeous usually tried to work on his history of the siege of Constantinople while Raffaele studied, and there was a half-filled page on the table in front of him. He had reached the point where he was describing the attempts by the Turks to tunnel under the Theodosian Wall.

But what if he lost his post as Raffaele's tutor? Could he find a position in another wealthy house? Even if he did, it was unlikely he would have time to work on his history. As his coughing seemed to worsen every day, he feared he might die before he could finish the story of what actually happened in the fire tunnel beneath the wall.

"How far have you progressed?" Thadeous asked.

Raffaele started. Then he looked down his page. "Canon 353," he said. "*Cardinales collegiali actione supremo Ecclesiae Pastori—*"

"Now translate."

"The cardinals especially assist the supreme pastor of the Church... Oh Thadeous, do you have any idea how boring Canon Law is?"

"You need to work," Thadeous replied. "Father Bernardo will be here soon."

"That old bag of horse farts."

Thadeous chuckled. He knew he should object, but the boy

was right.

Raffaele peered into the porcelain wine cup sitting next to his elbow.

"No more until you've finished," Thadeous said.

"Oh, dear God, please. Look, my hand is cramped." Raffaele dropped his quill pen, lifted his hand and stretched out his fingers. He leaned forward and peered at Thadeous's page. "Constantinople?" he asked.

Thadeous had told the boy about his book and about the three months he had spent in Constantinople twenty-five years before.

"Yes," Thadeous replied, picking up Raffaele's pen and handed it back to him. "If you stop after each canon and try to get me to tell you a story, you're not going to finish in time."

"I suppose." Raffaele sighed. He peered at the next sentence in the book and resumed work.

Thadeous tried to refocus on his own task, but his hand cramped, too. It reminded him of the days of work at a different table in a different house. But here, there were no crashing stone cannonballs. He looked down at the last sentence he had written and remembered. It was time to do what he had dreaded for days. Just as he hated the man, he hated to write his name. But he must.

Captain Giovan Battista da' Montesseco. The murdering bastard.

Twenty-Five Years Earlier

Thadeous, Lauro and Captain Giovan stood beside the hole just inside wall's inner face, peering down into the gloom, barely lit by a single candle far below. A rope, tied to a stake beside him, trailed into the depths.

Captain Giovan had been skeptical of Thadeous's suggestion about using ripples in the water buckets to detect Turkish mines. But when he, like Thadeous and Lauro, saw the ripples for himself and understood there was no other explanation, he quickly organized the digging of this mineshaft. After three days of excavation—first the vertical shaft and then the short horizontal tunnel beneath the wall—the miners had heard faint sounds ahead. They had detected an enemy tunnel whose purpose was to bring down the great Theodosian Wall.

Now, up and down this most vulnerable section of the wall, for over a Roman mile, women sat in front of bowls of water, watching for ripples that would indicate enemy miners were digging more tunnels.

There was a whistle from the hole. Two men with muscled shoulders and stripped to the waist heaved on the rope, lifting a flat wooden tub filled with loose dirt and stones. They emptied it, filled it with boards from a nearby stack and lowered it to the man below. The boards had been pulled from neighboring buildings.

Nearby, Giovan's mercenaries crouched or slept up against the wall of a house. Two men had built a small fire, and they held a skinned and skewered rat above its meager flames. Thadeous felt his mouth water despite the unpleasant, gamey odor.

"Ask him," Thadeous whispered to Lauro, who nodded.

"Captain," Lauro said, "I have a request. Do you know of the Greek named George Gemistus, also called Pletho? He's a philosopher." Lauro said. "Thadeous here is his protégé."

Giovan looked impatient.

"Pletho has written a book of laws called the *Nómoi,* and the Emperor ordered that he come to Constantinople and make him a copy. Thadeous was working on it when the siege began."

"You're wasting my time," Giovan said, turning away.

"Wait, Captain. Please," Thadeous said. "Today we finished the copying."

Giovan turned to Thadeous. "We?" He glanced back at Lauro.

"I've been helping," Lauro replied. "Instead of sleeping."

"You're paid to fight, not scribble."

"We haven't been paid for two months," Lauro said.

Giovan grunted. "True enough. Still, if the Turks come over this wall, none of that will matter. You both understand, right?"

"Yes, sir," they both replied.

"But it's done," Lauro added, "and it's time to present the manuscript to the Emperor, the man we fight to defend. Pletho has asked Thadeous and me to accompany him. Can we go? We'll only be gone for a few hours."

Giovan started to reply, but was interrupted as the giant Turkish cannon boomed again. Its stone ball whistled through the air overhead, just above the parapet, and crashed into the house behind them. Rock fragments showered down, and the air was filled with dust. Men shouted as the house's near wall collapsed, covering the sleeping soldiers with broken bricks and mortar.

Giovan rushed to help his men with Lauro and Thadeous close behind.

One soldier died from a crushed skull, someone that Thadeous did not know, but Lauro did. Several others had broken bones, and Thadeous did what he could to help. It reminded him of the time when he worked in the copper mine with his father and the ceiling had collapsed.

Later, when the dead man had been hauled away and the wounded tended to, Thadeous watched as Giovan walked to the water barrel and took a long drink. When he finished, he stood with his eyes closed, the cup dangling from his hand, his body swaying back and forth. Thadeous gazed at him, understanding something of the weight on his shoulders and of his profound exhaustion.

Nearby, the two soldiers who had been cooking the rat scrounged through the rubble, looking for their lost meal.

Giovan opened his eyes and shook his head. His eyes focused on Lauro and Thadeous.

"So you two have been spending your days together scribbling when you were supposed to be sleeping," he said.

Thadeous and Lauro glanced at each other.

"Yes, sir," Lauro said. "For the Emperor."

Giovan shrugged. "I need you here," he said to Lauro. To Thadeous, "You can go. But be back by sunset so you can help with wall repairs. Do not be late." He strode away, not waiting for a response.

Thadeous slumped against Lauro. "For a moment, I thought he knew about us," he whispered.

"Me, too." Lauro glanced around and then turned so he and Thadeous stood close, facing each other. He took Thadeous's hand and slipped it inside the front of his own tunic. "Death and destruction makes me hard," he said. Thadeous felt the truth of this.

"I'll try to come back early while Pletho stays with the Emperor," Thadeous whispered. "We can have the house to ourselves."

Chapter Five

Five Hours Until Dawn

Hunched over the little table, Giovan wrote.

> *Lorenzo told me: Go back to Imola. We will do all*
> *we can to—*

There was a pounding at the ironclad door, and Giovan looked up from his confession, both irritated and curious.

"What?" Alfeo shouted as he left his stool and stood before the door.

"Your wife is here," a muffled voice replied from the other side. "She has your dinner."

As Giovan heard the scrape of the bolt being withdrawn and the door creaked open a crack, he jerked upright, his entire body tense. Alfeo, the fool, had left Paulo's dagger on the table and turned his back. Giovan clenched his jaw with resolve. With the door unlocked, he could kill Alfeo, fight his way out, and escape to the countryside in the dark. Giovan grabbed the dagger and listened, trying to judge the best moment to spring.

"How is Matthias?" Alfeo asked, speaking through the narrow opening.

Matthias? Giovan was confused. His own son, dead nine years, was named Matthias.

"He's well," a woman's voice replied. "It was just a chill."

In the dim light of the single lamp, Giovan saw relief on his guard's face.

The door opened wider, and a woman's hand passed a cloth-wrapped bundle inside, followed by an unlabeled wine bottle.

"How much longer?" the woman asked.

Alfeo shrugged. "Dawn."

The woman's hand took Alfeo's through the gap and held

it for a moment. Then she was gone, the door closed, and the bolt shot home.

Giovan relaxed his grip on the dagger, realizing that he would not be murdering this man.

Alfeo turned, the bundle in one hand, the bottle in the other. He saw Giovan holding the dagger, and his mouth gaped open.

"You have a son named Matthias." Giovan said, standing. "So do I." The dagger was light in his fingers. He flipped it into the air, deftly caught it by the blade, and offered it to Alfeo.

Alfeo, his eyes big, set the bottle on the table and took the dagger. Sliding it back into his boot, he stared at Giovan for a moment, and then said, "Want some wine?"

Five Months Earlier

Giovan glanced up at the looming Palazzo della Signoria clock tower as he and Paulo hurried across the large piazza before it. On the clock face, the single gilded hand caught the setting western sun and indicated twenty-three hours had passed since the last sunset.

"Good, we're not late," Giovan said. "Rome needs a clock like that. You can see it from almost anywhere within the city."

"Are you worried about the duel?" Paulo asked.

"This is no duel."

Paulo had been striding along beside Giovan with his shoulders thrust back, his head high and his hand on the hilt of his sheathed dagger.

"A duel is governed by the *code duello*," Giovan continued. "This is just a street fight. No rules, no doctor, no square marked out with dropped handkerchiefs." Giovan glanced over at Paulo. "And no seconds, I'm afraid."

Paulo's shoulders slumped. "Not a duel. Will you kill him?"

"No. I'm sorry to disappoint you further. It does our mission here no good if I antagonize the Medici. I'll wound him, give him something remember me by. It shouldn't take long, and then it's back to Rome. You can see your mama again." He grinned at Paulo.

Paulo smiled sheepishly. "And Filiberto will be happy get back to his wife," he said.

"Better happy than drunk," Giovan replied. "We'll make an early start tomorrow to teach him a lesson." Back at the inn, Filiberto had drunk so much he was barely been able to stand, so they had left him behind.

They left the piazza, continuing down the dark street leading to the bridge, and the noxious smell of the river wafted over them. The Ponte Vecchio, the *old bridge*, was lined with the shops of butchers and fishmongers who dropped their offal and fish heads directly into the Arno.

The shops were closed and bolted as they stepped out onto the bridge. Ahead, there was an area with no buildings, open to the river on both sides, and a small crowd stood waiting. As Giovan and Paulo approached, Sandro Botticelli stepped forward.

"*Soldier,*" he shouted.

"*Artist,*" Giovan replied, his good humor lost, his heart beginning to race at the anticipation of combat. Giovan shrugged off his cape, and Paulo took it, along with his cap. Both he and Sandro drew their longswords.

"How is your chin?" Giovan asked, approaching Sandro.

Sandro moved his jaw back and forth, and Giovan knew his punch that afternoon had struck home.

"It's nothing," Sandro said. "Just what I expect from an old man."

Giovan clamped his mouth shut and bared his teeth in a tight grin. Enough words. He raised his sword, shifting the position of his hand on the grip so it pressed up tight against cross-guard. The balance was perfect. As there was plenty of room to maneuver on the bridge, he moved into his favorite position, turned with his left shoulder forward and his longsword held high and horizontal next to his head. It pointed directly at Sandro.

Unlike that afternoon, Sandro waited. He faced Giovan, moving to his left, his sword low in front of him. They circled each other with the crowd forming a ring around them. Both men waited for the other to make a move, and this went on for some time. The people began to call out encouragement to Sandro.

Giovan's excitement began to wane. This was getting boring. He stepped forward, prepared to swing—

The shouting stopped and in the silence Giovan heard the sound of hoofbeats. Out of the corner of his eye, he saw men leap out of the way as a powerful dark stallion charged through the onlookers, sparks flying from its iron shoes on the cobblestones. Giovan stepped back as the horse pulled up between him and Sandro.

What now?

"Stop," Giuliano di Medici shouted from atop the horse. With a flourish, he dismounted and handed the reins to Paulo. "My brother Lorenzo and I wish this illegal fight to cease at once."

Giovan did not move. "I honor you and your brother," he said, "but this does not concern you."

"The old man is right," Sandro called out.

Giuliano pulled a letter from his tunic and held it out for Giovan to see. "You told Lorenzo you wished to be of service in continuing the friendship between our family and Count Riario. We respectfully request you take this letter to the Count in Imola, along with our good wishes." He turned to Sandro and said, "Sandro, I know you care little for politics, but this is important."

Sandro lowered his sword, Giovan did the same and the crowd groaned. Giovan shook his head. Would he never rid himself of this silly artist?

"There is no dishonor in this," Giuliano continued.

Giovan glanced at Sandro and wondered, as he had earlier that afternoon, whether there was relief in the artist's eyes.

"This is the third time we have started to fight," Giovan said, "and the third time we have been interrupted." He slid his sword back into its scabbard. "The next time we meet will be the last."

Sandro glared at him. "So be it," he said. He turned away, and his friends gathered around him.

"How did you find out about this?" Giovan asked Giuliano, indicating Sandro and the crowd.

"I came to your inn, looking for you, and your man there told me I could find you here."

"Was he respectful?" Giovan asked, remembering the state Filiberto had been in when they left.

Giuliano laughed and slapped him on the back. "Respectful enough for a man pulling on his trousers in the back room with a whore."

Giovan sighed.

"You have the gratitude of my family," Giuliano continued, again serious. "Despite the diplomatic words between all parties, tensions are growing. Surely you've seen this in your travels."

"Yes."

So it was back to Imola. Dear God, would this never end? It was seven months now since this endeavor had begun, two since they had last seen Rome. I'm a soldier, not a diplomat.

He took the letter from Giuliano.

"Take care with this and have a good journey, Captain. My brother and I hope to see you again soon."

Giovan exchanged bows with him. At least the Medici brothers still seemed to know nothing of his dark purpose.

"So, Sandro," Giuliano shouted as he turned away. "A little wine? Some song? Would you like me to give you a lesson in swordsmanship?" He laughed and threw his arm over Sandro's shoulders, and they started back toward the city. Paulo scurried after to them and handed Giuliano the reins to his horse.

"That is a wonderful horse," Paulo said, returning to Giovan.

Giovan nodded as he watched the crowd follow Giuliano and Sandro. He was surprised that the crowd had lost their thirst for blood so quickly. It must be the popularity of Giuliano. It seemed the Medici brothers were the two most remarkable and popular men in Florence, perhaps all of northern Italy. And Giovan Battista da Montesecco, Captain of the Apostolic Palace Guard of His Holiness the Pope and also loyal to Count Riario, was compelled by his duty to murder them both.

He shrugged.

Fioretta sobbed as she stumbled over the old Roman road leading to Lucia's village. She wrapped one arm under her belly and prayed the baby would not be harmed by hours of walking in the cold December evening. Ahead of her, Lucia trudged forward, carrying the cloth bag and looking back every few minutes.

"How far?" Fioretta called out.

"Just over the next hill," Lucia replied.

"Thank you, Holy Mary." Fioretta made the sign of the cross with her free hand.

Soon they would be at the house of Lucia's family. Fioretta knew little about them, only that they were poor, struggling to feed a half-dozen children and so Lucia, the oldest, had left to make her own way. She sent money home when she had it.

Fioretta slowed as she struggled up this last hill, no longer crying, anxious to crest it and see the village where they could rest, eat a little and spend the night.

Lucia dropped back, grabbed Fioretta's hand and pulled her along.

By the time they finally reached the top, the sun had set, and they paused to catch their breath. It was almost impossible to see the scattered homes below them—they were light splotches against the slightly darker background of the surrounding fields. Fioretta realized that, unlike the city people of Florence, the people of the countryside rarely lit lamps when the sun went down.

"Where is your house?" Fioretta asked.

"We're not going there," Lucia replied. She took Fioretta's hand again and started down the hill. "First we need to find the woman who can help us—help you." Lucia paused, glancing at Fioretta's abdomen.

Fioretta froze, a dark suspicion washing over her. She yanked her hand away from Lucia and wrapped both arms across her belly. She had heard rumors. When they first saw the midwife, she had hinted something was possible, and Lucia had glanced at Fioretta as though she thought Fioretta might choose a different path.

"You want to kill my baby," Fioretta shrieked, pulling away, trying to turn back toward Florence.

"No, Fioretta, no," Lucia said. There seemed to be genuine surprise in her voice. She hurried to Fioretta's side, wrapping her arms around her. "That's not it, I swear. I want this baby for you." Her voice choked. "Truly."

Fioretta wanted to believe her.

"We call her Nóna," Lucia said, starting forward again, tugging at Fioretta. "But we need to hurry. We may already be too late."

Fioretta stopped, digging her heals in against Lucia's persistent pull. "Not a step farther until you explain." Even in the gathering darkness, she saw Lucia's exasperation.

"Tonight is the coming of the *Watcher of the South*," Lucia replied. "It's a star, marking the winter solstice."

"But, how do you know this?" Fioretta asked.

"Come, and I'll tell you," Lucia said, tightening her grip on Fioretta's hand and starting down the hill.

Reluctantly, Fioretta followed.

"Nóna lives outside the village. She knows of these things, and before I came to Florence, she taught me."

"You never mentioned this."

"Would your father have taken me in if I had?"

"Oh, Lucia. I thought we were friends. Surely you could

have told me."

Lucia glanced back over her shoulder. "It's as your friend that I bring you to Nóna tonight."

A few minutes later they moved through the silent, dark village, and then left it behind. Finally, when Fioretta thought she could not take another step, Lucia stopped.

The squeal of pigs came to them from a low ramshackle hut set back from the road, and Lucia, who had been so determined to get to this place, now held back. A door squeaked open, and the figure of a woman emerged with her arms stretched out in front of her. She carried a dead piglet and sang,

> *Poor little piggy, so sweet and wise,*
> *You sleep now, beneath the sky,*
> *Poor little piggy, with pretty eyes.*

The woman saw them and cried out, "Want to buy this piggy?" She came closer. "Fresh. Died just now, I swear."

"We have money, but not for that," Lucia called. To Fioretta she whispered, "That's her."

Nóna shrugged and turned away. Singing again, this time too low for Fioretta to hear the words, she jammed the piglet's rear leg onto a spike in the wall beside the door. In her other hand she carried large clay bowl that she placed beneath the piglet's head. Then, pulling a wicked-looking knife from her belt, she sliced through its neck, and the head dropped with a clunk into the bowl, along with a gush of blood.

The woman turned back to them and came closer, the bloody knife in her hand. She cocked her head. "Lucia?"

Lucia stepped forward and then stopped. The two women stared at each other, just out of arms reach. Nóna wiped the knife on a rag wrapped around her waist. Then she turned away and moved back to the door, where she took a quick peek into the bowl and grunted.

"I said we have money," Lucia shouted.

"I heard you," Nóna replied, entering the house.

"This lady needs your help," Lucia called out as she hurried after Nóna and disappeared through the door.

Fioretta stayed rooted in place. What was inside that dark door? She heard the grunt of a pig and the squeal of piglets. Come now, was she afraid of pigs? Trembling, her feet dragging in the dirt from exhaustion, she trudged to the house and entered, ducking under the door's low lintel.

Florence teemed with horses and donkeys and even a few cows, sheep and pigs, so Fioretta knew the sour, rotten egg odor of manure. But the stench inside the house was much worse, and if there had been any food in her stomach, surely it would have come up.

As Fioretta edged forward in the dark room, her face brushed against something hanging from the ceiling. She jerked back, and then realized it was a bundle of dried branches, smelling of willow. She pulled it close to her face, breathing in the clean fragrance.

"Try this," Lucia said, holding what seemed to be a small rock next to the single candle stub that provided the only light.

Fioretta leaned forward and sniffed—it was like church, with the altar boy swinging the censer, the aromatic smoke drifting out over the congregants.

"It's frankincense," Lucia added. "Like in the Bible."

"Put that back," Nóna shouted from the other side of a half-wall that divided the front from the back of the house.

Lucia returned the tiny pellet to a bowl next to the candle.

Fioretta peered over the half-wall and was not surprised to see pigs—a skinny sow laying in dirty straw, suckling four skinnier piglets.

Nóna poured some water from a wooden bucket into a hole dug in the dirt floor, and the sow struggled to its feet, staggered over to it and drank, the piglets left squealing behind her. "That'll do you for now," she muttered, stepping into the front room carrying the bucket. She lifted a rag, dipped it into the water and scrubbed her face and hands.

"You say you have money?" she said, turning to face them.

Fioretta had assumed Nóna was an old woman, a hag, but

her face in the flickering candlelight revealed she was only a few years older than Fioretta. Her eyes were gray and startling, and one eyelid drooped. She wore a patched peasant dress with a spray of pig's blood down its front.

Lucia pulled out the silver soldi the soldier had given them in the shop and showed Nóna, whose eyebrows twitched up. Nóna pointed at Fioretta's belly and asked, "You want to get rid of it?"

"No," Fioretta cried. She turned to Lucia. "You told me—"

"Stop," Lucia said, putting her hand on Fioretta's arm. To Nóna, she said, "No. You see, there is a man—"

"There always is," Nóna said, cackling.

"—who has lost his love for this lady," Lucia continued.

"Ah, that's different. Let me see the money again."

When Lucia held out her hand, Nóna leaned over and snatched the coin. "You come at a good time," she said. "You remember some of what I taught you."

Lucia said nothing.

"Come," Nóna said, pushing past them through the door and they followed her back outside.

The sky was clear, with a thin quarter moon, and Fioretta shivered. While it was good to be away from the smell, at least it had been warm inside.

"Show me the *Watcher*," Nóna said to Lucia.

Lucia gazed upward and stretched out her arm. She found the North Star, and then rotated to her right, stopping and pointing at a constellation above the trees on the horizon. "*The Southern Fish*," she announced. "And there, the brightest star. The *Watcher of the South*."

Nóna turned to Fioretta. "What's the man's name?"

"Giuliano."

"Giuliano," Nóna repeated. "Did you bring something of his?"

Lucia opened the bag she had brought with them, and took out a handkerchief. Fioretta remembered Giuliano had left a handkerchief in her bedroom.

"Good." Nóna took it. She ordered Lucia to drag dried brush from behind the house and pile it up in front. To Fioretta, she said, "You sit and wait," and then she disappeared inside.

Not knowing what else to do, Fioretta went back to the front of the house and sat down in the dirt with her back to the wall. Nearby, she heard the drip, drip, drip of the dead piglet's blood.

A few minutes later, Lucia stood beside a brush pile half her height. As Nóna had not reemerged, she came and sat down next Fioretta.

"How can she live like this?" Fioretta whispered.

"What do you mean?"

"With pigs in the house."

Lucia turned to her. "Because she must," she said. "We're in the country. Without our animals, we starve. My family has pigs and a milk cow."

"Oh."

For the first time Fioretta realized that, having never before left Florence, she knew nothing of life outside its walls.

They waited.

"Is she going to hurt me?" Fioretta asked.

"The demons might."

"Demons?"

"Stay close to the fire," Lucia said, "and the Goddess Diana will protect us."

"Goddess? Who is this woman?"

"She is *Strega*. She follows the Old Religion."

"Not a Christian?"

"Has your Jesus replied to your prayers?" Lucia replied.

Fioretta began to shiver.

Finally, Nóna came out with a bundle of branches under her arm and wearing a ragged black robe stitched with mis-shapen white stars.

"Lucia, bring out the candle and light the fire," Nóna said.

Soon the brush was blazing, with sparks climbing into the

solstice sky. Nóna tossed her branches onto the fire, and the sweet smell of willow, aloe and rosemary wafted over to Fioretta. When Nóna beckoned, Fioretta climbed to her feet and approached the fire. While she was glad of its warmth, she shivered with trepidation.

Nóna held something in her hands that Fioretta could not make out. Lifting it above her head, Nóna began to sing, twirling around, crying out words Fioretta didn't understand. In the fire, a branch cracked and more sparks spewed into the air. Beyond the flames, through the swirling smoke, shadows moved in the darkness.

Next to Fioretta, Lucia began to shake. Her eyes rolled back and saliva seeped from one corner of her mouth. Fioretta edged as close to the fire as she could stand, turning back and forth, trying to see the demons waiting to pounce on her and chew her bones.

Lucia dropped to the ground, still shaking.

Nóna ceased her singing and stepped in front of Fioretta. "Take these," she said, putting something sharp and cold into Fioretta's hand.

Fioretta looked down and in the firelight saw seven iron pins, the same kind as those she used for sewing.

Nóna lifted her other hand for Fioretta to see, and in it was a red clay doll, man-shaped, lying in Giuliano's handkerchief. She pressed it into Fioretta's other hand. "Take each pin, spit on it, and push it into Giuliano," she said.

"No. I want no harm for him," Fioretta cried.

Lucia groaned and staggered to her feet. Her eyes blurry, she looked into Fioretta's face. "This will not harm him," she said. "Push the pins into his heart. Don't you want him to love you?"

"Yes," Fioretta said, sobbing, but still she hesitated. This was not Christian. Would she go to Hell because of this. Would Giuliano? Was Giuliano's love worth the risk to her immortal soul? The words of Giuliano's love poem rose from the darkness of her memory.

I earn her fame, and every thought of mine,
only of her, and shared with no one else.

She opened the hand with the pins and, one by one, she spat on each and thrust it into the clay doll until it reminded her of the painting of Saint Sebastian she had seen in church.

Nóna wrapped Giuliano's handkerchief around the doll and then took a small glass vial from her pocket. "Lucia, pour this," she said.

Lucia took the vial from Nóna and poured it over the doll as Nóna again chanted words that Fioretta did not understand.

"Holy water stolen from the church," Lucia whispered.

The fire, with only brush to burn, began to die down. Fioretta held the doll in both hands, her arms stretched out before her.

Nóna wrapped her hands around Fioretta's. "Put this beneath your bed," she said, "and in seven days, Giuliano will return to you."

Hope swelled in Fioretta's heart. This Nóna woman seemed so confident. And wise in the ways of spells and spirits.

"I'm tired now," Nóna said. Without another word she returned to her house, singing,

Poor little piggy, with pretty eyes.
Poor little piggy, knows love and lies.

Lucia came to Fioretta's side and put her arm around Fioretta's waist. She said, "I saw a vision—a dagger with letters carved into its walnut handle. There was blood on the blade."

"I don't know what that means." Fioretta was exhausted, beyond caring.

Lucia shrugged her shoulders. "We'll go to my family's house now," she said. "You can sleep. And there will be warm milk in the morning."

"Nephew."

Thadeous had dozed off and his head jerked up. He was in Raffaele's untidy bedroom, and he was astonished to see Archbishop Salviati standing in the doorway. Raffaele leaped to his feet while Thadeous struggled to stand.

"Uncle?" Raffaele said. "We had no idea you were coming." He ran his fingers through his long hair, tucked in his shirt and hurried to greet the Archbishop of Pisa and master of this palazzo.

Thadeous bowed as deeply as he could manage as Archbishop Salviati swept into the room, his dust-covered traveling cloak swirling around him, followed by the rotund figure of Raffaele's confessor and theological mentor, Father Bernardo.

Why was the Archbishop here? Had he heard that his nephew was failing in his studies? Am I about to be dismissed?

Making a show of organizing the pages scattered around the table, Thadeous slid his own work on Constantinople out of sight. The Archbishop mustn't know that Thadeous had another interest besides tutoring Raffaele.

Salviati seemed ill at ease, his face working, changing between a scowl and a forced smile. He started to hold out his right hand so Raffaele could kiss the episcopal ring, but instead he offered his hand to Thadeous, who hobbled forward and kissed the ring as expected.

"Sit, my son," Salviati said to Raffaele, himself settling into Thadeous's chair. Raffaele gave Thadeous a quick look of apology as he resumed his seat. There were other chairs in the room, but Thadeous and Father Bernardo remained standing.

Salviati glanced around the cluttered bedroom, at the clothing on the floor and the disheveled bed, but his eyes seemed unfocused. They all waited.

Finally, Father Bernardo coughed and said, "With your permission, Your Eminence?"

Salviati gave a curt nod.

Bernardo turned to Raffaele and said, "Prepare yourself. We bring solemn news."

This didn't sound like he was about dismiss Thadeous. It must be news about the boy's family. He stepped close to Raffaele and put his hand on his shoulder.

"What?" Raffaele asked, alarmed.

"Forgive me. It's not bad news." Bernardo paused. Usually garrulous, he seemed at a loss for words.

"Spit it out, you fool," Salviati said.

"Young master," Bernardo said. "His Holiness, your dear uncle, in his great wisdom, has made a momentous decision."

"Just tell him."

"In short," Bernardo hurried on, "you are to be created Cardinal of the Church."

Nobody said a word. In the silence, Thadeous heard mice scurrying in the walls. He stared at Bernardo, certain he had misunderstood.

"But, but…" Raffaele sputtered.

"It's true," Archbishop Salviati said.

Thadeous shook his head. It made no sense. "He's only sixteen years old," he said. "Surely canon law…"

"It is unprecedented," Bernardo replied, now in his element. "Never in the history of the Mother Church has someone this young been made Cardinal. The previous youngest—"

"But I'm not even a priest," Raffaele cried.

"A difficulty, to be sure," Bernardo said. "However, as His Holiness is determined, we will find a way."

Raffaele, his face drained of color, turned to Thadeous.

"Your Eminence," Thadeous said, "Raffaele is undoubtedly reluctant to give up the pleasures of youth. Surely, His Holiness understands this."

Raffaele nodded vigorously as he turned back to his uncle.

"Yes, His Holiness does indeed understand this," Salviati replied. "My boy, do not be too dismayed. You will bear important responsibilities, but there are also privileges."

There seemed to be a note of envy in the Archbishop's voice, and Thadeous finally understood his foul mood. This boy—his nephew—would soon be his superior, at least in the eyes of the Church. As powerful as the role of archbishop was, a cardinal was second only to the Pope.

"Privileges?" Raffaele didn't appear to be reassured.

"You will be Deacon of San Giorgio," Salviati added.

"Where is that?" Raffaele asked. "Some Godforsaken village in the mountains?"

"No, no. It's charming diocese in Rome," Salviati continued. "You'll receive a good income from it."

Thadeous watched Raffaele as he leaned back in his chair with his eyes closed, a gesture Thadeous recognized. The boy was trying to think.

Father Bernardo seemed to want to say something, but a scowl from the Archbishop kept him silent.

A moment later, Raffaele said, "So I'll live in Rome? With my own palazzo, my own servants? And with money to spend as I choose?"

Salviati sighed and said, "Yes."

A smile spread across Raffaele pudgy face. Thadeous surmised that he knew that it was not uncommon for church leaders, especially wealthy ones, to have mistresses. He was a sixteen year old boy, after all.

There was further discussion of the details, including the date of his elevation, which wouldn't occur until some time the next year. Thadeous was relieved because, for the time being, they would remain in Pisa, and Raffaele would continue his studies.

"It's getting late," Archbishop Salviati said. "I'll sleep and start back to Rome before dawn." He gazed at Bernardo, Thadeous and Raffaele in turn. "No one is to know of this news for now. Or of my visit. Understood?"

They all nodded.

"A word with you, Professore Thadeous," he added, gesturing to the door leading to the hallway. They left Raffaele and Bernardo talking, with the older man trying to focus the younger on the spiritual implications of what would happen to his life.

Was the Archbishop going to dismiss Thadeous and wanted to do it out of the boy's sight? "Your Eminence," Thadeous said. "If there has been any concern about young Raffaele's studies..."

"What? No. Listen, I remember that you once lived in Florence," Salviati said, closing the door behind them. "And you tutored Lorenzo and Giuliano when they were young."

"I had that honor until the time when Lorenzo was married, eight years ago."

"And you remain friendly with them?"

"I was honored to receive a letter from Lorenzo recently," Thadeous said. "He had a question concerning the translation of an ode by Pindar, a Greek poet of—"

The Archbishop raised his hand. "You may be of use. His Holiness has commanded a—well, let's call it an endeavor—that concerns the state of Florence. When the time comes, we'll talk more."

Twenty-Five Years Earlier

Thadeous grasped the manuscript pages to his chest as they walked toward the Blachernae Palace. He had scrubbed himself from foot to head and wore the one shirt that was not stained from his nightly work on the wall. Neither he nor Pletho had shaved or cut their hair in months, but as there wasn't time to do anything about it, Thadeous hoped Emperor Constantine XI, with his city under siege, would not care.

Nonetheless, when they arrived at the palace gate, a courtier in flamboyant court dress tut-tutted as he inspected them, tugging at their sleeves and brushing nonexistent dust from their shoulders. A haggard guard searched them for weapons, even thumbing through the pages of the thick manuscript.

As they followed the courtier through endless dirty hallways, Thadeous gazed about in wonder. The palace was colossal, but almost empty.

"At one time, it was magnificent," Pletho said, "teeming

with a thousand servants and the greatest royal court in the world."

"Centuries ago," Thadeous said.

"Yes, sadly. We Greeks live in a world of fantasy, thinking we are still a great empire. Once Byzantium stretched around the Mediterranean Sea from Palestine to Iberia." Pletho's voice rose. "As the old western Roman Empire fell, the Byzantine Empire grew."

Despite his nervousness, Thadeous grinned. Pletho had slipped into his role as master teacher.

As they walked, he described the invasions from both the west and the east, and how the court became so bureaucratic and weak that the emperors were unable to defend their realm. Now there was only this city, some outposts on the Black Sea, and the Peloponnese. He sighed. "A vast garden of knowledge and power is now nothing more than a dried husk."

"But Mystras is safe?" Thadeous asked. Their home was in the far southern part of the Peloponnese peninsula.

Pletho smiled. "Yes, for now. May we see it again some-day soon."

Thadeous's nervousness returned when the courtier led them through a tall, arched entrance into the immense Throne Room, and toward a crowd gathered at the far end. There were no windows. A few candles provided such scant light that it didn't reach the ceiling far above their heads. Thadeous squint-ed through the gloom, but he saw little of the former glory of Byzantium in this chamber. Only the gilded throne, glinting in the candle light, hinted at a more magnificent time.

Thadeous's eyes were drawn to the man sitting on the throne. He had a long dark beard streaked with gray as it lay against his bejeweled breastplate, and he was listening to reports from the men around him, most of whom also wore armor. This was the Emperor Constantine, the eleventh to bear the name, going back to the founder of Constantinople over a thousand years before. Now fifty-three years old, Constantine had been a warrior for most of his life, fighting almost continuously to save his empire. His brow was furrowed. When he spoke to ask questions or give commands, his voice was hoarse.

The courtier left them, and Pletho and Thadeous remained at the back of the crowd, waiting to be noticed. In the cavernous chamber buried in the heart of the palace, it was difficult to judge the passing of time.

Thadeous remembered the touch of Lauro's hand back at the wall. To his embarrassment, felt himself become aroused. He must return to Lauro. If he could somehow manage to leave Pletho mired in conversation with the Emperor, then he and Lauro would have some time together, alone. He shifted the heavy manuscript from one arm to the other.

Finally, Constantine looked at Pletho and his face brightened. He spoke to a courtier who stood by the throne, and the courtier gestured that Pletho was to approach. Thadeous followed, his head down, his hands gripping the manuscript.

The Emperor smiled and said, "George Gemistus, you are a reminder of happier times."

Thadeous watched his master through the corner of his eye and matched his deep bow, worried the pages might slip from his hands and spill out across the cracked marble floor.

"My lord, it pleases me to hear you say that," Pletho replied.

"And who is this?" Constantine asked, indicating Thadeous.

"My protégé, Thadeous Phylacus. Alas, because of my poor eyes, most of the copying fell to him."

Not knowing what else to do, Thadeous bowed again. "And Lauro," he whispered to Pletho, who ignored him.

"Is this a good and true copy?" the Emperor asked.

"Yes, my lord." Pletho took the manuscript from Thadeous. He bowed again, saying, "I am honored to present to you my life's work, my *Nómoi,* the *Book of Laws.*"

Constantine gestured, and a courtier took the manuscript. "Master Pletho, George Gemistus, I accept this great work and give you my thanks."

Again Pletho bowed. Thadeous did the same, watching as the fruit of his and Lauro's labors disappeared into the gloom. With all the turmoil in the city, what would happen to it?

There was silence and Thadeous wondered if they were dismissed.

"It occurs to me," Constantine said finally, "that you are no longer needed in Constantinople. You are a treasure of the Empire, so perhaps it would be best if you left the city—with all its current inconveniences."

Leave the city? While Thadeous longed for this, it had seemed impossible that they might somehow escape. They were surrounded by a hundred thousand Turks on the land side and by fifty enemy ships in the harbor.

The Emperor continued, "I'm sending a diplomatic delegation to the infidel Mehmet to discuss a truce. Pletho, my friend, I want you to accompany them. Mehmet might behead you all, of course. But you will have a chance. Once outside the walls, you can attempt to make your way south, to safety."

Without waiting for a response, he turned to a clerk who sat at a small ornate table behind him, and said, "Write such an order for these two. And give him five stavratons." Then he said to Pletho, "Farewell, my friend." He stood and retired through a small doorway behind the throne, his courtiers scurrying after him.

Pletho glanced at Thadeous, a look of wonder on his face. Then he hurried over to the clerk's table.

They could return to Mystras. They could resume their old life of study and discussion and writing. There would be food in Mystras—and no giant cannon firing stone balls to crash down around them. There would be no backbreaking toil every night to repair the wall.

And there would be no Lauro.

"Look," Pletho said, turning away from the clerk. He had a sheet of parchment in one hand and held out the other, showing Thadeous five silver coins, stavratons. "It's a fortune. Just one of these should be enough to bribe the Turkish soldiers outside the gate. With luck, we can use the rest for passage on a boat south. We can be home in two weeks." He expression became serious. "But, the delegation leaves from the Golden Gate soon. It's miles to the south from here. We must hasten."

As they hurried back down the empty corridors and onto the street that would lead them to Pletho's house, Thadeous's thoughts were in a whirl. Could Lauro go with them? No, of course not. The Emperor's order would be specific to the two of them. And, Thadeous knew, Lauro would refuse. He was a professional soldier. His honor would keep him here.

At the house, they threw some clothing and a few other possessions into a bag, gathered up the pages of the original manuscript and stuffed them in too, on top of the clothing. Thadeous hefted the heavy bag onto his shoulder.

Back on the street, Thadeous said, "I must go to the wall, to see Lauro. I must, uh, we must thank him, and tell him what the emperor said."

"Impossible," Pletho said. "We may be too late already. Come or be damned!" The old man started down the street.

Pletho was his Master and had been so for ten years. He had no choice, he must follow. And he did.

The Golden Gate marked the southern end of the Theodosian Wall, and it was surrounded by the remains of an old fortress. Its three tall arched portals had been filled with brickwork during the siege, but the central one contained a massive oak door secured by a sliding iron bar. Archers manned the ramparts, and bedraggled Greek soldiers stood ready nearby.

Thadeous saw three elaborately dressed men—the Emperor's ambassadors. So they were not too late. Pletho had a hurried discussion with the one wearing the most ornate court robe, and showed him the parchment. The man nodded.

"We're just in time," Pletho said, hobbling back to Thadeous. "They're about to open the gate." The old man was wheezing, but his face was a mask of determination.

In the battlement above them, a trumpet sounded.

"It lets the Turks know we are coming out, that it's not a surprise attack," Pletho continued. "The chief diplomat is hopeful they won't harm us."

Thadeous held his breath as two soldiers slid back the iron bar, pushed the door open a crack and peered outside. Then they pushed it fully open, its hinges screeching, and the party moved through it, with Pletho and Thadeous in the rear.

For the first time in three months, Thadeous was outside the walls of Constantinople.

Ahead, a group of Turkish soldiers watched them, their lances and swords held ready. The diplomats strode forward, with Pletho following.

Thadeous started to follow, then he stopped. "I'm not going," he announced. He heard the creak of the gate closing behind him.

Pletho whirled around. "What? Are you mad?" he cried.

"I'm sorry, Master." Thadeous turned back to the gate. The door was almost closed, and he shouted, "Wait! I'm coming back in." But it continued to move. Desperate, he thrust the bag with their possessions into the gap, preventing the door from closing completely. He heard soldiers cursing inside. Then, with another loud screech, and the door opened. Thadeous grabbed the bag and squeezed through—back into the dying city of Constantinople.

With a thud, the door slammed shut, and Thadeous stood inside it, breathing hard. He had done it now. He was committed to Lauro and to fighting beside him, to trying to save this city and their lives. He had to get back to Lauro, back to their place on the wall. The street was getting dark, and he realized they would have not time together. In fact, he would be lucky to return before the sun set. What would Captain Giovan do if he was late?

Thadeous grabbed the bag, and as he slung it over his shoulder, only then did he realize that it contained Pletho's original manuscript. Both the original and the copy of this treasure were still inside the walls of Constantinople, surrounded by ferocious Turks lusting to sack the city.

Chapter Six

Five Hours Until Dawn

The wine was the cheapest possible, smelling of vinegar and sulfur, but Giovan took a deep swig and then passed the bottle back to Alfeo.

"Hungry?" Alfeo asked, holding out a crust of bread.

Giovan shook his head. What was the point? Better that Alfeo have it. Giovan looked down at what he had written and then resumed.

> *I went to Imola and I stayed for a few days as I had*
> *been told. On the way back, in Cafaggiolo, I again*
> *met Lorenzo the Magnificent and Giuliano...*

It was there that his mission began to unravel like a badly told lie. His head buzzing slightly, Giovan closed his eyes and remembered the horses at Cafaggiolo.

Four Months Earlier

Giovan gazed at the familiar countryside as he rode. To his left, olive trees stretched into the distance with geometric precision, starkly outlined against the midmorning winter sky. On his right, a dozen workers hunched over rows of dormant grape vines, pruning and retying them to their trellises.

They had passed this way before in their journeys. Another day's ride would see them in Florence, where Giovan had two final tasks to accomplish, and then—at long last—it was home to Rome after three exhausting months of travel.

"Paulo! Stop playing with that silly little knife. You'll nick your mule's neck."

At Filiberto's shout, Paulo shrugged and put away his dagger. He had been tossing it into the air and catching it as they rode.

Giovan, riding behind his two companions, glared at Filiberto's back, tired of his irascibility. Filiberto wanted to go home, of course, as did they all.

Two days before in Imola, Count Riario had read Lorenzo's letter and then tossed it down on the table. "It changes nothing," he said to Giovan. "Just polite words. We will proceed with our plans." He instructed Giovan to return to Rome via Florence, where he was to again attempt to recruit Jacopo de' Pazzi, Lorenzo's bitter enemy. He also gave Giovan another letter for Lorenzo, which Giovan knew contained nothing but empty compliments.

They crested another hill and there, amidst the grape fields and olive groves, stood the walled estate of Cafaggiolo, the legendary favorite country home of the Medici family. The white Medici flag with its golden family crest flew from a flagpole over the gate, meaning that one or both of the Medici brothers was in residence.

Filiberto, who had lapsed into sullen silence, perked up at the sight of the flag. "Do you think the Medici might give us lunch?" he asked. "Their wine is excellent."

Stopping at Cafaggiolo might be a good idea. If Lorenzo was there, Giovan could deliver the Count's letter. And since the plan for the assassinations had not been determined, some reconnaissance would be useful. Giovan noted the height of the whitewashed wall as they approached, and the tough-looking guards standing before the main gate. He wondered if there were archers—

The sound of dogs barking on the road ahead interrupted his thoughts, and he turned to see a party of four men on horseback trotting toward them, a dozen dogs yelping at their feet. Giuliano de' Medici was in the lead on a magnificent black stallion—Giovan recognized it as the same one that he had ridden at the Ponte Vecchio—followed by three men dressed in the same uniform as the guards by the gate. They all carried hunting lances. One of the men led a mule with the carcass of a wild boar slung on its back. As they got closer, Giovan heard Giuliano's voice singing.

> *'Let the boar go.' Come here, come here.*
> *She said, 'Hey no, hey no, because I fear.'*
> *But when I embraced her, she grabbed my spear.*
> *And led me to the woods right near.*

Giuliano laughed as he reined his horse before the gate. The mounted guards rushed forward to place themselves between him and Giovan's small party, but Giuliano waved them away. He maneuvered his horse to stand beside Giovan's mule.

"Giovan Battista da Montesecco," Giuliano said. "It's good to see you, my friend. Do you have a reply from our good friend, the Count?"

"I do, sir."

"Then let's go in. Lorenzo is here, so you can go to him now."

Giovan nodded. They all turned and passed through the gate and onto the villa grounds. A small flock of sheep grazed nearby on the wide grass lawn. Giovan's professional soldier's eye surveyed the main villa building with its crenellated battlements and towers. It was already clear to him that this fortress could not be easily taken by a frontal assault.

"Very impressive," he said to Giuliano.

"It's a good place to escape the intrigues of the city," Giuliano replied.

As they approached the main house, a chamberlain in bright red livery rushed out. "My lord," he cried. "It's happening. My lord Lorenzo is in the stable."

"Aha!" Giuliano shouted. He kicked his horse in its ribs and took off toward a nearby building built of whitewashed stone in the same military style as the house and outer wall. "Come on," he shouted over his shoulder to Giovan. They all hurried after him, including the mounted guards.

It was cool inside the stable building. Clean straw covered the flagstone floor of the aisle between two dozen closed stalls, and it stunk less of manure than any stable Giovan had ever been in. Ahead, he saw stable grooms clustered outside a stall partway down one side, all of them staring inside. Giuliano hurried down the aisle with Giovan following. The grooms jumped out of their way, and Giovan stood beside Giuliano, peering into the stall.

Lorenzo the Magnificent, his feet braced in the straw, his white cotton shirt covered with blood and mucus, straining so hard that his face flushed red and veins stood out at his temples, grasped the rear legs of a foal protruding from a large gray-dappled mare.

"That's trouble," Giuliano said. "It's turned around."

Giovan nodded. He'd seen this before and usually the foal died—and sometimes the mare, too.

An old stableman held the mare's tail and looked askance at his master's efforts. "Please, Excellency. Let one of the boys do that."

"No, Salvadore. I've got it now," Lorenzo replied through gritted teeth.

The mare staggered, pawed at the straw with her front hooves, and then her hips shuddered and her abdomen contracted. In a flood of bloody fluid, the foal suddenly erupted from its mother, landing on top of Lorenzo, and they tumbled back together into the straw. Lorenzo lay still, the foal unmoving on his chest. Then the mare turned and licked her baby's head, and it suddenly shuddered and took a breath. It slid off Lorenzo, staggering as it managed to stand.

Laughing, Lorenzo climbed to his feet, and as he wiped his face with his sleeve, he saw his brother. "Giuliano, look. It's a colt," he cried, pointing between the foal's legs. Giuliano laughed too, and Giovan grinned, finding himself caught up in the unrestrained joy of these two brothers.

"My Samuele is the sire," Giuliano said to Giovan, gesturing toward courtyard where they had left his stallion. "The mare is Lorenzo's. This colt will grow to be the finest horse in all of Italy."

The colt wobbled back and forth with its mother licking his back, and they all watched. Lorenzo put his bloody arm across the shoulders of the old groom, and together they bent down and peered beneath the colt's belly.

"Look Salvadore, already he's bigger than you are," Lorenzo said, pointing.

The old groom chuckled and then replied with a straight face, "And how would you know about the size of my cock, Excellency?"

"Your wife told me, of course."

Everyone laughed, Salvadore, the grooms, Giuliano, Lorenzo, and even Giovan as he struggled to understand this easy friendship that seemed to exist between the two most powerful men in Florence and the servants who worked in their stable.

"Many thanks, Salvadore," Lorenzo said. He went to each of the grooms and also thanked them for their help, mentioning their names. Then he noticed Giovan.

"Captain Giovan," he cried as he stepped out of the stall. "Forgive me for not embracing you," he added, indicating his smelly and soggy shirt. He quickly stripped it off and splashed water over his bare torso from a bucket held by one of the grooms. His body was pallid and weak looking, not at all like that of his athletic brother. "You bring news from our good friend, the Count?" he asked as he toweled himself with a rag.

"Yes, Magnifico, and a letter," Giovan replied, bowing.

"Excellent. Come, let's go to the house, and we can talk."

After a pleasant meal of sweet and sour wild boar along with asparagus and bread, Giovan, Lorenzo and Giuliano agreed to return to Florence together. They passed through the main gate in the outer wall with Giuliano once again on Samuele, still smiling with pride.

Giovan rode next to Lorenzo. "I was telling your brother that it's my professional opinion that Cafaggiolo could stand a siege of several months," Giovan said.

"Even if it were attacked with cannon?" Lorenzo asked.

"Well, it's unlikely that a cannon big enough to take down that wall could be brought here. In Constantinople, it took a thousand men to move the biggest cannon to the Theodosian Wall."

"A thousand men? That strains credibility."

"I saw it, Magnifico."

"You were at the fall of Constantinople?" Giuliano asked, clearly impressed. "How did you escape?"

Giovan looked over at Giuliano and then at Lorenzo, wondering if he should tell the story, if he should tell them about the young Greek scholar and his Milanese friend, about the fire tunnel and the final escape. It was, after all, a long ride to Florence with plenty of time to talk. But this was not something he talked about easily. He had told Rachele about it on his return. His friend and confessor back in Rome, Father Nicolo, knew about Constantinople, but not Filiberto, not Paulo, not anyone else.

I can't confide in these men. They're not my friends, despite their cordial words. They're the enemies of His Holiness and of my patron, the Count. And as I've sworn to assassinate them when the time finally comes, my duty requires that I shield myself from their friendship.

"I was fortunate," Giovan replied. "I managed to get aboard a Venetian ship." He shrugged.

Lorenzo gave him an appraising look. Then he said, "My grandfather Cosimo rebuilt Cafaggiolo many years ago. The truth is that I don't approve of turrets and crenellations on the houses of private citizens. They belong to the tyrant who fears malicious intent from his people."

Giovan thought that Lorenzo might be the only powerful man in Italy who believed this—if in fact, he truly did.

Ahead, a rider on a galloping horse came toward them, a trail of dust rising behind him. The guards, apparently recognizing him, let him pass, and he fell in beside Lorenzo.

"Some political business," Lorenzo said to Giovan. "Excuse me." Then, he added, "My brother has something to tell you."

Giuliano reined Samuele and fell back a dozen paces, with Giovan doing the same.

"Lorenzo loves politics and diplomacy," Giuliano said.

They rode in silence for a while.

"Your brother said you have…" Giovan prompted.

"Yes. We wish to tell you that the artist Sandro Botticelli is a great friend of our family. He's like a brother. It grieves us that you have this feud with him."

"It's not my choice."

"Sandro said the same thing. But it doesn't matter. Lorenzo wishes that while you are in Florence, you will not engage in any violence with Sandro."

"But if he confronts me?"

"Lorenzo has spoken with him. We do not ask that you become friends, merely that you avoid each other. Sandro is agreed."

Giovan took off his cap, placed it across his chest and nodded. "My first duty is to the Count and to His Holiness. As long as there is no conflict, I will honor your request."

Giuliano's friendly eyes hardened as he replied. "Beware, my friend. Do not underestimate my brother's authority. This is not a request."

"I understand," Giovan replied attempting to bow in his saddle. But, he said to himself, when my duty requires me to kill you, this promise will mean nothing.

"So who does the new colt belong to," he asked after a while. "You or your brother?"

Giuliano scowled. "Him. But we agreed the next one belongs to me." He reached down and stroked the stallion's neck. "This big boy did his job, and he'll do it again. Right, Samuele?" Straightening back up, he asked Giovan, "It seems a great thing to father a son. Do you have a son?"

Again, Giovan felt the urge to confide, and again he resisted. He would not discuss Matthias, dead now these nine years, not with this man. He shook his head.

Giuliano leaned over and whispered, "Soon I will have a son." He grinned. "Surely it will be a boy."

"The girl in the painting, the one who sews camicia?"

Giovan threw his hands up into the air. "What can I do? I love her, and she has taken me back."

"Sandro, you must promise me that Giuliano is not paying for this."

Fioretta sat on a tall stool so her face was level with Sandro's as he painted. Diffuse sunlight from the dirty windows on the far wall filled Sandro Botticelli's studio.

"Hush, my darling. We only have an hour of light left," Sandro replied as he peered around the edge of the canvas. "That's the problem with female models, they always want to talk."

"Humph."

The canvas was immense, taller than Sandro and half again wider. When they began, he had boasted that it would be the triumph of his career, great in its themes, symbolism and technique. Scattered around the studio were dozens of clay pots containing myriad species of flowers and other plants, each contributing to the strong floral aroma permeating the air. Sandro said he would incorporate over a hundred different kinds of plants into the painting's background.

Fioretta composed herself, forcing a quiet, serene expression onto her face as Sandro had commanded. She wore a simple linen gown that hid her belly which, while hardly noticeable to others, seemed to her to have swollen greatly in the past few weeks. As she often did now, she draped one arm across it. The midwife said it was too early to feel the baby move, but nonetheless, she found herself running her fingers along her abdomen, searching.

It would be just like Giuliano to provide the money Sandro was paying her. It was quite wonderful if he did, and even more wonderful that he hid it from her.

The visit to Nóna had worked. Two days later, Giuliano had appeared on her doorstep, kneeling in the mud of the street, crying out his love for her so loud she was embarrassed that her neighbors would hear. He was only a little drunk. Just as she had after the incident of the banner, Lucia told her to initially refuse him, to make him learn a hard lesson. Instead Fioretta had again thrown herself into his arms, and they had been together most nights in the month that had since passed.

"I'm still surprised you think I'm a good model for this painting," she said, glancing down at her breasts and belly. Sandro knew of her pregnancy.

"Nonsense. Now more than ever, your face has a radiance that I am desperate to capture."

"I wish you'd let me see it," Fioretta said, smiling with pleasure.

"In good time."

Sandro hummed tunelessly as he worked, first staring at her for a moment, and then dashing to the spot on the canvas where he was currently working. Usually he held a palette and brush, but occasionally he switched to a charcoal stick for sketching.

"This is taking so long," Fioretta said. Even though Sandro had provided the stool with a pillow, her bottom was getting numb. "When you did my portrait for Giuliano last year, it only took two afternoons." She had been sitting each afternoon for a week now.

"I will tell you something interesting about this picture if you will promise not to talk so much."

"Agreed."

"I am using your lovely face for more than one figure," Sandro said.

"Really? How many? Two? Three?"

"Four. The central figure of Venus and also the three muses."

"Oh, Sandro. Are you sure?" Fioretta asked. "Won't that make it boring?"

"I'm the artist, not you. Besides, it's more money. You do want the money, don't you? Wait, don't answer. Just be quiet for a while."

She did want the money, of course. Sandro had given her a generous advance payment, with the final amount to be determined by how much time it took. Her finances had improved in another way. The gentleman who had refused to pay had returned from Milan and decided he wanted his camicia, so they had finished the work and he had paid them after all. And they had another job, a bachelor friend of Giuliano's and Sandro's, so Lucia was busy sewing back at the shop.

Lucia. Why couldn't Lucia be happy? They had food and firewood now, and they had paid the back rent. Fioretta understood that after the horrible night when the odious Maffei attacked her, Lucia's life would never be as carefree as when they had skipped through the streets on their way to the jousting tournament. Fioretta smiled, also remembering how they had joked about the dour Stefano and how Lucia spent nights with him because she claimed she liked his bed better than her own. Now, when Stefano came to the shop with Giuliano, she ignored him.

Always tough, Lucia had become hard. And fearless. She had dragged Fioretta through the dark to see Nóna. She had stood between the sword tips of Sandro and that old soldier when they wanted to fight in the shop.

"Sandro?" Fioretta said.

"Hmm?" He was hidden behind the canvas.

"Remember the man you challenged in my shop?"

"Yes, but why bring him up now? I'm trying to paint, and you're making me angry again."

"Oh, phah," Fioretta said. "He seemed to be a nice old man who needed camicia. And you scared him away. I should be mad at you."

"But you made me look foolish in front of him." Sandro stepped out from behind the canvas and looked at her. "Perhaps, we can call it a draw," he said.

Fioretta nodded.

"In any case, he's back in Rome by now, I'm sure," Sandro continued. "We'll not see him again. There," Sandro shouted, as he stepped back from the canvas, flourishing his paintbrush. "We are losing the light, so that will do for now, I think. I need a cup of wine." He looked around, and seeing nobody else in the room, he shouted, "Wine. Bring us wine."

Fioretta knew Sandro's servants were not of the best quality. He really needed a wife to care for him and to organize his house.

"These poor minions plague me so," he said as he tossed his brush and palette onto a small table and stomped from the room. For once, he did not draw a sheet over the canvas.

Fioretta did not hesitate. She climbed down from the stool and rushed over to see the partially completed painting.

Much of the canvas was covered with drawings in charcoal, sketching in the outlines of nine figures, but Sandro had painted some of the faces. Her own face stared out from the center—Venus, Sandro had said. Fioretta's hand moved down to clutch the pendant hanging from her neck, tears welling up in her eyes. It was the pendant Giuliano had given her last year, and there it was, in the painting, the emerald shining in its frame of gold and pearls.

On the left side, she saw three women frolicking in the woods, and they all had her face, too. It was extraordinary. And there was a male figure on the far left, dressed as Mercury, reaching up as though he was trying to part the clouds. It was Giuliano.

Shaking her head and smiling, Fioretta stepped back so she could take in the entire canvas. In all, there were six female figures, and mostly their bodies were only sketched in charcoal. Fioretta began to laugh, hard—so hard that her hands wrapped themselves protectively around her belly.

Six women. And every one, it seemed, was heavy with child.

A door slammed behind her. "I am surrounded by

overpaid, lazy fools," Sandro said.

"Oh, Sandro," she called out as she turned, laughing even harder. "This is scandalous—"

She froze. She felt a sensation of warmth beneath her gown. Pain stabbed across the base of her abdomen, and Fioretta grabbed the little table holding the paintbrush and palette. It slid away from her, and she tumbled to the floor.

"Fioretta, what's wrong?" Sandro cried, hurrying to her, a bottle and cups still in his hands. He knelt beside her.

"I don't know. It hurts." The pain subsided, and she was again aware of the warm feeling. "Sandro, turn away. Please."

"But…" He gazed at her for a second and then did as she asked, staring across the studio at the dozens of potted plants.

Fioretta lifted the hem of her gown, fearing the worst. She pulled it up to her waist and saw the small, bright red spot on her undergarment.

"Sandro, please fetch Lucia," she said, her voice shaking with fear.

Twenty-Five Years Earlier

Thadeous hurried through the unfamiliar streets, his path lit only by the half-full moon. Now that he was remaining in Constantinople, Captain Giovan's order to return to the wall by sunset weighed on him, almost pushing thoughts of Lauro from his mind.

At last he recognized the street leading to the section of the great wall where he and Lauro had met and labored. Thadeous shifted the heavy bag he carried, and it occurred to him that Pletho would have no extra clothes for his journey back to Mystras. And, of course, he would not have his masterpiece, the *Nómoi*. Who knew what would happen to the Emperor's copy. Thadeous swore that if he lived through the coming days, he'd save the original manuscript—the one he now carried—and somehow return it to his mentor and friend.

He heard shouting ahead, and as he rounded the final corner, he saw Captain Giovan standing in torchlight beside the mineshaft.

Lauro was nowhere to be seen.

"You," Giovan shouted as he caught sight of Thadeous. He turned to a soldier. "Seize him."

The man gestured to another, and together they approached Thadeous.

"I ordered you to be back before sunset," Giovan said. "This is a flogging offense."

A third soldier unbuckled his sword belt, slid off the scabbard and swung the leather belt in front of Giovan, who nodded in approval.

Stunned, Thadeous dropped to his knees as the men stood on either side of him. "I'm sorry, Captain," he cried. "Please."

One of the soldiers grabbed the bag from his back, glanced into it and then tossed it aside. They yanked Thadeous to his feet, stripped off his shirt and turned him so his back was to the man with the belt. They tightened their grip and leaned away, stretching Thadeous's arms out spread-eagle on either side.

"The Emperor," Thadeous shouted, cringing, expecting the belt to slash across his exposed back. "He ordered me."

The blow didn't come. He was jerked around so he faced Giovan.

"What about the Emperor?" Giovan asked.

"He ordered me to accompany my master Pletho to the Golden Gate." The words rushed out of Thadeous's mouth.

"And why would he do that?"

"So my master could leave the city with a diplomatic delegation."

Giovan's eyes narrowed. "Your master—this Pletho—escaped the city?"

"At the order of the Emperor, sir."

"Why should I believe you?" Giovan asked.

"I could have gone with him. But I came back."

Giovan glared at Thadeous for a long moment and then said, "Let him go." He turned and walked back to stand by the hole.

A soldier handed Thadeous his shirt. The bag with the manuscript? Where was it? He saw it lying nearby next to a pile of rubble. He glanced around, and then pulled on his shirt as he hurried over to the bag and piled some broken stones on top of it. He walked back to stand next to Giovan at the hole.

"Are the miners getting close?"

Giovan growled, "Go back to working on the wall."

"Yes, sir. Is Lauro there?" Thadeous craned his neck to look up. Workers were barely visible at the top of the wall, and more men and women carried stones and bricks up the nearby steps.

Giovan glanced at him, his eyes cold. Then with a grim smile, he pointed into the hole and said, "No, he's down there."

Thadeous knelt beside the shaft, trying to see into its depths. Lauro must be deep beneath the wall. He felt himself jerked upright and Giovan spun him around.

"I said join the repair gang."

"Let me help with the tunnel. You found it because of my idea. And I'm the son of a copper miner. I spent a year in the mines myself back on Cyprus."

"You don't look like a miner."

"I'm not. I'm a scholar, a scribe. But I can help."

Giovan considered this and then said, "Go down and ask Lauro about their progress. Report back to me."

"Yes, sir," Thadeous replied. He stripped off his shirt and retied his sandals. If he lost one in the tunnel he'd be unlikely to find it. With his slight build, scrambling down the rope was easy, and he was careful not to bump the candle set in a carved-out niche at the bottom. Where was Lauro?

He bent over and squinted into the darkness beneath the foundation. Above the surface, the face of the wall was smooth, chiseled flat by unknown masons a thousand years before. But the bottom of the wall—the roof of the tunnel— was uneven, jagged, with loose stones threatening to fall.

Thadeous saw nothing, but he heard the regular scrape of the wooden tub on dirt as a miner dragged it toward him, the faint candlelight appearing in his eyes as he came closer. Thadeous pressed himself into a corner of the shaft as the man emerged, a rag over his nose and mouth as protection from the dust.

"How far?" Thadeous asked in Greek.

The man shook his head, not understanding. Thadeous would have to find out for himself. As soon as the dirt-filled tub was hoisted above them and was out of the way, Thadeous pushed past the miner and, crouching low, entered the tunnel.

Loose dirt and small stones fell from the underside of the foundation. Dust choked his lungs. He crept forward, step by step, counting as he kept one hand on the ceiling and the other on a sidewall, his body blocking any feeble light from the candle behind him. Every few feet, a crude wooden frame attempted to keep the dirt from the sidewalls from collapsing inward.

"Lauro?" he called out. He had come ten steps so far, perhaps a quarter of the thickness of the wall above ground. He stopped and listened. He heard the scrape and scrabbling of dirt in the darkness ahead. It must be their own miners working by hand and in the dark, afraid a light would expose them if they broke through into the Turkish tunnel. That meant they were very close.

Thadeous edged forward. "Lauro?" he said.

"Quiet," Lauro said from ahead, his voice a hoarse whisper. Then, "Thadeous?"

"Yes." His hands found bare shoulders. They embraced as well as they could, their bodies slick with sweat and dirt.

"You came back," Lauro whispered.

"Did you doubt me?"

Lauro wrapped his arm around Thadeous's narrow shoulders and pulled him tight. "Captain Giovan said you—"

"It's all right."

There was more Thadeous wanted to tell him: about the

Emperor, Pletho's escape, the manuscript they had both toiled to copy. But here, in a hole beneath the colossal wall of the Emperor Theodosius, he was content to huddle in his lover's strong arms.

A moment later there was a loud hiss, and it came from deeper in the tunnel. Lauro released Thadeous and crawled toward the sound. Thadeous hesitated, and then he followed.

He heard a man whisper to Lauro that when they stopped digging and listened, the sound of the Turkish miners was louder than ever. He feared they might break through into the enemy tunnel. He also made the point that he and his men were miners, not soldiers.

"Captain Giovan wants a report," Thadeous said, remembering his duty.

"Show me," Lauro said to the lead miner. "Thadeous, follow us."

They stood, stooped over, and moved forward another half-dozen steps and then halted. The man pulling the wooden tub came up behind them, and Thadeous indicated with a shush he should be quiet.

At first, Thadeous heard only the sound of his own breathing, and he struggled to control it. Then he heard something else: the steady, almost continuous crunch of iron shovels thrust into dirt and gravel. It sounded like many men were digging at once. They must have finished the approach tunnel and spread out to excavate the gallery. Once it was big enough, the Turks would set fire to the support timbers, the gallery would cave in and the thousand-year-old wall above would collapse.

The sound of digging ceased. Thadeous held his breath, but the pounding of his heart seemed to fill the space like the hammer blows of a blacksmith.

Ahead, a flicker of light appeared. It must be coming from the gallery!

"Thadeous, take the miners out," Lauro said, his voice a loud whisper. "If the Turks break through, I'll hold them."

Thadeous stood frozen, confused. Then he turned to the man who had brought the tub, and shoved him back toward the entrance. They both scrambled over the boards in the tub and, crouching low, ran back toward the their own dim candle light in the distance. Thadeous felt a hand on his back as someone followed him, pushing. He knew it must be a miner, not Lauro.

He tripped and crashed to the tunnel floor, gravel gouging into his forearms and knees. His head hit a wooden support and, for a moment, a blaze of light flashed in front of his eyes. The man behind him hardly slowed as he trampled over Thadeous, and the next man did the same.

Thadeous was alone. As he struggled to his feet, he felt blood running into his eye, and he tried to wipe it away. It was totally dark. The dim light of the distant candle was gone, perhaps knocked over by a fleeing miner.

Overwhelmed by the burning pain across his body and his head, Thadeous leaned against the tunnel wall. What should he do? Which way was the entrance? He had completely lost his bearings. He heard shouts coming from one direction, and the sound of iron clashing on iron. He started to turn away from the sound, away from danger. He took a step and stopped. Was Lauro fighting the Turks? Alone? In the narrow tunnel, perhaps he could take on one man at a time. Perhaps there were no soldiers among the Turkish miners. He had a chance.

Thadeous turned and moved toward the sound of the fighting, stumbling again over the wooden tub where it lay abandoned. He kept moving. Ahead, a light appeared, torchlight flickering through a small hole in the tunnel face. It outlined the figure of a man, Lauro, standing in a space too narrow for him to swing his sword.

As Thadeous came up behind Lauro, an iron-tipped pike plunged through the hole, and Lauro jumped aside, slashing down with his short sword as well as he could, striking the wooden shaft but not breaking it. He grasped the pike and pulled, at the same time thrusting his sword through hole, attempting to stab the unseen man on the other side. Thadeous couldn't tell if this was successful, but the pike was wrenched from Lauro's grasp, and it disappeared.

Lauro had stopped them. Thadeous's heart swelled with pride in this man he loved, this warrior, who was singledhandedly fighting back a horde of Turks. But it couldn't continue. Thadeous heard the ominous sound of digging. They were widening the gap, and soon they would swarm through.

"Lauro, the miners are out," he cried. "We need to go back."

As Lauro glanced over his shoulder, the pike head shot through the hole again and this time stabbed him in the chest, just above his armor. He gasped and fell back into Thadeous's arms. The sound of digging redoubled and guttural shouts from the other side filled the tunnel. The torchlight grew brighter as the gap widened.

"Run," Lauro gasped. "Leave me."

Panic clutching at his heart, Thadeous reached under Lauro's arms from behind and clutched him across the chest. Warm blood covered Thadeous's hands. He yanked Lauro away from the hole and dragged him back toward the entrance, Lauro pushing with his feet. Then his body went limp. Panting, desperate, Thadeous strained with all his strength, but once again he stumbled over the tub with its load of boards.

The torchlight dimmed and Thadeous realized that gap through which it streamed was partially blocked by the head and arms of a man. He held a curved sword and swung it back and forth as he labored to get through the hole.

The man was going to kill them both. Where is Lauro's sword? Thadeous couldn't see it in the dim light. He struggled to get out from under the deadweight of Lauro's motionless body, but his legs were trapped. He wailed in frustration.

The Turk was almost free.

We are going to die on top of this cursed tub. He closed his eyes and waited for the end to come.

Then Lauro's body magically lifted off him. As Thadeous struggled to stand, Captain Giovan pushed him aside, leaped forward and plunged his sword into the Turk's bare chest.

Chapter Seven

Four Hours Until Dawn

"Enough," Giovan said, throwing down his pen. His hand cramped from the strain of writing. How many hours had it been? More important, how many hours remained for him?

"You done?" Alfeo asked. He got off his stool and stood in front of the little table where Giovan worked. He surveyed the pages scattered across its surface, picked up the one Giovan had been working on and squinted at it.

"Do you read?" Giovan asked, guessing the answer.

Alfeo shook his head.

"It's my confession," Giovan explained.

"Like with a priest?"

Giovan shrugged.

Alfeo continued to stare at the page. Giovan had stopped writing about halfway down, and Alfeo pointed to the blank space. "It's not done," he said.

"It doesn't matter…" Giovan stopped, too tired to explain. But, of course the man was correct. He was not done.

Alfeo leaned over the table and looked into Giovan's face, his eyes sad. "If I bring a priest, will you tell confession?" he asked.

Ignoring him, Giovan snatched the half-finished page from Alfeo and positioned it on the table. He dipped the pen in the ink pot. He wrote.

> *That night Francesco came and he took me to Jacopo de' Pazzi.*

Four Months Earlier

Once again Giovan sat across from Jacopo de' Pazzi. They

were in the same room at the same inn, again with the fire burning before them. This time Francesco de' Pazzi, the banker from Rome, had joined them along with a priest that Jacopo had introduced as Father Maffei, who stood behind them against the wall. The priest's ankle-length cassock was wrinkled and stained.

"I bring a letter from my master, Count Riario," Giovan said, handing Jacopo the sealed letter. Please God, he prayed silently. Let this be the last letter. Let me begin to see then end of this onerous task.

"Tell me what it says," Jacopo said, without opening it.

"The Count and His Holiness do not agree to make you Duke of Florence. It's too much."

Francesco started to protest, but Jacopo quieted him with a wave of his hand. Giovan had not seen Francesco in months. The little man seemed to have grown even fatter and stupider. Now he sputtered and fidgeted, twisting his fingers through his long, straight, blond hair.

Ignoring his nephew, Jacopo said, "Go on."

"Instead, you will have at least three hundred soldiers, probably more, who will stay in Florence for one month after the assassinations. They will be under your direct command. You may do whatever you want without interference so that you may establish complete control."

"Good troops?"

"I've made the arrangements myself," Giovan replied. "From Perugia and Imola mainly. Some archers from Tolentino. His Holiness is also negotiating with the Duke of Urbino for more. He has the best troops in Italy."

Jacopo leaned back in his chair, deep in thought while Francesco squirmed. It had been clear to Giovan for some time that Francesco was not head of the Pazzi family, that he deferred to his uncle.

Giovan waited, knowing the commitment of Jacopo de' Pazzi was the last piece to fall into place. Without him controlling Florence in the aftermath, the entire endeavor was pointless.

"When last we met," Jacopo said, "I spoke of the gaming table, that if the risk is great, so must be the reward."

"I remember," Giovan replied.

"Franceschino, what do you think?" Jacopo continued.

The banker flinched at hearing this deprecating nickname, but he caught himself and replied, "The people of Florence will run through the streets shouting *Pazzi, Pazzi, Pazzi*. No other Gonfaloniere has been as popular as you. I think we may not need any soldiers at all."

Jacopo's face showed skepticism. "Well, I doubt that. But your point is well taken." To Giovan, he said, "You may tell His Holiness I put my life and fortune on the gaming table."

At last. After eight months of work, much of it traveling, the end was in sight. They would return to Rome, and this news would please His Holiness. All that remained was the final plan to bring about the deaths of Lorenzo and Giuliano.

All three men stood.

"Captain, you do not look happy," Jacopo said.

Surprised, Giovan said, "There is still work to be done."

"Of course." Jacopo turned to Maffei, who had been silent throughout. "A blessing, Father?"

Maffei nodded and raised his hand, making the sign of the cross over them. He muttered some words in Latin.

"This plan must remain a secret," Giovan said when the priest finished. "I'm sorry, Father, but I don't know you."

"Oh, you needn't worry about him," Jacopo replied with a tight, knowing smile. "He's from Volterra."

Outside the inn, two men who looked like thugs were waiting with horses. Jacopo explained that he was going back to the Pazzi family villa, a few miles outside of Florence. He mounted and with a nod to his nephew Francesco, he and his men trotted away.

"Well," Giovan said to Francesco and the priest, Maffei. "A most productive evening. I think I'll walk for a while."

"Let us accompany you, Captain," Francesco said. "It's safer with the three of us in Florence after dark."

"I don't need—" He stopped himself. Why argue? He shrugged and started striding up the street, with Francesco and Maffei trailing after him.

They walked together toward the center of the city, the gloom of the winter evening closing in around them. Soon it would be too dark to see without a lantern.

Squinting, Giovan looked back at Maffei, wondering about this priest from Volterra, remembering what Filiberto had said about the people of Volterra hating Lorenzo.

Maffei saw his glance. "You have met with His Holiness?" he asked, hurrying to come abreast.

"I have the honor of commanding his guard and his great fortress, Castel Sant'Angelo."

"So he blesses this endeavor?"

"Yes. I'll report to him as soon as I return to Rome, and I'm sure he will be pleased," Giovan replied.

"Perhaps a favor then." Maffei's voice was oily.

"You wish me to mention your name," Giovan replied, understanding. The man is ambitious.

"Please."

"What do you think, *Franceschino?*" Giovan asked, turning to Francesco, knowing that he would dislike this familiarity. "Should I do him this favor?"

Francesco drew himself up at the nickname. "Captain," he said, "you forget your place."

"My apologies, sir," Giovan replied, suppressing a smile. He turned back to Maffei. "When the deed is done, I will be happy to inform His Holiness of your role, whatever it may end up being."

"Thank you," Maffei said, bowing slightly.

Ahead, the facade of the Basilica di Santa Maria del Fiore —the Duomo—came into view, a black, hulking profile against the darkening sky.

"So, tell me, Father," Giovan said. "Does *God* bless this

endeavor?"

"Of course," Maffei replied. "How can you doubt it?"

"I don't doubt it," Giovan said. "But for the sake of this discussion, how can we know for sure?"

"His Holiness in Rome, whom you say gives his blessing, is infallible. Do you doubt this?"

Giovan didn't reply.

"Doubters cannot be true Christians," Francesco added.

Father Maffei nodded with approval.

"But at Gethsemane, did not Jesus pray to be relieved of his burden, to have the chalice taken from him?" Giovan asked. "And didn't he express doubt on the cross when he cried out, asking God why he had forsaken him. Surely if Our Savior can feel doubt, so can weaker men."

"You misunderstand the scripture," Maffei replied. "As a man, he may have despaired. But he never lost his faith in God."

"I understand that. But what about doubts concerning some earthly action?" Giovan lowered his voice. "How do we know for certain that this deed we plan is not sinful?"

"His Holiness gave his blessing," Francesco said.

Giovan thought back to what Sixtus had said months ago in the shadows of his unfinished chapel. In fact, he had initially forbidden any killing. But then he promised to forgive anyone who acted to accomplish this plan.

"Yes, I suppose this is true," he said.

"Then that is sufficient," Father Maffei replied. "Lorenzo and his dissolute brother deserve to die. Lorenzo especially."

Giovan stopped at the foot of the cathedral steps. "Gentlemen," he said, "I am going to pray for success," and they said goodnight. Francesco and Maffei continued up the street, their heads together.

As the hour was late, the interior of the Duomo was vast and dark, lit only by a few votive candles at one side of the entrance and by the candles on the distant altar. As Giovan walked forward, he passed between mammoth pillars bordering the central aisle, stretching high overhead and disappearing into the gloom.

He arrived at the main crossing, where the transepts met beneath Brunelleschi's famous dome. It felt like he was out of doors on a starless night. Even with flickering light of the altar candles, he could see nothing above him or to each side. The faint scent of incense hung in the air, reminding him of his home church, San Pellegrino, back in Rome.

There was no one at the altar. Giovan eased himself down, kneeling on the cold marble floor, and clasped his hands over his chest.

"Our Father…" he whispered.

The words came easily, as they always did. After two repetitions, he realized he was not concentrating on the prayer, that his mind was elsewhere: wondering how Jacopo de'Pazzi had lost two fingers from his left hand, remembering Filiberto's good humor as they left Cafaggiolo, a little drunk on Medici wine.

"Forgive me, Father," he said, and he started again.

But even as his mouth formed the words, he thought about the Medici brothers, remembering Lorenzo joking with the old stable groom and Giuliano talking about his love for that girl.

The edge of one of the marble floor tiles cut into his knee. He accepted the pain. The pain was good.

Giovan lifted his eyes, seeking the vision from San Pellegrino that so often came to him in times of doubt: Jesus Christ, his hand raised in blessing, against the golden sky. But instead, his eyes clouded over, and he saw his son, Matthias, lying on the Rimini battlefield, blood spurting from the arrow wound in his neck.

"Heavenly Father," he gasped. "What shall I do?"

Silence echoed through the dark and through his soul.

"My God, I pray to you. Take this chalice from me."

"There was an excess of air in your blood," the old doctor said. "So the humors were out of balance." He lifted a porcelain cup to his nose, sniffed and then dipped a dirty finger inside and touched it to his tongue. "Much improved," he added.

Fioretta stared at a spray of white alyssum next to her bed, its blooms so rare in winter. She forced a breath deep into her lungs, savoring their sweet fragrance. Every few days, one of Giuliano's servants brought them to the shop from Cafaggiolo, where they were raised in a hothouse.

"Just like your normal monthly menses," the doctor continued, "the bleeding is helpful in expelling the bad humors. I'll come by tomorrow and perhaps one more letting will be sufficient."

"She's always more tired after you bleed her," Lucia said, standing on the opposite side of the bed, her voice tense, barely controlled.

Ignoring Lucia, the doctor tossed his instruments into a bag and bowed to Fioretta. He left, and a moment later Fioretta heard the door close downstairs.

"Please let me fetch the midwife," Lucia said. "She has herbs that will help. That man is making you sick so he can get more money."

"Giuliano sent him," Fioretta replied. "He's the best doctor in Florence."

It had been two weeks since she had sat for Sandro's painting. During that time, there had been only a few occasions when cramps had attacked her and blood had spotted her undergarments. The midwife told them it was a common occurrence, but Giuliano insisted they consult the doctor.

Someone pounded on the front door downstairs, and Lucia went down to answer it.

"You!" Lucia screamed. "You dare come here?"

What was happening? Who was down there? Fioretta heard the muffled sound of a man's voice and then the door slammed. She thought the man had gone away, but then she heard a heavy tread on the stairs. Fioretta stared at the alyssum, not knowing what she should do.

"Good day, daughter," Antonio Gorini said as he entered the room, followed by Lucia. He wore his usual woolen tunic, old and patched by both Fioretta and Lucia. He held his worn leather cap in his hands.

"He brought that pig with him, that Maffei," Lucia said, her voice high-pitched, and her face red.

"A mistake," Gorini said. "I apologize. He's waiting in the street now."

Lucia came close to the bed, almost standing between Fioretta and her father.

"What do you want? Fioretta asked, trying to keep herself composed.

"I heard you were ill," Gorini said.

"So?"

"You are my daughter."

"Why should that be of importance to you now?"

Lucia still flushed, nodded in agreement.

Gorini didn't reply, seeming to be at a loss for words. He glanced around the room, his eyes lighting on the marriage chest that had belonged to Fioretta's mother, and he winced, as though he was surprised to see it. He swallowed and turned back to Fioretta.

"Since your mother died—" he began.

"No. You cannot use that as an excuse," Fioretta said. "You stopped being a father when I needed one. You made no provision for my dowry. You invited that awful Maffei into our home." She reached out and grasped Lucia's hand. "And you defended him when he attacked Lucia."

Gorini didn't look at Lucia. He said, "The business was failing. I had no money for the Monte."

The Monte delle Doti was the government fund that most Florentine families used to invest for their daughters' dowry.

"Liar," Fioretta cried, sitting up in the bed. "You put money in and then took it out."

"It's… It's…" Gorini stumbled. "It's the same thing…"

"No it's not. You stole my dowry. You knew that without

it, I'd never make a good marriage."

"The wool market collapsed. What could I do?"

"It broke Mama's heart." Fioretta spat out the words. "It killed her."

"No. That's not true. Is that what you think? Fioretta, my daughter, you've got it wrong, I swear. I did sell back our shares in the Monte, I admit it. I was trying to save the business. But that was *after* your sainted mother had passed away. When she got sick, the business was profitable."

He pushed past Lucia and knelt down next to the bed.

"Your mother," he continued, "as she lay dying, took comfort everyday thinking and talking about your future wedding. Don't you remember?"

A memory stirred in Fioretta. She lay snuggled next to her ill mother, listening as she talked about wedding dress she would one day sew for her daughter. She let Fioretta play with her pewter thimble as she talked. There would be yards and yards of silk. Mama laughed and said that her father would prefer wool, of course, but silk it would be. This must have been before the business had failed, and that made all the difference.

Fioretta saw tears glistening in her father's eyes. He clasped his hands on the bed beside her, as though in prayer. He was her father, after all, come to see her when she was sick. Realizing she still grasped Lucia's hand, she let go and placed her hand on top of her father's.

Lucia left the bedside and went to stand next to the window. She stared through the cracked glass panes down at the street below.

After a moment, Gorini cleared his throat. Groaning a little, he pulled himself to his feet and sat on the edge of the bed. "You are with child," he said. "So I've heard."

"Yes, Father."

"Perhaps a son, a grandson for me."

For the first time in many years, Fioretta saw her father smile.

"That's what I hope," Fioretta said.

"And your illness?"

"I just need rest."

"Of course. Well, I should go." He stood.

"Stop," Lucia said turning away from the window, her face now pale, her voice a hoarse whisper. "Don't you want to know who the father is?"

"Lucia!" Fioretta cried out.

Gorini looked back and forth between Lucia and Fioretta. "I thought that could wait. My purpose today—"

"It's Giuliano de' Medici," Lucia shouted. "She's been in his bed for over a year."

"What?" Gorini shouted. He stumbled back a step and grasped the doorframe to steady himself. "You know the Medici are my enemies."

"Father," Fioretta said. "Please. Giuliano is not your enemy. He loves me. He sent me these flowers. From Cafaggiolo, grown in the middle of winter."

"Cafaggiolo was built by stealing money from the citizens of Florence."

"No, that's not right," Fioretta said. "Not by Giuliano."

"Lorenzo ordered the sacking of Volterra. That ruined me. He keeps the government of Florence in his pocket, so that if you are not his friend, you starve. Fioretta, how could you do this to me? You spite me."

"No, no. Father, it's love. You do remember love, don't you?"

Again, her father glanced at the marriage chest, and the light blazing in his eyes seemed to flicker. But then he wheeled around and left the room, stomping down the stairs. They heard the front door slam.

Fioretta stared after him.

Lucia stayed at the window.

"Lucia," Fioretta said. "How could you do that? How could you tell him?"

"He brought Maffei with him."

"He apologized."

"That means nothing," Lucia said.

"You hate my father so much you would come between him and me."

"He invited Maffei into his house last year. They ruined my life. Both of them."

"Yes, I know it was awful—" Fioretta said.

"You *don't* know."

"What do you mean?"

"I visited my family after we moved here," Lucia said. "Remember?"

"Lucia, please don't stand over there. Come and tell me."

Lucia came to the bedside, trembling. "I went to see Nóna."

"But why?" Fioretta reached for her hand, but Lucia jerked it away.

"You are such a fool," Lucia said. "You understand nothing."

Fioretta didn't know what to say. Why was Lucia acting like this?

"You complain you'll never have a husband," Lucia continued, "that you have no dowry. But you have a child. You can have more."

"But so can you," Lucia said. "Stefano loves you."

"Not once he knows."

"Knows what?" Fioretta said. "Tell me."

"When I went to Nóna, I was with child." Tears flowed down her cheeks. "When I came back, I was not." Brushing the tears away with the back of her hand, she turned and went to the door.

Now Fioretta began to cry. Lucia had lost a baby. "But why?" she asked through her tears. "Stefano would have married you—"

"You still don't understand. The baby was not Stefano's. I know this."

"Oh, Dear God," Fioretta whispered. "Maffei."

"But still you do not know the worst. Because of what happened, Nóna says I may never have more children." She glared at Fioretta's belly.

"You're jealous of *my* baby," Fioretta said, now understanding. "You hate *my* baby."

"No," Lucia cried. Then in a quiet voice, "Yes." She ran from the room and a moment later the front door slammed.

Lucia was gone and Fioretta was alone.

The winter sun, having climbed over the surrounding walls half an hour before, warmed in the courtyard. Thadeous sat on a bench, a pewter cup of wine within reach as the Archbishop's servants worked nearby, sweeping the cobblestones, shaking out carpets, drawing water from the well in the corner.

If he kept his breaths shallow and slow he gained a little respite from the racking cough that plagued him and made life unpleasant for the people around him. For twenty-five years he had coughed, sometime so badly that he awoke lying on the floor, having lost consciousness. But today, sitting in the feeble sun, his lungs were quiet.

Raffaele had departed three hours before with his new friends, saying they were going to hunt boars. Since word had come of his future elevation to cardinal, the boy had grown restless with the life of a student. As he left, he made it clear to Thadeous that there would be no tutoring today. Thadeous hoped Archbishop Salviati would not blame him for Raffaele's change in attitude. But if Raffaele did not study or attend classes, what need did he have for a tutor? So far, the Archbishop seemed preoccupied in Rome and had let them be.

Someone hammered at the great ironclad door—a remnant of a more violent period in Pisan history—that lead from the courtyard out to the narrow street in front of the palazzo. A servant scurried to answer, and a moment later he returned, announcing that Signore Carpani wished to see him.

Thadeous had not seen Dante Carpani for over a month, not since that night when he had been expelled from the

Carpani house.

"Tell him I'm busy," he said.

"He has a book he wishes to give you, sir."

A book? "Oh, very well. Let him in."

The big man approached Thadeous with his brow furrowed, his hands gripping a large book. "I haven't seen you at the library," he said.

"Are you surprised?" Thadeous glared at him. "Does your wife know you are here?"

Dante bristled and said, "That is of no concern, to you."

"Ah, you sneaked to away without telling her."

"I came to see you because I have just acquired this." Dante held up the book. "But since you are so rude, I have changed my mind." He turned on his heel and started back toward the gate. Over his shoulder, he said, "It mentions George Gemistus."

Thadeous stared after him. *Pletho?* Dante had a book about his teacher, dead all these years? "Wait," he shouted. "Come back."

Dante returned and stood in front of Thadeous, his face expressionless. He held the book so Thadeous could see it. It was bound in gleaming leather, so different from the worn out, cracked volumes that Thadeous usually dealt with. "It's from Greece. It's a history of philosophers," he said.

"Including George Gemistus, you say?" Thadeous's hands twitched, wanting to snatch the book away from Dante.

"Yes."

Thadeous slid over on the bench. "Sit," he said.

Dante handed him the book and sat down.

"Have you read it?" Thadeous asked, running his fingers over leather cover. The book was heavy.

"Yes. Look at the marked page."

Thadeous opened the volume and leafed through the thick parchment pages, his eyes dancing across the blocky Greek script. Even in the university town of Pisa, books were rare and new ones even rarer. He found the scrap of paper Dante had used to mark a page near the end and opened to it.

The section about Pletho covered several pages, and it mentioned Pletho's death from natural causes in Mystras in 1454. Thadeous had heard that his escape from Constantinople had been successful and had been pleased the his old friend had made it home.

Then, on the last page, he found the answer to the greatest mystery of his life.

> *After the fall of Constantinople and the death of the Emperor, the only manuscript of the Nómoi came into the possession of Gennadius II, Patriarch of Constantinople. It is a sadness that in 1460, Gennadius burned it, saying it was a sacrilege against the word of God.*

Thadeous took a sudden, deep breath. A spasm of coughs exploded in his chest and went on for a minute, even after sipping from the wine cup that Dante lifted his lips. When the attack subsided, Thadeous felt drained, his face dripped with perspiration and tears blurred his sight. He dabbed his eyes with the corner of his sleeve, took the wine cup from Dante and took another sip.

"Your lungs are worse?" Dante asked, concern obvious in his voice.

"No, no. Lately it's been better." Thadeous took another sip. "Probably because I don't spend time in that dusty library of yours."

"A loss for me. I miss our discussions." Dante leaned over and gazed down at the page. "The *Nómoi*," he said. "Did you ever see it?"

"Oh, yes," Thadeous replied. He remembered those days sitting beside Pletho and Lauro, laboring to make the emperor's copy after long nights spent repairing the Theodosian wall. He remembered that time when Pletho was away and he and Lauro, exhausted as they were, had snatched a moment of love and pleasure in Thadeous's bed. And he remembered the day twenty-five years before, when Pletho had placed that manuscript into the hands of the last emperor of the thousand-year Byzantine Empire, while outside the Turkish army pounded the city walls with stone cannonballs.

But the wall had fallen, the *Nómoi* was burned, and Lauro was dead. Those months in Constantinople had been the most momentous of his life, and now there was almost nothing left but memories. He would finish his own manuscript, he would tell his story of Constantinople, of Pletho, the *Nómoi* and Lauro. And above all else, he would protect the stack of parchment pages hidden beneath his bed.

There was another pounding at the front door, and the servant dragged it open, admitting Raffaele and two older boys. Thadeous knew the taller one, Benedetto.

When they had left that morning, they had been in high spirits, brandishing their lances, shouting insults at each other, referring to each one's lack of skill in hunting boars and pursuing women. Now, as they filed into the courtyard, their faces were sullen, and Raffaele dragged his lance across the cobblestones.

Thadeous put his hand on Dante's shoulder and pushed himself to his feet, acknowledging the presence of his young master. Dante stood beside him.

"How went the hunt?" Thadeous asked.

"A disaster," Raffaele replied. "Benedetto's dogs were useless."

"What? The dogs found a boar didn't they?" Benedetto replied. "You were too busy talking to see him."

"Enough," said the other boy. To Thadeous, he said, "They've been arguing about this for an hour."

Benedetto punched the boy on his arm, hard. Then he turned to Thadeous, his face showing contempt. "So this old frocio has a boyfriend," he said, indicating Dante.

Months before, Benedetto and some friends had accosted Raffaele and Thadeous outside the university library. Then, he had called them both froci.

Dante, taller than any of these boys and strong as an oak

tree, stepped forward and gazed down on Benedetto. "I have five children and a happy wife," he said. "Young sir, I hope someday you can say the same."

Benedetto appeared confused, as though he wasn't sure whether he had been insulted. Dante bowed to him, and Thadeous was sure he saw a twinkle in the big man's eyes.

Raffaele said nothing during this exchange. He glanced at Thadeous with a look of apology, but then he turned away, mumbling something about going to his room. As he led the way to the archway at the back of the courtyard, they began to joke again and called for wine. Benedetto held back a moment, lifted his fist and made the sign of the fig, sneering at Thadeous with disgust.

"Raffaele is now friends with them?" Dante asked when they were gone.

"So it seems," Thadeous replied. He hesitated and then added, "His circumstances have changed, and he has more money now. From the Archbishop."

"Ah."

They both sat back down on the bench, and Thadeous opened the book again to the marked page. He felt Dante gazing at him, and he looked up to see that his old friend's face was troubled, as though he was searching for a way to say something.

"Dante," Thadeous said, "You are still worried that I am some kind of danger to your son, to little Luca."

Dante spread his hands before him, nodding. "If we are to be friends, I must first know. Have you ever... I mean... Have you ever been with young boys?"

Thadeous stared down at the book, unseeing. "When I was a boy myself back on Cyprus, I had friends, other boys..."

"I don't mean that. I mean since you have been a grown man."

Thadeous shook his head. "No. I swear to you. Never when I was a younger man and not now."

Dante looked him in the eye for a moment and then nodded.

"I am just a sick old man," Thadeous said, "who doesn't care about such things any more."

Chapter Eight

Three Hours Until Dawn

There was a pounding at the cell door and Giovan heard the bolt being withdrawn. He ignored it and continued to write.

In March I went to Rome where I met…

Alfeo opened the door a crack and peered outside. After a brief, whispered conversation, he turned to Giovan.

"Your priest is here."

Giovan kept his head down. "I told you, I need no priest."

"He's here for your confession."

"I need no priest. Send him away so I can complete my work."

"Giovan, it's me." It was the voice of Father Nicolo.

Nicolo? Giovan looked up in surprise.

"My friend," Nicolo continued, "I've traveled from Rome to see you. Paulo came to tell me what happened. He's here with me."

"I need no priest," Giovan shouted, wanting Nicolo to hear.

"But," Nicolo replied, "perhaps you do need a friend."

Alfeo nodded at this, and then turned to the door and started to tug it open.

"No!" Giovan sprang to his feet, pushed past Alfeo and threw his weight against the door, slamming it shut. The scoriada wounds on his tortured back screamed, and he bent over, gasping in agony.

"I need no priest."

Two Months Earlier

Wearing his best uniform, Giovan emerged from his modest apartment, built into the base of the outer wall of Castel Sant'Angelo. This defensive wall, with the bastions at its corners, surrounded the barrel-shaped central fortress, towering over the Tiber River. And between the curved fortress and the outer rectangular wall was a narrow, oddly-shaped alley paved with cobblestones.

Giovan squinted at the band of sky visible above him. It had rained the night before when he finally returned from another trip to Imola, and the sky was still overcast. Spring was at least a month away.

He turned, following the curve of the fortress until he came to the main gate in the outer wall, and then stepped through it. The Ponte Sant'Angelo stretched in front of him across the muddy waters of the Tiber, leading into the heart of Rome.

As always, guards were posted on either side of the gate. One of them failed to see Giovan and continued to slouch against the wall, dozing. Giovan stepped up close and cuffed him across one ear with the flat of his hand.

"Guard," he shouted.

The soldier jerked up straight, stared at Giovan and then saluted. Giovan was pleased to see that the man's lips trembled.

"If I catch you asleep again on guard duty," Giovan said, "you'll be flogged. Understand?"

The man nodded, saying nothing.

"Hello, Captain Battista."

Giovan recognized the voice of his friend, Father Nicolo, and he turned to greet him. They embraced.

"Paulo brought your message," Nicolo said. "The boy is growing into a man." He put his hand on Giovan's shoulder and added, "I'm glad you're home."

"Yes, finally."

They turned away from the guard who was still saluting, and Giovan led Nicolo inside the gate. When they were out of earshot, Giovan said, "I'm afraid I've been away too much these past months. Discipline here is getting lax."

"You'll soon put that right."

Father Nicolo turned towards Giovan's living quarters, assuming they would have a cup of wine and talk, as they usually did. But instead, Giovan took his elbow and led him through the arched entrance into the interior of the fortress. They descended through the tunnel, which was only lit by sunlight from the entrance behind them and a flickering torch in the chamber ahead. Midway, in the semi-darkness, Giovan stopped and turned to Nicolo.

"I've never been inside the fortress," Nicolo said.

"I need your help," Giovan said.

"Anything."

"We're going to meet with His Holiness."

"What?" Nicolo said. "Here in Sant'Angelo? You should have sent word to me with Paulo." He tried to smooth his coarse woolen cassock. "How do I look? Oh, it's too dark." He hurried forward into the dim chamber in front of them.

Giovan followed, bemused. "You look fine," he said.

Nicolo licked his fingers and ran them through his sparse hair.

"This way," Giovan said, pointing to another dark tunnel leading out of the chamber. The floor sloped upwards and curved to the left, following the circular outline of the fortress. There were no side passages or rooms, and they soon left the light from the entrance chamber behind and were again plunged into darkness.

"Sant'Angelo was originally the tomb of the Emperor Hadrian," Giovan said. "This part is over a fourteen hundred years old. We are walking on the original marble, just like Hadrian did."

"You said you need my help," Nicolo said, puffing a little as they climbed.

Giovan was silent for a moment. Then he said, "You know His Holiness has given me a task."

"That's why you've been traveling. But you've told me nothing more."

"I've come to have doubts. Grave doubts."

"About an undertaking for His Holiness?" Nicolo asked.

"Yes."

They came to a passage on their left. Giovan followed it, and they found themselves in a high vaulted room with large niches cut into the walls on each side.

"This is the Chamber of the Urns," Giovan said. "We're in the center of the old tomb, where Hadrian's ashes were kept. And many emperors after him. There's nothing left now, of course. We store supplies here."

Wooden barrels were stacked nearby along with sacks of grain, and Giovan heard the scratch and scuttle of rats.

"Grave doubts?" Nicolo said.

"His Holiness has ordered me to kill two men," Giovan replied.

Nicolo considered this. "Killing is not always a mortal sin. As a soldier, you know this, of course."

"Yes. I've killed many men. I've always thought it was necessary."

"And now?" Nicolo asked.

"I suppose it's necessary in this case, too." Giovan replied.

"Then what is the problem?"

Giovan didn't know what to say. Father Nicolo was his confessor and his friend. He was also unquestioningly loyal to Sixtus. Could he be trusted?

Instead of answering, Giovan led Nicolo to a doorway on the other side of the chamber and up a flight of stairs. Finally, they stepped out onto an open courtyard paved with new marble, surrounded by walls with ornate doors and shuttered windows. The sun was still covered by dark clouds.

"This is called the Courtyard of Honor," Giovan said. "It gets its name—"

"Giovan, my friend. Tell me. What is the problem?"

"I have made a mistake," Giovan replied. "The men I am

order to kill have befriended me."

"I see."

"What am I to do?" Giovan asked. "Advise me, please."

"Who are these men?"

"Lorenzo de' Medici and his brother."

"Of Florence," Nicolo said. "So, it's a political killing," Nicolo said, stroking his chin as he gazed up at the overcast sky.

"His Holiness has promised absolution for whatever needs to be done."

"Ah. Well that's the key, isn't it," Nicolo said.

"Yes, I understand. But…"

"You hesitate because they are, perhaps, good men?" Nicolo asked.

"In forty years as a soldier, I'm sure I've killed many men," Giovan replied. "And surely, some of them were good men. So why do I feel this way now?"

"You have come to know these two brothers."

Giovan remembered standing next to Giuliano in the stable at Cafaggiolo, watching as Lorenzo joked with his old groom. They had all laughed together. Giovan nodded to Nicolo.

"So it's a selfish concern," Nicolo said. "His Holiness has decided on this path. He has promised absolution so you know your soul is not in mortal danger, but you wish to avoid it because it will be unpleasant."

"You say I would shirk my duty because it's unpleasant," Giovan said, glaring at Nicolo. "Do you know me?"

"You asked for my help."

A liveried servant stepped out of a doorway, spotted them and approached.

"Captain Batista, His Holiness commands your presence."

Giovan nodded, straightened his uniform and stepped forward, following the servant. At the door, he glanced back at Nicolo, who was trying to brush lint from his cassock.

"I feel trapped," Giovan whispered.

* * *

As commandant of Sant'Angelo, Giovan had often been in this room. Pope Nicholas V had built it and the adjoining chambers directly on top of the imperial mausoleum just twenty odd years before. Tapestries with lush depictions of flowers and green foliage covered the plastered stone walls. The floor was tiled in gleaming brown terra-cotta. While the room was not nearly as sumptuous as the papal apartments in the Vatican Palace, Pope Sixtus seemed to like it, and often used it for meetings that required privacy.

Under a large window, one of the few in Sant'Angelo, Sixtus sat on a gilded, high-backed throne with Archbishop Salviati next to him in a chair that was only slightly less tall and ornate. They leaned toward each other in quiet conversation.

As Giovan stepped forward, Sixtus looked up and smiled. He wore a wrinkled white robe, as he often did when not holding court, and he was bareheaded. "Captain Batista," he said. "It's good to see you. We hope your journeys have not been too burdensome."

Giovan knelt and kissed the proffered papal ring. Standing, he replied, "Not at all, Your Holiness."

"And you brought Father Nicolo," Sixtus said. He paused.

Salviati leaned toward him, and Giovan heard him say, "Pastor of the Church of San Pellegrino."

"Yes, yes. Of course," Sixtus said. "Welcome, my son."

Salviati watched with narrowed eyes as Nicolo kissed Sixtus's ring.

"His loyalty to you is beyond question, Your Holiness," Giovan continued. "So I have confided in him about the task that you have set for me."

Sixtus nodded and said, "Even a hardened soldier such as yourself needs spiritual guidance."

"Yes, Your Holiness. And I look to him for advice."

Salviati spoke. "Give us your report, Captain."

Giovan spent several minutes recounting his travels and his conversations with political and military leaders in Imola,

Perugia, Tolentino and other cities, and especially with Jacopo de' Pazzi in Florence. They discussed the number of troops available, their reliability, and agreed that they would be adequate to control Florence while a new government was being established.

"And so, Your Holiness," Giovan said in summary, "while it has taken almost a year, all is finally in readiness."

"We are most pleased," Sixtus said.

Giovan bowed.

"But," Salviati said, "Lorenzo and his brother still rule Florence, do they not?"

"Yes, Your Eminence. Of course that is true," Giovan replied.

"Then, with all the pieces in place," Salviati continued, "what prevents you from returning to Florence and completing your work?"

Sixtus watched Salviati as he talked, and now he turned to Giovan with questioning eyes. "Indeed. Is there some problem, Captain?" he asked.

Giovan swallowed. He had served this Pope for many years, and he believed that they had built at least a small rapport.

"I wonder, Your Holiness," he said, "if the deaths of Lorenzo and Giuliano are necessary."

Salviati's eyebrows shot up.

"What do you mean, Captain?" Sixtus asked, appearing puzzled.

"Perhaps they could be kidnapped—"

"This is not for a soldier to decide," Salviati snapped.

Sixtus raised his hand and Salviati leaned forward in his seat, his eyes hard and beady, staring at Giovan.

"When first we spoke of this, Your Holiness said you wanted no killing," Giovan said.

"Yes, we did—" Sixtus started to say.

"They must die," Salviati cried, leaping out of his chair. "This has been decided."

Giovan looked at Sixtus, who seemed surprised at this outburst, and then at Salviati, who was breathing hard and staring back at Giovan. It was clear to him now. For the archbishop, this is not about loyalty to His Holiness's wishes. He wants revenge on Lorenzo for opposing his appointment to the bishopric of Pisa. And he lusts for political control over Pisa, now dominated by nearby Florence. If Lorenzo and Giuliano die, both goals will be obtained.

"Compose yourself, Archbishop," Sixtus said, his voice now stern.

Salviati resumed his seat, pulled a handkerchief from his sleeve and wiped his brow.

"Captain, you are correct," Sixtus said. "It would be better with no killing. But we also promised dispensation for any acts that are necessary. Surely, you remember that."

"Yes, of course," Giovan replied. "But if I can find a way —"

Sixtus threw up his hands and sighed with frustration.

For a moment, nobody spoke.

Then Salviati leaned forward again, his eyes calculating. "You want money," he said.

"No, Your Eminence."

"Then what, Captain?"

Giovan pulled himself up straight and faced Sixtus. "I only want to serve my Pope with honor," he said.

"I don't believe you," Salviati said. "There's something more."

How could Giovan tell them that he did not want to kill the Medici brothers? What could he say?

"Forgive me, Your Holiness, Your Eminence," Nicolo said, creeping forward a step, his voice shaking. "If I may speak, I humbly beg to remind you that Captain Batista's son, Matthias, died without being in a state of grace."

"Ah," Salviati said. He leaned back in his chair, a clear look of satisfaction on his face. He smiled at Giovan.

"Tell us what you are thinking," Sixtus said to Salviati.

"Holiness," Salviati replied, "I think there is a solution to the problem of the Captain's reluctance to do what must be done. Perhaps an indulgence for his son?"

"Oh," Sixtus said, surprised. He asked Giovan, "Do you believe your son is in Purgatory?"

"Yes, Your Holiness, since his death nine years ago."

"Such a shame." Sixtus turned back to Salviati. "I think an indulgence can be arranged, don't you, Archbishop?"

Salviati nodded and replied, "That would seem to be most appropriate."

Stunned, Giovan dropped to his knees in front of Sixtus. "Thank you, Your Holiness. It never occurred to me that I could ask for such a great gift." After years of prayer, it seemed that Matthias would finally be taken from Purgatory and would join Jesus Christ in Heaven.

"It brings us joy to bestow such a beneficence on our worthy servant," Sixtus said.

"Please, Your Holiness. When might this be done?" Giovan asked, still kneeling.

"These things take time, Captain," Salviati said. "You must have patience."

"Yes, Your Eminence, of course."

"So it is settled," Salviati said. "That brings us back to the topic. When can you complete your holy mission?"

Giovan climbed to his feet, thinking. "We need to set a date. And then we can send messages to the lords who are providing the troops, and to Jacopo de' Pazzi in Florence."

"A date," Sixtus said. "Of course." He glanced at Salviati.

"Soon," the Archbishop said.

Sixtus thought for a moment. "Captain," he said finally, "we wish this thing to be done by Easter."

Giovan tried to remember the date of Easter for that year.

"The twenty-second day of March," Nicolo said, his voice just above a whisper. "Three weeks."

Easter, Giovan said to himself. That reminded him of something he had heard about Lorenzo. Yes, that might work.

"Upon my honor," Giovan said. "Lorenzo and Giuliano de' Medici will be dead by Easter. You may rely on me, Your Holiness."

Sixtus raised his hand and blessed Giovan.

Salviati stood and accompanied Giovan and Nicolo to the door.

"Captain," he said, "I hope there is no misunderstanding about this matter." His voice was steely hard. "The indulgence for your son is contingent on the deaths of Lorenzo and Giuliano. If they live, your son stays where he is, continuing to suffer our Lord's redemptive wrath."

Giovan led Nicolo, still a bit dazed, through the outer courtyard to a wooden drawbridge, which they crossed over to the top of the outer defensive wall directly above the main gate. They stood with their arms resting on the parapet, looking down on the Ponte Sant'Angelo and across the river, where a thousand columns of smoke ascended into the sky as the people of Rome cooked their noon meal. At this time of day, it was impossible for Giovan to distinguish whether some of these spires came from the marble burners.

"I often stand here, especially in the morning," Giovan said.

"How well do you know Archbishop Salviati?"

"I first met him almost a year ago, when we started this task."

"Do you trust him?" Nicolo asked.

Giovan thought. "He seems loyal to His Holiness."

A soldier approached, marching along the top of the wall, his uniform tidy and his halberd held rigidly across his shoulder. Giovan and Nicolo watched as he saluted, and marched past them, his eyes staring straight ahead.

When he was out of earshot, Nicolo chuckled. "The word has spread. They all know you're back now."

Giovan smiled. "Nicolo, my friend. I knew I was right to have you join me today. Thanks to you, poor Matthias will finally join our Lord in Heaven."

"God be praised. So you are at peace with the killing of these men?" Nicolo asked. "These good men?"

"They are enemies of His Holiness. As I said before, a soldier kills, and sometimes he must kill good men. I do it as a duty for my Pope, my honor, and my son. When the times comes, I won't hesitate."

"It's best that you do not," Nicolo said. "All depends on your success. Perhaps even your own life."

"True enough. But what good is a soldier who fears for death at the hands of his enemies?"

"I fear the risk may come from your allies."

"I will trust in God," Giovan replied.

He heard footsteps on the drawbridge behind them, and Archbishop Salviati joined them. Giovan forced himself to look respectful, a skill he had perfected after years of soldiering.

Salviati had no interest in taking in the view, and he ignored Nicolo. He held out a brocaded purse to Giovan and shook it so the coins inside jingled.

Giovan put up his hands in protest.

"Don't be a fool, Captain. Take the money. Why shouldn't you?"

Giovan eyed the purse, tempted. Then he shook his head.

Salviati put the purse on the parapet. "Captain," he said. "Have you had any thoughts on the details of the attack?"

"Yes, Your Eminence. I understand that Lorenzo usually travels to Rome for Easter."

"Go on."

"With him outside Florence," Giovan continued, "it would be a simple matter to attack his party with a modest number of soldiers."

"And Giuliano?"

"If he accompanies Lorenzo, all the better. If not, we will find him on the streets or even in his house. If the attack on Lorenzo is done correctly, it will be some time before word gets back to Florence. He will not be forewarned, and he can be killed without difficulty. My troops will seize the city government, and Jacopo de' Pazzi will raise the citizens against the last of the Medici supporters."

Salviati said nothing for a moment. Then he said, "His Holiness is quite serious about having this completed by Easter."

"I understand."

"Perhaps," Salviati continued, "I might contribute something to your plan."

"Please, Your Eminence."

"Have you heard of the recent elevation of the Cardinal of San Giorgio?"

"No, Your Eminence. I have been traveling," Giovan said.

"He's sixteen years old," Nicolo said.

"That is correct," Salviati said. "He lives in my house in Pisa, and he's my nephew. And he has an old Greek tutor."

"Yes?"

"He used to teach Lorenzo and Giuliano. I think we might use him as a spy."

"That would be useful," Giovan said.

"You will hear more from me about this soon. Good day, Captain."

As Salviati turned and walked back across the bridge, Giovan picked up the brocaded purse and handed it to Father Nicolo. "For the church," he said. "Repair the fresco, repair the golden sky."

"Signore Giuliano is here," Bruna said, sticking her head inside Fioretta's door. "Do you feel well enough to see him?"

"Of course," Fioretta replied. "Quick, fetch my brush and Venetian mirror." She tossed the almost-completed baby nightdress that she had been embroidering onto the bed beside her and slipped her mother's thimble into a pocket of her gown. As Bruna held the polished steel hand mirror for her, Fioretta ran the silver-handled brush that Giuliano had given her through her hair. "How do I look?" she asked.

"Well enough."

Fioretta pinched her cheeks, took one last look in the mirror and then shouted, "Giuliano," knowing he could hear her. "Giuliano, please come up."

Bruna scowled at her lack of formality, but Fioretta didn't care a fig about that. Giuliano had sent Bruna to her after Lucia had left, and while the old woman did all the work that could be expected of her, she clearly had reservations about Fioretta. Fortunately, her loyalty to Giuliano and the fact that she was Stefano's mother, made her reliable and discreet.

Giuliano bounded into the room, a bouquet of calla lilies in his outstretched hands. "Look what I've brought you from the hothouse. The first lilies of Spring."

Fioretta grinned as she accepted his tender kiss.

"You look ever more lovely each day," Giuliano said, sitting on the bed and handing the flowers to Bruna. "How is our son?" They had gotten into the habit of speaking of the baby as if they knew it would be a boy.

"Still quiet."

"And how are you feeling?"

"Very well," Fioretta replied. "Still no bleeding or cramps —"

Giuliano blushed at this, uncomfortable as he always was with the details of her pregnancy.

"—and I feel good. In fact, I'm bored. I'm sick to death of embroidering. I want to get out of bed and stand at the window. Or go downstairs. Or for a walk outside. But Bruna won't let me."

It was true. With perhaps three months left before the baby came, she felt much better. Fioretta suspected that this was because the doctor Giuliano had sent was no longer bleeding her. Lucia had been right about that.

Fioretta noticed that Stefano had followed Giuliano into the room and stood next to his mother by the door.

"Stefano, how is Lucia?" she asked.

"She is well enough, lady," Stefano replied. He glanced at Giuliano, who nodded. "Please, lady," he went on. "Can't you make up your quarrel with her so she can come back to you? She drives me mad with her complaints and her nagging."

Fioretta felt like laughing but suppressed it, not wanting to be cruel to poor Stefano. She saw that Giuliano's eyes were bright with amusement.

"It's Lucia who left me," she replied, and her lightheartedness evaporated. Did she want Lucia back? Could they live together again? Did Lucia hate her baby? Fioretta shook her head.

Stefano's shoulders slumped.

"Leave us now," Giuliano said.

When Stefano and Bruna had gone downstairs, Fioretta leaned forward and gave Giuliano a long, deep kiss, and he enveloped her in his arms. His hand touched her breast, grown plump with her pregnancy, but then he stopped. For him, passion and pregnancy were incompatible. But Fioretta loved the fact that he was tempted.

"Poor Stefano," she said.

Giuliano laughed. "All he has to do is cast her out of his bed," he said. "There are other places where she can sleep."

"I think he loves her," Fioretta said.

"Perhaps. True love is rarely easy." Giuliano stood up and walked to the window. He examined the rotting frame and tapped one of the cracked panes. "I'll have this window fixed," he said. His eyes swept around the room, alighting for a moment on the marriage chest. He glanced away. "I have some news," he said.

As Fioretta waited, her hand slipped into her pocket and grasped her mother's thimble.

"I must travel to Piombino," Giuliano continued.

"Why?"

Giuliano turned and looked out the window onto the street below. "My brother has arranged my marriage to the daughter of the lord of Piombino."

Fioretta closed her eyes and forced herself to take deep breaths. It had finally happened, just as she feared. When the midwife visited, she brought the gossip of the city, and as always, much of it was about the Medici brothers. Fioretta tightened her fist around the thimble.

"It's a political marriage, of course," Giuliano continued, still not looking at her.

"Of course." The thimble pressed deep into her palm. She kept her voice even, calm.

"It will change nothing," Giuliano continued.

"Is she beautiful?" Fioretta asked.

"I don't know."

"But surely your brother's negotiators brought you some kind of likeness—a cameo, a portrait," Fioretta said.

Giuliano turned around and looked at her. "I thought you'd be angry," he said. "None of this will make a difference." He sat on top of the closed marriage chest. "You'll always—"

This was too much for Fioretta. "Get away from that!"

Giuliano leaped to his feet.

"You liar," Fioretta continued, her voice now shrill. "You'll marry this woman, make love to her, live with her, have children with her. You'll have no time for me. Or for our son."

"That's not true, I swear." He started to kneel at her bed, but she pushed him away. The thimble dropped to the floor.

"I cannot stand to see you," she cried.

Giuliano stooped, picked up the thimble and set it on the bed next to her. Then he backed away, opened the door and stood next to it. His face showed relief. "Of course this makes you angry. I understand. I'll come back tomorrow, when you've—well, I'll come by tomorrow." He fled.

Fioretta buried her face in her hands, sobbing. Giuliano. How could he do this to her? She hoped the girl in Piombino was fat and stupid, and that thought slowed her tears. Yes, fat and stupid—just what Giuliano deserved. The great fool.

The door opened and Bruna leaned in. "Are you well,

lady?" she asked.

"Leave me alone," Fioretta said, wiping her tears with her sleeve.

Bruna closed the door.

Fioretta picked up her mother's thimble and slipped it over her finger, taking some comfort in its familiar feel, in the memory of her mother wearing it for countless hours as she worked at her sewing or embroidery.

Fioretta threw back the bedcovers and swung out her feet. Steadying herself by gripping the bedpost, she stood, and for a moment, the room swam before her eyes. Then it steadied, she let go, and with confident steps, she walked to the marriage chest. Fioretta sat down and looked around. For the first time in weeks, she saw her world from a different aspect.

She had known for years that she would probably never marry, not to Giuliano, nor to any man because she had no dowry. But now she understood that knowing something in your head is very different from knowing it in your heart.

Fioretta stood up, almost without thinking about it. She turned to the window, unlatched it and pushed it open. Cold, bracing air blew into the room. Leaning out, her belly against the sill, she watched a woman carrying a baby as she hurried up the street with another young child trailing behind her. Fioretta gripped the window sill.

She had no mother, no father, no husband, no friends. And soon she would have no Giuliano. What kind of life was this? What could she do?

Then, a miracle happened.

Inside her, something moved. Astonished, Fioretta placed her hands across the top of her abdomen, waiting. It happened again. Just a little twitch, but the meaning of it flooded through her consciousness. Finally, the quickening. Her baby, previously an abstract idea, an inconvenience, had finally came alive for her.

Yes, she was alone today. She had been abandoned by everyone she had ever loved. But this baby was hers, he needed her, and he would love her until the end of her days.

Now was the time to rise up, to be strong, be a she-wolf, a lioness, a mother. All her life, she had let the winds of fate blow her way one way and another, but that must end today.

Wrapping both arms beneath her belly, cradling her child, Fioretta stared out the window.

But what to do? Her baby would need more than her love. He would need food, a safe home, teachers. How could she provide these things? Giuliano said he would help, but that wouldn't last. He'd be caught up in his new wife, his new family. Somehow she must guarantee that her son would have security. After all he was a Medici. A Medici...

The sound of a bell clanging the hour came to her, and she raised her eyes to the Signoria tower peeking over the top of the building across the street.

And she knew the solution. It was simple, obvious and it solved everything. It was also impossible.

Despite Lorenzo, despite Giuliano's irresolution, despite the world conspiring against her—Giuliano must marry her.

Yes, it was impossible. They had discussed it many times. Lorenzo would not allow it because he needed a political marriage.

But it was said that Lorenzo loved his brother.

So she would somehow convince Lorenzo of Giuliano's love for her. She had the sonetto that Giuliano had written to her. Surely that would help.

Once Lorenzo approved, Giuliano's doubts would end. They would marry. They would be together, raising their son, in safety and comfort for the rest of their lives.

Her heart swelled with hope.

But what to do?

And it came to her. While Giuliano was in Piombino, she would go to see Lorenzo.

Twenty-Five Years Earlier

Passing a group of soldiers, Thadeous scrambled to the top

of the wall where Lauro stood next to Captain Giovan. Thadeous knew he shouldn't be there. But he was worried about Lauro who, despite his wound, had refused to leave the wall. Behind him, the sun was rising over the city.

"You should be working," Giovan said as Thadeous stepped beside Lauro. Giovan gestured at the hundreds of soldiers and civilians nearby who were hauling stones and dirt to the top of the wall, struggling to repair the previous day's damage.

"They're almost finished for the night, sir," Lauro said before Thadeous could answer. "The bombardment will start soon." He wore his full armor and clutched his helmet under one arm.

Giovan grunted and turned back to look at the thousands of Turks on the far side of the wall. Out of Captain Giovan's view, Lauro put his hand on Thadeous's buttock and squeezed. It seemed that Lauro was feeling fine.

"There, see that dark line?" Captain Giovan said, pointing.

Thadeous squinted into the gloom, trying to see.

"It's the top of a trench, sir," Lauro said.

"Right. Look carefully. Do you see any change from yesterday?"

"The color of the dirt."

Giovan nodded with approval.

"It's the dirt they're digging from the tunnel," Thadeous said. "That's the entrance."

After Lauro's heroic defense, the Turks had not attacked through the tunnel far below their feet. Instead, they'd blocked the smaller Greek tunnel so they could continue to expand their gallery. Bringing down the wall was their goal, not a minor skirmish.

"Yes. They spread it out during the night, hoping we won't notice," Giovan replied.

"We're ready, sir," Lauro said. Behind him, soldiers waited, short swords in their hands.

"What? I don't understand," Thadeous said.

"They won't expect a sortie now," Lauro said. "We'll kill the miners and block the entrance."

"But that's suicide. And even if you succeed, they'll just bring in more miners and dig out the entrance."

"It'll gain us a day," Giovan said. "Giustiniani sent word that we must hold the wall—no matter what is required. The Pope's ships are expected soon."

Lauro stood taller at this and drew his sword. Giovanni Giustiniani was also from Genoa, and Emperor Constantine had appointed him commander of all the defensive forces.

"But what if there's a better way?" Thadeous asked, thinking desperately. "What if we can destroy that big area beneath the wall—"

"The gallery," Lauro said.

"—yes, the gallery. What if we can set fire to their timbers. It would collapse. That would set them back for many days."

"That only works if we can do it soon," Giovan said. "In a few more days the gallery will be so big its collapse would bring down the wall. We'd be doing their work for them."

"Besides," Lauro added, "how do we fire the timbers? The gallery must now be large enough to hold both soldiers and miners. We could only send in one man at a time through our small tunnel."

"Lauro," Thadeous said. "Have you read the biography of Emperor Alexios?"

Puzzled, Lauro shook his head.

"What has this to do—" Giovan said.

"Hear me out, Captain," Thadeous said. "It describes a weapon, a kind of liquid fire sprayed from a ship to burn others. Greeks have used it for hundreds of years."

"I've heard of this," Giovan said. "We call it *Greek Fire*."

"That's it," Thadeous said. "We could spray the fire into the gallery from our tunnel. It will kill the miners and soldiers, and burn the support timbers."

Giovan considered this. "And after that, they'd be afraid to try again for some time, perhaps for many days. But is there any in Constantinople?"

"You say it's used on Greek ships?" Lauro asked Thadeous.

"Yes."

"If there is any here, it will be in the Golden Horn."

The Golden Horn was the wide river bordering the north side of Constantinople. A massive iron chain stretched across its mouth, protecting scores of anchored Greek vessels from the Turkish ships stationed outside in the Bosphorus Straights.

"Captain, give me ten men," Lauro said. "I'll go to the harbor, and I will find this Greek Fire."

"If you are not back by nightfall, we will attack the entrance," Giovan said. "And Thadeous will go with us."

Captain Giovan snored on Pletho's pallet.

Thadeous lay on his own, trying to get some sleep, trying to force the image of burning timbers and screaming miners from his head. He tried to think of Lauro instead. How long would it be before Lauro returned? Would he bring the Greek Fire? And would it be in time? Giovan had said that Thadeous would participate in the attack on the Turkish tunnel entrance if Lauro was late. Surely, he didn't mean it. He must know that Thadeous would be useless. He must be trying to motivate Lauro to hurry. Did that mean Giovan knew about them? Did he know Thadeous and Lauro had snatched passion and love when they could, and it was in the same bed where Thadeous now lay?

No, Giovan didn't suspect. When Thadeous had suggested they rest in Pletho's house, Giovan had agreed without hesitation, and he was not self-conscious as they each stripped before climbing onto the straw pallets.

The snoring stopped. Giovan sat up and glanced over at Thadeous. "Did you sleep?" he asked.

"Not really."

Giovan grunted, stood up naked and scratched himself. He walked to the doorway, had a brief conversation with the sentry posted outside and returned.

"Mid-afternoon," he said. "No news. Do you have any food here?"

Thadeous shook his head.

"It's getting hard to find even rats," Giovan said. "As in any siege, the main danger is starvation."

Thadeous rolled over in his bed, careful to keep his blanket covering his nakedness. "What will happen if the wall falls, and the Turks take the city?" he asked.

"There is no *if*."

"What do you mean?" Thadeous asked.

"The Turks will certainly take Constantinople."

"No! What about the ships sent by the Pope? If they arrive in time—"

Giovan shrugged. "If they are coming, and I doubt that, they won't make it past the Turkish warships. Did you see them? There are hundreds blockading the city. And even if the Pope's ships do get through, how many soldiers will be aboard? A few hundred? And how much food can they carry? Maybe rations for a few more days."

"Then why continue to fight? What's the point?" Thadeous asked.

"We fight for Christ. And I am paid to fight."

"So when the city falls?"

"We will die. Hopefully it will be a quick death." Giovan began to pull on his underclothes and armor. "Get dressed."

"I thought there was hope," Thadeous said as he rose from his bed and began to put on his own clothes.

"There's always hope. We must put our faith in God."

"So you admit you don't want to die."

"Of course. I have a wife at home who was with child when I left. I would like to see my son."

"Or daughter."

"Phah," Giovan said. He thumped his chest armor with his fist. "I am Captain Giovan Battista da Montesecco. Of course I will have a son. And he will be strong and brave and smart—a great soldier some day."

"I pray that you live to see him, Captain," Thadeous said.

There was a commotion outside, and the door flew open. Lauro stumbled into the room, his face covered with dust and rivulets of sweat. "I've got it," he said. "I brought the apparatus and the fuel. And a man who knows how to use it."

Lauro sagged against the doorframe, and both Giovan and Thadeous rushed to assist him. He shook them off and led them outside.

Lauro's men stood in the street, eyeing the strange paraphernalia. There was a wooden half-barrel, a leather hose and three clay amphorae. Lauro introduced a Greek sailor who was clearly unhappy at being away from his ship. The sailor explained what must be done, speaking rapidly and looking over his shoulder, back toward the harbor.

Thadeous peered into one of the amphorae. The dark liquid inside had a surprisingly sweet smell, reminding him of a time back in the copper mines of Cyprus. His father, working at the face of the mine, exposed a seam of coal and this same sweet aroma had floated back to where Thadeous labored.

Thadeous knew from his reading that the recipe for this Greek Fire was a state secret guarded by the Byzantines for hundreds of years. The sailor pointed at the half-barrel, into which the contents of one amphora would be poured. The leather hose ran from the bottom of the half-barrel to a bulky bronze nozzle with a handle. When the handle was pumped, the liquid squirted out. The sailor claimed the nozzle had been cleverly crafted so that with vigorous pumping, the flames would shoot out ten yards or more. The liquid stream was lit as it exited the nozzle using a candle or taper.

"We'll need him to operate this," Giovan said, pointing at the sailor.

"I promised him he could return to his ship if he came with us," Lauro said. "Please, Captain. I gave him my word of honor."

"Then you better make sure you understand how to work

this contraption," Giovan said. "Because you're going to take it into the tunnel."

"Yes, sir," Lauro replied, his voice dull.

Thadeous stepped over to stand next to Lauro. The poor man was wounded and exhausted. Thadeous put his arm across Lauro's shoulders, no longer caring what Captain Giovan thought. He hugged Lauro to him.

"No. Captain," he said, turning to Giovan. Releasing Lauro, Thadeous picked up the nozzle and worked the handle back and forth. "I understand how this works. I'll go."

Chapter Nine

Three Hours Until Dawn

Giovan had been writing for five hours, and his head began to nod and his eyes close. Then he jerked awake and stared down at what he had just written.

Because Lorenzo wasn't coming, they then deliberated...

He stopped, set down the pen and collapsed onto the cot, staring up at the arched, brick ceiling overhead. Hot irons seem to burn into his back, but he remained silent, willing himself not to move.

"Done writing?" Alfeo asked.

"Let me rest for a while."

Alfeo said nothing.

Giovan closed his eyes, but after a moment, a piece of paper swirled up behind his eyelids. It was covered with script in his own hand. The page floated this way and that, and then it was joined by another, and another. They danced before him. Giovan squeezed his eyes tight, but it didn't help. A page surged closer, its text smudged, unreadable. But one word grew, and its letters burned with bright red flames, searing into Giovan's conscience. The word was *Thadeous*.

Giovan's eyes snapped open.

Thadeous Phylacus. Giovan remembered the boy he had met in Constantinople, twenty-five years ago. Then, just one month before this night, they had met again in Pisa, and even though Giovan had saved Thadeous's life in Constantinople, still the old man hated him.

Ignoring his pain, Giovan sat up and saw the unfinished page on the table. In the writing of this confession, he had come to the point where he must speak of the attack and list the conspirators.

One Month Earlier

Careful to keep his expression neutral, Giovan watched the church's newest and youngest Cardinal. His Eminence Raffaele Sansoni Galeoti Riario, elevated to this office just two months before, could hardly sit still in a big upholstered chair while Archbishop Salviati patiently explained what was to be done.

They were in the *sala* of Salviati's palazzo in Pisa. This largest room in the house spanned the entire width on the second floor above the front door, and the four large windows admitted very little light as the street in front was narrow and gloomy. It had high ceilings and a gleaming Terrazzo floor. A poorly painted portrait of Sixtus looked down on them.

"So, Your Eminence, I suggest you write the letter today," Salviati said. "I can help with the composition, if you like."

It was clear to Giovan the chair occupied by Raffaele belonged to the archbishop. Giovan suppressed a smile, knowing that Salviati had no choice but to defer to his sixteen-year-old nephew. It was a mystery as to why His Holiness would elevate this boy to the most powerful position in the Church, second only to the Pope, but it didn't matter as long as Giovan was able to perform his military duties. As it turned out, Archbishop Salviati had found a way to use this development to their advantage.

Giovan had been forced to abandon his plan to assassinate Lorenzo on his way to Rome, as Lorenzo had decided at the last minute to stay in Florence for Easter. His Holiness was furious with all the conspirators, especially Giovan and Archbishop Salviati.

As a soldier, Giovan had long understood that in any military campaign there were setbacks, but the failure of his plan stung him to his heart. He had failed both his Pope and his patron, Count Riario. And try as he might, he had not been able to find an alternative scheme in the three weeks since

Easter.

Then Salviati had summoned Giovan to Pisa and proposed his own plan. And fortunately, it seemed to have a chance of success. The plan required that Raffaele write to Lorenzo suggesting he'd like to visit Florence. Even with all his political power, Lorenzo would not dare to ignore a Cardinal, and he would surely send a formal invitation. But Lorenzo wouldn't know that amongst the Cardinal's large retinue there would be the fifty soldiers Giovan had obtained from Perugia.

Raffaele must know nothing of this plan. Even though he was part of the immensely powerful Riario family—along with His Holiness and Salviati—it had been decided that the boy was too young, inexperienced and innocent to take part in the assassinations of the Medici brothers.

"Lorenzo has the best collection of art in Italy," Raffaele said. "I so look forward to meeting him. And his brother Giuliano is said to be amusing."

"Indeed," Salviati said.

Something about Raffaele tugged at Giovan's memory. Raffaele was a little chubby and had an air of dissoluteness. Of course. Raffaele reminded him of his own son, Matthias, dead at sixteen, the same age as this boy before him.

"And then on to Rome, and San Giorgio, and my own palazzo," Raffaele said, almost hopping up and down in the chair with excitement.

"Perhaps Your Eminence would like start the letter to Lorenzo now?" Salviati asked. He stood. "And you might find it more comfortable to work in your own bedroom?"

"Of course. I know just what to say," Raffaele replied, leaping up. Without a word to Giovan, he rushed from the room.

Salviati took a deep breath and then moved over and sat in the chair vacated by Raffaele. "Captain," he said, gesturing to a bench nearby.

Giovan sat.

"Tell me about the troops," Salviati said.

"In addition to the fifty Perugian foot soldiers, there are thirty crossbowmen from Imola, and a score from Tolentino. And most important, Federico, Lord of Urbino, has promised His Holiness he will send six hundred more soldiers, one third of them mounted."

"And you are confident of these promises?"

"Yes, Your Eminence," Giovan said.

"Lorenzo will no doubt host a banquet honoring our young friend, probably after Mass on Sunday. Giuliano would surely be there, too. You can kill both of them during the dinner. You'll have sufficient troops nearby to rush in and do whatever needs to be done."

Giovan thought this might work. "And then I'll lead my men to the Signoria and take control of the city government," he said. "Meanwhile, Jacopo de' Pazzi will rally the people in the streets."

Salviati nodded, and then he stared at Giovan, his eyes drilling into Giovan's, not speaking.

He's wondering about my loyalty after that audience with His Holiness in Sant'Angelo. It was a mistake to express my concerns about killing Lorenzo and Giuliano, a mistake to let my feelings for these men interfere with my duty, my honor. I know what must be done. Once these men are dead, and His Holiness grants the indulgence for Matthias, all will be well. That's all I need to think about.

Giovan stared back at Salviati, meeting his eyes.

Salviati nodded and then gave Giovan a death's head smile. "And so, Captain, after a year, we approach the culmination of this solemn task given to us by His Holiness. I pray that it goes well, for the sake of both our souls."

It seemed Salviati was worried. "Yes, Your Eminence." Giovan started to stand, but Salviati gestured for him to sit back down.

"There is another matter," Salviati said. "In Rome, I mentioned we need someone inside the Medici household who will keep us informed."

"A spy," Giovan said, nodding with approval.

"Exactly." Salviati spoke to a servant standing near the door. "Send him in."

A moment later, a old man shuffled into the room.

"Ah, Professore Thadeous," Salviati said. "A chair for him."

Thadeous? Giovan stared as old man hobbled forward, stooped to kiss Salviati's ring and then sank into a chair provided by the servant. He wore a shabby teaching gown. Every breath rattled in his chest. Twenty-five years had passed and, if Giovan had not heard the man's name, he would not have recognized him. The last time Giovan had seen Thadeous was at Galata on the Golden Horn.

"Professore Thadeous was a tutor in the Medici household many years ago," Salviati said. "He taught Lorenzo and Giuliano."

"Yes, well…" Thadeous said. He turned his gaze from Salviati to Giovan and, as his eyes focused, they widened in astonishment. "Captain Giovan," he cried, standing back up, his face working in rage.

Giovan was surprised at this. Twenty-five years had passed, after all.

"You know each other?" Salviati asked, amused.

Thadeous stared at Giovan, his mouth twisting in anger, unable to speak.

"Yes," Giovan said. "Many years ago in Constantinople."

"How interesting," Salviati said.

Giovan remembered the Greek Fire.

"Thadeous was a great help in defending the city," Giovan said. "And in the end, he fought bravely."

"There, Professore," Salviati said. "Surely such fine words can heal whatever quarrel you have with the Captain."

"He tried to kill me. He killed…" Thadeous began to cough, and grasping the arm of the chair, lowered himself into it. Salviati told the servant to pour Thadeous a cup of wine, and this seemed to help.

Giovan shook his head. "You remember it wrong, Thadeous."

"No matter," Salviati said. While he had seemed to be amused by this exchange, now he was getting impatient. He told Thadeous about the proposed visit by Raffaele to Florence, leaving out any mention of the plot against the Medici.

Thadeous seemed to only half-listen, and he continued to glare at Giovan the entire time.

"I want you to accompany the Cardinal," Salviati continued. "As his tutor and advisor, you'll live with him in the Medici palazzo. And we want you to report everything you hear and see to Captain Giovan."

"You want me to spy on my master, the Cardinal?" Thadeous said, turning to Salviati.

"No, no. Mostly we want to know what is happening with the Medici."

"And report to this man?" Thadeous said, pointing at Giovan.

"Yes."

"I refuse. I'll have nothing to do with it."

Salviati leaned forward and fixed Thadeous with an unsympathetic stare. "Professore," he said. "I think perhaps you misunderstand your situation. You are an employee of my household. If you refuse to assist us in this matter, then I'm afraid your service will no longer be required, and I will make sure you do not find another position. You'll be out on the street."

Thadeous's mouth opened as he struggled to keep his breath and his eyes widened.

"On the other hand," Salviati continued, "if you help us, you can look forward to a long and comfortable position as councilor to a young Cardinal. In Rome, no less."

"Listen to him," Giovan said, speaking to Thadeous for the first time. "He speaks for His Holiness."

Thadeous stood up and, with difficulty, pulled his body

erect. "I refuse," he said, and then he turned and left the room.

"It's not possible," the servant said to Fioretta. "You must leave."

He started to shove the door shut, the door through which Fioretta had passed so many times when she had spent the night with Giuliano. Exhausted from walking, she had been leaning against Bruna in the alleyway behind the Medici palazzo, but now she stepped up close to the servant and showed him Giuliano's love poem.

"Lorenzo, your master, will want to see this," she said, her voice hard with determination. "It's news about Giuliano."

"So you say. And I have said it is not possible." He stepped back and slammed the door shut.

Bruna wrapped her arm around Fioretta's waist. "Come child," she said. "You need to rest."

"I'm well enough."

That was true. For the last week, she had been moving around the shop, and had even taken some short walks in the nearby streets with Bruna's help, always wearing her red cloak to hide her pregnancy. The midwife encouraged this.

That morning, Fioretta had decided that with Giuliano now in Piombino, this was the day—the day to see Lorenzo and convince him to let Giuliano marry her. She had tried writing to Lorenzo, asking to see him, but the letter had not been answered. If she could only see Lorenzo, she would show him the poem, and he would recognize Giuliano's handwriting. This must convince him she was not some harlot trying to extort money from the richest family in Florence. It must.

With Bruna's help, she had walked the mile to the Medici palazzo, but it had been for nothing. She wanted to cry, but she clenched her teeth instead. I must find a way.

"Sit, lady," Bruna said, and she helped Fioretta sit on the step before the door. "Rest here." Then she turned and opened the servant's door, reminding the servant inside she was in service to the Medici house. He let her pass.

Fioretta wondered what Bruna was doing. Stefano, her son, was traveling with Giuliano, of course, so she could not be visiting him.

A few minutes later, the door opened and Lucia stepped out onto the street with Bruna behind her. Lucia knelt down next to Fioretta.

"Are you well, lady?" Lucia asked.

"You must not call me that," Fioretta said.

"And what am I to call you?"

"My name. Fioretta."

Lucia gazed at her for a moment. "How is the baby, Fioretta?"

Fioretta felt tears welling up, but she smiled and said, "He kicks now, very hard some times."

Lucia started to reach out toward Fioretta's swollen abdomen, but she pulled her hand back.

"The midwife says all is well," Fioretta continued. "We should see him in another month or so."

Lucia said nothing, but her eyes were soft and glistening.

"And you?" Fioretta asked. "How is it with Stefano?"

"He's a good man." Lucia shrugged. "And he wants me to marry him." She glanced back over her shoulder at Bruna and then whispered, "But he doesn't know what happened to me."

"I think you should tell him. If he loves you, it won't matter."

"What if you are wrong and he forsakes me?"

"Then you can get a clay doll from Nóna and stick it with pins like I did," Fioretta said, suddenly laughing. "You can put it under your bed so he will love you."

Surprised, Lucia laughed, too. "But we share that bed. How would that work? Would he fall in love with himself?"

"Such talk," Bruna said, interrupting them.

"Oh, Bruna," Fioretta said. "Your son just needs a little help to marry the woman he loves. Don't you want that?"

"He needs no help from a witch. And you two don't either."

Fioretta and Lucia glanced at each other, and then replied at the same time, "Yes, Bruna." This made them giggle again.

"We should go back," Bruna said.

Fioretta struggled to stand, and Lucia helped her up. For a moment, they looked at each other, not speaking. Fioretta remembered why she had come to the Medici palazzo. "Lucia," she said, "please help me. I need to see Lorenzo. I'm sure I can convince him to let Giuliano marry me—"

"Stop, Fioretta," Lucia said. "You know it's impossible. Giuliano is visiting his future wife even now."

"She's right," Bruna said.

"But I have this poem Giuliano wrote to me." Fioretta held up the piece of paper. "You remember. Surely when Lorenzo sees it…"

Lucia shook her head. "It won't matter. Giuliano has told you this."

"So you won't help me?" Fioretta said, her voice rising. "You are loyal to the Medici after being in their service for two months, but you have none for me?"

"What you are trying to do is mad. Besides, why should I have loyalty to you? Your family, your father—and yes, especially you—have caused me only grief. It's better I stay here."

"No one is asking you to leave this place," Fioretta said. "Certainly not me."

"Good," Lucia said, whirling away. She stepped through the door and started to push it shut. But she stopped and gazed at Fioretta through the gap, and Fioretta returned the look.

Then Lucia closed the door.

Twenty-Five Years Earlier

Deep beneath the great Theodosian Wall, Thadeous's hands shook as he clutched the brass nozzle. His breaths came in quick succession, like the thumping of a horse's hooves. He had been in this narrow tunnel before, but this time it was completely dark because there was no candle at the entrance shaft behind him. When they broke through to the gallery, there must not be even a hint of light to warn the Turks.

Just ahead, Thadeous heard their own miner digging away loose dirt using only his hands. And behind Thadeous, Giovan crouched, holding a tin lantern taken from Pletho's house. It held a lit candle and was covered by a thick, dark cloth. The leather hose, connected to the nozzle, snaked beneath Giovan's feet to the half-barrel, empty for now, behind him. And on the other side of the barrel, three soldiers cradled the amphorae filled with the mysterious liquid that would set fire to the timbers in the enemy gallery. If all went well, the gallery would collapse while it was still small, and the wall would stand for a few more days.

The digging sounds from the miner stopped. Yesterday, Thadeous had crouched near this spot, and today he again heard the muffled scraping of many shovels. Was the remaining distance to them a few yards—or just a few hand breadths? Thadeous reached forward and touched the back of the miner, causing him to jump and give a suppressed squeal of fright.

"That's enough," the miner whispered as he pushed Thadeous out of the way, scrambling toward the entrance shaft and safety. Earlier, it had been necessary for Giovan to draw his sword and hold it to the man's throat to convince him to do even this much work. Now this miner was escaping to safety while Thadeous remained.

Thadeous moved to the front of the tunnel while Giovan followed him, straightening the hose. Setting down the nozzle, Thadeous groped for the tunnel face in the darkness. He dug into the earth at chest level, scooping it back so it fell at his feet. As he worked, he paused frequently, listening to the sounds of the Turkish miners. Their digging was steady—they were not suspicious.

Thadeous's hand broke through, and he felt nothing but air on his fingertips. He jerked his arm out, leaned forward to peer through the opening and saw a flicker of light. It was the gallery. Thadeous reached back and tapped Giovan twice on the shoulder, and as they had agreed, Giovan thumped the barrel twice with his hand. Soon the tunnel was filled with a sweet smell as the first soldier emptied his amphora into the barrel. There was a momentary glint as Giovan peeked beneath the cloth covering the lantern to confirm the candle was still lit. He tapped Thadeous's shoulder three times, and Thadeous knew all was ready.

He lifted the nozzle's lever and pumped it. He heard only a wheezing sound. The sailor had told him this would happen until the hose filled. Then Thadeous heard a gurgle and liquid dribbled onto the dirt at his feet. He stopped pumping.

The moment had come. Giovan, holding the covered lantern, came up beside him. At the signal from Thadeous, he would remove the cover and pull out the lit candle. While Thadeous worked the lever, Giovan was to hold the candle near the emerging stream, lighting it, and once it was lit, Thadeous would shove the nozzle into the narrow gap, so the liquid fire would spew into the gallery.

Thadeous took a breath, and he heard Giovan do the same.

"Now," Thadeous whispered.

Giovan pulled away the cloth, and it seemed as though the tiny space was flooded with light. As Giovan lifted the candle, Thadeous saw his face, streaked with dirt and sweat.

The Turkish miners might notice the light at any moment, but Thadeous hesitated. He could still try to escape. Lauro was waiting for him. Giovan had said Constantinople would fall anyway. And yet Giovan was here, prepared to give his life, because he was a soldier with honor.

Giovan lifted the candle, shaking it to show his impatience.

Thadeous began to pump. Again there was the wheezing sound, but the liquid began to flow from the nozzle tip, first as just a dribble, but then with sudden force, spraying a large quantity into the dirt at their feet. Giovan lifted the candle just as Thadeous lowered the nozzle toward it, they bumped against each other, and the candle fell. The spilled liquid at their feet burst into a blue hot flame, waist high, and Thadeous screamed as it scorched his bare legs and his hands. He jumped back, more liquid spilling from the nozzle, and the flames flared even higher. He gasped, and hot gas seared into his lungs.

After a moment, the fire consumed itself and died. Trying to ignore the pain in his hands and legs, Thadeous stepped forward again. He coughed, lost his balance and recovered. He heard shouting and the crunch of shovels in front of him. The Turks knew they were there. Soon they would open the passage wide and soldiers would pour through.

The tunnel was not completely dark, and Thadeous was surprised to find a small blue flame still burned at the tip of the nozzle, apparently feeding on some residual fuel inside. Pumping again, he saw the flame blaze out in front of him, and realized all was not lost. He could still do this.

He lifted the nozzle to the hole leading into the enemy gallery and began to pump. The flame blazed through the hole, and Thadeous heard screams from the other side. He pumped harder, jammed the nozzle deeper, and smoky fumes smelling like cooked meat poured back out through the gap. He felt them burn the inside of his chest, but still he pumped and heard more screams.

The nozzle sputtered and the stream of fluid died down to a trickle, barely burning. He needed more fuel—the soldiers needed to pour another amphora into the half-barrel.

"More," Thadeous tried to shout, but only a rasping sound emerged. He flailed around, trying to find Giovan, but he wasn't there. He couldn't catch his breath. His eyes swelled nearly shut. "Captain," he croaked, but there was no response.

Thadeous dropped to his knees, letting the nozzle and hose fall beside him. The flame had gone out completely, starved for fuel.

Thadeous struggled to breathe, every breath an agony. He heard the crackling sound of burning wood, and smoke billowed through the gap in the tunnel face, illuminated by the flames behind it.

Thadeous felt himself slipping into unconsciousness. Where was Captain Giovan?

A breeze blew down the vertical shaft and cooled Thadeous's face. Above, the stars shone in a clear sky and were as bright as goatherd campfires on a distant hillside.

Thadeous lay in the bottom of the wood tub the miners used, and the lifting rope had been attached. Lauro stood beside him, shouting to the men at the top of the shaft. The tub shifted as they began to haul him up. As Thadeous rose, his face came level with Lauro's. Thadeous reached out and touched his cheek.

A muffled roar and a blast of hot air erupted from the tunnel, sweeping over them. The tub twirled around and dropped a bit as the blast struck the men at the top of the shaft. But they recovered and held on.

"Lauro, the gallery collapsed!" Thadeous gasped. He peered up at the wall, visible through the shaft opening above him. The ancient Theodosian Wall still stood. They had succeeded.

Lauro didn't reply and darkness overcame Thadeous.

Twenty-Five Years Later

Thadeous was grateful to young Raffaele. When the boy returned from Rome after his elevation to Cardinal, he had used his new prestige to insist that Thadeous be given a room on the ground floor. No longer was Thadeous forced to climb three flights of stairs, coughing and wheezing, to the tiny attic room with its single window. Now, he sat on a soft bed and gazed out onto the inner courtyard with its pleasant bench, just a few steps away.

But Thadeous could not enjoy his room now. After a quarter of a century, Captain Giovan Battista—the man who killed Lauro—had come back into his life. And Salviati insisted that Thadeous spy on the Medici, reporting to this man.

He had spent three years in Florence, tutoring the young

Giuliano and Lorenzo. They were both remarkable students, with Giuliano showing an appetite for the poems of Ovid and Lucretius, as well as a gift for writing ballads of his own, often salacious. Lorenzo was the better student, loving the stories of Greek philosophers, including Thadeous's old mentor, Pletho, but he was often absent. His father frequently sent him, even at his young age, on diplomatic missions all over northern Italy.

Unfortunately, Lorenzo married a simple religious woman from a powerful Roman family who had no tolerance for classical history or modern ideas. When Lorenzo's father died soon afterwards and Lorenzo came to power at age twenty, he had been forced to dismiss Thadeous in order to keep his new bride happy. But Lorenzo had also provided a generous pension that had supported Thadeous until he had come into the service of Archbishop Salviati.

No, Thadeous would not do as Salviati asked. He would not spy on Giuliano and Lorenzo, and he would not work with Giovan. He had to hope Raffaele would stand by him. Even if Salviati dismissed him, Thadeous hoped Raffaele would employ him in Rome once he established his new household. The boy was immature and caught up with his newly acquired prestige and wealth, but he was good at heart. Thadeous had to hope so. As a sick old man, his greatest fear was being turned out onto the street.

Without a knock, the door swung open, and Salviati walked in. Thadeous stood but made no motion to kiss the Archbishop's ring.

"Look under your bed," Salviati said.

Thadeous stared at him in consternation.

"Go ahead, old man. Look."

"You've stolen it," Thadeous cried out, his voice weak and breathless. There was no need for him to look. It felt like a hole had opened in his chest where his heart had been. He dropped back onto the bed.

Salviati nodded.

For twenty-five years, Thadeous had carried Pletho's

original manuscript, now the only copy of the *Nómoi*. And as he had so often done before, he had hidden it beneath his bed in its leather case, along with his own manuscript about the fall of Constantinople. Looking at the smug Salviati, he knew that both manuscripts were gone.

"Raffaele tells me you've worked on your history for some time," Salviati said. "So many pages. And just the one copy, I'm sure. It would be a shame if something happened to it."

Thadeous stared at Salviati. The man didn't know about the *Nómoi*. Even though his Constantinople history was written on paper, and the *Nómoi* was on parchment, the pages were roughly the same size. Salviati had no doubt glanced at the first few pages and concluded it was all one thick manuscript.

"Where is it?" Thadeous asked.

Salviati turned to leave. "It's safe enough for now. I've entrusted it with your old friend, Captain Battista. While you are in Florence, he will use it to insure your cooperation."

As Salviati left, Thadeous collapsed onto his soft bed, staring through the window at the courtyard, seeing nothing.

Chapter Ten

Two Hours Until Dawn

Giovan awoke because of the cold. He kept his eyes closed, not thinking, just feeling the chill in his feet and hands. It reminded him of when he was a young soldier, lying beside a burned-out campfire in bivouac, just as the sun started to show. As he had done so many times, Giovan started to curl his body tight, trying to conserve warmth—

Once again, pain shot across his back, his wool winter camicia chafing at the scoriada wounds. He opened his eyes and was dismayed to find himself back in the cell, high in the tower above the Palazzo della Signoria. Ignoring the pain, he pushed himself upright on the cot. There was so little time left.

Alfeo set the wine bottle on the table, and Giovan swilled what was left, swirling it around in his mouth, trying to clean away the grit and scum.

"You write?" Alfeo asked.

"Yes, yes, I'll write. There's not much left to tell."

"Maybe two hours to dawn," Alfeo added.

The partially filled page lay before him, and Giovan squinted at his scrawled handwriting, reading the last sentence he had written. What was next? Oh, yes. What to say about Thadeous?

Eight days ago, that broken-down old man had betrayed him. If Giovan mentioned Thadeous in the confession, saying he was part of the conspiracy, that would be the end of Thadeous Phylacus. Just one short sentence would do the job. He dipped the pen in the inkpot.

Instead, he wrote about the endless, last-minute planning, including what had happened that last day before the deed was done.

"...on Saturday at two o'clock, they changed their minds again."

Someone hammered at the door.

"Leave it," Giovan said, continuing to write.

"Captain Giovan. It's me, Paulo."

Giovan's head jerked up.

"I'm alone. Please open the door."

Alfeo looked at Giovan.

"Oh, let him in," Giovan said, throwing down his pen. "But not the priest if he's there."

Alfeo shouted to the guard outside. Giovan heard the iron bolt being withdrawn, and Paulo pushed into the room. In the year since they had started their travels around northern Italy together, the boy had grown at least a handbreadth. His arms and chest were heavier now, and he stood solidly on his feet, as though he was ready for a fight. He carried a leather satchel slung over his back.

But for all that, tears streamed down Paulo's cheeks. "Oh, my Captain," he said as he tossed his satchel on the floor.

"Wipe your face."

Paulo did as he is told.

"Now sit. Here, next to me," Giovan said and Paulo sat. "It seems your fall did you no great harm."

"I didn't fall. You pushed me."

"True enough."

"Why won't you see Father Nicolo?" Paulo asked. "I went all the way to Rome to fetch him, and he's waiting outside."

Giovan shrugged. "You wouldn't understand."

"But you're going to die. You need to confess."

"Perhaps. Listen to me, Paulo. I know my situation is difficult." Forcing a smile, Giovan added, "How do you think I feel about it?"

This did not cheer Paulo. "It's wrong," he said as he glanced over at Alfeo. "They searched me outside, but I see a knife in his boot. Together, we can take it and kill him."

Giovan shook his head. "Alfeo," he said, "please show the

boy your dagger."

Without a change in expression, Alfeo placed the dagger on the table, the word carved into its hilt clearly visible.

"Sicarius!" Paulo cried out. He snatched it up and took a fighting stance, as Filiberto had taught him. "I can kill you," he said to Alfeo. "Tell the guard outside to unbolt the door."

Alfeo took a step back. He gazed at Paulo for a moment and then glanced at Giovan with a hint of a smile.

"Give the dagger back," Giovan said.

"There are only two guards in the stairwell." Paulo was breathing hard. "We'll kill them and escape into the city. We'll be in the countryside before dawn."

"Tell me Alfeo, would you do as he asked?" Giovan said. "Would you tell the guard outside to unbolt the door?"

Alfeo shook his head.

"So the boy will have to kill you."

"He can try."

Nine Days Earlier

Giovan pushed the empty plate away and gulped down the last of the wine in his silver cup. He glanced across the table at Francesco de' Pazzi who, unlike his uncle Jacopo sitting at the head of the table, was fastidious in his eating habits, using a fork instead of his fingers and wiping his mouth with a napkin. Giovan smiled as he imagined this blond dandy eating moldy bread and rotting cheese during a military campaign.

The Pazzi family villa was just a few miles outside of Florence. Earlier, Francesco had strutted around the house and grounds, showing off art and architecture that he declared was the most refined in all of Europe. Having seen the Medici palazzo in Florence and Medici villa at Cafaggiolo, Giovan knew the emptiness of these claims.

Now, they sat at the dining table in the house's sala, with gaudy red silk upholstery and heavy tapestries on the walls depicting knights on horseback in battles and in tournaments. Behind Giovan, a low fire burned in an enameled fireplace.

Archbishop Salviati sat at Jacopo's right hand, the priest Maffei sat on Jacopo's left, next to Giovan. Giovan had edged his chair away from Maffei at the beginning of the meal because the priest stank. As Maffei ate using his fingers, he wiped his hands on his cassock, his head hidden inside the cassock's hood.

The cardinal, young Raffaele, had been left in Florence, happy in the bosom of Lorenzo's hospitality. Thadeous was with him.

It was Saturday afternoon, the day before the High Mass and the planned attack at the banquet afterward. A servant entered and came to stand next to Giovan. "This just arrived, sir," he said as he handed Giovan a note. Giovan broke the seal and read it.

> *Giuliano did not attend the luncheon. He is said to be sick. There is a rumor he is mourning a woman named Simonetta.*
>
> *Thadeous*

Giovan knew that Lorenzo had hosted an informal luncheon for Raffaele earlier that day at the Palazzo Medici.

"Gentlemen," Giovan said as he stood. "I have a message from our spy." He read the note.

"So he may not attend the banquet tomorrow," Francesco said. "Our plans are ruined."

"Calm yourself, Franceschino," Salviati said.

Jacopo ordered the servants to leave the room and told the guards outside that they were not to be disturbed. Turning back to the table, he said, "My nephew exaggerates. But still, our plan may be jeopardized."

"Who is this Simonetta?" Giovan asked.

"I remember her, Simonetta Vespucci," Jacopo said.

"Yes, *La bella Simonetta*," Francesco said. "Years ago, all of Florence talked of Giuliano and the most beautiful woman in Italy. Last year it was rumored that he fell into a melancholy on the first anniversary of her death. It may have happened again."

Salviati waved his hand impatiently. "So perhaps he won't be at the banquet tomorrow. What do we do?"

"It makes no sense to kill Lorenzo alone," Jacopo said. "If Giuliano lives, then we cannot take control of the city."

"So we need to get both men out of the Palazzo Medici together, so we can strike them down at the same time," Salviati said. "Everything depends on that. We must act quickly. His Holiness is furious. It's been five weeks since Easter."

"And," Giovan said, "the six hundred Urbinese soldiers are marching on Florence. They will be outside the walls tomorrow morning. It will be impossible to keep them secret then. We must act now."

No one spoke. For a moment, Giovan thought they might be at an impasse.

"There is a way."

Giovan glanced up and saw the priest, Maffei had spoken for the first time. His face was still hidden beneath his hood.

"Go on," Salviati said.

"Unless Giuliano is on death's bed, surely he will be at Mass tomorrow, along with Lorenzo," Maffei said. "It would be an unforgivable affront to the Cardinal otherwise. They will be together, away from their house, unguarded."

"Perhaps outside the church," Francesco said, his voice high in excitement, "before they go in or, better yet, as they come out."

"No," Jacopo said, shaking his head. "They may arrive and leave separately. And they'll be heavily guarded outside."

"So inside," Salviati said.

"In the Duomo?" Jacopo whispered. "Dear Jesus."

Giovan struggled to understand what these men were saying. Were they truly going to murder Lorenzo the Magnificent and his brother inside a church? Inside the greatest church in all the world? Beneath Brunelleschi's dome?

"It's sacrilege," Giovan said, unable to restrain himself. "In front of God—"

"His Holiness promised to forgive whatever must be done," Salviati said. "You were there. And I trust you remember *all* the consequences if we fail."

"Yes, but, but… There must be a better way."

"Please, Captain," Salviati said. "Tell us your better way."

Giovan felt everyone's eyes on him. "Let me think," he said. He stood, stepped away from the table and gazed into the fireplace. The flames were low.

So, they wish to kill Lorenzo and Giuliano in a church. Giovan put his hand on his sword's hilt. Can I draw this sword and strike Lorenzo down with God watching? Is that sacrilege? Is it honorable? I thought I could do this. And what if I do not? The plot will fail, Matthias will stay in Purgatory and my own life will be in jeopardy. I must do this—for my honor, for His Holiness, for Matthias.

Riding back from Cafaggiolo, Giuliano had said he expected to have a son. And that girl, Fioretta Gorini, was carrying his child. Giovan remembered her lovely face in the portrait in Giuliano's room. He remembered her determination as she stood between the tips of his and Sandro Botticelli's swords in her little shop. What would happen to her? To her child?

Behind him, Jacopo was speaking. "We'll need two assassins," he said. "And they must strike together, at the same exact moment. But Lorenzo and Giuliano may not be next to each other inside, so there must be a signal."

The fire in the fireplace was almost out. Giovan used the iron poker to rearrange the embers so a flame burst out again.

"At the sound of the Sanctus Bell," Maffei said.

Giovan turned around. The Sanctus Bell, signaling the commencement of communion. Dear God, forgive us for even talking of such a thing.

"So two assassins, each striking at the sound of the bell," Salviati said, his voice both cold and approving. "Who will kill Giuliano?"

Francesco de' Pazzi pushed back his chair and climbed to his feet. "I will do it," he said, puffing out his chest. "My family, the Pazzi, the most illustrious and ancient family of Florence, has suffered many indignities from these Medici upstarts for too long. I will kill Giuliano de' Medici."

Jacopo stood and clapped his nephew in the back. "Yes," he exclaimed. "You must represent our family in this holy endeavor."

Archbishop Salviati also stood, and made the sign of the cross before Francesco. "Bless you, my son," he said. "You do God's work."

They all returned to their chairs. Francesco poured more wine into his cup.

"And so, there is Lorenzo," Salviati said.

The moment had come, as Giovan knew it would. He stepped away from the fireplace and came back to the table.

"Gentlemen," he said. "I will not kill Lorenzo."

They stared at him.

Salviati stood. "Captain, do you remember," he said, his voice barely controlled, "when we discussed this very subject in Rome?" He leaned forward, his fists on the table.

"Yes. I said, *I am Lorenzo's assassin.*"

"Precisely. And yet now you will break your word. Have you no honor?"

Giovan drew his sword and, extending his arm across the table, placed the tip against Salviati's chest. "You know nothing of my honor," Giovan added, his voice low, "because you have none yourself. Do not tempt me."

Salviati glared down at the bright blade. His face flushed, but then he took a breath and put his hands up. "There is no need for this, Captain." His eyes showed shrewdness, calculation.

Giovan laid his sword on the table amongst the pots and plates, its tip still pointing at Salviati. "Now listen to me, gentlemen," he said. "Have no doubt about my determination to complete this task His Holiness has set for us. I will lead the Perugians and capture the members of the Signoria. Someone else must kill Lorenzo."

"And if we do not agree?" Salviati asked.

"This task will fail. And we all suffer the consequences. Including you, Archbishop."

"But, if you refuse to kill Lorenzo, why do we need you?"

Giovan smiled. "The soldiers are loyal to me. I've been traveling for a year gathering military support. It was I who received commitments from the lords of Tolentino, Imola and Perugia."

"Still, I am Archbishop of Pisa. I represent His Holiness. They must acknowledge my authority."

"You are one of many archbishops. I am the Captain of His Holiness's Apostolic Palace Guard, the commander of all his military. These soldiers will follow my orders, not yours."

Salviati glared at Giovan.

"He's right," Jacopo said. "Archbishop, listen to him." Francesco nodded his agreement.

"And afterward?" Salviati asked.

"I will place my life and my soul into the hands of His Holiness. If we are successful, He will see that I have served him well."

"Archbishop, we have no choice," Jacopo said. He looked back and for the between Salviati and Giovan. "Both of you sit. Captain Giovan, we are agreed."

Salviati stood for a moment longer and then dropped into his chair.

Leaving his sword on the table, Giovan also sat.

Everyone looked at Salviati. He took a sip of wine, and said nothing.

Jacopo glanced around the table. "So, as the Archbishop said, there is the matter of Lorenzo. I would do it, of course, but I have other duties. Only I can raise the citizens of Florence."

Salviati stared at Giovan. "Then who?" he asked.

Next to Giovan, Father Maffei stood and threw back his hood. His thin, dog-like lips trembled. His eyes were wide and wild. "For Volterra!" he cried out, "I will be Lorenzo's assassin."

Maffei? Could this weasel of a man kill Lorenzo de' Medici?

"A priest," Jacopo said. "Who better? He can stand near Lorenzo and no one will suspect."

Giovan was skeptical. So everything would depend on a fop and a priest. He turned to Francesco. "Are you skilled with a knife?"

"Of course," Francesco replied. Then he whipped out a dagger from beneath his tunic, flipped it into the air and caught it by its bare tip. The dagger had a golden hilt adorned with pearls.

Giovan turned back to Maffei. "And you?"

"I'm a poor priest. I have no dagger, and I have no experience with one. But God will guide my hand."

The door swung open and Paulo charged in, followed by Filiberto who was trying to restrain him.

"Take this," Paulo cried as he held out his dagger. "I call it Sicarius."

"You told Paulo about Volterra," Giovan said. "And about our mission."

"Yes, I'm sorry," Filiberto said.

They stood in Giovan's room after the meeting with the door closed. Paulo and the priest had gone to the stable, where Paulo would attempt to teach Maffei something about using his dagger.

"You were listening at the door," Giovan said. "What else did you hear?"

"Tomorrow Lorenzo will get what is due him."

"For Volterra. Tell me, my friend. Will this make your wife happy?"

Filiberto thought about this. "She's happy now. Or she will be when this long campaign is over and I am home again."

"Will you tell her that you had a part in Lorenzo's death?"

"I think not," Filiberto said, shaking his head. "Twice I

have been welcomed by the Medici household. I think Lorenzo must pay for Volterra, but I don't hate him."

"Nor do I," Giovan said. "It's difficult. But we do it for our Pope, for our honor. And I do it for another reason."

Filiberto appeared as if he was going to ask Giovan a question.

"I want to show you something," Giovan said. He turned and lifted his saddlebag from a hook on the back of the door, laid it on the bed, and unbuckled its strap. Inside was a leather case from which Giovan pulled a stack of pages. He took it closer to the window. When Salviati had given this to him in Pisa, he had not taken time to examine it.

The top page was in Latin, written in a careful, neat script. Salviati had told him this was a history written by Thadeous.

"You don't read Latin?" Giovan said, knowing Filiberto could barely read his own name.

Filiberto snorted at the idea.

The stack of pages was thick, four finger-widths at least. Giovan flipped through them and realized they were actually two manuscripts, the first on paper, and the second on crackling parchment.

Giovan squinted at the scrawled, blocky letters on the first parchment page. They were not Latin letters. Greek perhaps? A memory of twenty-five years before rose to the surface of his mind like a bubble in a wine cup. He had seen these same pages before; they were spread out on a table with the young Thadeous standing before them. This was the manuscript he had copied for the Emperor.

"You know Thadeous Phylacus, the teacher in Cardinal Raffaele's retinue?" he asked Filiberto.

"Yes. The man hates you."

Giovan sighed. "That's true. A long time ago, I committed a crime against him. Or so he believes." Giovan gathered the pages together and put them back in their leather case. "Filiberto, I have a task for you."

"You want me to go help Paulo teach that priest to use a

dagger?"

"Well, yes. That would be good. But there's something else." Giovan put the case back in his saddlebag and turned back to Filiberto. "If anything happens to me tomorrow, I want you to return these pages to Thadeous."

"One year," Fioretta cried out as she paced in her room from the door to the wedding chest to the window and back.

It was one year ago that she and Lucia had gone to the jousting tournament to see Giuliano compete. She remembered hurrying through the streets of Florence in her red cloak, the cloak he had bought for her and that matched the color of Giuliano's team. For a time, she had been happy. Even Lucia had been happy.

Then she had caught sight of Giuliano's banner, and her happiness turned to despair. The banner had been painted with the image of Simonetta Vespucci. Giuliano had fallen into melancholy on that first anniversary of her death.

And tomorrow, Sunday, would be the second anniversary.

According to Bruna, Giuliano had returned from Piombino yesterday. But he had not come to her, and he had not sent a message. Was he brooding over Simonetta again? Or, she wondered, has he finally abandoned me after meeting his future wife? It was maddening not to know.

She felt dizzy. I have to stop this. This not good for the baby, and the midwife said it's possible he could come early, any day now. Fioretta sat on the wedding chest and took deep breaths.

What was she to do?

Her hands gripped the carved edge of the chest lid. Not only had Giuliano abandoned her after the joust, but he had also done so five months ago, when she told him about the baby. Only Nóna's clay doll had brought him back.

Nóna!

Fioretta stood, turned and threw open the marriage chest lid. Where was it? She rummaged through baby clothes, her own garments and sewing materials. There it was, the red clay figure Nóna had given her, still wrapped in Giuliano's handkerchief and with seven iron pins stuck into its heart. After Giuliano had come back to her, she had taken it from beneath her bed and tucked it away in the chest.

Now holding the doll at arm's length, Fioretta stared at it. Should she put it back under the bed? Should she go and visit Nóna again? Would Nóna come to her? No, no, no. None of that mattered. Lorenzo was the problem. If only she could talk to him. She had failed at his house. There must be another way.

The window was closed, but still she heard the sound of church bells ringing through its cracked glass and rotten wood. The bells summoned her.

Church—that was the answer. Tomorrow she would go to the Mass and before God and the citizens of Florence, she would confront both Giuliano and Lorenzo. It was mad, but what else could she do?

Standing, she crossed to her bed and lay down, leaving the doll behind on top of the chest.

Twenty-Five Years Earlier

Thadeous opened his eyes and saw Giovan leaning over him. "You'll live," Giovan said.

"What happened?" Thadeous asked, his voice a feeble wheeze, his head swirling and his eyes struggling to focus. He lay on the ground and the stars were again visible overhead next to the still-standing wall. They must have pulled him out of the vertical shaft. "Where's Lauro?" he asked.

"Here," Lauro said nearby, his voice a whisper.

With difficulty, Thadeous craned his head around and saw Lauro lying next to him, a gaping slash across his forehead bleeding into the blood-soaked dirt beneath his head.

"What happened?" Thadeous asked.

Lauro's eyes fluttered and closed. A woman, one of the laborers who worked on the wall, bent down and wrapped a bandage around his head.

"Lauro!" Thadeous tried to cry out, but his breath seared his lungs. He curled over on his side, his eyes squeezed shut in agony, his body wracked with deep, scalding coughs. It seemed they would never stop.

"Give him water," Giovan said to the woman who had finished bandaging Lauro.

It seemed to help a little.

"Lauro," Thadeous said again. "How bad is it?"

Lauro did not move.

"He's dying," the woman replied. "I'm sorry."

"What?" Lauro dying? Thadeous reached out and found Lauro's hand. It was warm, but it did not respond to his touch.

"Captain Giovan," Thadeous gasped. "You killed him. If you hadn't run away, he wouldn't have come for me. He was already wounded."

"When the fire started, I—" Giovan started to say.

"Captain! A message."

Thadeous saw a soldier run up, panting. Giovan drew him aside and as Giovan listened, his shoulders slumped. After a few questions the messenger left, following the wall south, undoubtedly to pass the message on. Giovan climbed atop a broken stone and shouted, "Soldiers of Italy."

Around them, the mercenary soldiers of Giovan's company approached, each of them weary, dirty and dull-eyed.

"Grave news," Giovan said to the gathered men.

Managing to prop himself up on one elbow, Thadeous twisted around to see if Lauro was listening. Lauro lay still with his eyes closed.

"A Turkish banner flies over Kerkoporta Gate," Giovan said.

A groan went through the men.

Despite his pain and the difficulty breathing, Thadeous realized what this meant. If the Turks had captured a gate, the city would fall soon, most likely in a matter of hours. The barbarians were finally coming, despite all their efforts.

"We have done our duty," Giovan cried out. "The Emperor thanks you. Now, we fight for ourselves."

Thadeous tried to understand what Giovan was saying. He watched Giovan's men, and they seemed confused, too. "Will we return to Italy?" one of them shouted.

"God willing," Giovan replied.

"How?" another shouted.

"I don't know yet."

Next to him, Lauro said something.

Ignoring his pain, and willing himself not to cough, Thadeous bent around and put his ear next to Lauro's mouth.

"Tell him..." Lauro gasped, his cerulean blue eyes now open.

"Yes? What?"

"Tell him to go to Galata."

And with those words, Lauro died.

Chapter Eleven

Two Hours Until Dawn

"Give it to him," Giovan said again to Paulo.

"But it's *my* dagger," Paulo said, his voice plaintive.

Giovan was reminded again that Paulo was not quite a man. "True enough. Alfeo, would you do me a service? Tomorrow, after it's over, please return the boy's knife to him."

Alfeo nodded. Still sullen, Paulo handed him the knife, and Alfeo returned to his stool.

"I could have killed him," Paulo whispered. "You should have let me try."

"Perhaps. But he's a good man," Giovan said, nodding at Alfeo. "I'll not be responsible for the killing of another good man."

"You've said that sometimes it's necessary."

"Yes, but not by me. Not any more."

Giovan looked down at the pages on the table, and realized he would not be naming Thadeous as a conspirator. To name him in the confession would be a death sentence. Enough.

"Did you bring any wine with you?" he asked Paulo.

The boy shook his head.

"Ah, well. I am almost finished with this," Giovan said, gesturing at the pages. "I think I'll tell you the story of another good man. Alfeo, you can listen."

Alfeo turned and pulled his stool near.

"I've told you a little of my time in Constantinople. I was a mercenary, one of hundreds from Italy, contracted by the Emperor to defend the city from the Sultan Mehmed and his Turks. I had under my command a man named Lauro from Genoa. You remind me of him, Paulo. He was a good soldier. He had a friend, a young scholar named Thadeous."

"The old man?" Paulo asked. "The one who hates you?"

"Yes."

Giovan told them about the discovery of the enemy tunnel and gallery beneath the great wall, and about Thadeous's suggestion to use Greek Fire.

"Thadeous and I," he continued, "went into our own tunnel with the Greek Fire and three soldiers who carried the apparatus. When it came time to light the fire with a candle, I mishandled it, and a fire erupted in the tunnel. I jumped back, and saw Thadeous standing amongst the flames. Then I noticed my soldiers had fled, and so I went after them."

"You were afraid," Alfeo said.

Giovan glared at him. "There is no shame in fear. But there is in running away. I should have stayed with Thadeous. Together, we could have managed."

"What happened?" Paulo asked.

"At the tunnel mouth, I met Lauro. He had heard the men crying out about the fire as they escaped, and, even though he was wounded, he came down into the tunnel to help. I told him to assist Thadeous, and I would follow him as soon as I had gathered some men." Giovan spread his hands, palms up as he looked at Paulo. "Lauro pulled Thadeous out just as the gallery collapsed. Thadeous lived. Sadly, Lauro did not."

"So that old man saved the wall," Paulo said.

"Yes, that old man. But, alas, Constantinople still fell. When the word came that the Turks had captured one of the main gates, I gathered those Italians I had left, and we fought our way to the river known as the Golden Horn, north of the city. At night, we stole boats and rowed to the port of Galata on the other side, which was still controlled by the Genoese. I got my men aboard a ship bound for Genoa."

"Not you?" Alfeo asked.

"I found another ship sailing for Venice. I was going home to Montesecco. When I had left six months before, my wife was with child."

"But how did you get through all the Turkish ships?" Paulo asked.

"The Sultan was happy to have the mercenaries leave. He let us go."

"And Thadeous?" Alfeo asked.

"He went with the men."

"You sent Thadeous to Genoa?" Paulo asked. "He was dying."

"I couldn't leave him. My men liked him. He was courageous. He stood in fire and fought—deep underground—alone. I couldn't just leave him behind..." His voice trailed off.

"Because you left him before," Alfeo said. "In the fire."

Both Giovan and Paulo turned in surprise to look at the big man, perched on his stool.

"Yes," Giovan said. "I couldn't do that again."

Eight Days Earlier

"I'm worried about the priest," Giovan said.

He and Francesco de' Pazzi stood on the steps in front of the Duomo, its plain facade and immense central door looming up behind them. The street was filled with people. Some, such as the wealthy merchants and members of the old Florentine families, were elaborately dressed in silks and fine wools. Mixed in were the workers wearing their best clothes: carders, weavers, farmers from the countryside. The weather was clear and bright, so thousands were coming to see the young Cardinal and the pageantry of High Mass. Giovan had been in the Duomo only once, at night, and he remembered the dark echo of the cavernous sanctuary. It would be crowded today.

Archbishop Salviati had already gone inside to make sure all was ready for Mass, along with the nervous priest, Maffei, who was to position himself near Lorenzo.

"God will guide him," Francesco replied.

Giovan hoped this fool was right. Everything depended it on it.

"There's Lorenzo," Francesco said. "And the Cardinal is with him."

"And our spy," Giovan added, seeing Thadeous hobbling along behind, trying to keep up with the large entourage accompanying Lorenzo and the young Cardinal.

Giovan turned away, not wanting Lorenzo to see him. And he didn't want to look upon the face of the man who had been so hospitable to him, a good man who would soon be dead thanks to Giovan's year of planning, traveling and scheming.

Stop. I must not think these thoughts.

Thadeous approached them, breathing hard. "Giuliano is still sick," he said. "He's not coming."

"That will ruin everything," Francesco cried.

"What does he mean?" Thadeous asked Giovan.

"It's nothing. Go inside."

Thadeous seemed to want to ask another question, but then he shrugged and did as he was told.

"What are we going to do?" Francesco asked as he reached inside his cloak, checking that he had his dagger for what seemed like the hundredth time.

"Stop doing that," Giovan said. "Just stand here without fidgeting."

"Captain, you forget yourself—"

"Quiet. Let me think."

They couldn't proceed without Giuliano. As disinterested as the younger brother was in politics, the people of Florence would still rally around him if Lorenzo was killed. They had to do something to get Giuliano into the Duomo.

"Filiberto," Giovan called out.

Filiberto, who had been positioned nearby, hurried over. They had left Paulo back at the inn with their baggage and the mules. Thirty armed Perugian troops, ostensibly part of the Cardinal's retinue, hid in an alleyway nearby, and a hundred more soldiers were ready outside the city walls. Unfortunately, the six hundred from Urbino had not yet arrived, but time was running out. They had to go ahead with the men they had and pray to God they were enough.

"Stay here with your men," Giovan told him. "If the Archbishop comes out, tell him we've gone to fetch Giuliano."

Filiberto nodded.

"Come," Giovan said to Francesco. "We haven't much time."

The Palazzo de' Medici was only a few blocks up the Via de' Martelli, and Giovan remembered walking this street after his first meeting with Lorenzo and Giuliano back in December.

"What will we do?" Francesco asked, huffing along behind him.

"That's up to you. Just convince Giuliano he needs to come to Mass."

The palazzo rose up in front of them, its rusticated, three-tiered walls towering over the smaller houses and shops around it.

Francesco hammered on the main door and soon a servant appeared.

"Tell your master Francesco de' Pazzi and Captain Giovan Battista have come with an important message from Lorenzo," Francesco told the man.

The servant disappeared and returned a few minutes later. "Only Captain Giovan may come in," he said.

Francesco started to protest, but Giovan whispered, "We don't have time to argue." As he followed the servant inside, he glanced back and saw Francesco reach inside his tunic and touch his dagger.

The servant showed Giovan to Giuliano's room. It was as Giovan remembered, both opulent and untidy as befitted a bachelor. This time Giuliano lay on his rumpled bed wearing a wrinkled sleeping gown, his hair disheveled.

"What do you want?" he asked, bleary-eyed.

"Your brother sent Francesco de' Pazzi and me to fetch you," Giovan replied.

"But why would he send you and that idiot Francesco?"

Giovan steeled his heart. "I'm trying to help. You and Lorenzo have been so kind to me in the past."

"Why does Lorenzo need me?"

"It's Cardinal Raffaele," Giovan said. "You've insulted him by not attending Mass. He's heard a rumor you are not really sick, that you merely suffer from silly melancholy about some woman two years dead."

"He means Simonetta Vespucci," Giuliano said. *La bella Simonetta.* It's not true. I no longer mourn her. I am truly sick." He swung his legs out onto the floor. "But not so sick I want to insult the Cardinal. I suppose I must do what must be done. Stefano," he called. "Come dress me."

The servant hurried in and assisted Giuliano with pulling off his gown. While Giuliano used the chamber pot, Giovan turned away and noticed the portrait he had admired when he was in this room before. It was the girl, Fioretta, the one Giuliano had claimed to love. For a moment, Giovan smiled, remembering when he met her in her shop—he had been trying to arrange for some new camicia.

"Why did you ask me to come in alone?" Giovan asked.

"Francesco is a fool," Giuliano said as he came to stand by Giovan, wearing only his own camicia. His face was pale. "Did you know Lorenzo sent me to Piombino to meet a woman he wants me to marry? It would be a good diplomatic move. But, I've been vomiting since I ate a meal prepared by that woman. And she's a fat cow with a matching personality."

He gazed at the girl in the portrait as Stefano dressed him. "It's true, you know. I did love Simonetta, and I will always remember her. But that's the past."

"We should hurry," Giovan said.

Stefano held up a opulent red tunic, brocaded with gold threads, suitable for a man of Giuliano's rank attending High Mass.

"Giovan, my friend," Giuliano said, slipping into the tunic. "She is with child. Soon, I will have a son."

Giovan stared at him. Dear Jesus. He called me his friend. This horrible task only becomes harder with every minute. No, I must not think of this.

"In Piombino, I decided I must tell Lorenzo," Giuliano continued. "I'll do it today, at the banquet after Mass. I will acknowledge my son, and I will marry dear Fioretta. My brother cannot stop me. If he will not accept this, I'll take her and leave Florence forever."

Back outside on the street, Francesco greeted Giuliano as if he were a great friend, wrapping his arm across his shoulder and hugging him. Giovan noticed Francesco's hand patting Giuliano's chest and ribs, apparently checking whether he wore armor under his tunic. Satisfied, Francesco led them back down Via de' Martelli, trying to joke with Giuliano, who ignored him.

At the Duomo steps, Archbishop Salviati stood waiting. He moved aside as Francesco guided Giuliano to the open door, and his face showed a tight smile of satisfaction.

Giuliano turned in the doorway and looked back at Giovan. "Aren't you coming in, my friend?" he asked. "Let's see how well this young Cardinal performs."

Giovan struggled to breathe. It felt like an iron band had bound his chest. *My friend*, he had said again. Giovan shook his head and turned away, hiding his face as he had done with Lorenzo. He knew this would puzzle Giuliano, but there was nothing he could do. He heard the cathedral door close.

"Excellent," Salviati said. "Now we can proceed."

Giovan rubbed his hands across his face. I must think of my own son, think of Matthias. And I must do what needs to be done. Clamping his jaw, he waved for Filiberto and his men to follow him. The Palazzo della Signoria was just a few blocks south.

I'm a soldier. Now it's time to do soldier's work.

Fioretta pushed through the crowd at the back of the cathedral's vast nave, wearing the flowing red cloak that hid her pregnancy. If it became necessary, she would cast it aside and show everyone, especially Lorenzo, what Giuliano had done. She clutched Giuliano's love poem in her hand.

"Lady, you shouldn't be here. Let's go back," Bruna pleaded, as she had during the half-hour walk from the shop.

Fioretta ignored her and continued to press forward. She had never been inside this immense house of God before as her father had always taken her to Saint Joseph's, the small church near their house.

On both sides of the narrow aisle, the people of Florence stood gazing at the far end, straining on their tiptoes to see the young Cardinal of San Giorgio. The sweet smell of incense mingled with the sour odor of the people. Fioretta caught sight of the Cardinal on the raised platform before the altar. He began to read from an ornate missal held by two altar boys, and around her, the faithful knelt and made the sign of the cross. He had a strong voice, so Fioretta was able to recognize a few Latin words even at this distance. The Cardinal was reading the Eucharistic Prayer.

Fioretta started forward, passing through the kneeling and praying worshippers. She cringed as she heard whispers and felt their eyes upon her. Where were Giuliano and Lorenzo? They must be near the altar under the dome, surrounded by their political allies and friends. Fioretta squinted, unable to see them.

Halfway, she stopped, trembling, the only person standing, and it felt as though all Florence was watching. She was a tiny woman in the cavernous nave of the largest church in all of Italy. She looked behind her and saw Bruna by the door. Bruna gestured for her to come back, and Fioretta wanted desperately to go. The sound of the Cardinal's voice faltered and then continued. This was madness. Surely she would be exiled to the poor nunnery outside the town walls where the insane citizens of Florence were sent.

Then she saw a man stand up near the altar. He stared at her. It was Lorenzo. Their eyes met, and he scowled. Of course he would not approve of any disruption during such an important religious and political event. Lorenzo would refuse to speak with her; his friends would not even let her approach.

Perhaps her mission here was pointless. Perhaps Bruna was right.

She slipped one hand inside her cape and rested it on her belly. Her son moved beneath her fingers. She started forward again.

Lorenzo was still staring at her. And then his face softened and he gestured, beckoning her. He kept his eyes on her as she hurried forward.

The Cardinal reached the end of the prayer, and the people began to stand. She lost sight of Lorenzo for a moment, but then she saw him as he stepped toward her.

"Magnifico," she said when she stood before him. Now the moment had come, and she was uncertain what to say. When she attempted to curtsy, she felt dizzy.

"I know you," he said, taking her arm and steadying her. "The painting in my brother's room."

"Yes," Fioretta cried. She lifted the slip of paper containing Giuliano's love poem, trying to give it to Lorenzo, and as she did, her cloak fell open.

Lorenzo jaw dropped as he stared at her swollen belly for a moment. He seemed to be thinking. Then he muttered, "She'll ruin everything." Turning away, he told a man standing next to him, "Remove her."

The poem fell to the floor. Behind Lorenzo, an altar boy lifted high a golden bell.

Lorenzo's friend took her elbow.

"No," Fioretta shouted as she pulled her arm free. "I will be heard."

The man seized both her arms and began to drag her toward a side door.

The Sanctus Bell rang out.

Fioretta wrenched herself loose, and as she again turned to confront Lorenzo, she saw a man coming up behind him. Father Maffei! And he clutched a dagger, holding it high. His eyes glinted with hatred.

"Assassin!" Fioretta screamed.

Everything seemed to stop. Maffei stood panting, the dagger raised, his face white. Lorenzo appeared frozen in place. His friend stood beside Fioretta, his hand reaching for his sword. The only sound that Fioretta heard was Maffei's rapid, shallow breathing.

"Assassin!" Fioretta screamed again.

Spinning around, Lorenzo ducked, grabbing for his own sword just as Maffei lunged. Lorenzo deflected the stab with his forearm, but the dagger sliced into his neck, and he fell back, blood streaming down the front of his tunic. Maffei raised his arm again, but the man who had held Fioretta leaped forward, putting himself in front of Lorenzo while still struggling to pull his sword from its scabbard. Maffei stabbed him in the chest, and he fell twitching at Fioretta's feet.

Fioretta wrapped her arms around her abdomen and backed away.

More men rushed to protect Lorenzo, swords drawn, forming a wall between him and Maffei. Lorenzo clamped his hand over his wound, and blood oozed between his fingers.

Maffei stared at the men protecting Lorenzo and his jaw went slack. Then he turned and ran toward a nearby side door, swinging his dagger back and forth. After a moment of confusion, some men ran after him, but Fioretta saw him disappear.

"Don't kill him," Lorenzo shouted. He was pale, but still he stood. "Giuliano? Where are you?" he called over his shoulder as friends pulled him away, still shielding him with their bodies.

Yes, Giuliano! Fioretta swung around, searching the crowd, and saw Sandro on the far side of the altar. Oh, Sandro, please keep Giuliano safe, Fioretta prayed as she hurried toward him. Sandro was staring down at something on the floor. Behind him, a man with long blond hair broke lose from the crowd and, like Maffei, ran for a side door.

The cathedral was in turmoil, with women screaming and men shouting. In front of the altar, the young Cardinal stood open-mouthed while an old man tugged at his arm. The panic spread, and Fioretta heard a man shout out, "The dome is falling. Run." People surged toward the doors, pushing and tripping over each other.

Fioretta didn't think about the dome, keeping her eyes fixed on Sandro instead as she hurried toward him. He knelt down as she reached him, and she saw Giuliano laying on the floor, gaping bloody stab wounds in his chest. Fioretta dropped to her knees. Desperate, she pressed her hands over the largest gash and warm blood oozed between her fingers. She couldn't staunch the flow. Next to her, Sandro wept.

Giuliano's eyes flickered open, and a trickle of blood escaped the corner of his mouth. Fioretta heard a wheezing sound, and through her tears she realized that air was bubbling in and out of the chest wounds. His eyes were wide, and they darted around, seeming to search for something. He was terrified, desperate. His lips quivered as he struggled to speak.

Fioretta touched his cheek with her bloody hand and leaned forward, her face close to his. His eyes found hers and became quiet, peaceful. The sounds from his wounds became a whisper, then ceased, and the light of life left Giuliano forever.

Fioretta collapsed beside his body, her mouth gaping wide with a wail that had no sound.

Sandro stood up, brushed his sleeve over his face and drew his sword.

As Fioretta lay next to the only man she had ever loved, an abyss of darkness enveloped her. She heard nothing, saw nothing. Time ceased.

Then a voice echoed in the distance.

"It's me," Lucia said.

Thadeous watched as Medici supporters, swords drawn, encircled the wounded Lorenzo and hustled him through the doorway leading to the sacristy. The big bronze door slammed shut, and more men stayed outside, their weapons ready, watching the crowd.

Thadeous hurried to Raffaele's side. The boy stood in front

of the altar, his mouth agape.

"What's happening?" Raffaele asked.

"I think someone attacked Lorenzo."

It seemed to Thadeous that the crowd was beginning to thin. Most of the congregants, some crying out that the dome was falling, had managed to scramble out onto the street.

"What should we do?" Raffaele's voice trembled.

Thadeous didn't know what to say. He caught sight of a woman in a red cloak sprawled across the floor. Next to her, a girl in servant dress pulled her to her feet, and Thadeous saw a body. He hobbled toward them. It was Giuliano, lying in a pool of his own blood.

"Come," the servant girl said. "We can do no more for him." An older servant woman joined her, and together they pulled the sobbing woman in the cloak away from Giuliano.

One man stood with his sword drawn, staring down at Giuliano's body. Thadeous recognized him as Sandro Botticelli, a friend of both Lorenzo and Giuliano.

"Who did this?" Sandro cried. Others nearby responded with animal, guttural cries. They lifted their drawn swords into the air.

"I saw him," a man shouted. "It was Francesco de' Pazzi, the banker."

"Yes," another replied. "I saw him, too. He ran away."

"The Pazzi," the men cried. "We all know the Pazzi hate the Medici. To the Pazzi palazzo. Revenge for Giuliano."

"Wait," Sandro shouted. "It's not just the Pazzi. Where's Archbishop Salviati?"

"He left before the start of the Mass," someone called out.

"He's a Riario," Sandro said. "The Riario false pope makes no secret of his desire to conquer Florence. Salviati Riario brought that boy Cardinal into Florence so they could attack us. It's the Riarios, I say."

The men murmured, considering what Sandro had said.

Thadeous turned and hurried back to Raffaele. "We must leave," he whispered. "They're blaming the Riario family. You aren't safe."

"Death to Salviati," the men began to shout. "Death to the Riarios." They all were facing Sandro, but Thadeous knew that soon they would remember Raffaele, a Riario, stood only a few feet from them. Thadeous grabbed Raffaele's arm and pulled him. The boy seemed to come to his senses, and they retreated through a nearby side door and out onto a raised porch, a few steps above the street. A mob of Florentine citizens milled about. Women wept, crying out, 'Lorenzo! Giuliano!'

Thadeous guided Raffaele to one side. "Let the Cardinal through," he said, his voice wheezing.

The crowd started to part, but then Sandro and some armed men came out of the church. "The Pazzis and the Riarios have killed Giuliano," Sandro shouted to the mob. He saw Raffaele. "You. You're a Riario. You're part of this plot."

The men with Sandro surged toward Raffaele, who burst into tears. "I know nothing of any plot," he cried. "Lorenzo is my friend."

Two men grabbed his arms and held him. Sandro lifted his sword and moved toward Raffaele.

"Stop," Lorenzo shouted as he stepped out of the cathedral and stood between Sandro and Raffaele. He was pale, but his voice was strong and commanding. Thadeous took a deep breath, relieved. Lorenzo was not dead, and it seemed he was not badly wounded.

Sandro froze, and then he turned and knelt before Lorenzo. "Magnifico," he said. "This boy is a Riario. The Riarios have killed Giuliano."

"I know," Lorenzo said. He had a blood-soaked scarf wrapped around his neck.

Someone on the street shouted, "Lorenzo. He lives," and Lorenzo lifted his arm in acknowledgment. The crowd cheered. More people came running through the streets from all directions, drawn by the commotion.

Thadeous saw the woman in the red cloak as she too

emerged from the door behind Lorenzo, followed by the two servant women. She approached Lorenzo and stood beside Sandro. Her hands were covered with blood and there was a smear of it on her cheek.

"Fioretta, now is not the time," Sandro said, attempting to take her arm.

The woman shook him off. She stared at Lorenzo and he met her gaze. "I know who attacked you. I saw him. It's the priest named Antonio Maffei."

"I saw it was a priest," Lorenzo replied. "Now I know his name." He faced the crowd. "Citizens of Florence," he shouted. "A great crime has been committed against our republic and my family. My beloved brother, Giuliano, is dead."

As the sound of Giuliano name, a cry went up from the crowd.

"The time for retribution will come, my friends," Lorenzo continued, "and it will come soon. Bring me the Pazzi. Bring me the false archbishop Salviati Riario. And bring me the priest named Antonio Maffei. Bring them all to the Palazzo della Signoria, and they will meet the fate they deserve."

"Death to the Pazzi. Death to the Riarios," the crowd shouted, many shaking their fists at Raffaele. "To the Pazzi palazzo," someone shouted, and many ran off in that direction. "Find Salviati, find Maffei!"

Lorenzo turned to Thadeous and Raffaele. Yesterday at the luncheon, Thadeous had spent a moment with Lorenzo, who had professed his pleasure at seeing his old tutor again.

"I swear, Magnifico," Thadeous said, "the Cardinal and I had no knowledge of this."

Lorenzo considered this. "I want to believe you," he said. He turned to Raffaele. "But you are a Riario. You must be involved."

"No, no," Raffaele cried.

"Don't harm him," Lorenzo said to Sandro. "But take him to the Palazzo della Signoria." Lorenzo started down the steps to the street.

"Magnifico," the girl said, grabbing his arm. "Please hear me out."

"I have no time for this," Lorenzo said, shaking free. With a dozen men surrounding him, he hurried up the street toward the Palazzo Medici.

"But I saved your life," Fioretta called after him.

Lorenzo did not seem hear her.

Chapter Twelve

One Hour Until Dawn

"So you saved Thadeous," Paulo said. "And yet he hates you."

"He has reasons. He still blames me for killing his friend long ago. Because I…" Giovan stopped, blinking. "Paulo. Is that the satchel you used when we traveled?" He stood and pointed at the leather bag Paulo had dropped by the door when he came in.

"Yes, Captain. I wanted to show you—"

"Does it have a manuscript?" Giovan asked.

"Yes. I took it out of your saddlebag just before we were attacked. I thought maybe I would read it while the mules grazed, work on my Latin. It would keep me awake." Paulo retrieved the satchel, pulled the pages from it and placed them on the table. "I left the other manuscript, the one called *The Nómoi*. I couldn't save it."

"I know." Giovan put his hand on Paulo's shoulder. "You did well." Then Giovan peered down at the first page. Yes, it was Thadeous's history of Constantinople. He remembered puzzling over the Latin with poor Filiberto. The page blurred before his eyes. Alas, Filiberto. Giovan swayed. Paulo grabbed him and eased him back down onto the bed.

"You rest," Alfeo said.

"I will. But first I must finish this." Giovan pushed aside Thadeous's manuscript. He found the last page he had written, one of seven, each covered with his tiny scrawl. He added at the bottom.

> *Everything that is written here is true and it is written by my own hand.*
>
> *Giovan Battista da Montesecco*

"There, it's done," he said. "Now I think I would like to see my old friend Nicolo."

Both Alfeo and Paulo brighten at these words.

"But first," he added. "Alfeo, give me the knife, give me Sicarius."

Alfeo handed him the dagger.

Giovan hefted the dagger in his hand and then with a quick downward stab, buried its tip into the table. "Put your hand over mine on the handle," Giovan said to Paulo.

The boy did so.

"I have two final orders for you. Swear to me that you will follow them," Giovan said.

"Anything, Captain. Anything."

"Tomorrow you must find Thadeous and return this manuscript to him."

Paulo nodded. "What else?"

"You must not harm Thadeous."

"Why would I harm a sick old man?" Paulo asked.

"Because he betrayed me to Lorenzo."

Eight Days Earlier

Giovan, along with Archbishop Salviati, Filiberto and thirty Perugians, left the Duomo behind and hurried down the Via de' Martelli. The streets were almost empty now that High Mass had begun. The few Florentines they passed eyed their armed party with suspicion, and Giovan was relieved when they reached the piazza without any problems.

The Palazzo della Signoria, the seat of the Florentine government, had been built as a fortress. As they crossed the wide piazza before it, Giovan gazed up, admiring the high facade, the crenelated parapet above it, and finally the massive bell tower, with its clock marking the hours since sunset the day before. Above the clock was a small window, high enough so it must provide a commanding view of the city and the surrounding countryside. Giovan wondered if the missing soldiers from Urbino were visible from it.

Somewhere inside was the Gonfaloniere of Justice and the other members of the Signoria. Giovan and his soldiers were to find them and hold them incommunicado while Jacopo de' Pazzi brought troops into the city and took control. It was not enough to kill Lorenzo and Giuliano. The city government must be captured and the people rallied around the Pazzi family. Only this would satisfy His Holiness.

During their first visit to Florence last summer, Giovan and Filiberto had explored the palazzo as well as they could, Giovan anticipating this day might come. The inside, he knew, was a maze of small rooms, long hallways and stairs surrounding two courtyards and the base of the tower. The problem was to find the Signoria without delay.

Two guards stood at the main door. They drew their swords when they saw armed men coming toward them and then one dashed inside.

"I demand to see the Gonfaloniere of Justice," Salviati announced. He wore his archbishop's Eucharistic vestments. Not prepared to argue with dozens of armed men, the remaining guard stepped aside.

Giovan ordered six of his men to stay behind and hold the door against any attack, from inside or out.

Salviati led Giovan, Filiberto and the remaining men down a short corridor and out into the first courtyard, where a man wearing a robe trimmed in yellow confronted them. Giovan assumed he was a government official.

"Your Eminence," the man cried. "You cannot bring armed men in here."

"I demand to see the Gonfaloniere of Justice," Salviati said.

"The Gonfaloniere and the rest of the Signoria are dining," the official said. "You must wait."

"Nonsense," Salviati said. "We bring a message from His Holiness, the Pope."

Now the man looked confused.

Giovan put his hand on his sword hilt and said, "I am a

servant of His Holiness, the Castellan of Castel San'Angelo and the Captain of the Apostolic Palace Guard. Take us to the Gonfaloniere immediately."

"Yes, yes, of course," the official replied. "But please, only His Eminence, the Archbishop."

Salviati looked appalled at this. He pulled Giovan aside and whispered, "What can I do alone? We need to take control —and soon, before word comes from the Duomo."

"We need this man to show us to the Signoria," Giovan replied. "If we push on past him, we'd have to search every room on three floors." He turned back to the official. "As His Holiness's representative, I will also attend. My men will wait here."

The official considered this, glanced at the troops waiting behind Giovan, and said, "That will be acceptable. Please follow me."

"Filiberto," Giovan said, hanging back. "Keep the men here. Stay alert."

Filiberto nodded.

Salviati whispered, "What are you doing?"

"Once we locate the Signoria, I'll come back here and fetch the men."

The official led Giovan and Salviati up a stairway to the second floor, and down a hallway to a second staircase. Giovan began to worry his men were too far away. What if Signoria guards attacked them? He'd have to trust Filiberto's judgment.

Finally, at the end of another long hallway, the official stopped in front of a heavy paneled door. "Please wait," he said and he slipped inside.

Salviati sputtered. "He can't leave me waiting out here. I'm the Archbishop of Pisa."

Should Giovan go get his men now? Were the members of the Signoria on the other side of this door? He had to know for sure.

Giovan stepped to the door and tried the handle, but it was

locked. What was happening inside the room? He knocked on the door. "Open in the name of His Holiness," he shouted.

There was no response.

Giovan pressed his ear to the door. There were men talking inside. As he raised his arm, prepared to hammer on the door with his fist, there was a click and the door swung open.

"I am Cesare Petrucci, the Gonfaloniere of Justice," announced a man wearing a dark crimson coat, trimmed with fur. He glared at Giovan. "Who dares disturb the Signoria?"

Salviati pushed past Giovan into the room, saying "You know very well who I am."

Giovan started to follow him, but he froze when he saw three men, swords drawn, wearing the same uniform as the guards at the main door. A group of well-dressed men cowered in a corner. The Signoria. There was another door on the far wall behind a large table strew with cups and plates, and more guards were streaming through it.

"Run," Giovan shouted as he jumped back from the door. Guards surrounded Salviati, and one pressed his sword to the archbishop's throat. Giovan turned and dashed down the hallway. "I'll fetch the men," he shouted over his shoulder.

Guards chased after Giovan. He drew his sword as he ran.

"Ring the alarm bell," Petrucci cried out behind him. "Ring the *Sonare de Palagio.*"

Giovan flew down the first stairway. If he could bring his men upstairs quickly, he should have enough of them to capture the Signoria. But he had to be fast. Soon the alarm bell would sound, and the citizens of Florence would flock to the Palazzo della Signoria.

"Filiberto," Giovan shouted, panting as he ran down the next hallway, knowing he was still too far away. Over his own gasping breath and pounding steps, he heard the muffled ring of a bell coming from the tower high above his head. As Giovan reached the top of the final stairwell, the bell was drowned out by the sound of shouting and the clash of steel on steel. The Signoria guards had attacked his men.

"Filiberto," he shouted.

"Here," Filiberto cried from below.

Giovan launched himself down the stairs, his sword ready. After a year of endless frustration and doubt, finally he would do what he did best. He would fight.

Halfway down, he caught sight of Filiberto and the Perugians below him in the hallway. They were fighting with guards, and at their feet lay several men, both Perugians and Florentines. Giovan heard a shout and the thudding of boots on the stairs behind him. His pursuers had caught up. Two guards from the floor below started climbing toward him. He was trapped.

Turning just in time to see the first man above lunging toward him, Giovan parried the man's long dagger, and smashed him on the side of the head with his sword hilt. Giovan caught his limp body and swung him around so he crashed into the men on the stairs below.

He climbed the steps toward the next guard above him. This one was left-handed, but he also was no match for Giovan, who had fought all kinds of soldiers for forty years. Giovan pulled his sword blade back over his left shoulder and then swung, striking the man in the side of his head before he could react. Again he threw the body down the stairs. The last man above him backed away, shouting for help.

Giovan wheeled around. Guards from the floor below were picking their way over the fallen bodies of their comrades. Giovan charged forward, sword held horizontally before him, plunging down the steps to leap over the bodies. He stabbed one man, but his feet slipped in spilled blood and he fell forward, his arms flailing. He crashed into another guard, lost his balance and fell down onto the steps. Giovan rolled to one side, but someone kicked the sword from his hand. A heavy boot crashed into his ribs, and his breath burst from his chest. Giovan raised his arms to cover his head, waiting for the fatal blow to fall. His cheek pressed into a pool of blood.

"Captain!" It was Filiberto. He was nearby.

A body landed on top of Giovan, lifeless, further driving the air from his lungs. Protected for the moment, Giovan reached out, searching for his sword. His hand closed over the familiar blade. Gasping, he tossed the body aside and climbed back to his feet, reversing the sword so he gripped its hilt.

"The Captain lives," someone shouted. Filiberto and his remaining soldiers must have thought he was dead.

The only guards still moving were above him now, and they backed up the stairs, apparently deciding to wait for reinforcements.

Giovan emerged from the stairwell into the hallway and stood next to Filiberto, whose longsword dripped blood at his side. At the far end of this hall, another small group of guards eyed them, but they did not advance. No sound came from the stairway. It seemed they had a moment of respite.

"What happened?" Filiberto asked, panting.

"They guessed our plan," Giovan replied. "The Gonfaloniere called guards into the room through another door, and they attacked."

"Salviati?"

Giovan shrugged. He looked at the few remaining Perugians standing nearby and at the bodies scattered up and down the hallway. He forced himself to think. By now, the Signoria will be surrounded by even more guards. I don't have enough men left to fight them. What can we do? It all depends on what happened in the Duomo. If Lorenzo and Giuliano are dead, there is still hope Jacopo de' Pazzi can raise the people, and his troops will be enough. We have to fight as long as there is hope.

"Our men at the door," Giovan said. "We'll join them."

They rushed the guards at the end of the hallway, bursting through to the courtyard beyond and managed to get back to the front door of the Palazzo, losing one more Perugian.

Giovan stepped through the door and gazed out over the Piazza della Signoria. It was half-filled with men milling around, along with a few women and children. They had been summoned by the Sonare de Palagio, whose rapid clang in the tower above him still rang out across the piazza, the city and the surrounding countryside. More people were streaming in from the side streets.

"Half the men inside, half outside," Giovan said to Filiberto. "If the crowd attacks, we'll pull inside and bolt the door."

A few men in the crowd watched them with suspicion. One, in a shoemaker's apron, had a rusty sword, and two young men beside him brandished daggers. Giovan also saw a man carrying a shovel and another with a wood-splitting axe. So far, none of them seemed inclined to come closer.

A shout went up on the far side of the piazza. Giovan squinted and saw a man on horseback trotting through the crowd with a large group of armed men on foot behind him. It was Jacopo de' Pazzi with the soldiers from outside the wall. As planned, he had brought them into the city at the crucial moment. Jacopo stood in his stirrups, turning his head back and forth, searching.

"Here," Giovan shouted, waving his sword above his head.

Jacopo saw him, and as he urged his horse forward toward the palazzo, he shouted, "Citizens of Florence. The Medici have enslaved you. Join us. Restore Florence to its former glory."

The crowd quieted, their faces turning toward Jacopo.

"Pazzi, Pazzi," Giovan shouted. He gestured to his men that they should join him. "Pazzi, Pazzi," they shouted, and some of the people nearby took up the clamor. The shoemaker lifted his old sword above his head and yelled, "Pazzi, Pazzi!"

Then a silence descended on the piazza. The shoemaker stared up at something above Giovan's head. Giovan edged forward, craned his head around, and saw two men standing on the balcony just above the door. One of them was Gonfaloniere Petrucci, easy to identify because of this crimson coat. The other looked familiar. Where had Giovan seen him? It was Giuliano's servant, Stefano. The man was sobbing.

"Our beloved Giuliano is dead," Petrucci shouted. "Killed

by treachery."

A gasp went up from the crowd. The shoemaker stared in disbelief. A woman nearby burst into tears.

Petrucci raised his arms, and the people quieted.

"But Lorenzo lives!" he shouted.

A joyous cheer went up. The shoemaker glared at Giovan, who backed away, retreating toward the door.

We have failed. No, I have failed. In my heart, I feared Maffei would not succeed, and yet we went ahead. If I had done my duty, if I had killed Lorenzo as I promised, we would have succeeded. Instead, Giuliano is dead and Lorenzo lives. The worst possible outcome. A good man, who had called me his friend, has died for no purpose, killed by that idiot Francesco. I will lose all I have gained. Certainly my position with His Holiness. And most likely my life. And Matthias will stay in Purgatory.

"Get them," a woman shouted.

Giovan looked up and saw the crowd moving toward him, the shoemaker leading them and the woman who had been crying now screaming, urging them on.

Giovan lowered his sword and stepped forward. Let them do their will. It no longer mattered. The shoemaker raised his old sword above his head, grasping it with both hands, and swung.

Giovan felt the breath knocked from his lungs as he was jerked backward. The shoemaker's sword fell, slicing through the front of Giovan's surcoat, its tip scraping against his chest armor.

"Captain," Filiberto shouted in his ear. "Get back."

Filiberto dragged Giovan through the palazzo door. Just before it slammed shut, Giovan saw the soldiers running away and the screaming crowd pulling Jacopo de' Pazzi from his horse.

"Bolt the door," Filiberto ordered as he released Giovan. "Captain, what do we do?"

What indeed?

"Captain, we need orders. We're surrounded."

Giovan shrugged. "Look for wine," he said.

Filiberto stared at him. "But…"

Giovan noticed an old man, stooped over and coughing nearby. It was Thadeous Phylacus, the tutor. How did he get here?

Thadeous saw Giovan and glared. "You!" he shouted, lifting an arm and pointing with a crooked shaking finger. "I should have known."

Giovan stared at Thadeous for a second, and then turned away, thinking about Constantinople, a quarter century ago. A great endeavor had failed. He had been left with a small band of men in a hostile city. But still, he had survived.

"Filiberto," he said, his voice commanding again. "This old man must have come in through a back door. We'll find it, fetch Paulo and the mules, and fight our way out of the city."

Fioretta collapsed onto her bed, no longer crying, but exhausted, haunted by the image of sweet Giuliano's face, blood seeping from the corner of his mouth, trying to speak to her.

Lucia sat down next to her. She leaned forward and whispered, "He was a good man. He loved you."

But lost in her grief, Fioretta doubted this was true. Hadn't he abandoned her again? If he loved her, why had he not come to see her when he returned from Piombino? She gave a shuddering sob and then was quiet again.

After a time, Lucia stood and went downstairs, returned and again sat next to Fioretta. "Drink this," Lucia said.

Fioretta glanced up at the cup in Lucia's hand and shook her head. "I don't want it."

"Fioretta," Lucia said, "remember the baby."

Yes, the baby. She sat up and let Lucia hold the cup to her lips. It was watered sweet wine. Her throat was parched, so Fioretta put her hands over Lucia's and gulped down half the cup.

"I found some food," Lucia said, holding a wooden platter with slices of bread and cheese.

Fioretta realized she was famished. She had eaten nothing that morning, and it was past noon. She began to stuff a piece of bread into her mouth, but she stopped. How could she think about food now? Now that—

"For the baby," Lucia said.

Fioretta wolfed down the food, gulped the remaining wine, and wondered if there was more. Bruna would know. "Where's Bruna?" she asked.

"She went to find Stefano," Lucia said.

Oh God, poor Stefano. He had served Giuliano for so many years. The man must be shattered. "Lucia, you should go to Stefano. He needs you."

Lucia nodded. "Yes. But for now, I'll stay with you."

"Oh, Lucia, why would anyone want to kill my beloved Giuliano?" Fioretta buried her face in her hands and started to lay back down on the bed.

Lucia grasped her by the shoulders and pulled her back upright. "People are saying it was the Pazzi and the Riarios," she said.

"What people?" Fioretta asked, a stab of anger pushing aside her grief.

"The people in the streets. Didn't you see the crowds? They are crying out to kill the—"

There was a loud hammering at the front door below. Lucia rose and went to the window, unlatched it and leaned outside to see the door. "Show yourself," she shouted.

The only response was another hard pounding on the door.

"He's hiding in the doorway," Lucia said to Fioretta. Leaning back out, she looked from side to side. "There's nobody else on the street right now." Again, she shouted, "Let me see you."

Again, they heard only pounding.

"I'll go look," Lucia said.

"Be careful."

As Lucia walked past the wedding chest, she glanced down at Nóna's doll, wrapped in Giuliano's handkerchief, laying on the closed lid. She gave Fioretta a questioning look and then left the room, descending the stairs to the shop.

"Who are you?" Lucia shouted below.

"I bring a message from Lorenzo," The voice was muffled, but familiar.

Lorenzo? He must have decided to acknowledge Giuliano's son. God be praised. Fioretta pulled herself to her feet and stood at her bedroom door, looking down into the shop.

"Let him in," she said.

"But how do we know—"

"Let him in. Please, Lucia."

Lucia lifted the iron latch.

The door flew open, and Father Maffei burst into the room, knocking Lucia back onto the stairway's bottom steps. He looked around, his eyes wild, and then slammed the door shut and latched it.

"You!" Fioretta shouted from the top of the stairs. "You tried to kill Lorenzo. I saw you."

"And were it not for you, I'd have succeeded," Maffei shouted back. He held a dagger, and Fioretta guessed it was the same one he had used in the Duomo. He pointed it at Lucia and said, "Up there, now."

Fioretta backed into the room and sat on the bed as Lucia came in, trembling with Maffei behind her, poking the tip of the dagger into her back. He wore his usual filthy ankle-length cassock, surely the same he wore that terrible night almost a year ago. Lucia looked terrified, more frightened than Fioretta had ever seen her. This man, this beast, had attacked her, had raped Lucia. And he had left her with a monster child growing inside her.

Lucia dropped onto the bed, and Fioretta took her hand. It was shaking.

"You had to let me in this time," Maffei said, snarling. "Today, you can't leave me standing in the street like a beggar."

Maffei had come with her father that time when he had visited.

"And fair Lucia," Maffei continued. "Aren't you happy to see me?"

Lucia looked away, her lips trembling.

"Why are you here?" Fioretta asked. "What do you want?"

Maffei didn't answer. Instead he cocked his head to one side, listening. Then he crossed the room to the window and peeked out.

"They're coming," he said.

Fioretta heard it, too. It was the sound of a mob, crying out for vengeance in the streets, just as they had when she and Lucia had come from the Duomo. She remembered now.

"They won't find me here," Maffei said. He swung the window closed, its loose panes rattling in the cracked frame, latched it and stepped away. "We had the chance to rid Florence of the Medici curse, but they've forsaken our efforts. I would have avenged Volterra. But now they roam the streets, crying out they will kill all the Pazzi, kill all the Riarios." He pointed the dagger at Fioretta. "And because of *you*, they also shout my name."

Fioretta wanted to tell Maffei she was proud to have named him to Lorenzo, but she stared at the dagger, too terrified to say anything. Next to her, Lucia gripped Fioretta's hand so tightly it ached.

Maffei passed his hand over his face and swayed on his feet. Clearly he was exhausted. He started to sit on the closed marriage chest, but he noticed Nóna's clay doll lying on top. He picked it up and unwrapped Giuliano's handkerchief, exposing the iron pins piercing the doll's heart.

"Witchcraft," he shouted. "I should have guessed. Giuliano had low tastes, and now I know why. You used this to bewitch him." His eyes narrowed as he looked back and forth between Fioretta and Lucia. "Hear me, you two. If you don't keep me hidden, if you help them, I'll tell them about this." He held up the doll. "All Florence will know you are witches. Here's the proof."

Fioretta shuddered at the thought and felt Lucia trembling, too. Witches were sometime burned alive—three witched had been burned in Valtellina just a few years before. But even if she and Lucia were spared, Lorenzo would never acknowledge Giuliano's son if there was even a hint of witchcraft about her. It would be the end of all hope.

The shouts of the crowd came through the closed window. It sounded like they were coming down the street. Maffei turned and peeked out.

"Bastard," Lucia screamed as she launched herself off the bed and threw herself against Maffei, her hands grasping for the dagger. Twisting around, Maffei tried to fight her off.

Fioretta sat frozen on the bed, astonished, terrified.

Maffei staggered back toward the window, trying to shove Lucia away, but she clamped her hands over his on the dagger's hilt. He lifted the dagger above his head and swung her body back and forth, but she held on.

The sound of the crowd rose outside the window.

Fioretta leaped up and charged toward Maffei, who saw her coming, saw her face, and shrieked. Lucia wrenched the dagger from his hand just as Fioretta's shoulder smashed into his chest. Lucia joined Fioretta, and together they threw themselves against Maffei.

Screaming, Father Antonio Maffei tripped backward over his cassock, and crashed through the closed window, glass and wood exploding outward, and fell into the passing crowd below. The doll slipped from his fingers and disappeared.

Lucia stood at the shattered window, shaking the dagger above her head. She screamed, "It's Antonio Maffei! He is Lorenzo's assassin!"

The arches of the Loggia della Signoria soared over Thadeous's head as he sat on the top step at their base. The facades of the Loggia and the Palazzo della Signoria formed the southeast corner of the immense piazza, and from his perch Thadeous was just high enough to see over the raging crowd.

Hours had passed since Lorenzo's men had brought Raffaele from the Duomo to the palazzo. Thadeous had followed as well as he could, but when they took Raffaele up into the tower, they had set a guard and refused to let him go any farther. Then that bastard Giovan Battista and his soldiers had found him and had forced him at sword-point to show them to the palazzo's rear door. After they slipped away, Thadeous had managed to escape through the turmoil and find this place to rest.

Thadeous knew he should go back and try to help the boy, but he was so exhausted that he wasn't sure he could even stand. His breath rattled in and out of his lungs.

He heard shouts from the crowd—they wanted blood. They knew of Giuliano's death and that someone had attacked Lorenzo in the holiest place imaginable, before the altar of the Duomo. Men and women wept. Others shook their fists at the palazzo, knowing some of the captured conspirators were prisoners inside. A half-dozen dead bodies, reputedly Perugian soldiers, had been brought out of the palazzo and thrown onto the street.

"Thadeous! There you are."

Thadeous glanced up and was astonished to see his friend Dante Carpani, a head taller than the people around him, pushing his way through the mob.

"I've been looking everywhere for you," Dante said, shouting over the roar as he climbed the steps. He put his hand on Thadeous's shoulder, preventing him from rising and knelt down so he could make himself heard. "I came to Florence to see the High Mass. And to see you." He looked back at the tumultuous piazza. "Alas, this isn't what either of us expected, is it?"

"Dante, thanks be to God you are here," Thadeous replied. "Raffaele—the young Cardinal—is in there somewhere." He gestured toward the palazzo. "I fear for his life. He's a Riario."

Just then, the crowd roared and many pointed up toward the roof of the palazzo, at a figure standing high above in one of the crenels of the parapet.

"Help me," Thadeous said, and Dante assisted him in getting to his feet.

"Franceschino, Franceschino," the crowd chanted.

"That's the banker, Francesco de' Pazzi," Thadeous said. "I can see his long blond hair. He killed Giuliano."

Francesco had a rope around his neck, which looped down in front of the wall below him. His hands were tied at his back. He turned, pleading with someone out of view behind the parapet.

"Good God," Dante said. "They're going to hang him."

"Franceschino!" The crowd was screaming now.

The crowd went silent as someone pushed Francesco de' Pazzi, and he plunged down, his scream echoing across the piazza as he gathered speed. The scream ceased when he hit the end of the rope, and both Thadeous and Dante flinched at the faint, sharp *crack* as his neck broke. Dante crossed himself.

A great shout of triumph rose from the people in the piazza.

"Lorenzo will show no mercy," Dante said.

"That's why I fear for Raffaele."

At the top of parapet another bound man was pushed into the crenel. Thadeous squinted to see better and saw the man wore an ankle-length cassock. "It's the priest, Maffei," he said.

"Hang him, hang the assassin," the people cried.

And, as if in answer to their entreaties, Father Antonio Maffei fell from the parapet. Unlike Francesco, his body swung to one side, and did not jerk when it reached bottom. Maffei still lived, swinging back and forth, his feet thrashing. Finally, the swinging stopped, and he came to rest next to the lifeless lump of Francesco. He twitched for a moment and then was still.

There was a pause for several minutes. The people began to get restless, waiting for more conspirators to plunge to their deaths before them, their thirst for revenge not yet sated.

"Cardinal, Cardinal," someone yelled, and others took it up.

It was as Thadeous had feared. *I've got to do something. They're going to hang Raffaele next.*

The palazzo's main door, guarded by men with drawn swords, was close by on their right, but the intervening space was filled with angry, milling Florentines.

"I'm going find the boy and plead for his life," Thadeous said. He started down the steps.

"Wait. First you must think," Dante said, grabbing Thadeous's shoulder. "If you identify yourself with Raffaele, they might throw *you* off that wall."

"I know."

Thadeous continued down to the piazza, feeling Dante let go of his shoulder. Immediately, he was surrounded by the crowd, and as he tried to move forward, he was jostled back and forth. Some boys stood directly in front of him and, as Thadeous tried to get through them, they laughed and screamed, their voices shrill with excitement. They did not make room for him; perhaps they couldn't because of the press of the crowd. Thadeous lost sight of the palazzo door. It was hopeless.

"Make way. Make way for this man." Dante's voice boomed out as he stepped around Thadeous and shoved the boys aside. The big man plunged forward through the crowd, and Thadeous followed in his wake, like a rowboat towed by a galley ship.

The crowd thinned as they approached the palazzo door, and Thadeous saw the dead Perugian soldiers. The people had stripped them naked and defiled them, kicking and stabbing them so that their blood spread out across the paving stones.

Thadeous and Dante stepped over the bodies. When they were confronted by Lorenzo's guards, one of them recognized Thadeous from his days as a tutor in the Medici household. Thadeous claimed he had a message for Lorenzo, and the man let them through and gave them directions for getting to the parapet. They would need to climb halfway up the tower, to the same level as the immense clock.

Inside, Thadeous and Dante found the inner courtyard and the doorway leading to the tower steps. There were no guards here. They started up the narrow stairs with Dante taking Thadeous's arm.

It seemed to take forever for them to reach the landing on the second floor. Thadeous began to cough and his legs collapsed beneath him.

"Sit on the step for a moment," Dante said.

Though reluctant, Thadeous did so. There was a window nearby and through it he heard a cheer go up. Another conspirator must be standing at the parapet. He feared the worst.

"Jacopo, Jacopo," the crowd shouted.

Thank God. It wasn't Raffaele. Not yet.

The cheering swelled and then quieted. Jacopo de Pazzi must have jointed his nephew and Maffei.

"We must go on," Thadeous said.

They climbed until they reached the third floor. One more flight of stairs remained. Thadeous paused for a moment, listening, but he couldn't hear the crowd. The final steps stretched out before him. He closed his eyes, trying to find some last reserve of strength. Dante waited beside him.

A great cheer penetrated the palazzo walls. "Cardinal, Cardinal!"

"Come on," Dante said. "I see sunlight ahead." He pulled Thadeous's arm across his shoulders and lifted. Thadeous placed one foot on the next step, and they climbed toward the sun. Finally, they came to the doorway leading out onto the parapet, where Dante's strength gave out, and he lowered Thadeous to the floor. Behind them, the great clock of Florence ticked and clanked.

Supporting himself by his hands in the doorway, Thadeous stared out at the narrow walkway between the outer parapet and the low inner wall that looked down on a courtyard. His fears were confirmed. A dozen feet away, a group of men crowded around Raffaele, still in his Eucharistic vestments, standing in a crenel. The boy must be terrified, but he wasn't crying. Instead he stood resolute. Behind him, the crowd in the piazza three stories below continued their cry, "Cardinal, Cardinal, Cardinal."

Sandro Botticelli stood in front of Raffaele, sword in hand, and seemed prepared to force Raffaele over the edge. Lorenzo stood beside him, his hand on Sandro's chest.

"He's a Cardinal of the Church," Lorenzo said. He looked uncertain.

"For Giuliano," Sandro replied. "He considered me to be his brother, too."

"I know." Lorenzo dropped his hand to his side.

"Cardinal, Cardinal!" the mob shouted.

Sandro stepped closer to Raffaele and placed the tip of his sword against his chest. "Die, Riario," he said with a snarl.

"It was Giovan Batista," Thadeous said, his voice a rasping whisper.

Sandro didn't hear him. He pushed with the sword, forcing Raffaele back until he teetered on the edge of the wall.

"Giovan Batista," Thadeous said again, but he knew it was hopeless.

The crowd noise swelled up as they sensed Raffaele would soon join those who had gone before him.

"Thadeous Phylacus says it was Giovan Batista," Dante boomed out. Thadeous looked up at him, his heart full of gratitude.

Sandro swung around. "Batista," he said. "That bastard, my enemy, was behind this treacherous plot? Who says this?"

Lorenzo stepped over to Thadeous and helped him to his feet.

"Thadeous Phylacus taught both myself and my brother," Lorenzo said to Sandro. To Thadeous he said, "Tell us what you know."

"Magnifico," Thadeous said, regaining some of his voice.

"I saw Giovan Batista leading a group of armed men here in the Palazzo della Signoria."

A man wearing a crimson coat stepped forward, and Thadeous recognized him as Gonfaloniere Petrucci. "Describe him," he said.

"He's almost bald with a little beard. And he has bandy legs."

"This man speaks the truth," Petrucci said, pointing at Thadeous. "That man was with Salviati, but he escaped. Now we know his name."

"And I know him well," Sandro said. "It's only been a few hours. Wherever he went, I can catch him."

"Yes," Lorenzo said. "Take some men. I trust you more than anyone to track him down and bring him back to Florence. Alive."

Sandro sheathed his sword and turned to Thadeous. "Where he might have gone?"

"He was from Montesecco."

Sandro bowed to Lorenzo and started down the stairwell.

"Take Samuele," Lorenzo shouted after him.

It seemed to Thadeous that everyone had forgotten Raffaele.

"Magnifico," Thadeous said. "I am the close confidant of His Eminence, the young Cardinal. I swear to you on my loving memory of Giuliano, he was not involved in this terrible treachery."

Lorenzo glanced back and forth between Thadeous and Raffaele, who still stood in the crenel, although he had edged away from the brink.

"He's a Riario," Lorenzo said.

Nobody said anything for a moment, and the shouts of "Cardinal, Cardinal" again rang out.

"He might be more useful to you alive," Thadeous said. "As a hostage, perhaps."

Lorenzo nodded. "Yes. That may be true. But still, the crowd…"

"Magnifico, there is another Riario," Petrucci said. He gestured, and two soldiers dragged forward Archbishop Salviati Riario. Like Raffaele, he was still clad in his vestments. His hands were bound in front of him.

Lorenzo turned to Thadeous. "What do you know of this man's role in my brother's death?"

Thadeous stared at Salviati.

"My dear Thadeous—Professore." Salviati said, his voice oily. "I urge you to remember I employed you when you where on the street. You lived in my house, ate my food. I paid you out of my purse."

Thadeous nodded. Yes, this was true. But you stole my manuscript and also Pletho's Nómoi. And you blackmailed me into spying on my former students. Because of you, Lorenzo suspects me, and Raffaele might soon be hanging from this wall.

"He planned it along with Giovan Battista," Thadeous said.

Salviati lunged forward, his bound hands outstretched, grasping for Thadeous's neck. "You ungrateful *frocio*." Lorenzo and Petrucci grabbed him and held him back. "You want to save that boy because you share his bed!"

"No," Thadeous said, his cracking.

Lorenzo looked over at Raffaele.

"Never, I swear, Magnifico," Raffaele said, his voice strong and calm.

"Take the noose from the Cardinal and unbind him," Lorenzo said stepping back. "Put this man up there in his stead."

A moment later, Raffaele was at Thadeous's side, and Salviati stood on the wall.

"Your brother was nothing but a degenerate whoremonger," Salviati shouted.

Lorenzo leapt up beside him and smashed him in his face with his fist. "For Giuliano," he shouted, and he pushed Salviati off the parapet. A moment later, the rope, which was looped around a merlon, jerked tight. The throng below screamed with delight.

Lorenzo leaned over the edge and gazed down for a moment. Finally, with exhaustion clear on his face, his shoulders slumped, he turned around and glanced at Raffaele.

The boy stood up straight next to Thadeous. His mouth was firm as he returned Lorenzo gaze.

"Gonfaloniere," Lorenzo said to Petrucci, "announce to the people that retribution has ceased for today. I think they've gotten their fill."

Chapter Thirteen

Just Before Dawn

"So, Giovan," Father Nicolo said as he stepped into the cell.

"Forgive me, old friend," Giovan replied. He came forward and embraced Nicolo. "I've been rude."

"You are *in extremis.* An enormous weight rests upon you."

As Giovan and Nicolo sat on the bed, Paulo went to stand next to Alfeo.

"Are you prepared to confess your sins, and receive the Sacraments of Penance and Communion?" Nicolo asked.

"I've refused Communion for many years."

"As I well know," Nicolo said. "And perhaps now you will finally tell me why."

"Yes, Father." Giovan took a deep breath. "For the past nine years past, I have not been in a true state of grace."

"But you confess to me regularly."

"But I never confessed my one great sin."

"I see," Nicolo said. "And this *great sin* concerns your son Matthias?"

"I've told you he also died without being in a state of grace."

"And so we pray for his soul in Purgatory every day."

Giovan closed his eyes for a moment and then nodded. "But I never told you what he did. Or what I did."

All night, the oil lamp had burned, hanging on an iron hook near the door. Now, it sputtered and went out, leaving the lingering smell of burnt olives. The room darkened, and a thin, golden shaft of morning light appeared, stretching from the window across to the wall next to the door, motes of dust dancing in it. They all saw it.

"Nine years ago, I fought for the old pope at Rimini," Giovan said. "The night before we were to attack, I found Matthias…" Giovan paused and then glancing at the shaft of light, continued. "I found him lying with another boy."

Alfeo snorted in disgust. Nicolo glared at him, and he turned away.

"I think now, I must have suspected his sin before," Giovan said.

"His sin is not yours," Nicolo said.

"Yes. But the next morning, as we attacked the enemy, I pushed him forward. It was his first battle, and of course he was afraid. But I had no compassion for him—for my son. I just kept pushing him, forcing him toward the enemy."

"You were angry with him."

"And then he was struck by an arrow. In the throat. He died at my feet."

"And this is your great sin?" Nicolo asked.

"I killed my son! And he is condemned to Purgatory because he had no time to confess and do penance." Giovan threw his arms into the air and looked around the room, his eyes wide. "And now, I have done another terrible thing. I've caused the death of a good man, and that has brought me here. I did it to save my son, but because I failed, it was for nothing." He buried his face in his hands.

"Why did you refuse to see me?" Nicolo asked.

Giovan looked up. "Because I thought I should not die in grace when I denied it to Matthias."

"You said let the priest in," Alfeo said.

"Yes," Giovan replied. "As dawn breaks on the day of my death, I feel the Hell fires of eternal damnation closing in on me. I fear the wrath of Almighty God. Please, Father. Let me fully confess my sins so I may, at long last, take Communion before I die."

The light from the window grew brighter as the sun rose, filling the small room with its golden glow.

"There isn't much time left," Nicolo said, glancing at the

cell door. He positioned himself in front of the table, as though it was an altar, and said, "Paulo, my bag."

Giovan eased himself down onto the floor, kneeling before Nicolo.

Paulo took out the plain blue stole that Giovan had seen many times and draped it over Nicolo's shoulders. Then he and Alfeo stepped to the far end of the cell and turned their backs.

"May God, who has enlightened every heart," Nicolo said, "help you to know your sins and trust in his mercy."

"Amen," Giovan replied.

Giovan whispered his confession, saying he had caused his son to be needlessly killed, and he was killed without redemption. After a moment of thought, he added that he had killed or caused to have been killed many men, and some of them were good men. He particularly regretted the death of Giuliano de' Medici.

Father Nicolo listened, his face serene and kindly. When Giovan finished, Nicolo said, "I absolve you from your sins in the name of the Father, and of the Son, and of the Holy Spirit. Amen."

Giovan stared at Father Nicolo in confusion. I feel nothing. After all these years, I have confessed my sin against Matthias. And for what? Where is my salvation?

Paulo returned and placed a loaf of bread and a pewter chalice on the table. He offered a prayer missal to Father Nicolo, who waved it away. Nicolo tore a small piece from the loaf. He lifted it and the chalice above his head and recited the Eucharistic prayer from memory.

As Nicolo finished, Giovan looked up in alarm. "No Sanctus Bell!"

"Do not fear, my son," Nicolo replied. "The bell is not required."

Father Nicolo held the Eucharist, and Giovan tried to prepare his heart to receive it. I felt nothing from my confession. Am I not truly in God's grace? Is there something else I must do? There is no time. Soon they will come for me.

Nicolo leaned down, his hand outstretched. *"Hoc est corpus meum."* This is my body.

Giovan opened his mouth and felt the Body of Christ placed on his tongue. It was soft, weightless, warm. The warmth spread to his cheeks, his lips. The Body swelled and then shrank to nothing. And with it went his fear, slipping away, meaningless. God loved him and that was sufficient.

Nicolo offered the chalice, saying *"Hic est sanguinis mei."* This is my blood.

Giovan received the Blood of Christ. It too was warm in his mouth, and a wave of fever swept over him, his body shook. He gasped for air. His vision narrowed. The cell, Paulo, Alfeo, they all faded away so Giovan saw only Father Nicolo's loving face bathed in the morning light. Another wave crashed over Giovan. Only the light remained. The golden light. It was familiar, comforting, it was the light illuminating Jesus Christ in Nicolo's church in Rome, Giovan's church. Jesus Christ stood before him. He raised his right hand, blessing Giovan. Jesus reached out and as Giovan felt a touch to his cheek, he collapsed to the floor, exhausted, filled with the certain forgiveness of his Lord Jesus Christ.

Nicolo knelt down, placed his hand on top of Giovan's head and said, "May Almighty God bless you, the Father, and the Son, and the Holy Spirit. Amen."

Giovan lay quiet for a moment.

There was a noise outside the door—the sound of many men climbing the stairs.

"Thank you, Nicolo," Giovan said as Paulo helped him to his feet, his body weak.

"God's forgiveness will give you strength for what is coming," Nicolo said.

"Yes. But I still grieve for Matthias. How will he ever be brought out of Purgatory?"

"Have faith. I believe he will leave Purgatory soon."

* * *

Five Days Earlier

Giovan's mule stumbled. This was a bad sign as their three mules had always been surefooted on these narrow mountain paths. On Giovan's left, the earth rose steeply with thick brush and scattered *pino* trees, while on his right, the slope was more gentle, leading to a stream full from the spring rains, tumbling through the valley below.

Three days ago in Florence, Giovan, Filiberto and the remaining Perugian soldiers had fought their way out of the Palazzo della Signoria onto the back streets of Florence. Then the Perugians had left them, fearing Lorenzo's wrath and not willing to wait while Giovan and Filiberto went collect Paulo and the mules. They set out for their home city, hopeful of sanctuary there.

Since then, Giovan, Filiberto and Paulo had stopped only twice for a few hours sleep, and then only when hidden far off the road. Giovan assumed Lorenzo's men must be searching for them, and would not be far behind. Giovan hoped their pursuers would overlook the obscure mountain path they were following now.

Filiberto wanted to return to Rome, of course, but there was no safety for Giovan there. He had failed. He remembered that day when, standing atop the wall of Sant'Angelo, Father Nicolo had warned him that his life depended on success. Now, everything Giovan had worked for was gone. Before, he was the Captain of the Apostolic Palace Guard and Castellan of Castel Sant'Angelo. Now he was a criminal desperate to find refuge. Even Count Riario, safe in his castle in Imola, would deny sanctuary to Giovan.

Giovan's last hope was that he would find safety in Montesecco, his home village and the home of Rachele, the mother of his son.

"We need to stop," Filiberto called out from behind. "The mules can go no farther."

Giovan turned in the saddle. "There must be a village somewhere ahead. We'll get new mules there." He still had three gold florins and some silver in his purse.

"I'm stopping, Captain," Filiberto said, and he pulled back on his reins. Paulo's mule, just behind him on the path, bumped into Filiberto's, and Paulo looked up, confused. He must have been dozing as he rode. He stared at Giovan, waiting, his face blank and haggard.

It would be agreeable to stop. Even with the months of traveling by mule during the past year, his old bones screamed at him. His own mule sensed that his comrades had halted and did so, too. Giovan didn't have the heart to kick his sides again. With every joint burning, he dismounted.

"Paulo, find forage back there." He gestured the way they had come and then handed the reins of his mule to the boy. Filiberto did the same. "And keep a careful watch. I'll relieve you soon."

Without a word, Paulo pulled his reins around and headed back down the trail, leading the two other mules.

Two nights before, when they had stopped to rest in an isolated copse of juniper trees, Paulo had come to Giovan and said, "I want my dagger back."

"I'm sorry," Giovan replied, trying to find a comfortable spot to sleep amongst the tree roots. "I fear you'll never see that dagger again."

"Then I want a longsword. How can I fight if they catch us?"

"You don't need a weapon. If we are attacked, you must run."

"I'll never run," Paulo said.

Giovan had turned to Filiberto, sitting next to him. "Both of you should leave me," he said. "There's nothing for you in Montesecco. You and Paulo must go to home to Rome. You should be with your wife."

"I would go," Filiberto replied. "But the boy must go with me. He'll be safe with his family and Father Nicolo."

They both looked up at Paulo, whose lips had trembled even as he stood resolute and determined to be brave. "I won't desert you, Captain," he said. "You can't force me."

And so, because Paulo refused to leave Giovan and Filiberto refused to leave Paulo, the three of them had traveled together for two more days.

As Paulo disappeared around a bend in the trail, Giovan and Filiberto relieved themselves beside the path.

Paulo had bought stale bread at the Arezzo market when they passed through that morning. Now Giovan and Filiberto ate, their backs against the hillside, their feet stretched across the path, their longswords unsheathed and close at hand. They passed a bottle back and forth, filled with muddy water from a stream they had crossed earlier. Filiberto set aside an entire bread loaf for Paulo.

Giovan didn't want to take Paulo to Montesecco. If I arrive with him, Rachele will think I have found a new son, a boy to replace Matthias, whose body was burned at Rimini. I cannot do that to her.

Nine years before, despite Giovan's efforts, the forces of the old pope had lost at Rimini, and Federico Montefeltro's men had burned the bodies of the dead. The smoke of the pyres climbed straight into the windless sky—like the white plumes of the marble burners over Rome.

When Giovan had arrived in Montesecco alone, Rachele had screamed at him, attacking him with her fists while Giovan stood silent, accepting her blows. He tried to embrace her, to pull her arms to her sides, but she fought him off. When she ran into the kitchen and returned with a knife, he had fled, his hands over this face, covering his own tears. That was nine years ago, and he hadn't seen her since.

Now, sitting next to Filiberto, Giovan covered his face with his hands.

Once he had loved Rachele, and she had loved him. He tried to remember those times, before Matthias was born and after, when he was a beautiful, chubby baby. Giovan shook his head. It was so long ago. Then he had lost his family, and now he had lost his life as a soldier.

Going home to Montesecco was the only thing he could think to do. Perhaps Lorenzo's power would not reach to the eastern coast of Italy. Perhaps, in time, the wrath of His Holiness would cool, and a spirit of forgiveness would prevail. And perhaps Rachele would also find it in her heart to finally forgive him.

"Horses are coming," Paulo shouted as he came running up the path. He carried his saddlebag.

Giovan and Filiberto leaped to their feet, grabbing their longswords. There was just enough room on the path for them to stand side by side, shoulder to shoulder.

"Paulo, get behind us," Giovan said. "How many?"

"I saw five. There may be more," Paulo replied has he slipped past them. "I know the lead horse. It's Samuele."

Giuliano's stallion? Was Giuliano alive after all? No, that was impossible.

Minutes went by. Where were they? They must have seen the mules.

Paulo was right. Finally, Samuele rounded the bend in the trail, walking. Giovan stared at the rider. It was Sandro Botticelli.

"*Soldier!*" Sandro called out. He swung down from Samuele.

"*Artist!*" Giovan replied. "We meet again." He grinned. Yes, this was good. Finally he would dispose of this arrogant fop who had caused him so much aggravation. Yes, killing Sandro Botticelli today would bring him a brief moment of joy.

"Leave him to me," he said to Filiberto without turning his head. He sensed Filiberto taking a step back.

They had faced each other with drawn swords three times before: in Sixtus's unfinished chapel, in that girl's shop, and on the Ponte Vecchio. Three times they had been interrupted. But not today.

There was no room on the trail for them to circle as they had done before. Giovan knew how to fight like this—it was like the fight on the staircase back at the Palazzo della Signoria. Sandro would have no clue.

"Lorenzo wants you alive," Sandro said. "I ask you one time to put down your sword. I have a dozen men behind me."

Giovan laughed. "Then we will kill a dozen men today. And one artist."

This was another advantage of being on the path. Like the staircase, only one or two of them could attack at a time. And unlike the staircase, there were no enemies at his back. And he had Filiberto. Yes, they could survive this.

"So be it," Sandro said. He lifted his sword.

Giovan raised his own sword. As he always did, he shifted the position of his hand on the grip so it pressed tight against the cross-guard. The balance was perfect, as he knew it would be. The sword tip drew him forward, hungry for blood. As the trail left little room to maneuver, he stood with his right foot forward, his weight centered, the sword guard low, and the blade vertical in front of his right shoulder.

There was fear in Sandro's eyes. Giovan had seen it there three times before, and a hundred times in other men. Staying out of range, Sandro positioned his own sword so the blade slanted down and outward.

Giovan smiled, knowing what was coming.

Sandro leaned forward, moving his sword in front of his left thigh, still keeping the point low, still staying just out of range. He was threatening a low thrust to the belly.

When Sandro took a step closer, Giovan slid his right foot forward, closing the gap and coming into range. He launched a cutting attack at Sandro's head with the sword grip high, and his wrists swinging the blade in a flat arc.

As Giovan expected, Sandro's hands shot up, catching Giovan's blow on the cross of his sword. Sandro tried to lever his sword point over Giovan's left forearm, attempting to stab him in the face. But Giovan pushed his own sword's guard under Sandro's blade, lunged forward and shoved both blades high. They struggled in this awkward position, neither able to swing or retreat.

Giovan had been in this position before and guessed that Sandro had not. He swung his knee up into Sandro's belly and, taking his left hand off his own sword grip, reached between Sandro's forearms, grabbing the pommel of Sandro's sword. Giovan's blade swung toward Sandro's head and as he ducked, Giovan jumped back, jerking Sandro's sword out of his hands. Giovan tossed Sandro's sword behind him and, with both hands back on his own sword's grip, held his blade held straight out in front, the best stance against an unarmed opponent.

"At last, *artist*," Giovan said, breathing hard. He started to draw back his blade for another swing at Sandro's head, this one sure to be successful.

"Captain," Filiberto called out behind Giovan. "Look out!"

Giovan glanced over his shoulder and saw men on foot with drawn swords stumbling down the mountainside above and behind him. The fop was smarter than he looked. He'd sent his men above the trail, out of sight while he created a diversion by fighting Giovan.

Giovan turned away from the disarmed Sandro and shouted, "Run, Paulo."

Paulo stood frozen on the trail, the saddlebag on his shoulder. Above them, the attacking men paused. There were four of them, far fewer than the dozen that Sandro claimed. They were disheveled and dirty, but Giovan still made out the red and gold Medici colors on their uniforms.

"Paulo, I said *run*," Giovan shouted.

Instead, the boy picked up Sandro Botticelli's sword and turned to face Lorenzo's men.

The men hesitated. Now it was four against three. Filiberto, his sword held ready over his shoulder ready to swing, made a daunting appearance.

"Come on," Filiberto shouted. "We'll make your mothers weep for you."

Giovan stepped beside Paulo, who held Sandro's sword tip

low and on his right, a good defensive position. The boy had learned something of sword fighting.

Giovan froze. He remembered his own son, Matthias, standing with a sword in hand nine years before. The arrow was one of a hundred launched at them as Giovan led his men forward, pushing Matthias ahead. The arrow struck Matthias in the neck, above his armor. His son's blood sprayed across Giovan's face and he had tasted salt.

"Run, Paulo," Giovan said, but the boy ignored him.

"Attack, you fools," Sandro shouted behind Giovan.

Lorenzo's men began to creep down the hillside.

"I'm sorry," Giovan said. He took one hand off his sword grip, swung and clipped Paulo on the jaw. The boy staggered back, dropping Sandro's sword. Giovan stepped on the sword blade as Paulo recovered and tried to grab it.

"Let me fight," Paulo cried.

Behind Giovan, Sandro shouted. "Attack now."

Giovan knew the men would see that he was distracted and Paulo was unarmed. He grabbed the front of Paulo's shirt and whirled him around. Paulo's feet scrabbled at the edge of the trail as he struggled to keep his footing. He stared at Giovan, his face contorting in anger and fear.

"Go home," Giovan said. He gave Paulo a push and released him. Paulo stumbled over the edge and slid down the muddy slope to the stream a hundred feet below. He splashed into the shallow water, climbed to his feet and glared up at Giovan. Giovan guessed he wouldn't be able to climb back up and hoped he wouldn't try.

"Captain," Filiberto shouted.

Giovan swung around just as two of Lorenzo's men reached the trail, landing on either side of Filiberto. Filiberto was ready, but he had no room to maneuver. He spun back and forth, his sword tip forward, trying to keep them at a distance.

The remaining two men stayed a dozen feet above the trail, ready to assist, and perhaps wary of attacking Giovan after seeing him fight Sandro.

As Giovan moved to assist him, Filiberto swung around and for the briefest of moments, Giovan and Filiberto looked into each other's eyes. Then the man behind Filiberto struck, slicing through his hamstring.

Filiberto went down.

Giovan howled as he swung his sword at the nearest man, who turned, his own sword ready. His comrade lifted his longsword, its hilt above his head and the tip pointed down at Filiberto's chest.

Giovan froze. "No! I yield!" He dropped his sword. "Don't do it. I yield."

The man hesitated.

"Kill him," Sandro Botticelli said.

The man plunged his heavy sword down into Filiberto's chest. Filiberto trembled for a moment and then was still.

Enraged, Giovan reached for his sword at his feet, but Sandro had come up close behind him, and he kicked it over the side of the trail into the valley. Just as Giovan gathered himself to plunge after it, the men tackled him. Giovan ceased to struggle.

Soon he was back on his mule, his hands bound before him so he could grasp the saddle pommel. Sandro rode ahead on that big black horse. And as they retraced the way they had come, Giovan turned and saw Filiberto's body, still laying where he had fallen on the path. Then, as well as he could, he searched the valley below. In the distance, he saw Paulo, trudging beside the stream, head down, saddlebag slung over his back, heading south toward Rome.

Three Days Later

A stone struck Giovan's shoulder, but he ignored it.

Sandro Botticelli rode Samuele ahead of Giovan, accepting the accolades of the Florentine citizens who lined the Via de' Martelli. The cheers became angry threats and jeers as the people turned their attention to Giovan, stumbling along behind on foot, his hands tied. He tried to lick his lips, but his tongue was as dry as old parchment. They had given him nothing to drink since dawn, six hours before, when they had resumed their journey back to Florence.

The Palazzo Medici rose up before them, and they approached the main door where Giovan and Francesco had come to fetch Giuliano just eight days ago. This time the door was wide open and crowded with Medici supporters.

A woman wrapped in a red cloak stepped out of the throng and stood before Giovan. He recognized her from her portrait and remembered that day so many months before when he had met her in her shop. Giuliano had said she was with child, but the cloak hid it now.

"You're the man who killed my Giuliano," she screamed at Giovan.

"Fioretta," Sandro said, wheeling the horse around and dismounting.

Yes, he remembered that her name was Fioretta. And he remembered her as being lovely, her skin almost too pale, offsetting her auburn hair. Now that face was contorted in hate.

Despite his bound hands and his aching joints, Giovan dropped to his knees in the street before her. "I did not strike the blow," he said, "but I am filled with remorse for my part in his death. I humbly beg your pardon, my lady. Giuliano de' Medici was a good man."

"Don't you dare speak his name," she said.

Sandro stood at her side. "He'll pay, dear Fioretta. Lorenzo will see to that."

"Yes. Lorenzo." Fioretta turned to Sandro, quieter now, but her eyes flashing with determination. "Sandro, I need your help. You've been gone. Lorenzo still refuses to see me. I need to convince him to acknowledge Giuliano's son."

Giovan, still kneeling, looked up at Fioretta as she pleaded with Sandro. He thought back to his last conversation with Giuliano, eight days before. It had been in Giuliano's bedroom as he dressed to go to the Duomo—to his death. While gazing at the girl's portrait, Giuliano had said that he would tell Lorenzo that he loved Fioretta, that he would insist on marrying her, and this would legitimize their child.

Giovan said, his voice cracking, "When I last spoke with Giuliano—"

"Silence," Sandro shouted, turning on Giovan.

"—he told me—"

Sandro struck Giovan on the side of his head, knocking him sprawling onto the cobblestones.

"You filthy pig." Fioretta snarled down at him. "You'll soon get worse than that." She turned back to Sandro and looked into his eyes. "You've changed," she said.

Sandro shrugged.

"You're taking him to Lorenzo now?" she asked.

"Yes."

"Please, Sandro. Take me in as well."

Sandro gazed at her, his face showing both his concern and uncertainty.

"For Giuliano's son," she said.

Sandro took a handkerchief from his sleeve, wiped Fioretta's cheeks and offered her his arm.

"Please, my dear," Sandro said. "Remain out here in the hallway for now. Wait until we finish this business." He gestured at Giovan who stood nearby between two guards.

Fioretta nodded. She peeked through the door into a large, high-ceilinged room, and what she saw dulled her anger and anguish for the moment. Lorenzo stood staring into an enormous marble fireplace, his back to the room, wearing a high-collared jacket that hid the wound on his neck. His shoulders were slumped, and he paid no attention to the men—friends and advisors—gathered around him, including a man in a crimson coat. Nearby, a large window overlooked the Via de' Martelli and the only woman in the room, dressed entirely in black, stood alone beside it, gazing out.

The heat from the blazing fire didn't reach Fioretta as she

stood outside the door shivering beneath her cloak. Just inside, a wheezing old man stood hunched over, and she wondered where she had seen him before.

"Magnifico," Sandro announced, striding to the center of the room.

Lorenzo turned from the fireplace. His face was drawn and dark.

"On your orders," Sandro continued, "I have captured the devil and traitor, Giovan Battista da Montesecco." He turned and called out, "Bring him in."

Fioretta jumped aside as the two guards dragged Giovan forward.

I could kill him. As Giovan passed close to her, she reached for Maffei's dagger hidden inside her cloak. No, wait until I can talk with Lorenzo. Somehow I'll convince him to help me. If he denies me again, that will be the time to avenge my poor Giuliano. It will prove my love for him. And besides, there will be nothing left to lose.

The guards pushed Giovan into the center of the room, where he stood, gazing around, his feet apart and his hands still bound.

Addressing Lorenzo, Sandro described days of hard riding, a surprise attack on a mountain trail, and the final fight in which one of Giovan's men was killed.

"You've done well, Sandro Botticelli," Lorenzo replied. He turned to Giovan, and his eyes flashed with anger. "I gave you my hospitality. My beloved brother, Giuliano, considered you his friend. You are the lowest of all vermin. You have no honor. Your family is shamed and will deny you."

"I served His Holiness, the Pope," Giovan said, dropping his gaze. "I was in an impossible position, and I regret that I found no way to resolve it with honor."

"Ha!" Lorenzo said, sneering. "You know nothing of honor."

Yes, Lorenzo understands. Fioretta smiled. He will see that Giuliano gets justice.

Lorenzo turned to the man wearing the crimson coat and said, "Gonfaloniere of Justice Petrucci, what is your verdict?"

"He is guilty without any doubt, Magnifico," Petrucci replied. "A trial is unnecessary."

"How do you sentence him?"

"Death by beheading, tomorrow at dawn in the Podestà."

What? Fioretta glared at Petrucci and then at Lorenzo, appalled. If they chopped off his head, he'd die quickly. He'd hardly suffer. She slipped her hand insider her cloak and then pulled it back out. Wait. Wait. First I must confront Lorenzo. Then we will see what needs to be done.

"Very well," Lorenzo said. "Take him to the Signoria Tower." He turned to Giovan. "I once told you of the cell above the clock. I'm sure you'll be comfortable."

Fioretta took a breath. Now is time to speak up. She took a step forward. She opened her mouth.

"Forgive me, Magnifico," Sandro said. "Before he is taken away, I must show you something."

Fioretta stopped next to the old man. Sandro had asked her to wait until this business was completed. No one seemed to have noticed her—except the woman in black by the window. She stared at Fioretta, her brow furrowed.

Sandro gestured to one of his men who handed him a leather saddlebag, and he pulled out a thick packet of pages. "He was carrying this," he said, setting it on the table.

Lorenzo picked up the top page, studying it in the firelight. "It's in Greek," he said. "On parchment."

The head of the old man next to Fioretta jerked up, and he gaped at Lorenzo. He hobbled forward, saying, "Magnifico, may I see that?"

Lorenzo looked up. "Professore Thadeous. An expert in Greek if ever there was one." He offered the page to the old man. "Do you recognize this?"

As Thadeous examined the page, he staggered and put a hand on the table to steady himself. "Yes," he said, nodding. He set the page down and spread out the other others, searching through them. "They all seem to be here," he added.

"What is it?" Lorenzo asked.

Thadeous pointed at something on the first page. "Magnifico, you were my best pupil. I hope you remember enough Greek to be able to pronounce this name."

"George Gemistus," Lorenzo read, astonished. "Pletho."

"My mentor, as you know," Thadeous said. "This is the original copy, the only one remaining, of his masterwork. Its title is *The Nómoi, the Book of Laws.*"

"God in Heaven," Lorenzo whispered. "I've heard rumors if this. They say the only copy was lost."

Fioretta didn't understand why Lorenzo was so concerned about some old scribbling. Had he forgotten that this pig Giovan, standing so quietly off to one side, had killed his brother?

"This is the original, written in my master's hand." Thadeous said. "The copy that was lost was the one I made for the Emperor. Pletho entrusted this to me in Constantinople, twenty-five years ago, while the city was under siege."

"Then how did Giovan Battista come to have it?" Lorenzo asked.

"Salviati Riario stole it from me and gave it to him."

"Why?"

"So he could blackmail me," Thadeous replied. "He wanted me to spy on you and your brother."

"You spied on me? On Giuliano?" Lorenzo said, his voice hard. "By God, you're the traitor, not that boy."

"No, Magnifico, I swear. Neither I nor the young Cardinal had knowledge of this heinous plot against you."

"He tells the truth," Giovan said, his voice croaking.

Lorenzo whirled around to face Giovan. "Why should I believe you?"

"What have I to gain by lying now? He tells the truth. He and the boy knew nothing of our plans."

Lorenzo was silent, staring at Giovan. Finally, he put his hand on Thadeous's shoulder. "My old friend. My teacher. I believe you."

Thadeous bowed his head. "Thank you, Magnifico. And the Cardinal?"

"He's a Riario. This changes nothing. But it suits my purpose to keep him alive."

"Thank you." Thadeous again looked through the pages on the table, spreading them out with shaking hands.

Lorenzo turned back to Giovan and said, "Take him away."

As the guards moved to take Giovan, Fioretta edged forward. She reached for front of her cape.

"Wait," Thadeous said. "Please, Magnifico. One question for him first."

Lorenzo nodded.

Thadeous stepped to the center of the room, in front of Giovan. "The other manuscript. In Latin on paper. Where is it?"

"Enough," Fioretta cried. She strode past Thadeous and Giovan and stood before Lorenzo. It was like the time in the Duomo, nine days ago. This time, Lorenzo *must* acknowledge her.

Fioretta threw open her cloak.

Many in the room gasped, and Thadeous was reminded of the absurd reaction Italian men had to seeing a pregnant woman.

Lorenzo stood silent, gaping at her bulging belly.

Sandro came to stand beside Fioretta. "This woman, Fioretta Gorini, is my friend. But more important, she carries Giuliano's child."

Lorenzo turned and gazed into the fire. "Send her away," he said.

"Cover yourself, girl," Petrucci said.

Sobbing, Fioretta pulled the cloak around her.

Two liveried servants came forward. Each took one of Fioretta's arms.

"I saved your life," Fioretta cried out. She dropped to her

knees, her hands clasped as if she were praying.

Thadeous, who stood at Lorenzo's side, was perhaps the only one in the room who heard his whispered response.

"And I wish you had not." Without turning, he gestured that she be taken away.

"Wait!" The old woman in black came away from the window. She gazed at Fioretta's face. "I have seen you a hundred times," she said. "In Giuliano's room." She glanced at Sandro. "His portrait does not do you justice."

"Mother, you must let me deal with this," Lorenzo said, turning.

"No. This is a family matter, not politics. My son, my beautiful Giuliano, your brother, is dead. You cannot marry him off to some high-born woman now just to make an alliance with a neighboring city. It doesn't matter anymore. All that matters is that he has a child, perhaps a son. And this girl, who I think loved Giuliano, is the mother of that child."

"But—"

"Lorenzo, we will take her in. When the time comes, you will see that the child is legitimized. I am serious. Do not obstruct me in this."

Lorenzo looked around the room, clearly embarrassed that his mother would treat him this way. He looked trapped.

The sound of a crowd came through the window, and Lorenzo crossed to it and looked out. "The mob knows Giovan Battista is here," he said. "We will need to make an announcement about him soon." He turned to Fioretta and asked, "What would you have us do with him?"

Fioretta reached inside her cape and pulled out Maffei's dagger. As guards hurried forward to protect Lorenzo, she whirled around and pressed the dagger's tip into Giovan neck beneath his chin. "Whip him," she said. She tossed the dagger onto the marble floor.

Lorenzo stared at her in surprise for a moment and then nodded in agreement. "Gonfaloniere, tell the people he will be whipped and then executed."

"Yes, Magnifico."

Then facing the room, Lorenzo announced, "It appears that Giuliano has an heir."

There was silence for a moment. Then Petrucci said, "Wonderful news, Magnifico," and there was a scattering of applause and murmured approval. Petrucci gestured to one of the men who was guarding Giovan. "Alfeo, take him away. See that he is whipped with the scoriada until he agrees to write a full confession."

"There's no need," Giovan said. "I will write and tell everything I know."

"Whip him anyway," Lorenzo said.

Fioretta smiled as Alfeo grabbed Giovan's arm.

"Wait," Thadeous cried. He approached Giovan. "My own manuscript. Written on paper. You had it last. Where is it?"

"I'm truly sorry. I don't know."

"You lost it." Thadeous turned to Lorenzo, who was talking with his mother. "It was my last attempt at scholarship."

"I'm sorry, Professore," Lorenzo said, shrugging.

Fioretta's dagger lay on the floor nearby. Twenty-five years of hatred stormed into his heart. *I can finally kill this man. Nobody will blame me.*

Alfeo, the guard, bent down and picked up the dagger. As he pulled Giovan toward the door, he slipped it into his boot.

Chapter Fourteen

Dawn

The clock below them struck ten times—ten hours since sunset.

Father Nicolo said, "Saint Augustine taught us that the prayers and sacrifices of the faithful aid the departed, and move the Lord to treat them in mercy and kindness."

"Yes, and you know I have prayed daily for Matthias's soul," Giovan replied.

"Even so, you fear our prayers alone have not been enough."

"What else can we do?" Frustration crept into Giovan's voice.

"I was with you in Sant'Angelo when we spoke with His Holiness, remember?"

"Yes, of course."

"Why did you agree to attempt this scheme for which you'll be soon lose your life?" Nicolo asked.

"You know why—to save my son. But, His Holiness will never grant an indulgence now."

"Giovan, Saint Augustine told us prayers and *sacrifices*."

"I don't understand."

"You put your own life at risk to gain the indulgence for your son. More than that, now you will sacrifice your life."

Giovan stared at him. "My death will save Matthias?"

"God be praised," Alfeo cried.

"But how can I be sure?" Giovan asked.

"You cannot. This is the essence of faith. You must put this in God's hands, confident of His love for you and for Matthias."

Yes. Nicolo is right. This is beyond any earthly concern. Faith in God is the only answer.

The tension drained from his body. He felt limp. Giovan knew Peace.

Someone pounded at the door. Alfeo's eyes widened and his mouth gaped open, but he didn't move.

Giovan stepped close to him. "The time has come, my friend." He turned and pulled the door open himself.

"Make way for Gonfaloniere of Justice, Cesare Petrucci," the outside guard shouted.

Petrucci bustled into the room and confronted Giovan. "Have you finished writing your confession?" A half-dozen men dressed in clerical garb stood in the stairway behind him.

"I have, Your Excellency." Giovan gestured at the pages stacked on the table. Paulo had put Thadeous's manuscript back in his satchel, which he carried.

"We are here to bear witness."

As they all crowded into the cell, Giovan guessed at the reason for so many churchmen. Lorenzo was now in an open struggle with Sixtus, and he needed support from as many Florentine men of God as possible.

The formalities were tedious. Giovan read out his confession and the witnesses signed it, each adding a lengthy endorsement. Finally, Petrucci stood before Giovan, who pulled himself up straight and returned his gaze.

"Giovan Battista da Montesecco, I am compelled to ask whether you have confessed your sins to God and received His Holy Sacraments."

Giovan nodded in Father Nicolo's direction and replied, "I have."

"Then the time has come."

Giovan turned and glanced around the cell. The quill pen lay on the small table, along with the inkpot and a few remaining empty sheets. "One moment." He sat again and picked up the pen.

"We have no time for that," Petrucci said. "Alfeo, bring him."

Alfeo looked confused for a moment, then he lumbered

over to stand between Petrucci and Giovan. He said nothing, his arms crossed over his broad chest.

Petrucci scowled, but he waited.

Giovan finished writing. He blew the ink dry and folded the sheet in half. "Paulo, my son."

Paulo, who had remained in the shadows, stepped forward, his face contorted as he struggled to control himself.

"One last request. Find the girl named Fioretta Gorini and give her this."

Paulo nodded and took the note. Giovan embraced him.

"Now, Alfeo, my friend," Giovan said. "I am ready."

Giovan shivered as he stood in the portico's shadow, his hands bound behind his back. Through the archway before him he saw the courtyard of the Podestà, filled with the people of Florence, all of whom, he knew, had come to see him die.

Giovan remembered the Palazzo del Podestà from his reconnaissance visits in the months before. It housed the *Capitano del Popolo*, the constable of the Florentine people. He surmised that its courtyard was also used for executions.

Nicolo stood at his side, repeating a prayer in Latin that Giovan didn't recognize, and Petrucci was nearby with the clerics who witnessed his confession. Alfeo, his hand on Giovan's shoulder, stood behind him. Giovan assumed Alfeo was making sure that there will be no foolish attempt to run, but he felt comfort from the big man's touch.

They were waiting for something. Giovan smiled to himself. I'm not a patient man and I never have been. In my military life, this was my weakness and aggravation. Soldiers often must wait for orders and should do so in silence, but it often seemed that waiting would drive me to the edge of madness.

Giovan turned to Nicolo. "So, today I learn patience."

Nicolo interrupted his prayer, crossed himself and gazed at Giovan. There were tears in his eyes.

"Oh, come now, my old friend," Giovan said. He felt the urge to reach out to Nicolo, but his bindings prevented this.

"It's in God's hands now."

Nicolo nodded.

There had been a constant babble of excitement from crowd, and now it swelled to a clamor. Gonfaloniere Petrucci came to stand before Giovan. "Lorenzo has arrived," he said. "Prepare yourself."

Giovan took a breath and nodded. God's will be done.

A moment later, they emerged in procession from the darkness of the portico with Gonfaloniere Petrucci leading, followed by the solemn witnesses, and then Giovan, Nicolo and Alfeo. Nicolo was again praying at Giovan's side, and Alfeo's hand still grasped Giovan's shoulder. The people cried out as they caught sight of Giovan. They glared, their faces filled with hate, their fists raised and shaking in anger. Someone threw a rotten orange, and it struck Giovan on the chest.

In the center, a hooded man stood next to a wooden block.

Giovan raised his eyes and saw the bright blue of the spring sky. On one side of the courtyard a stone staircase led up to a balcony. This balcony was also filled with people, and Giovan noticed that they were dressed more colorfully than the common people below. They were the elite of Florence.

The witnesses ascended the staircase as Petrucci led Giovan, Nicolo and Alfeo to the block and the hooded man. The executioner wore a leather vest leaving his muscular arms bare. He held a long, odd-looking sword vertically before him, it's tip on the ground, his hands resting on the pommel.

"May I see the blade?" Giovan asked.

The executioner hesitated and then lifted the sword blade. Giovan had seen executioner's swords before. Unlike most swords, its blade did not taper along its length, and the tip was wide and blunt. This gave added momentum to the stroke.

"Is it well-honed?" Giovan asked.

The man did not answer. Instead, he lifted the blade and touched it lightly to his own forearm. A trickle of blood appeared.

A proper sword with a sharp edge and a strong

executioner. It was as good as Giovan could hope.

"Thank you," Giovan said. He turned to Nicolo. "Father, please bless this man."

Nicolo looked puzzled for a moment. Then he lifted his hand, making the sign of the cross as the executioner knelt. Nicolo said, "*Pater noster, benedic hunc et huius opus.*"

Giovan had heard this blessing before. Holy Father, bless this man in his work.

The executioner stood.

Gonfaloniere Petrucci climbed up onto the block. There was a murmur of excitement from the people in the courtyard. He took a page of parchment from inside his coat and squinted down at it. The crowd quieted. Petrucci began to read the official declaration of Giovan's crime and his punishment.

Giovan stopped listening and scanned the balcony above, looking for Lorenzo. His eyes were drawn to a splash of red, a young woman in a cape.

Lorenzo's mother, Lucrezia, put her hand on Fioretta's as they stood on the balcony overlooking the Podestà courtyard. Fioretta smiled at her, grateful for the older woman's kindness. Below them, Gonfaloniere Petrucci pontificated to the people of Florence, standing atop the execution block.

"I wish you had not worn that cloak, my dear," Lucrezia said. "It's not suitable for mourning." She was dressed completely in black, for Giuliano. On the other side of Lucrezia stood her remaining son, Lorenzo, his face pale. He had said nothing since arriving a few minutes before.

"Giuliano gave this cloak to me last year," Fioretta replied, "and this red is the color of his jousting team. Besides, today I do not mourn. My red cloak celebrates the execution of the beast, Giovan Battista."

Lucrezia didn't reply.

Fioretta gripped the cold stone balustrade as she stared down at the people who fill the courtyard. Off to one side, Lucia stood with Giuliano's servant, Stefano. To Fioretta's great relief, Lorenzo had agreed that Lucia and Stefano would care for her during the remainder of her pregnancy and help with the child once he was born.

Lucia turned to Stefano and said something. Fioretta blinked, not sure whether she could believe what she saw. Lucia was heavier, her breasts, always ample, had grown and her belly was bigger. Tears welled up in Fioretta's eyes. Nóna was wrong! Lucia is with child. How could I not have noticed? Oh, God, is it possible that the child was Maffei's? No, no, of course not. That was almost a year ago. Fioretta smiled as she wiped her tears away. Of course, this child is Stefano's.

Bending down, Stefano listened to whatever Lucia was saying. Then, to Fioretta's surprise, the usually dour Stefano smiled. He took Lucia's hand and together they turned back to watch Petrucci drone on.

Oh, Lucia. I pray you find happiness with Stefano and have many healthy babies.

Next to her, Lucrezia's reserve failed and she wept, pressing her face into her hands. "My poor, sweet Giuliano."

Lorenzo, on her other side, remained motionless, making no effort to comfort her.

As Fioretta put her hand on Lucrezia's shoulder, she felt no urge to cry. She had cried for Giuliano for the seven days since he had been murdered and would surely cry many more days in the future. But not this day. Today, like Lucia, she would be strong. And in the days to come, she would be an indomitable mother, defending her baby from the all the evils of the world.

Inside the cloak she wore the emerald and pearl pendant that Giuliano gave her. She clutched it as she remembered Giuliano's face in the Duomo, full of fear, his eyes searching. Did he truly love her? She will never know.

It was the girl, Fioretta. Giovan recognized the cape and, of course, that lovely face, now contorted with anger and grief.

Next to Giovan, standing atop the executioner's block, Petrucci finished reading and paused. The crowd, which had grown restless, fell silent again.

"Citizens of Florence, a great tragedy has struck our city..."

Giovan realized that Petrucci was taking this opportunity to make a political speech, and again he stopped listening. He caught sight of Lorenzo, standing near Fioretta on the balcony. Lorenzo was pale, stiff. Even from this distance, Giovan saw Lorenzo's hands were white on the balustrade. Next to him stood the old Greek, Thadeous, hunched over as usual.

Fioretta, Lorenzo and Thadeous. I have done horrible harm to all of them. God forgive me.

Giovan met Lorenzo's eyes and bowed. Lorenzo started, his face puzzled. His eyes left Giovan's, and he gazed up at the clear blue sky.

Thadeous stared down at Giovan, surprised. The man had bowed to Lorenzo. Glancing over at Lorenzo, Thadeous saw that his face was ashen, and he was staring up at the sky, lost in thought.

Lorenzo was under terrible pressure, Thadeous knew. Not only had his brother been killed, but now war with Rome and Imola threatened Florence. While the people of Florence seemed as devoted as ever to him, still Lorenzo must never take them for granted. His grandfather Cosimo, the man the people now called the *Pater Patriae*, the father of his country, was once imprisoned and exiled because he involved Florence in an ill-advised war against Lucca.

"Professore Thadeous?"

A boy stood next to him. Thadeous recognized Paulo, who had accompanied Giovan to Pisa and Florence, and had run messages during the days leading up to the attack.

"Yes, son?"

"My master, Captain Giovan, commands me to bring you this." He handed Thadeous a leather satchel.

Thadeous looked at it in amazement. Was it possible? Was it his Constantinople manuscript? It must be. Somehow, it was saved! He was unable to speak. He pulled back the satchel's flap and peered inside. *Yes, it all seems to be there.*

"Paulo…" Thadeous struggled to talk. "Paulo, on a grim day, you bring me joy."

He must have spoken more loudly than he intended because Lorenzo turned to him. "This man's death brings you joy, Professore?"

"No, Magnifico. Something else, a small thing." Thadeous explained as he held out the satchel, open so Lorenzo could see the pages inside.

Lorenzo stared. And he continued to do so for some time, lost in thought while Thadeous awkwardly held the satchel. Finally, he turned back to the courtyard and said, "Perhaps Captain Giovan is not wholly a devil."

"Yes, Magnifico," Thadeous replied. "I have been thinking that myself."

"What? How can you say such a thing?" It was the girl, Fioretta, standing on the far side of Lorenzo. The girl pushed past Lucrezia and Lorenzo and stood before Thadeous, her face filled with outrage.

"My lady," Thadeous said, bowing. "I share your grief. As do all these people gathered here."

Lucrezia put her hands on Fioretta's shoulders, trying to pull her away.

"He is a devil and nothing more," Fioretta said. "If you say otherwise, you are a traitor to Giuliano's memory."

"My lady, you are wrong."

It was the boy, Paulo, who had been standing nearby.

Her eyes flashing, Fioretta turned.

"You don't know Captain Giovan…" Paulo stopped. His face showed despair, as though he understood the futility of what he was trying to say. He held out a folded piece of paper.

"What's this?" Fioretta asked.

"Please, take it. I cannot stay. I cannot bear to watch." He pushed the paper into her hand and hurried away, averting his eyes from the courtyard.

Below, Petrucci's speech continued.

Fioretta unfolded the note and read its scrawled message. The note slipped from her fingers and she collapsed against Lucrezia, who turned and enfolded Fioretta into her arms. Thadeous picked up the note and read.

> *My dear lady Fioretta,*
>
> *I spoke with Giuliano on the morning of his death. He expressed to me his love for you and his intention to speak to Lorenzo and to acknowledge you and your son. He said he would marry you no matter what the consequences.*
>
> *Giovan Battista da Montesecco*

"Enough," Lucrezia said. "We're leaving now."

"No!" Fioretta cried out. "We could have married. My son would have had a father. I could have been happy. That beast down there stole everything from me. I *will* witness this. I *will*." She grabbed the railing and stood like a rock, a great towering tree, a marble statue of Diana.

Below them, Petrucci finally finished his speech and climbed down from the block.

"Are you able to find any forgiveness in your heart, Professore?" Lorenzo whispered.

"I think, perhaps, he was a good man who found himself trapped. He bears responsibility for what he did, but I am surprised that I no longer seem to feel hatred for him."

Lorenzo said nothing to this. After a moment, he turned to a servant standing nearby and whispered something to him. The servant dashed away.

Thadeous wondered what this meant. Was it possible that Lorenzo was going to stop the execution, was going to pardon Giovan? Thadeous leaned forward against the balustrade and looked out. He couldn't see what happened to the servant. Then he noticed that Giovan was again looking up. He eyes met Thadeous's. Thadeous nodded.

Then the executioner placed a black bag over Giovan's

head. The big guard who had been standing behind him took his hand from Giovan's shoulder, turned and without looking back, hurried through the crowd and out of the courtyard.

The executioner eased Giovan down onto his knees beside the block.

What did it mean? Lorenzo spoke to a messenger who then hurried away. Is he coming to save me? Am I going to live?

The block was hard beneath the side of Giovan's head, and it was not fully dark inside the black bag. The bag smelled of sweat, fear. The sounds of the crowd had faded. They were waiting. Giovan heard only his own breathing. He closed his eyes.

The messenger does not matter. Lorenzo probably sent for wine. I am in God's hands.

His breathing slowed and he whispered.

Pater noster, qui es in cœlis, sanctificatur—

A hand shook his shoulder.

"Papa."

Giovan opened his eyes and he saw light. The bag was gone.

"Papa, stand up."

His hands were no longer bound. There was no pain in his joints as he climbed to his feet.

Matthias stood before him. He looked just as he had nine years before. His face beamed with love.

"It's a miracle," Giovan cried.

"Yes, Papa." Matthias reached out and took Giovan's hand. "Papa, look up."

Giovan looked up. The sky had turned to gold.

Epilogue

November 19, 1523

Forty-Five Years Later

Stefano, now seventy-five years old, pulled the silk camicia down over the head of the man he had served for forty-five years. When Cardinal Giulio, son of the beloved Giuliano, poked through the neck opening, his hair was mussed, and Stefano reminded himself to brush it before they finished.

"I've been thinking about Lucia," Giulio said, putting his hand on Stefano's arm. "I wish she was here to witness this day."

Stefano nodded. He and Lucia had cared for Giulio since his mother, the sad and beautiful Fioretta, had died. Lucia had been a mother to Giulio, and for the first years of his life, he had been raised alongside their own six children in the Medici household.

Lucia had succumbed to the *piaga bianca*, the white plague, five years before. The love of his children, grandchildren and many great-grandchildren, as well as his daily duties for Giulio, had barely been enough to keep Stefano from succumbing to deep despair.

"I think she would have been pleased," Giulio continued. "And fussing about my camicia." He glanced down at the silk shirt. With a sigh and a shrug, he turned his attention to the array of white cassocks hanging in front of him. "What do you think?"

Stefano examined each one, measuring it with his practiced eye and visualizing it on his master's body. "This one, Excellency," he replied, lifting a cassock from its hook.

Giulio fingered the fabric and had Stefano hold it up against him, trying to judge its length. "I don't know."

"We cannot dally," Stefano said. "They're waiting."

Giulio laughed. "I assure you, Stefano, they aren't going to proceed without me."

"Yes, Excellency. Of course," Stefano replied, dutifully smiling.

"Let's try it." As Stefano assisted him, he added, "I wish Raffaele was here."

Cardinal Raffaele Riario had been sixteen years older than Giulio, but they spent a decade together in the Vatican as fellow cardinals and political allies. Raffaele had died two years earlier.

"Yes, Excellency."

They said nothing more as they completed dressing. Finally, Giulio turned to kneel before a window in the room's small alcove.

Stefano stood motionless, watching as his master prayed, knowing he would need the guidance of God. War was raging in Italy as France and Venice fought England, the Holy Roman Emperor and the Church's own Papal States. In Germany, the Augustinian friar Martin Luther was preaching that popes were the Antichrist, and that Holy Mother Church was a new Babylon. There was a rumor that English King Henry VIII wanted his marriage to Queen Catherine to be annulled.

The problems facing Cardinal Giulio di Giuliano de' Medici, soon to be known as Pope Clement VII, were myriad.

Weeks before, when old Pope Adrian's health had begun to fail and there were rumors of Giulio's possible election, he and Stefano had visited the stunning chapel built by Sixtus IV on the other side of the door to this chamber. On that day, Cardinal Giulio had wept, gazing up at the magnificent frescos of Moses and Jesus painted by the man he had called Uncle Sandro. Then he had turned to stare at the immense fresco above the altar, and the weeping had stopped. In its lower right corner was a portrait of Pope Sixtus IV, dead for thirty-nine years.

Now, Giulio climbed to his feet and crossed himself. His

face was troubled. "I find it difficult to pray," he said. "I wish to prepare my heart for this burden that God thrusts upon me. But I cannot help but think about my Father—and Uncle Lorenzo. Stefano, you've told me that once my uncle was a happy man, taking joy in literature, art, politics, his family. But I only saw vestiges of that. The Lorenzo I knew was angry and tired. The bastards who assassinated my father also assassinated Lorenzo's spirit."

"Yes, Excellency. I saw much the same thing."

Stefano brushed Giulio's hair. "Now you are ready." He reached for the door leading into the chapel.

Giulio lifted his hand. "Wait, take this." He slipped Fioretta Gorini's thimble from the tip of his little finger. "I cannot wear this out there. Take care with it and return it to me tonight."

Stefano tucked the thimble away in an inner pocket.

"Remember when I showed you the fresco over the altar?" Giulio gestured toward the door and the chapel beyond. "I think I'll ask my friend Michelangelo Buonarroti to do something different with that space. Perhaps a portrayal of the Resurrection or the Last Judgment."

"You wish to paint over the image of Pope Sixtus?"

"This is my chapel now." Giulio's eyes were dry and hard.

The End

Appendices

Acknowledgements

Writing a book is essentially a solitary activity. However, by the time it is finished, it seems like a hundred people have contributed in a dozen different ways.

My wife, Pamela Simpson, was often the first reader of new pages, especially during the second draft. Her enthusiasm and line editing skills have helped immensely during the four years of this project.

I needed realistic sword fighting scenes and fortunately my oldest son, John Aaron Van Roekel, is a Renaissance sword fighting enthusiast. He provided much of the choreography and helped with the research.

Writing workshops, also known as read and critique groups, have been an essential part of my process since I started writing historical fiction in 1994. I've been in ten or twenty, depending on how you count them. While I will probably omit some important workshop participants who have provided insightful feedback for *Lorenzo's Assassin*, I particularly want to thank Kim Keeline, Joy Saler Drees, Maureen McNair, Amy Ohlson, Robert Love, Paula Margulies, and especially my writing buddy, Moana Evans, who gave me a high-five when I typed "The End" on the first draft.

I have been fortunate to have many excellent writing teachers at the UCSD Extension and at San Diego Writers, Ink. In particular I want to thank, Judy Reeves, Tammy Greenwood, Jennifer Lane, Marni Freeman and especially Rich Farrell. I knew my knowledge of writing had advanced when I was able to hold my own in discussions with Rich on the use of ellipses and free indirect discourse.

I appreciate the support I've received from writing friends such as Jill Hall, Susan McBeth, Janene Roberts and many others.

Thanks to my copy editor, Cory Steiner, pen name Cora Lee. Any mistakes you may find were undoubtedly made by me after her edits.

Lori Mitchell painted the two images used for the cover. We had an unveiling celebration at Inspirations Art Gallery, and at that time I said that the challenge for me was to make the inside of the book as good as the cover. These painting now hang in our home.

Thanks to Jenny Gherpelli, who did the new translation of Giovan's confession.

The two maps were drawn by Chris Erichsen for this book.

Thanks to the gang at Dime Stories including David Raines, Brad and Noah Davidson, Shannon Bates and Joanna Gorman, who sat patiently as I read what seemed like the entire manuscript in monthly three minute excerpts.

And finally, thanks to the readers of *Braver Deeds* and *Prisoner Moon*, and especially to you, the readers of *Lorenzo's Assassin*.

Abbreviated Bibliography

Acton, Harold. *The Pazzi Conspiracy: The Plot Against the Medici.* Thames and Hudson, 1979.

Alberti, Leon Battista. *The Family in Renaissance Florence.* Waveland Press Inc, 2004.

Bartlett, Kenneth R. *The Civilization of the Italian Renaissance.* University of Toronto Press, 2011.

Basbanes, Nicholas A. *On Paper: The Everything of Its Two-Thousand-year History.* Vintage, 2013.

Bernardini, Maria Grazia. *Castel Sant'Angelo National Museum.* L'Erma Di Bretschneider, 2012.

Boccaccio, Giovanni. *The Decameron.* Trans. J. M. Rigg.

Brucker, Gene A. *Renaissance Florence.* Univ of California Press, 1969.

———. *The Society of Renaissance Florence.* University of Toronto Press, 1998.

———. *Giovanni and Lusanna.* University of California Press, 2005.

Capponi, Gino. *Storia Della Repubblica De Firenze.* Casa Editrice Barbèra, 1876.

Castiglione, Baldassare. *The Book of the Courtier.* Dover, 2003.

Cecch, Alesandro. *Palazzo Vecchio.* Scala.

Crowley, Roger. *1453.* Hyperion, 2006.

Currie, Elizabeth. *Inside the Renaissance House.* V and A, 2006.

de Roover, Raymond. *The Rise and Decline of the Medici Bank 1397-1494.* W. W. Norton, 1966.

Durant, Will. *The Renaissance.* Simon and Schuster, 1953.

Frick, Carole Collier. *Dressing Renaissance Florence: Families, Fortunes, and Fine Clothing.* Vol. (3) JHU Press, 2002.

Gino, Capponi. *Storia Della Repubblica Di Firenze.* Anno Ii, Fase I, 1875.

Grimassi, Raven. *Italian Witchcraft: The Old Religion of Southern Europe.* Llewellyn Worldwide, 2000.

Hibbert, Christopher. *The House of Medici, Its Rise and Fall.* Harper Perennial, 2003.

Jones, Jonathan. *The Lost Battles.* New York: Knopf, 2012.

Kaborycha, Lisa. *A Short History of Renaissance Italy.* Prentice Hall, 2010.

King, Ross. *Brunelleschi's Dome: How a Renaissance Genius Reinvented Architecture.* Bloomsbury Publishing USA, 2013.

Kohl, Benjamin G., Ronald G. Witt, and Elizabeth B. Welles. *The Earthly Republic.* University of Pennsylvania Press, 1978.

Leibs, Andrew. *Sports and Games of the Renaissance.* Greenwood Publishing Group, 2004.

Leland, Charles Godfrey. *Legends of Florence.* D. Nutt, 1896.

Lev, Elizabeth. *The Tigress of Forlì: Renaissance Italy's Most Courageous and Notorious Countess, Caterina Riario Sforza De'Medici.* Houghton Mifflin Harcourt, 2011.

Loth, David. *Lorenzo the Magnificent.* Brentano's Publishers, 1929.

Machiavelli, Niccolo. *History of Florence and of the Affairs of Italy.* The Echo Library, 2006.

Maggi, Armando. *In the Company of Demons: Unnatural Beings, Love, and Identity in the Italian Renaissance.* University of Chicago Press, 2006.

Martines, Lauro. *April Blood.* Oxford University Press, 2003.

Mayor, Adrienne. *Greek Fire, Poison Arrows, and Scorpion Bombs.* Duckworth Publishing, 2009.

Muccini, Ugo. *Palazzo Vecchio. Guide to the Building, the Apartments and the Collections.* Scala Group, 1989.

Nichols, Francis Morgan. *Mirabilia Vrbis Romae: The Marvel of Rome, or a Picture of the Golden City.* Ellis and Elvey, 1889.

Nossov, Konstantin. *Ancient and Medieval Siege Weapons.* Lyons Press, 2012.

Parks, Tim. *Medici Money.* W. W. Norton and Company, 2005.

Partington, J. R. *A History of Greek Fire and Gunpowder.* JHU Press, 1960.

Pernis, Maria Grazia, and Laurie Adams. *Lucrezia Tornabuoni De'Medici and the Medici Family in the Fifteenth Century.* Peter Lang, 2006.

Phillips, Mark. *The Memoir of Maro Parenti.* Broadview.

Plumb, John Harold. *The Italian Renaissance.* Mariner Books, 1985.

Poletti, Federico. *Botticelli.* Prestel Pub, 2011.

Runciman, Steven. *The Fall of Constantinople 1453.* Cambridge University Press, 1990.

Scaglione, Aldo Domenico. *Knights At Court: Courtliness, Chivalry, and Courtesy From Ottoman Germany to the Italian Renaissance.* University of California Press, 1991.

Simonetta, Marcello. *The Montefeltro Conspiracy.* Random House of Canada, 2008.

Strozzi, Alessandra. *Selected Letters of Alessandra Strozzi, Ed. And Trans.* Heather Gregory (Berkeley: University of California Press. 1997), University of California Press, 1997.

Terpstra, Nicholas. *The Art of Executing Well.* Truman State University Press, 2008.

Trexler, Richard C. *Public Life in Renaissance Florence.* Cornell University Press, 1991.

Unger, Miles J. *Magnifico.* Simon and Schuster, 2009.

Van Wyck, William. *Florintines.* Ruskin House, 1923.

Victoria, Albert Museum, and Elizabeth Currie. *Inside the Renaissance House.* Victoria and Albert Museum, 2006.

Warr, Cordelia. *Dressing for Heaven: Religious Clothing in Italy, 1215-1545.* Manchester University Press, 2010.

Webb, Matilda. *The Churches and Catacombs of Early Christian Rome: A Comprehensive Guide.* Sussex Academic Press, 2001.

Windsor, Guy. *The Swordsman's Companion: A Modern*

Training Manual for Medieval Longsword. Lightning
    Source, 2013.
————. *Swordfighting for Writers, Game Designers and
    Marital Artists.* Lightning Source, 2015.
Wirtz, Rolf C, and Clemente Manenti. *Art and Architecture,
    Florence.* Könemann, 2000.
Zeri, Federico. *Botticelli, the Allegory of Spring.* NDE Canada
    Corp, 2000.
Zucchi, V. *The Museum of Palazzo Vecchio.* Mandragora,
    2013.
Zucconi, Guido. *Florence: An Architectural Guide.* Arsenale,
    1995.
Zupko, Ronald Edward. *Italian Weights and Measures From
    the Middle Ages to the Nineteenth Century.* Vol. 145
    American Philosophical Society, 1981.

Historical Characters

Lorenzo's Assassin has both historical and fictional characters. The historical characters are listed below. Any characters *not* listed here are products of the author's imagination.

Giovan Battista da Montesecco
Lorenzo had Giovan's confession printed and widely distributed throughout Italy as proof of the Pope's complicity in the assassination plot. There is no record of where Giovan was buried.

Francesco Salviati Riario, Archbishop of Pisa
Salviati's body was left to hang from the Palazzo della Signoria parapet until it rotted.

Francesco de' Pazzi
For their role in the conspiracy, the Pazzi family was permanently exiled from Florence and all their property confiscated.

Girolamo Riario, Count of Imola and Forlì
Count Riario survived the aftermath of the conspiracy and died in 1488 when he was assassinated in a plot by the Orsi family in Forlì.

Francesco della Rovere, Pope Sixtus IV
After the failed conspiracy, Sixtus allied with Naples to attack Florence, but was thwarted when Lorenzo slipped out of Florence secretly and negotiated a peace with Naples.

Fioretta Gorini
Gave birth to Giuliano's son, Giulio, one month after the assassination attempt. She died sometime afterward.

Antonio Gorini

Lorenzo de' Medici
Perhaps the greatest historical figure of the Italian Renaissance. He died in 1492 as Savonarola was gaining

influence in Florence. He never fully recovered from the death of his beloved brother, Giuliano.

Giuliano de' Medici
Giuliano and Lorenzo's bodies are in plain tombs in the Medici Chapel. Visitors there are often confused because two relatives with the same names are in the same room, and their tombs have ornate statues by Michelangelo.

Sandro Botticelli
Sandro finished his *Primavera* circa 1482 and went on to paint other significant works, including *The Birth of Venus*. Sadly, he came under the influence of Savonarola and burned some of his paintings in the infamous Bonfire of the Vanities in 1497. He completed his frescos in the Sistine Chapel, but they are upstaged by the work of Michelangelo.

Jacopo de' Pazzi
Jacopo's body was left to hang and rot next to Salviati's until it was finally buried in Santa Croce. But then it was dug up by children, abused and finally thrown in the Arno.

Antonio Maffei
Historically, Maffei was caught seven days after the attack and then hanged from the Palazzo della Signoria parapet.

Federico da Montefeltro, Duke of Urbino
Federico was the great Italian military figure of the fifteenth century. Recent research has shown that he was more involved in the Pazzi Conspiracy than was previously thought.

Gonfaloniere Cesare Petrucci

Lucrezia Tornabuoni Medici
Lorenzo and Giuliano's mother, Lucrezia was a powerful influence in Florence, especially after the death of her husband, Piero. Among the property she personally bought was a resort near Volterra.

Simonetta Vespucci

Raffaele Sansoni Riario

Raffaele became an active Cardinal and patron of the arts until his death in 1521.

George Gemistus, Pletho
Historically, Pletho was not in Constantinople during its fall. He died in Mystras around that time.

Constantine XI Dragases Palaiologos, Emperor of the Byzantine Empire
Died during the defense of Constantinople in 1453.

Giovanni Giustiniani

Giulio di Giuliano de' Medici, Pope Clement VII
Lorenzo arranged for Giuliano's son, Giulio, to be legitimized and well-educated. He became a powerful figure in Rome and was elected Pope in 1523. He papacy was tumultuous, filled with war and intrigue. In 1527, Rome was sacked by the forces of a rival cardinal. Clement also known to history as the pope who refused to annul Henry VIII's marriage to Catherine of Aragon.

Mehmed II, Sultan of the Ottoman Empire
After a fifty-seven day siege, the forces of Sultan Mehmed II captured Constantinople and made it the capital of the Ottoman Empire. This marked the end of the thousand-year-old Byzantine Empire. Mehmed continued to conquer areas in Anatolia and as far west as Bosnia. The Ottoman Empire lasted until the end of World War I.

Historical Notes

Amazing Facts

Part of what inspired me to write *Lorenzo's Assassin* were some amazing historical facts I came across while reading about the Italian Renaissance and Constantinople:

- The attack on Lorenzo and Giuliano did take place during High Mass in the Duomo.
- In Constantinople, Turkish tunnels beneath the Theodosian Wall were detected using ripples in water buckets.
- Greek Fire was used to collapse Turkish galleries beneath the Theodosian Wall.
- Raffaele Sansoni Riario was, at the age of sixteen, appointed Cardinal by Sixtus IV.
- Fioretta's baby did become Pope Clement VII.

Historical Accuracy

As a work of historical fiction, *Lorenzo's Assassin* is based the actual events now known as the Pazzi Conspiracy. It contains deviations from historical accounts, while remaining true to the overall story. Some of the more significant changes are:

- There were more individuals involved in the conspiracy than are depicted in the story, including a second priest who helped Maffei attack Lorenzo.
- There is no evidence that Giovan participated in the attack on the Palazzo della Signoria. Further, the details of that attack have been altered in the story.
- Maffei and Jacopo de' Pazzi were actually executed several days after the attack.
- Most of Sandro Botticelli's role in the story is fictionalized.
- The jousting contest in Chapter One is fictional. The

referenced earlier contest, when Simonetta Vespucci was alive, is historically correct.

- George Gemistus, also known as Pletho, did write his great masterpiece, the *Nómoi*, while at Mystras. However, he was not summoned to Constantinople and no copies of the *Nómoi* have survived.

Locations and Their Names

Over five hundred years have passed since the time period of *Lorenzo's Assassin*. Some of the places mentioned in the story now have different names.

- The Church of San Pellegrino is still in use and is now used by Vatican gendarmes and firefighters.
- The Palazzo della Signoria was renamed to Palazzo Vecchio by Duke Cosimo I de' Medici. He did this to repudiate the days of the Florentine Republic.
- Similarly, the Loggia della Signoria was renamed Loggia dei Lanzi.
- The Podestà is now known as the Palazzo del Bargello.
- The Cathedral of Santa Maria del Fiore is commonly referred to as the Duomo, both at the time of the story and today.
- The original facade of the Duomo was relatively plain. The current ornate facade was added in 19th century.
- Salviati's palazzo in Pisa now contains apartments.
- Constantinople is now known as Istanbul.

A Note About the Signoria Tower

The prison cell above the clock in the Palazzo della Signoria exists and was occupied by Giovan during the night before his execution. It may still be visited if you know where to look. It's mainly known today because it held Savonarola in 1498 before he was hanged and burned. Lorenzo and Giuliano's grandfather, Cosimo de' Medici, was also imprisoned there in

1435.

The current tower clock is conventional with two hands. A single hand clock like that described in the story may still be found inside the Duomo above the main doorway.

Miscellaneous Facts

- The bawdy Tenth Tale of Day Three in Boccaccio's *Decameron* was commonly bowdlerized, and it is still difficult to find an unexpurgated translation.
- Giuliano's hunting song is based on *caccia* songs whose lyrics have survived.
- Giuliano's love poem to Fioretta actually by Francesco Petrarch.

Giovan Battista da Montesecco's Confession

Introduction

Much of what we know about the Pazzi Conspiracy comes from the long confession written by Giovan Battista da Montesecco during the night before he was executed. Historians generally consider it to be an accurate account of the conspiracy because Giovan knew he would be executed and had nothing to gain by lying.

The author commissioned a new English translation by Jenny Gherpelli of the confession from the Italian as it was published in *Storia della Repubblica de Firenze* (see the bibliography).

Paragraphing, capitalization and punctuation have been added for readability and do not appear in the original manuscript. Much of the confession is confusing and out of sequence, due undoubtedly to the haste with which it was written.

Giovan's confession was printed and distributed by Lorenzo throughout Italy.

The selections from the confession quoted in the story text have been edited for clarity and sometimes changed for dramatic effect.

The Confession

This is the confession, written by Giovanni Battista da Montesecco's own hand, in which he clearly states to everyone the requirements and the way to change the status of the City of Florence, commenting from beginning to end without leaving anything behind, including all those he had previously spoken with and narrating in detail the precise words they actually said.

Firstly I spoke about this in Rome with the Archbishop and Francesco de Pazzi, in the Archbishop's room, who wanted to

share with me a secret and a thought he had kept in his heart
for a long time; he also wanted me to promise with sacrament
not to mention it to others or to talk about it when not necessary except when they wanted and liked me to do; thus I
promised him so.

The Archbishop started to talk, explaining how Francesco
and himself wanted to change the state of Florence, they were
determined to do so and they wanted me to help. I replied I
would have done any possible thing for them, but being a
soldier of the Pope and of the Count, I could not intervene.
They replied, 'How can you think we could do such thing
without consent of the Count? All we are looking for and all
we do is to exalt and glorify him and to keep him in his state;
I'm telling you that if we don't do this, there will be nothing
more to do for his state because Lorenzo de Medici wants him
dead, and I don't know any other man on this world he wishes
worse. Once the Pope would be gone, he will do nothing else
but try to take away his little state and to put him in trouble
because he feels greatly insulted.'

As I wanted to know the reason why he made such an
enemy of the Count, he told me many things, about the De-
pository, the Pisa's Archbishopric and many others more that
would take me too long to write about. His conclusion was
that, for their own sake and for the sake of the Count, for his
honor and his profit, I had to do anything possible to fulfill
whatever they would order me in the name of the Count. Both
the Archbishop and Francesco agreed, adding that at one of the
following day we should have all met with the Count to decide
what to do; there we left it.

I didn't hear anything for a while, although I'm aware that
Francesco, the Archbishop and the Count have spoken about it
many other times.

One day, the Count asked me to join the Archbishop and
himself in his room, where he started to talk again about this
thing. He asked me, 'The Archbishop told me you have already discussed the matter in our hands: what do you think?'

I replied, 'Sir, I don't know what to say, I still don't understand it; once it is clear to me, I will say what I think.'

And the Archbishop, 'What? Didn't I explain to you how we want to change the state of Florence?'

I said, 'Of course you did, but you didn't tell me exactly how you want to do it; therefore not knowing that, I don't know what to say.'

Then they both walked outside and started to discuss the amount of hostility and malevolence Lorenzo had in their regards, about the danger the state of the Count would have been in if the Pope had died; that they had to change the state, to eliminate every potential enemy and that they were up to anything to achieve it.

When I asked about the way, they told me, 'We have this way: The House of Pazzi and The House of Salviati, which have half of the people outside the city on their feet, are in Florence… Good; have you thought of a way? Let them to it! They don't desire anything but cutting Lorenzo and Giuliano in pieces; right after, those men-at-arms would have to be prepared and they would have to get into Florence without raising any suspicions, as only if we manage to do it without suspicions, we will do a good thing.'

I replied, 'Sir, you decide what to do. I admit, this is a huge thing; I'm not sure whether you will be able to do it because Florence is a great city and Lorenzo's magnificence is enormous, I think.'

The count said, 'Those people think the opposite, that he lacks in grace and he is hated by many; and the day he dies, they will all raise their hands to Heaven.'

The Archbishop came out saying, 'Giovan Battista, you've never been in Florence; we know better than you about Lorenzo and all his things, and we are well aware of the benevolence and malevolence he has among the people; do not question this, it will happen, that's why we are here, to decide how to do it. So, in what way? The way is to warm up Messer Jacopo, which is colder than ice; and as soon as we have him on our side, this thing is sorted, no more doubt about it, end of it!'

I commented, 'Oh well, and how would He take this? Will he like it?'

They answered, 'Our Sir will always do what we ask him to; His Holiness hates Lorenzo more than any other, and He wants this more than anything. Did you ever speak to him about it? We did; and we will make sure he will tell you his intentions. We will also think how to put together all the soldiers without raising any suspicion, done so that it will all go well.'

It was then agreed how to put the show on, how to move the soldiers from place to place, how to send Napolione's soldiers to Todi and Perugia, and those of Giovanfrancesco from Gonzaga; and so the orders were given.

Then it was the turn of the Count Carlo, not easy to deal with as they all cared about him for different reasons. His camp was in Siena and it couldn't have lasted long; therefore deliberation was made to go to Montone, and keep it under siege as long as possible, to give them time to order the expedition; this is the reason why Francesco de Pazzi came to Florence: he was running away.

Francesco, who stayed for a couple of days, wrote to the Archbishop in Rome explaining how things were going, and they they had to warm up and sting Messer Jacopo and get him to understand all the benefit of such thing, etc.... the way the soldiers were moving, the benefits; he needed to understand all this clearly because once he understands all this, he will realize for himself that things will end up in the right way.

During that time Count Carlo, who was severely ill, got to the end of his days. The Archbishop and the Count had their reservation about his death, therefore they used it as an excuse to send me here, so that I could have a chance to see the City and Lorenzo the Magnificent. They wanted me to talk to him so that he would know that the Count wanted to get his state back, namely Valdeseno, and he wanted to know what the Magnificent and the Republic would do to help; I also had to make clear that the Count was putting all his hope in no other person in this world but the Magnificent himself, and he was longing to know his opinion and to receive his advice. He had to know that, even if they previously had some arguments, he wanted to put them aside and forget about all those things, he wanted him on his side as an uncle, and many other pleasant words, which were indeed fake.

Anyway, I arrived late that night and I could not speak to the Magnificent. I went to see him the following morning, he came downstairs, dressed in mourning for the loss of Orsino; he replied as if he was the father of the Count, with such love, to the extent that I was surprised, after all that I had heard, to find him so toward him. There could not be any other lovable way to speak to a brother as he did about him.

He told me, 'Go back to Imola, see how things are, let me know what you think we should do as we will do all we can to please the Count; for this and for everything else from now on I will do my best to always please him… with the most loving memories a father can hold of his child, memories that I shall hold within and not talk about.'

I then went to the Campana's Inn to have lunch; as I also had to speak with Francesco de Pazzi and Messer Jacopo. While I was having lunch, I mentioned it around saying I had letters from the Count. They told me Francesco went to Lucca so it wasn't there; then I send someone to tell Messer Jacopo that I needed to talk to him about few important things; if he wanted me to go to his house, I would have gone; if he wanted to come down to the Inn, I would have waited for him.

Messer Jacopo came to the Campana's Inn, we went to a secret room where I greeted and comforted him on behalf of Our Sir, and on behalf of the Count Gerolamo and of the Archbishop that respectively gave me a credential letter. I gave them to him. He read the letters and then said, 'What shall we say, Giovan Battista? Shall we talk about the state?'

I nodded.

He replied, 'I don't want to know anything about this,

these people are going mad, they want to became Lords of
Florence; I know these things better, don't speak about it, I
don't want to hear.'

I managed to convince him to listen. 'What do you mean?
I'm comforting you on behalf of Our Sir, whom I spoke with
before I left; His Holiness told me, in presence of the Archbishop, to hurry to tell you about this Florence cause, as he
doesn't know for how long it would be possible to hold and
keep so many soldiers so close to your territory. Hesitation is
dangerous thus he comforts you to do so. His Holiness would
like to change the state without losses,' I said to him, still in
presence of the Archbishop. 'Holy Father, could we ever do
such thing without losing Lorenzo and Giuliano and many
others?'

His Holiness replied, 'I do not want anyone to die; although Lorenzo is a boor and not nice to us, I do not want his
death, but I do want to change the state.'

The Count answered, 'We will do all we can to avoid it;
but if it happens, Your Holiness will well forgive whoever is
responsible?'

The Pope, in response to the Count's words, said, 'You are
a beast, I'm telling you: I do not want anyone to die but I do
want to change the state. Thus, I'm telling you, Giovan Battista, I really would like to change the state of Florence and to
take it away from Lorenzo's hands, who is a boor and a bad
man that doesn't respect us. Once he will be out of Florence,
we will be able to do what we want for the Republic, and we
will have credit for that.'

Both the Count and the Archbishop said, 'His Holiness is
saying the truth, as when Florence will be in your hands and
you will dispose of it at your pleasure, His Holiness will rule
half of Italy and everyone would like to be on your side. Thus
you must be pleased that we will do anything to achieve it.'

His Holiness replied, 'I'm telling you what I do not want:
go and do whatever you like as long as no one dies.'

After this, we left His Holiness concluding that we were

indeed keen to use the soldiers and whatever else we needed. The Archbishop said: 'Holy Father, you should be happy that we are in this boat because we lead it well.'

And Our Father said, 'I'm happy.'

We then went to the room of the Count where we kept discussing the plan further and where we concluded that there was no way to do this thing without the death of Lorenzo the Magnificent and of his brother. When I argued it was not a good thing, they said that there was no other way to do such a big thing; they made lots of examples that I'm not going to report. They concluded that to find out the way, we had to come here and speak to Francesco and Messer Jacopo, decide how to and then give the order.

Therefore here I came. Being that Francesco wasn't there, he - I mean Messer Jacopo whom I was talking to - didn't want to come to a conclusion other than telling me 'Go to Imola, come back with Francesco and then we will deliberate all we have to do.'

I went to Imola and I stayed for a few days as I had been told. On the way back, in Cafaggiolo, I met Lorenzo the Magnificent and Giuliano; having previously said to him all those things about the Count, he told me the most lovely and kindest word of this world, that he had already done what he could for the Count and that he wanted to be a dear friend of him. As he was going back to Florence, we decided to go back together. Along the way he kept telling me how well dispose he was toward the Count, but I will not say as it would take to long to write.

I arrived in Florence with Francesco, who was ordered not to leave that day, so that we could meet and speak to Messer Jacopo later that night. So we did. That night Francesco came and he took me to Messer Jacopo's room. We spoke about that thing and we concluded that many were the things to do for this expedition. First of all, the Archbishop had to be here, but he had to come with a licit excuse not to raise any suspicions, an excuse that himself and the Count had to figure out. Once he would arrive they will decide what to do next. They had to come up with credible facts and figures (having found favor of the Pope's people) ... Such thing would not be done; to do it properly, one of the two brothers had to be away; as soon as this would happen, they will go ahead. Both Lorenzo the Magnificent and the Lord of Piombino were related to Giuliano; for their plan to work, one of them had to go there. Since both were in the city, he didn't want to do anything as he was sure that he couldn't do such thing. Francesco however kept saying that they had to find a way. He kept thinking about it, when he was playing cards, at Church, at a wedding. He just needed them to be in the same place and he would have found the courage to do it, nor he needed people with him, least of all myself that I didn't want what he was going to do. He said he would have found a way and that he just needed more time. I had to send the Archbishop there, the expedition would have gone well and he would have advise me about all I had to do.

After he concluded, I went to Rome and I reported everything to the Count and to the Archbishop; the Count immediately made his deliberations. The Archibishop had to go to Faenza, and I was ordered to go to Imola with a hundred of infantrymen and a small group of soldiers that had been prepared to their requisitions, as well as their people, etc...

I went to Imola, then to Montugi, where I spent a night with Messer Jacopo and Francesco, reporting the orders that were given to each band about this expedition, and on behalf of, etc... The Count wanted to go ahead with the expedition before the camp got split. They replied that I didn't need to spur them as they would have act soon and that I had to prepare myself because they would soon advise on what to do, and that I won't have to put anything before their advise. I told them I would have certainly done it and then I left. Since the Count Carlo was there and he was staying at The Martinelli's house, they didn't have a chance to do it; they decided to leave it for a while and ordered me to divide the camp. So I did. Nothing more has been said about this thing for a while.

I went to Imola looking for Valdiseno and I brought him back. In March I went to Rome where I met the Count, Giovanfrancesco da Tolentino, Messer Lorenzo da Castello, Francesco de Pazzi, etc... which were all talking about this thing and the fact that the expedition time was about to come. Thus I asked in what way and he told me: 'Lorenzo is coming here this Easter but as soon as Francesco would hear about his departure, he will make sure to leave as well. The other one will have to wait for his return and at that point we will have to properly think what to do with him.'

I said, 'Will you kill him?'

He answered, 'Oh no, that is not what I want, I do not want to cause any pain but before he leaves everything will be ship-shape, in a way you will like as well.'

I asked to the Count, 'Is Our Sir aware of this?'

He told me, 'Of course.'

I said, 'Hell yes, it's a great thing to have his consent!'

I was told, 'Don't you know we will get him to do what we want? As long as things will turn out right.'

And so they remained, waiting for him to come.

Being he wasn't coming, they then deliberated to do this thing anyway before the end of May, etc... As I already said, the above was discussed in the Count's room, and any other time they were short of material, they would get back to the matter; when one of them was meeting the others he would immediately say that things couldn't last that way, because it would all become too evident and many people would have known about it. So they had to go ahead with the expedition. For this reason Francesco had to go there, Giovanfrancesco da Tolentino and I had to go to Imola, Messer Lorenzo da Castello, etc... to give orders and then return to Castello. Everyone had to be prepared to receive orders from Messer Jacopo, the Archbishop and Francesco and to swiftly do whatever they would command. All of this was ordered by the Count in Rome. Then the Bishop of Lion came, and once again he ordered that we had to be prepared to fulfill their requisitions without too many difficulties.

So we did, although we never received any order until one Saturday at two o'clock at night; on Sunday they changed their mind again. This is the way things were managed, constantly reminding us to be prepared to do anything possible for Our Sir and for the Count.

Hence with this order on Sunday morning, on the XXVI of April MCCCCLXXVIII, in Santa Liberata we did what is known to the world.

In the same way, on my way back from Romagna and on my way to Rome, among the many things we were talking about, Our Sir told me, 'Well, Giovan Battista, the Archbishop and of Francesco, who said he wanted to do many things and that a state like Florence shouldn't have been change, I also believe that you should never put three eggs in a pan, if not with blabbers. Sad and poor those who will get stuck.' In the same way, as the Count told me many times, Our Sir has a strong desire to change the state, as much as we have; and if you could hear what he says when it's just him and I, you would say exactly what I am saying.

I, Giovan Battista da Montesecco, truly confess and declare all the things written in this one and a half papers to be true, those written above, and what I wrote about what I said to Messer Jacopo in Florence about the opinion and the will of the Pope... and all those things are really true. I was present when His Holiness said them, and everything that is written here, it is written by my own hand.

Witnesses

I, Matteo Toscano da Milano, Knight and Sovereign of the magnificent City of Florence, I was present, together with the Reverend of the Country, at the time the young Battista said what is written above - in one paper and a half plus this one, which will all be put together – was written by his own hand and when he confessed. Therefore upon my own word I declare that what written above is the truth. On the IIII of May MCCCCLXXVIII, in Florence.

I, Friar Battista d'Antonio, Prior at San Marche of Florence, belonging to the Order of Preachers, was present to the said confession, and upon my own word, I guarantee that all Giovan Battista has declared to be written by his hand, it is the truth what in such writing is enclosed. On said day.

I, Benedetto d'Amerigo of Florence, Monk and unworthy Prior of the Abbey of Florence, upon my own word I declare I was present when Giovan Battista da Montesecco confessed he wrote by his own hand what is written here and the things on the other side of this sheet mentioned in the underwriting of the Sovereign and of Friar Batipsta. Upon my own word, it is the true what this papers contain. Thus I did this by my own hand. On said day.

I, Friar Nofri d'Andrea from Florence, of the Order of Preachers, I was present when Giovan Battista confessed that said writing were written by his own hand and it is the true what in it is contained. Also I make clear I wrote the above by my own hand.

I, Don Miniato of Francesco d'Andrea from Florence, Monk and unworthy Prior of the Abbey of Florence, I was present when Giovan Battista confessed that said writing were written by his own hand and it is the true what they contain. Upon my word I wrote the above by my own hand, on said day.

I, Don Antonio di Domenico, monk of Cestello of Florence, upon my word I declare I was present when Giovan Battista confessed that said writing were written by his own hand and it is the true what they contain. Upon my word I wrote the above and signed by my own hand, on said day.

I, Don Marco di Benedetto, of the Order of Cestello, I was present when Giovan Battista confessed that said writing were written by his own hand and it is the true what they contain. Upon my word I wrote the above by my own hand, on said day.

About the Author

In 1994, John Van Roekel finished reading Nathan Miller's excellent biography *Theodore Roosevelt: A Life*, and the next morning he told his astonished wife Pam that he was going to write a novel. Miller's description of the African-American cavalry troopers who fought beside Roosevelt in Cuba inspired John to write *Braver Deeds*, published fifteen years later in 2009.

In 2002, John started work on his World War II home front novel, *Prisoner Moon*. It tells the story of a young German soldier who is captured in France after D-Day and finds himself in a POW camp in Michigan. It was published in 2012.

John completed his third historical novel in 2016. *Lorenzo's Assassin* is set against the backdrop of the Pazzi Conspiracy when Pope Sixtus IV plotted to murder Lorenzo the Magnificent. Not withstanding the religious themes in *Lorenzo's Assassin*, John is not religious.

In addition, John has edited the World War II letters of his father, Paul Van Roekel. They are available on his web site: johnvanroekel.com/warletters.

After a forty year career as a software engineer, John retired in 2012. Much of his life now revolves around his wife, Pam Simpson, as well as writing, hiking and attending classes at SDSU and UCSD. He is currently working on a screenplay adaptation of *Prisoner Moon*.

John is a proud member of San Diego Writers, Ink, a nonprofit organization dedicated to supporting San Diego writers. He urges all writers to visit sandiegowriters.org.

More information about John is available at johnvanroekel.com and facebook.com/johnvanroekel. John is available for readings and book club discussions in the San Diego area. Please email john@johnvanroekel.com.

CPSIA information can be obtained
at www.ICGtesting.com
Printed in the USA
LVOW10s1601300317

529063LV00013B/852/P

2

9 780692 729175